"A faithful portrayal of the story of Jacob and his two wives, *Rachel* will make you feel the agony of two sisters in love with the same man. Jealousy, betrayal, heartache, and deceit cannot prevent the invisible hand of God from leading His people inexorably toward the fulfillment of their destiny. Smith has the knack of making her fiction feel truly authentic to the world of the Bible."

—**Tessa Afshar**, award-winning author of *Harvest of Gold*

Praise for *Rebekah*

"In her second Wives of the Patriarchs book, Smith makes biblical fiction unforgettable and worthy of our attention. This incredible author's ability to re-create biblical settings and transform dialogue delivers a God-given message that is just as relevant today as it was thousands of years ago."

—*RT Book Reviews*, 4 stars

"With attention to detail in every aspect of her writing, Jill makes this story sing with love, human frailty, and triumph. *Rebekah* is a powerful story that supports the biblical account and proposes a reasoned and moving story of what could have been. *Rebekah* is biblical storytelling at its finest and is well worth adding to your shelves."

—**Rel Mollet**, Relz Reviews

Praise for *Sarai*

"The scriptural account of Abraham and Sarah is not only a testament of God's faithfulness to His promises, it's a story of love. Smith skillfully captures both, and the essence of living in Old Testament times, by combining biblical facts with research-based interpretation and her own imagination to create a detailed drama that will leave readers eagerly awaiting the second book in the series."

—*CBA Retailers+Resources*

"Smith is at her best in handling the triangulated relationship between Abraham, Sarah, and Hagar . . . Smith breathes new imaginative life into a well-known sacred story."

—*Publishers Weekly*

Rachel

Books by Jill Eileen Smith

THE WIVES OF KING DAVID

Michal

Abigail

Bathsheba

WIVES OF THE PATRIARCHS

Sarai

Rebekah

Rachel

Rachel

A Novel

JILL EILEEN SMITH

Revell

a division of Baker Publishing Group
Grand Rapids, Michigan

Published by Revell
a division of Baker Publishing Group
P.O. Box 6287, Grand Rapids, MI 49516-6287
www.revellbooks.com

Printed in the United States of America

Library of Congress Cataloging-in-Publication Data
Smith, Jill Eileen, 1958–
    Rachel : a novel / Jill Eileen Smith.
        pages cm. — (Wives of the patriarchs ; book 3)
    ISBN 978-0-8007-3431-2 (pbk.)
    1. Rachel (Biblical matriarch)—Fiction. 2. Jacob (Biblical patriarch)—
Fiction. 3. Bible. Old Testament—History of Biblical events—Fiction.
4. Women in the Bible—Fiction. I. Title.
PS3619.M58838R33 2014
813'.6—dc23   2013033531

Scripture quotations are from the Holy Bible, New International Version®. NIV®. Copyright © 1973, 1978, 1984, 2011 by Biblica, Inc.™ Used by permission of Zondervan. All rights reserved worldwide. www.zondervan.com

This is a work of historical reconstruction; the appearance of certain historical figures is therefore inevitable. All other characters, however, are products of the author's imagination, and any resemblance to actual persons, living or dead, is coincidental.

Published in association with the Books & Such Literary Agency, Wendy Lawton, Central Valley Office, P.O. Box 1227, Hilmar, CA 95324, wendy@booksandsuch.biz

14   15   16   17   18   19   20   7   6   5   4   3   2   1

❋✜❋

To my sister Elaine.

Rachel and Leah's relationship has taught me much,
to appreciate all that God has given.
I am so grateful God gave me a sister,
and I am glad that sister is you.

❋✜❋

Part

1

Then Jacob continued on his journey and came to the land of the eastern peoples . . .

When Jacob saw Rachel daughter of his uncle Laban, and Laban's sheep, he went over and rolled the stone away from the mouth of the well and watered his uncle's sheep. Then Jacob kissed Rachel and began to weep aloud. He had told Rachel that he was a relative of her father and a son of Rebekah. So she ran and told her father.

Genesis 29:1, 10–12

Now Laban had two daughters; the name of the older was Leah, and the name of the younger was Rachel . . .

So Jacob served seven years to get Rachel, but they seemed like only a few days to him because of his love for her.

Genesis 29:16, 20

❧ 1 ❧

The spindle moved in an almost sacred rhythm as Rachel's hands kept time with the pace of her feet. The sun spilled down at a midmorning angle over her father's small flock as she walked, whistling a tune the sheep would recognize, pausing every now and then to look behind her.

They came to a grassy knoll, and she settled on one of the low hills where her perch allowed a better view of the animals as they grazed not far below. She set the spindle and distaff aside and reached into her pouch for a hunk of bread and cheese that she had packed early that morning. How relieved she had been to escape the confines of the house where Leah's look of censure and biting words had heated her blood.

"There is no need for kohl when you are only attending those few sheep. You waste it. Do you not care for the expense it costs our father?" Leah had stood in the door to Rachel's bedchamber, hands folded, her expression carrying that smug, older-sister look Rachel had grown to despise. If Leah cared more for her appearance and used a bit of kohl herself, she might have found a husband by now. But Rachel bit back the unkind words.

"I don't waste it. A small amount in the right places protects my eyes from the harsh sun." She glanced from the bronze mirror to Leah's scowling face. "And Father has gold enough to afford this small luxury." That this particular kohl had been bought from merchants of Punt and cost her father more than he would normally consider for such a frivolous purchase did not trouble her. Leah worried too much.

Rachel gathered up her leather pouch and fastened it to her belt, then strode toward the door where Leah stood. "It would not hurt you to use some cosmetics now and then, you know." At the narrowing of her sister's pale eyes, she amended, "Most of our friends do so."

The comment had done little to ease the tension. Leah was usually the quiet sort but, where Rachel was concerned, seemed too quick at times to voice her motherly opinion. That there were ten years between them might have accounted for her to become Rachel's self-appointed adviser, but Rachel was weary of being told what to do.

She nibbled the cheese, her keen senses long attuned to the deviously quiet hills. She paused, listening. A moment later a small flock of birds took flight as one of the lambs drew too near. She leaned back against the trunk of a tamarisk tree.

If only Leah would marry and move away. Life would have been far easier for Rachel if she'd been her father's only daughter. With her father's two wives, not to mention a household of female servants, there were women enough to do the household chores and see that the men were well fed. The tension came in Leah's presence. Would they get along better if they'd had the same mother?

She finished the cheese and water from the goatskin at her side, then took up the spindle again. There had to be a way to soften the strife with her half sister. And hadn't she tried to be kind, to take care not to flaunt her beauty in Leah's presence?

Leah seemed to have no trouble criticizing her in every other way, from Rachel's culinary skills to her work with the loom.

Only Leah knew how to make such fine garments from their father's wool. Only Leah could bake sweet treats that were crisp, tasty, *and* light as fine flour.

The thought stung. She was not some shallow-minded child. She was a woman as any other and had learned to cook and weave as well as the next woman. But Rachel far preferred to spin and shepherd the flock than be cooped up in the house with Leah and her mother, Farah. Farah, the first wife. Leah, the first daughter. While Rachel was the last born, and a girl at that, to a lesser wife. If not for her beauty, she would be counted as worth very little in her father's eyes.

She blinked, tasting the salt of bitterness in an unexpected tear that slipped down her cheek. She brushed it away and lifted her chin. She would not weep over Leah or her father's expectations or the tension of Laban's house.

But as the sun drew its pathway to the west and the time came to take the sheep to the well for watering, Rachel could not help the earnest longing that filled her. To marry. To leave her father's house and start anew. Away from the bitterness and strife of her father's two wives. Away from her half brothers and the image they had of her as spoiled baby sister.

To be rid of Leah and her sharp tongue.

Leah sat at the loom, threaded a rich poppy-dyed woolen weft strand through the warp, and drew it through with practiced ease. Her father's second wife, Suri, Rachel's mother, sat at another loom in the opposite corner of the weaving room, her nimble fingers moving as swiftly as Leah's. A subtle tension filled the air between them, as it always did when Suri chose to weave at the same hour as Leah. Competition to create the better garment was passed off as friendly, but in her heart, Leah knew the rivalry was more out of envy than camaraderie.

She released a long-suffering sigh, her thoughts still mulling over her conversation with Rachel that morning. The girl was incorrigible! Always flaunting those dark eyes at every male who passed, even using her haughty charm on Leah's older brothers. That the family coddled her was undeniable. Was it any wonder that Leah felt compelled to help the girl use some common sense and not waste the family's resources on frivolities?

Rachel heard none of it, of course. *"It would not hurt you to use some cosmetics now and then, you know."* As if kohl could change the color of Leah's pale eyes . . . or give her the confidence she lacked.

She surveyed the row, irritated with herself. How had she missed that strand? A soft curse escaped as she undid the weaving and went back to fix the missed spot. She must stop trying to help Rachel. The girl cared not one whit what Leah thought and rarely listened to her elders. Leah winced at the thought. She was ten years Rachel's senior and still she waited for a man to take her from this place. Had her father made inquiries with the newcomers to Harran? Surely even a passing merchant or a distant cousin from Ur could be sought.

But Laban seemed more interested in the fine cloth she produced and the sweet breads she baked him than in finding a man to cover her, to give her his name. Was she never to wed then? She would die a worthless one!

"You're a quiet one today." Suri's voice grated Leah's already heightened senses like coarse sand on skin. "Having trouble with the loom?" Suri's voice held a hint of kindness, but Leah was in no mood to share her thoughts, especially with her rival's mother.

"I'm fine," she said, resisting the urge to dampen Suri's cheerful spirit. Despite her own mother's feelings toward Rachel's mother, Leah could not bring herself to ruin the atmosphere of the day.

Suri nodded, resuming her work. "Some women at the well told of a caravan come up from Babylon to Harran. Brought some settlers with them." Suri tied off the end of a thread and drew another color from a basket at her side. "Perhaps your father will make use of the knowledge." She glanced at Leah, her look telling.

"Why should a group of settlers concern my father?" Though she couldn't deny the little kick such news brought to her heart. Might a suitable husband be found among them? "Have you told him? My father, I mean?" Her voice sounded anxious and much too curious. She busied herself with the threads, finishing the red and extracting one of bright gold.

"He had already heard. He met some of the men at the city gate as they entered." She paused, her look pitying. "There were several younger men among them."

Leah bit her lip, not wanting to be baited into asking what she longed to ask. She hated being the last to hear the latest gossip, but it was a price she paid for avoiding treks to the well. Even her visits to town were few.

"Unmarried men?" she asked at last, hope making her tongue loose.

Suri's smile held a hint of triumph, but then she quickly grew thoughtful. She gave a brief nod. "Some of the younger ones were unwed, boys about Rachel's age."

Too young for her. She choked on a bitter sigh.

"But some of the others might be willing to take a second wife." Her hands paused in the work of weaving as she faced Leah. "I know your mother resents me, Leah. But it is not the worst thing that could happen to wed a man who already has one wife. At least it would give you the chance to bear children. To wed is a good thing." She offered Leah a smile that held too much sympathy. And yet Suri herself had wed her father, a man who had already had a wife and had laid to rest a concubine.

Still, Leah was the oldest. She deserved the status of first wife, and she wanted to marry a man who would love her. Only her.

"Perhaps one of the younger ones would suffice." Leah

shrugged as though the subject was of no concern to her, though she knew Suri would not be fooled.

"Perhaps," Suri said, though she did not look convinced. "I thought the same for Rachel. I will speak to your father."

"No need to speak on my account." She looked away and concentrated on her work. "I can speak with him myself." And if he didn't listen to her, she would send her mother. Never mind that Suri had her father's ear. Her mother had been fairly cast aside since the woman had come into their home, if her mother was to be believed.

But as the afternoon shadows lengthened, Suri's words flitted through Leah's thoughts, her offer more troubling than Leah would allow. The God of Shem, whom her father fancied he worshiped along with his other household gods, was said to have created men and women to marry, one man to one woman. Male and female. To leave father and mother and be joined to a wife, a husband. The number of her father's wives surely did not meet with God's approval.

She wanted better when the time came.

If only it had already come.

Jacob stopped at a well on the outskirts of Luz to draw water for himself and the beast at his side. If there had been time, if he had not been forced to flee like a thief from the hand of justice, his father might have sent him off with camels and jewels and gold enough to purchase the bride he was sent to seek. But the truth of his fugitive situation weighed him down with every hurried step away from Beersheba and his father's camp, away from the safety and security of all he had known.

The sun's bright rays that had borne down on him as he trudged over hot sands had lost their potency as the round orb dipped beneath the earth's surface. He was tired. Weary beyond a normal day's work. He had spent days away with the sheep, but always with the knowledge that he could return to warmth and familiarity and a hot meal. Now his senses were attuned to the wild, every nerve ending heightened, and he could not stop the continued glances over his shoulder. Surely Esau would not follow.

But the fear and the doubt lingered.

If only he had found another way to secure the blessing. A way that did not involve cheating Esau and deceiving his father. If God had truly promised his mother that the covenant blessings would be his, then why was the ruse necessary?

He tied the donkey's reins to a nearby tree branch, then moved the stone that covered the well and lowered his weighted goatskin to the depths until he felt the rope grow heavy beneath his grip. He pulled the full skin to the surface, then filled the trough. The work was slow going without a larger jar to do the filling, and by the time he had looked around for a stone smooth enough to use as a pillow, built a small fire, and rested on the nearby grasses, he had to force himself to eat some of the dates still left in his sack. He was nearly faint with hunger yet had no appetite. He felt old and worried with sorrow.

Would he find Harran and Paddan-Aram? Was Laban still living, and would any of his daughters be yet unwed? Would his uncle welcome him once he heard the truth of why he had fled? He looked up into the blackened heavens and tried to count the stars.

Are You really there, God of my fathers?

He closed his eyes against the nagging doubts, drifting into sleep.

His thoughts jumbled in his head as he slept, and the faraway sound of music filled his ears. Confusing visions moved in his mind's eye, and in the distance, growing closer as sleep deepened, a large ziggurat loomed before him with steps reaching to the heavens. Bright light swirled over every step, curling into flowing white robes of glowing men . . . but no, not men, though their faces reflected the idea of a man. Their appearance was ethereal yet solid, beings moving up and down the ziggurat stairs.

The vision held him fast, and he knew in a moment he was awake yet not awake in a dream he could not escape, nor did he wish to. His gaze followed the angels' gliding walk until it reached to the very top of the ziggurat where a Being stood in shining glory.

"I am Yahweh, the Elohim of your father Abraham and the Elohim of Isaac. I will give you and your descendants the land on which you are lying. Your descendants will be like the dust of the earth, and you will spread out to the west and to the east, to the north and to the south. All peoples on earth will be blessed through you and your offspring. I am with you and will watch over you wherever you go, and I will bring you back to this land. I will not leave you until I have done what I have promised you."

The words flowed through him like rushing wind, leaving him weak. He jerked awake, the vision gone. "Surely Yahweh is in this place, and I was not aware of it." His heart thumped fast and loud in his ears. "How awesome is this place! This is none other than the house of Elohim. This is the gateway of the heavens."

The knowledge that he had seen God in the dream shook him, the fear as fathomless as the depths of the nearby well. His father, Isaac, had feared Elohim after the encounter on His altar, and now Jacob knew that same fear and the raw dread of Yahweh in such dazzling glory. He tried to stand but could only manage to roll onto his stomach and splay his arms and hands in front of him. *I am unworthy.* The thought hovered over him, piercing him, shaming him.

But as morning's dawn burst like a bridegroom from his tent, flinging its pink and yellow arms toward the waiting sky above, Jacob at last had the strength to stand. The sun's kiss on his damp cheeks felt like a gentle touch, carrying with it a sense of the glory of Elohim in the dream. He lifted the stone that had been his pillow and propped it upright, then gathered more stones to brace it.

He reached into the donkey's saddlebag, retrieved a flask of oil, and poured it on top of the stone. "This place shall be called Bethel," he said to the empty space around him, yet he sensed he was not as alone as he had once thought.

He glanced heavenward, longing once more for the dream, and more so for the Being who had captured his heart, his imagination. He raised one hand to the skies, his thoughts working to form the words he needed to say, words he had crafted in the night in his awe, his fear.

"If Elohim will be with me and will watch over me on this journey I am taking," he said, placing a hand over his heart, "and will give me food to eat and clothes to wear so that I return safely to my father's house . . ." He paused once more, feeling that the weight of worry had somehow shifted, his faith strengthened. "Then Yahweh will be my Elohim and this stone that I have set up as a pillar will be Elohim's house, and of all that You give me I will give You a tenth."

The sun shifted, catching the pillar in its glowing rays. Jacob watched it but a moment, this "house of Elohim," Bethel, then packed up his provisions and headed toward Harran.

✳⚜✳

The sun dipped past the midday point as Rachel led her flock toward the large well in the field between Harran and Paddan-Aram. Wind whipped the veil that covered her hair and face, her protection from the elements and, when she chose to use it, from the scrutiny of men. Especially from some of the younger shepherds who seemed too eager to gain her attention. She should be grateful for the interest, and more than one had hinted that he would soon speak to her father for her hand. Perhaps she had been too coy with them. She had cast the slanted looks their way innocently enough—to garner help with the well's heavy stone. But she feared perhaps Leah was right. Perhaps her kohl-rimmed eyes made her seem more beguiling than she intended.

She released a deep sigh as she crested the ridge and looked down on the valley where the well stood. Three flocks of sheep, along with those eager shepherds, sat waiting for her. She squinted, raised a hand to her brow. A fourth man stood speaking to them. A foreigner, by the look of him. A donkey stood nearby with few bags hanging from its sides. A traveler, and likely a needy one.

She glanced behind her and called to the sheep to follow her down the ridge. They needed no coaxing, however, and hurried past her. She stood her ground and slowly approached, assessing the stranger as she walked. When she drew near enough to make out his features, she caught her breath. A handsome stranger at that!

He looked up and stilled. His dark, nearly black hair poked beneath a striped turban, and his colorful cloak bespoke the garments of a prince. His bearded face needed trimming, and his sandals were coated in dust, a sign that he had come a long distance. He stared at her, and she could not pull away from the deep curiosity and appreciation in his gaze.

A slow smile appeared around the edges of his beard that did not match the look of anticipation—relief, even—that filled his dark eyes. His gaze lingered in a suspended moment but at last pulled free of hers to examine the flock in her care.

He moved closer to one of her ewes and touched its head as though he knew well the care of sheep, then without a word he walked over to the large stone covering the well, braced himself, bent low to shift his weight, and rolled the stone. The familiar grating sounds of stone on stone made her cringe, but the discomfort passed quickly as the large rock rested at an angle against the raised lip of the well. He grasped the sturdy rope that hung nearby and lowered the stone water jar to the stream below ground, lifted it with practiced ease, and carried it to the trough.

She glanced at the men, her fellow shepherds, behind the man, reluctant to allow this stranger to water her sheep before theirs. But the look of censure she expected from the shepherds toward the newcomer did not come. She stepped closer to the troughs as the man worked, admiring the sheer strength he possessed. Moving the stone without help was a feat no other had managed.

He paused for breath as he lowered the jar once more to the depths, watching her. Shyness swept over her. Surely she had

had her share of admirers, but this man looked at her like he knew her. The thought was disconcerting.

"You are Rachel, daughter of Laban, son of Bethuel?"

She nodded, certain her fellow shepherds had pointed her out to him the moment she crested the ridge. Warmth heated her cheeks beneath the veil. Her affirmation seemed to strip him of his confidence, and his strength faltered slightly as he finished watering the last of the sheep.

He set the jar aside and walked toward her, then leaned close and kissed first her right cheek, then her left. His dark brows drew down and his mouth twitched as he struggled to keep his composure. "I am Jacob," he said. "Son of your father's sister, Rebekah. I am come from Beersheba where my father, Isaac, son of Abraham, resides. I am your own flesh and blood. Your cousin." The words came out choppy, mingled with tears, until at last the man broke down. Covering his face with both hands, he wept. "Forgive me." But the tears continued.

Stunned, Rachel could only watch, her mind whirling. Her cousin? He had come from so far! Questions filled her mind, aligning with memories of stories her father had told of a cousin Isaac whose father Abraham had sent his servant to find a bride for his son. Had Jacob come to Paddan-Aram for the same purpose? To find a wife from among his mother's brother's daughters?

A little thrill passed through her at the thought. This man could be the answer to her prayers, her dreams. If his father lived in Beersheba, surely Jacob would want to return there to live with his family. He was simply a traveler looking for a bride to return home.

She must tell her father.

As Jacob's tears subsided, Rachel stepped closer and gently touched his arm. "I must go home and tell my father you have come. He will welcome you and you will stay with us." She glanced at the sky, knowing it would be dark soon. She should take the sheep first to the pen, but she couldn't leave the man waiting. And it would not be proper for her to lead a strange man into town alone.

"I will tend the sheep until you come," he said as if reading her mind. "Do not worry. I will wait." He swiped at his tears, his look embarrassed.

Rachel nodded. "I know you will." She turned, picked up her skirts, and ran home.

Jacob sank onto a large stone opposite one of the water troughs, his thoughts muddled. One of the other shepherds took his turn lowering the jar into the well to water his flock while Jacob waited for his uncle Laban to come from the city. Would his uncle embrace him and accept him as Rachel had indicated? Doubts nagged him, but he was too spent from the release of emotion to give thought to them.

As the moments ticked past, he rose on shaky legs and retrieved the goatskin from where it hung at the donkey's side. He drank deeply, refreshed, then walked to the well to refill it. As he lifted the sack from the well's mouth, he glanced in the distance toward the city gates. Still no sign of Laban. Anxious now, he walked among the sheep, giving quick inspection to Laban's flock. Most were sturdy and strong, though some appeared feeble. Did his uncle keep the feeble from breeding with the strong?

Shadows hid the sun for several moments, and he glanced once more toward the city gates. There, a lone figure, a man in billowing robes, ran toward him. Had he not even bothered to gird himself? Yet that he would run to meet his nephew meant that he must have accepted Rachel's word. Jacob stepped away from the lamb he was inspecting and walked toward the man to greet him.

Laban approached him, looking him over as though he were one of the sheep. "You are Jacob, Rebekah's son?"

Jacob nodded. "Yes, my lord. I have come from Beersheba, a great distance from here. It is where my mother and father live to this day."

Laban leaned forward and kissed Jacob's cheeks, then motioned to the stones near the water troughs, where they sat facing each other. The other shepherds had finished watering their sheep and were some distance from them now, leaving Laban and Jacob blessedly alone.

"Tell me everything," Laban said. "Why have you come?" He flicked a glance at the donkey and Jacob's meager possessions, then met Jacob's gaze.

Jacob held Laban's assessing look, not wanting to appear desperate. "My father bid me come, to seek a wife from the daughters of Laban. He did not wish for me to take a wife from among the daughters of the Canaanites among whom we lived, as my brother has done. They do not worship our God and are displeasing to my parents. My father blessed me and sent me here."

Laban's expression held a calculating edge, and his smile did not quite reach his eyes. "Your father blessed you, you say. Yet you are the younger son, are you not?" That Laban would know the birth order of his sister's twins came as no surprise. News traveled between the camps, even if the people did not.

"The God of my fathers chose me for the covenant blessings over my brother." He did not wish to convey to Laban just how he had secured that blessing.

"And yet you come with so few possessions." He glanced again at the donkey and the obvious lack of bulging sacks at its sides. "When your grandfather's servant came seeking my sister, he had camels and jewels and many gifts to pay a bride-price.

And yet you come to me seeking a wife with so little? Unless it is gold you have hidden in those sacks?"

Jacob quickly deduced that Laban cared a great deal about how much he would profit from the loss of a daughter. But Jacob did not have even one gold piece left from his travels to cover the bride-price. He glanced into the distance, aware of his own inadequacies. He would have to confess all if his uncle were to believe him.

A bitter sigh escaped him. He met Laban's penetrating gaze.

"The God of my fathers promised my mother before I was born that the older would serve the younger," he said. "I was the younger. My mother raised me to understand that it was I who deserved the birthright, foreordained to me by Elohim Himself. But when it came time to receive it, I knew my father preferred my older brother. So I found a way to take the birthright from Esau. It was obvious that he despised it, in any case." He folded his hands and rested them in his lap, glancing at them once, seeking strength.

"After I received the birthright, the blessing should have come to me without question. But again, my father chose Esau over me. So my mother, your sister, devised a plan for me to take the blessing from my brother. Together we convinced my father that I was his firstborn, and my father granted me the covenant blessing of Abraham." He paused, gauging Laban's reaction, noting the sudden gleam in his dark eyes.

"My brother was furious when he discovered the ruse and threatened to kill me once my father rests with his fathers. My mother, fearing for my safety, requested that my father send me off to secure a wife and to get me away from my brother. I have come to ask for your protection and, if I find favor in your eyes, to marry your daughter."

Laban shifted his weight on the stone and smoothed a hand over his robe, all the while holding Jacob's worried gaze. "You are my own flesh and blood," he said, smiling. "You are my sister's son." He stood and offered Jacob a hand. Jacob took it and Laban embraced him. "Come, stay with me and all will be well."

"Thank you, my lord. And your daughter? Is she unmarried and able to become my wife?" He followed as Laban turned his face toward the city once more.

"I have two daughters," Laban said, his voice suddenly strained. "But there is time enough to discuss your future." He glanced over his shoulder and motioned with one hand. "Come. Let us get you settled and enjoy a warm meal. Meet my family and partake of my table and tell me how my sister fares." Laban walked on, and Jacob grabbed the donkey's reins.

Two daughters. But he already knew that Rachel was the one he wanted. Rachel, whose dark eyes had captured his, whose gentle touch had held no pity when emotion overcame him. Rachel, who was a shepherdess, as he was a shepherd.

His heart lifted with the possibility. Irrational as it might seem, he would do whatever it took to have her.

Rachel walked past the cooking rooms and sniffed, greeted by the scent of ground cinnamon and baking bread. Her stomach rumbled in anticipation of the sweet treats yet quickly soured at the knowledge that Leah was at her best, trying to impress Jacob with her baking. Jacob, for his part, had been appreciative, but his attention always returned to Rachel, his look gentle, longing.

At first his interest had almost amused her, no different than other men she had known. Hadn't her many brothers acted in a similar way toward the women they'd married? Hadn't every man and boy who passed her at the market or spoke to her at the well when she was with the sheep acted the same? Men were predictable, if nothing else.

Yet as the weeks turned to a month, she did not find Jacob's looks or the way he acted toward her amusing in the least.

Here was a man who valued her, who considered her a woman of worth.

She smiled, comfortable in the knowledge yet pricked by irritation at Leah whistling while she worked. Rachel hurried on toward her rooms. The men would be in from the fields soon, and she wanted to change her tunic, dirty as it was from helping her mother weed their large garden.

Rachel enjoyed the study of plants and their uses on her treks through the fields and hills with the sheep. She had come across rare mandrakes once when she was in the fields and quickly offered them to her mother. Their use, it was said, could aid in fertility, but her mother had told her she had no wish to bear another child at her age. Still, she had taken them from Rachel's hand, declaring her too young to know about such things, and later admitted to offering them to Laban, who did not hesitate to catch her meaning. Unfortunately . . . or fortunately for her mother, no child had followed.

She moved from the hall that led to her bedchamber and met her maid, Bilhah, coming from the weaving room, a tunic draped over one arm. "Come, help me dress," she said.

"Yes, mistress." Bilhah obediently quickened her step as Rachel led her to her spacious room.

Rachel sank onto a low stool before a table that held her cosmetics and lifted the brass mirror. "Look in that chest and find me a fresh tunic." She held the mirror to her face, noting the smudges of dirt across her nose. She wiped them clean with a cloth.

"This yellow one would look nice on you."

Rachel turned as Bilhah held the garment for her approval. "No, not that one." She pointed to the chest, holding back an impatient sigh. The girl was young and new to Laban's house. It would take time to teach her. "Find the blue one. It's Jacob's favorite." She turned back to the mirror, then set it down and went to the low table that held a clay basin with brackish water.

This would never do. But she rinsed her dirty hands in it just the same, then crossed the room to the chest with her clothes.

"Never mind the tunic. I'll find it myself. Go, draw me some fresh water to wash with."

She sighed as Bilhah hurried off, turning her attention to the small stack of tunics. That she had several to choose from was a testament to her father's wealth and her sister's skill with the weaving. She ought to be more grateful to Leah for the fine clothes, but all she could think of was the way Leah had been putting too much effort into gaining Jacob's attention. Everyone knew Jacob cared for Rachel. He barely gave Leah a second glance. But though Leah rarely looked him in the eye, she watched him from the shadows, and Rachel heard the whispers and comments she made to her mother, Farah, or the other new servant, Zilpah.

Rachel pulled her best blue tunic from the pile, then chose a thick circlet of gold to cinch the waist, to accentuate just enough without causing her father to raise a brow. She would use the imported kohl to enhance the wide angles of her dark eyes and would place a small amount of ointment made from crushed poppies to bring out the color of her lips.

If Leah was going to bake her prized cinnamon pastries to tempt Jacob's ardor, she would do what she knew best and tempt him with one well-placed glance. She would allow her beauty to do the rest.

The meal that night held a festive tone. Jacob listened to and laughed with Laban and his sons while Laban's wives and daughters served them. At meal's end, Leah carried a tray of sweets to the table and placed them before her father. Laban motioned to Jacob to eat while Leah slipped into the shadows.

"Ah, Leah, my daughter, what fine treats you make for your poor father." Laban glanced behind him and waved his arm to draw her close once more. "My Leah is a marvel with dough and spices, and her weaving rivals your own mother's." He smiled, and Jacob felt suddenly uncomfortable with his perusal. "You will find no worker more dedicated than this girl." She bent closer at his insistence, and he kissed her cheek. "What say you, my boy? Are her baked goods not most appealing?"

Jacob took a bite of the sweet pastry and nodded his appreciation. They *were* good. But he caught the subtle undertone in Laban's words. He did not wish to take Leah to wife. He glanced at Leah, who looked beyond him, unwilling or unable to meet his gaze. The girl had no confidence, and though one might consider her pretty, she was not beautiful like her sister. What man would want a wife who wouldn't look him in the eye or glance at him with something more than wistfulness?

"Your daughter is quite skilled in her work. The sweets are most appreciated." He glanced her way again and caught the slight smile she seemed reluctant to give.

"Thank you," she said, her words strained as though something were stuck in her throat. She backed quickly away and stood once more in the shadows.

Jacob tilted his head. Curious girl. He turned his attention back to his uncle.

"You have been with me a month now, my son."

Was Laban rethinking his hospitality? Custom demanded a host offer to house a man three days before that man should no longer infringe on the host's kindness but offer his services, to work for his food and a place to sleep at night. But Jacob had worked for his uncle since the first day.

"Yes, my lord. The time has passed quickly." What more did his uncle want from him?

"Just because you are a relative of mine, should you work for me for nothing? Tell me what your wages should be," Laban said, helping himself to another of Leah's treats, his look pointed and assuming. Laban knew Jacob wanted to marry his daughter

Rachel. He was offering a way for him to pay the bride-price for her. But by his actions this night, Laban clearly wanted him to seek Leah's hand in marriage.

Jacob glanced across the room where Rachel stood some distance apart from her older sister. Lamplight bathed her face in a soft glow. Her robe was of the softest wool, and he imagined her skin was far softer. Longing filled him. How beautiful she was! And how much he wanted to spend his life at her side, listening to her words, her laughter.

He slowly pulled his gaze from her, a gaze she willingly returned with the confidence Leah lacked, a hint of mischief in her dark, alluring eyes. He looked again at his uncle. "I'll work for you seven years in return for your younger daughter Rachel."

The room grew still, and Jacob felt the gazes of all resting on him. It was a slight against Laban, who had clearly tried to place Leah before him. Yet Laban knew it was Rachel Jacob wanted from the first day. Surely he would not deny him! Seven years would seem like nothing if it were but Rachel who waited for him in the end.

Laban's expression clouded for the slightest moment, but as the air grew heavy around them with anticipated dread, Laban smiled. "It's better that I give her to you than to some other man. Stay here with me." He lifted his silver cup and Jacob did the same, their cups meeting in the middle of the table. "Seven years," he said.

"For Rachel," Jacob said, wanting to be sure everyone understood to what it was he had agreed.

"For Rachel," Laban agreed.

It was a trust. A betrothal. A contract between them. Rachel now belonged to him, as long as he kept his part of the bargain. In three and a half years he could pay the bride-price with the amount Laban would pay to shepherd a flock of sheep. He had offered seven, double the amount. To be sure Laban would give him his desire. To be sure he was not cheated.

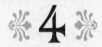

4

SEVEN YEARS LATER

Rachel stood at the gate as she did every night, waiting for Jacob to return from the fields, her heart beating with fresh anticipation. This day marked the end of Jacob's seven-year agreement with her father, which meant . . . he would ask for her soon. He had said as much as he left for the fields that very morning.

"Soon, beloved." His words were soft, a caress against her ear as he bent low, close enough for her to feel the heat of his breath on her cheek. They had kissed several times in the seven years of waiting, but rarely, for fear of her father's censure. The betrothal meant she belonged to Jacob in every legal sense, but still, they could not come together as man and wife until her father escorted her, veiled, to the marriage tent where Jacob would unveil his bride and they would be one.

She longed for that day with every fiber of her being. And now the day had arrived at last. Jacob would speak to her father after the evening meal, and her father would plan a feast by week's end. Her pulse quickened at the thought of all she had left to do. She would enlist Bilhah's help to bake the sweetmeats Jacob loved, and perhaps even Leah would be generous enough to offer her help. Surely the bitterness of Jacob's refusal had passed. It was her father who should never have encouraged Leah's hopes or put her in such a plight to suffer Jacob's rejection.

She stood on tiptoe and raised a hand to her brow, shading her eyes from the angle of the late afternoon sun. There! He crested the hill and hurried toward her. She burst through the gate and ran to him but stopped short at his side. How she longed for him to catch her and swing her about in his strong arms! *Another week*, she told herself. *Just one more week.*

"How beautiful you are, my bride!" Jacob winked, his lazy smile making her insides melt. He took her hand and rubbed soft circles along her palm. "Soon we will be together at last." His dark eyes held the fire of passion she had glimpsed on these rare moments alone, before a servant or sibling somehow appeared from some unseen hideaway, watching. Always watching. As if Jacob could not be trusted. But she knew he would never take her until the proper time.

He released her hand and led her toward the gate. "I will speak with your father this night." He glanced at her as if gauging her reaction. "Does this please you?"

She smiled, then glanced away, suddenly shy to speak of it. "Yes, my lord."

His fingers gently grazed her arm. "I love you, Rachel."

She looked up at that. "I love you, Jacob." Her heart did another flip at the look in his eyes. "Will you take us back to Canaan right away?" She had told him how willing she was to return to his father's house, how she longed to move away from her father, from Leah.

He stopped at the gate and turned to face her, but she didn't miss the shadow that crossed his face. "I do not know . . . that is, I hope so. Surely my brother's anger has passed. I will send word to my father to see if the time is right." He leaned in yet kept a safe distance. "I would be most happy to take you with me, just the two of us."

"But with provisions and servants." She smiled. He could

not possibly mean to travel alone without aid. They could never manage. And they could not return to his father empty-handed.

"Of course," he said. But he didn't look convinced. "Go now and prepare the meal for your father. After we partake, I will speak to him."

She nodded, smiling. "Yes, my lord." And she hurried to do his bidding.

❊❊❊

Jacob reclined at the table with Laban and his sons an hour later, sipping the last of the wine, full and anxious to speak. At last the women returned from the cooking rooms and stood along the walls. Jacob reached for the flask of wine and poured Laban a drink, then filled his cup as well. He met Laban's gaze, his heart thumping hard. In the seven years he had worked for the man, he had found Laban to be less than honest in his dealings. If not for the fact that the family had witnessed the betrothal, he would have expected the man to change the terms of that agreement as well. He seemed to have little respect for keeping his word.

But with the family in attendance, Jacob spoke with confidence. "Give me my wife. My time is completed, and I want to lie with her."

Laban looked at him, but his face was unreadable. He glanced toward his oldest son, Tariq. "Seven years is completed already?"

Jacob held his breath. What game was this? Laban knew very well the time had reached completion.

"Seven years to the day, my father," Tariq said, easing Jacob's anxious thoughts.

"Very well then. It is time we held a feast and brought this man his bride!" Laban lifted the cup Jacob had poured for him, suddenly smiling. Jacob did the same, his confidence slowly returning. "By week's end, you shall have your bride, my son."

Jacob lifted his cup and both drank freely. Laughter bubbled from a place deep within him. Soon Rachel would at last be his!

Leah paced her spacious bedchamber, her heart beating fast with each weighted footfall. Already runners had been sent throughout the town announcing the wedding feast that would take place at week's end. How could her father have allowed it to come to this? She was the firstborn! She was the one who truly loved Jacob. Rachel was too childish and flippant to really care about the man's heart. Rachel wanted someone to rescue her from their father's house, and to live like a princess over her own domain.

But Rachel didn't love Jacob like Leah did. How could she? The girl was far too vain and self-important to care about another.

Leah paused at the sound of footsteps and glanced quickly at the bronze mirror so often neglected on her cosmetic table. Lately she had found more use for the kohl and ointments, but still Jacob did not notice. She leaned close to the mirror, noting her flushed cheeks, and touched one, hoping the action would cool them. A knock sounded at her door. She jumped. Her nerves were frayed and fragile, her emotions too close to the surface. She would not weep. She would not give Rachel such satisfaction!

Dragging in a ragged breath, she smoothed imaginary wrinkles from her pristine robe and opened the door. "Ima."

Her mother, Farah, stood in the archway, her brows drawn close, heavy storm clouds brewing, her mouth pulled into a familiar frown. She moved past Leah and closed the door behind her. She faced Leah, arms crossed. "Your father is a fool." No welcoming embrace to allow Leah to weep over her loss.

"My father made a promise." She choked on a sob. "Oh, Ima, how can he do this? Rachel doesn't love Jacob! And how can he let her wed before I do? Am I such poor fruit on the vine that he can find no man worthy of me?" She covered her face, ashamed of her honest words.

"You are not poor fruit. The fault is your father's, not yours."
Farah touched Leah's shoulder, her tone suddenly softening.
"Whether Rachel loves the man or not, the truth is Jacob loves
her. No man works for a maid as long as he has done without
love. Lust alone would be too impatient." She stepped closer
then and wrapped Leah in her sturdy arms. "You mustn't fret,
my girl. There might yet be something we can do."

Leah stilled at her mother's words, leaning away to look at
her, to assess her meaning. "What can we possibly do, Ima?
Everyone is invited, and the wedding is in two days. Even if my
father found a man this night, we could not possibly wed before
Rachel. I will be a laughingstock!"

Farah pulled her close again and patted her back. "Hush now.
It is not so difficult as you think." She held Leah at arm's length
again. "Does not the bride go to her husband fully veiled?"

Leah stared wide-eyed, her mother's meaning suddenly clear,
and yet she could not voice the thought. It was both too exciting
and too terrible to utter. "What are you saying, Ima?"

"Only that your father owes you a husband. You are ten years
Rachel's senior, and she, the daughter of a lesser wife!" Farah's
words came through clenched teeth, the tone a fierce whisper.
"I will not stand by as my husband gives that haughty, spoiled
child everything she wants while you are denied." She touched
Leah's cheek. "No, my daughter. This will not be." She glanced
toward the door and leaned close. "I will speak to your father.
You will go to Jacob under the wedding veils. You will take your
sister's place and reign as first wife in Jacob's household. I only
ask one thing, my daughter."

Leah's mind whirled with the thoughts, unable to take it all in.
She swallowed past a suddenly dry throat, her pulse quickened
with longing. To become Jacob's wife? His first wife before
Rachel? And yet he would still take Rachel. That, her father
could not deny the man.

Farah's fingers tipped Leah's chin to force her to meet her

mother's gaze. Leah glanced beyond her first, then at last looked into her mother's dark eyes. "Can you share this man with your sister? You will be first, but you will not be his only. And he loves your sister. You know this. Can you marry a man who may never love you?" Her mother's gaze probed hers, searching.

Leah looked away, her thoughts churning, uncomfortable, and her mother released her hold. Could she? The words sent a pang to her heart. She had loved Jacob in silence for seven years. Surely once he took her to wife she would make him see how much she could do for him, how blessed he would be to have her. She would add to his household and feed him from the finest storehouses. She would give him sons. Pray God that were true.

Though the truth stood that Rachel could do every one of these things. There was no denying it. Rachel had grown and matured since the first days of Jacob's arrival. She was ready to wed the man, no matter how much Leah tried to pretend otherwise.

"Can you do this, Leah? Can you marry a man who will not share your love? I warn you, my daughter, it is a bitter herb to swallow to share a man." She touched Leah's cheek again, but Leah could not meet her gaze. "When your father married me, I was young. He was handsome and charming, and I begged my father to give me to him. But we were not married long, soon after your brother Tariq was born, before your father's eyes roamed and he took Refiqa as his concubine. She died before you were born. He married Suri soon after." She released a deep sigh. "Your house will be one of turmoil, and strife will not end between you and your sister if you do this. You must choose now, my Leah. If you would have Jacob, I will go at once to your father and demand he protect your honor and do as I say. He will listen to me. But I will not act unless you tell me you are willing." She brushed loose strands of hair away from Leah's forehead and waited.

Leah stood still, her gaze flitting from her mother to the bedchamber and its contents. She would forfeit this home and its comforts to live in tents with Jacob and Rachel in one of her father's fields just outside of the town. They would still be near her father's family, even part of his household, until Jacob returned them to Canaan.

Canaan. Rachel had talked of it often, and Jacob assured them he wanted to return there one day. Could she leave all she loved to travel there? Oh, but if only she could be the one to go with Jacob alone! She and Jacob and their children. But the overarching truth remained. Wherever Jacob went, Rachel would follow. Leah might be first wife, if they could follow through with this ruse and not be discovered. But she would not be the one he loved. And if Jacob should discover that it was Leah in his bed before she could get him to sleep with her, she would be worse than a laughingstock. She would be ruined!

And yet . . . if she did not take the risk, she would lose Jacob for good. For once he left for Canaan, she could not follow. No man would marry her once Rachel was wed, for they would see her as undesirable, the older sister, quickly forgotten.

She swallowed the bitter taste of it all and drew in a long, slow breath. At last she met her mother's gaze and forced herself to hold it. "I will do it. If my father will agree, I will wear the veils and marry Jacob in my sister's place."

Laban strode in from the fields, bone weary and longing for his clay pipe and some of the aged wine he'd been saving for the coming feast. He would lose Jacob by month's end. For once he wed Rachel, he would be free to leave Laban's employ and return to his father. While his sons might not miss the man, Laban had seen with his own eyes the difference in his flocks since Jacob took over as primary shepherd in charge of their care. Few lambs had miscarried and the stock was heartier, stronger, increasing Laban's wealth. If Jacob were to leave . . . He left the thought unfinished. Jacob couldn't leave. Not yet. But he had no way to hold him, to keep him in Paddan-Aram, especially when he talked so frequently of Canaan.

He rubbed the back of his neck to forestall a headache, with little relief. As he drew closer to the city gates, he squinted, seeing a lone figure rushing toward him. Farah. He braced himself, already sensing what was to come, the truth he had avoided for far too long.

She approached, her frown deepening as she drew near, and stopped short in front of him, hands on her ample hips. "How can you possibly allow that foolish child of a lesser wife to wed before our daughter?"

"Is that any way to greet your husband after he has worked a long day?" Why couldn't she sweeten her words as Suri did with honeyed tone and gentle smile? Even the scent of Farah's sweet perfume, usually meant to entice him, did nothing to soften his sudden ire. "Have you not nagged me about this often enough? What good does it do to remind me of my failures now? Do you think I want to see Jacob take my daughter and return to his father? But there is nothing to be done. I have given my word."

Farah huffed. "Since when does your word stand for anything?"

He bristled at the insinuation. He kept his word. He only shaded the meaning when the need arose. But no matter which way he looked at this situation with Jacob, he could not find a way to change the meaning of their agreement. "What would you have me do?" There were no men lining up to wed his oldest daughter. He had waited too long, had thought to gain a higher price than she could command, and now there were few her age left in Harran who were not already wed. He could consider the widower Sohrad, but Leah had already scorned the man.

"Give Leah to Jacob instead of Rachel. With her fully veiled and led to his tent, he will not know the difference until it is too late."

Laban blinked, not sure he had heard correctly. "You want me to give Leah to Jacob instead of Rachel." By her look he knew she thought him daft. Her bitter spirit had poisoned him so much over the years that he often forgot how well she understood him. How much alike they were in thought, in craftiness.

"It is a good plan. You know it is." Farah's mouth tipped only slightly in a cunning smile.

"Jacob is no fool. He will demand Rachel as well."

Farah shrugged. "Then give her to him. After Leah's wedding week. Make him work for you for Leah another seven years." Her laugh held sarcasm, but her knowing look went straight to his heart.

"What am I supposed to do with Rachel while Jacob lies with Leah in the huppa?"

"Seclude her. Threaten her. Take her away. She will listen to you. You are her father. She has no choice but to obey."

"My *wife* has no choice but to obey either, but she doesn't seem bothered by that fact." What was he supposed to tell Suri then? She would turn against him, toss nettles in his bed. There were ways a woman could ruin a man, head of the family or not.

He looked at Farah, calculating. "You just want to put Suri in her place."

Farah shrugged again. "It is no matter to me what you do with your concubine."

"Wife."

She inclined her head. "She is secondary. Leah is your first daughter of your first wife. You have an obligation."

She was right about that. He felt the dowry weighing heavily in his leather pouch. Jacob had paid for Rachel. *Give me my wife.* But he had not named her specifically. Just "give me my wife." He could feign ignorance. He shook his head. Jacob would never abide such a thing.

But the plan could still work. Laban nodded. "Very well then. Bring Rachel to me. Dress Leah in Rachel's wedding clothes."

"No need. She has made her own."

Laban smoothed his face to reveal no response, but his heart kicked over with the sense of one who has just beaten his opponent. He was not the only one who wanted to keep Jacob around, nor the only one who felt the need to keep control of his daughters. It was time he did something to please Farah, and Leah should marry before Rachel. He would simply tell Jacob that was the way they did things here. He would be none the wiser.

But what words would convince Rachel? She held sway over Laban's actions, and he had given in to her pleading all of her life. How was he to command her to keep silent? He could have Tariq take her to the house in Harran while the feast took place in Paddan-Aram. Or he could bind her and lock her away until Leah's night ended.

He tasted the bitter gall of the fate that awaited his little girl. What a foolish father he was! But there was no other way to keep Jacob from leaving. There was nothing else he could do.

5

Rachel passed through the courtyard and surrounding grounds where servants worked to transform the place into a flower-bedecked, musical world. Scents of yeast and cinnamon mingled with the smells of cumin, garlic, and fennel. Stews and sweet-meats, bread, and her father's finest wines had been pulled from his storehouses. Rachel did a little twirl, giggling like a young child, and caught Bilhah's arm.

"The huppa awaits you, mistress, like a jewel uncovered in the field," Bilhah said as they hurried on, nearly knocking into a servant carrying an armful of unlit torches.

Rachel stopped to look at her slave girl, a gift her father promised would accompany her into her marriage to Jacob. "I will admit, I am nervous to enter it." She smiled, her heart doing a little flip. "But come, let us hurry or we won't be back in time to help with the meal."

Their arms were loaded with stacks of linens Rachel would soon need after her wedding week. Jacob had told her he would be out in the fields today, and she could start to arrange her side of the tent whenever she liked. Warmth heated her cheeks at the familiar way he had looked at her and the intimate kiss that followed. Tonight they would be together as man and wife. Her pulse quickened at all that she knew awaited her in the marriage tent, things her mother had intimated and the servants had teased her about since the night Jacob announced his desire to lie with her.

They approached the black goat's-hair tents at the edge of her father's fields just over the hill, Rachel's hope rising with each footfall. The flaps were down to protect Jacob's meager belongings from being swept away by high winds or taken by greedy passersby, though in truth, he had little to take. His efforts had gone into paying her father for her hand in marriage. Together they must work to build Jacob's house until it rivaled her father's vast estate.

She lifted the flap and let her eyes adjust to the semidarkness. Little light, even the bright light of the morn, passed through the black goat's hair, but they wouldn't be here long enough to light a lamp. There was too much yet to do to prepare for the feast and the wedding guests who would be arriving by nightfall.

"Will we really leave for Canaan soon?" Bilhah's question caught her up short. Rachel lifted the lid on a carved wooden chest that her father had delivered to Jacob's tent on her behalf and filled it with the tunics and sheets that she and Leah had labored over in strained silence. A sigh escaped as she took Bilhah's stack of loincloths and undergarments and tucked them neatly out of sight. How glad she would be to get away from Leah!

"As soon as Jacob feels it is safe to return, yes." She touched the carved wood of the lid as she lowered it, feeling the smooth craftsmanship beneath her fingers. They would have to leave such a chest behind or fit it onto an oxcart to transport. But she couldn't fault her father for the gift. He knew how much she loved beauty.

She moved from her side of the tent, the room Jacob had partitioned off for her, and entered the spacious open room where they would eat and entertain guests. Colorful rugs of various stripes covered the floor, and cushions lined the tent walls. A fire pit sat in the area marked off as a courtyard outside the tent's door. In the cool of the evenings they would be able to sit by the fire or under the awning and gaze at the stars, as she had often done in the fields with the sheep.

"We should get back, mistress. Your mother said we would leave soon for the river to wash." Bilhah stepped to the side to allow Rachel to exit the tent first. Rachel took one last wistful look at the place she would soon call home and stepped into the bright light of day.

She blinked as her eyes readjusted, then looked back toward her father's house, where smoke slowly rose from cooking fires and young boys turned spits, sending the succulent scents of roasted lamb in her direction. But her heart did a little flip at the sudden movement coming from the direction of the stables. She would recognize her father's portly form even with the field between them. And he was coming straight toward her.

"What could he want, mistress?" Bilhah had been with them long enough to recognize her father's agitation. "Do you think something has happened?"

A lump formed in Rachel's throat as myriad possibilities formed in her thoughts. Had something happened to Jacob? She once heard of a woman whose betrothed husband drowned in the Euphrates the night before they were to wed. He had been laughing and imbibing and had slipped into the river whose current was high and running too fast at that time of year, and his witless friends tried in vain to pull him out before it was too late. But no, Jacob would not imbibe in the daytime, and the only friends he could name were her own brothers. Besides, he was with the sheep . . . unless a lion or bear had come upon him unsuspecting . . .

"I'm sure my father is just worried and wondering where I've run off to." Though her father should not even be thinking about such things. Her mother was the one who had warned her to hurry back. "You go on ahead and tell my mother I am coming. I will see what my father wants."

Bilhah nodded, probably not the least sorry to leave her with Laban, for Rachel knew her father intimidated the poor girl, who was as insecure as Leah but not nearly as prickly or opinionated.

As Bilhah left her, Rachel moved away from Jacob's tent and met her father at the edge of the courtyard, accepting his kiss. "What has you so agitated, my father? Is something wrong? Is it Jacob?"

She looked into her father's eyes, searching, but he would not meet her gaze. "Jacob is fine," he said, obviously to appease her. He motioned her back toward Jacob's tents. "Your mother told me you were here. Are you alone?"

"I sent my maid back to the house. Yes, except for you, I am quite alone." A niggle of fear crept along the back of her neck. "What is so urgent on my wedding day, Father? My mother is waiting to take me to the river."

Laban did not speak as he lifted the flap and motioned for her to precede him into the tent. Darkness settled once more, and Rachel blinked, adjusting to the dimness. She whirled on him, arms crossed. "Why are we here? What have I done?" He had chastened her but a few times in her girlhood, but today of all days she did not deserve to be singled out with such obvious alarm and concern.

"You have done nothing, my child. It is I who have been the fool." He looked at her then, his brow creased with sorrow. "But I am afraid it is you who must bear the consequences of my foolishness." He looked away and walked farther into the room. "I should not have given in to you so often as a child." He slowly turned. "If you had been more obedient, less spoiled, it would make what I am about to tell you easier to bear. Though you must know that it pains me to tell it, despite what you think of me."

The fear took wing inside of her. "Speak plainly, Father. Please. I cannot bear such riddles, today of all days!"

It was then that she saw the rope swinging loosely from his side. Her father fingered it, and her heart skipped a beat at the commanding look in his eyes.

"I am going to have to alter my agreement with Jacob," Laban said, his voice suddenly hardened stone, a tone she had only heard from him when he was angry or implacable.

"What are you talking about—alter your plans?" She clasped suddenly trembling hands in front of her, willing them to be still. "You cannot even think to go back on your agreement. He has paid the bride-price!" Her voice had risen in pitch, and she could feel the anxiety rising within her.

Laban nodded and stepped closer, placed a hand on her arm. "No, no, I am not going back on my agreement, dear child. He has paid for a wife from among my daughters, and I intend to give him that."

His words swirled in her head, but she quickly caught his meaning. "He paid for me, Father. Not just any wife."

"It is not fitting that you marry before your sister."

"My sister is not betrothed. You cannot make me wait until she is. Jacob will not wait." The shaking grew within her at his look.

"Jacob will not have to wait. But I am afraid, my daughter, that you must wait a little longer." He stepped away from her and crossed his arms over his ample middle, his expression brooking no argument. But argue she must!

"What do you mean?" Anger surged, heating her blood. "I am to be wed this night."

"Leah will take your place."

Reeling, she took a step back, stumbling in her sudden weakness. Her father caught her arm to steady her, but she shook it away.

"What do you mean, Leah will take my place?" Her words were hoarse, as though they had been driven over rough sands.

Laban walked to the tent's door and looked out, as if assessing whether they were still really alone.

"What's the matter, Father? Are you afraid Jacob will return to his own tent and find you plotting his ruin?" As he turned to face her once more, she met his gaze with a determined one of her own. "You cannot do this."

"I can and I must. And you, my daughter, will accept my decision." He walked closer to her, his tone firm, his expression unmoving.

"And if I don't? One word from me, from my mother, from anyone, and Jacob will know of the ruse. Leah will be ruined. Is that what you want?" Why would Leah even agree to such a thing? Jacob would surely notice the difference between the two of them once he removed the wedding veils. Leah was similar in height and build to Rachel, and her hair was dark, though not quite as dark, but surely one look into her eyes . . . Leah would not look at Jacob, not share the intimate looks Rachel and Jacob had already shared. He would notice immediately . . . Surely he would notice . . .

"Your sister loves Jacob. She is willing to take the risk."

The words rocked her. Jacob loved her, Rachel, and she him. Leah should not have even looked in Jacob's direction, knowing he was bound to her sister. Was Leah so hateful?

"Was this her idea?" The words tasted sour on her tongue.

Laban shook his head. "You must not blame your sister."

"How can I not? You are telling me that she is to wed my husband!" Her voice shook as the words rose in volume again. "What of me? I am to just sit by and watch?" Tears rose so quickly they blurred her vision.

"You do not have to watch, dear child." His tone was placating, soothing, but she would not accept his comfort. "Give Leah her wedding week. Then I will give you to Jacob as well."

"It is my wedding week! This is my wedding everyone is planning, and Jacob is expecting me!" She choked on the words. "How can you do this to me?"

"Leah is the firstborn daughter of my first wife. I cannot let you wed ahead of her."

"Then why didn't you give her to another years ago? Why

give her *my* husband? I want to get away from her, not be forced to live with her the rest of my days!" Emotion rose so strong it took her breath. Never had she hated another human being with such force as she did her father and her sister in that moment.

"I should have. This is why I told you it is I who am the fool. And now we are at a point that something has to be done or your sister will never wed. I cannot put Jacob off another year while I look for a man to wed your sister. He might take you in dishonor and leave Paddan-Aram." Laban bobbed his head as if he somehow expected his words to placate her.

"Jacob would never dishonor me. Though you seem to have no trouble doing so."

She felt the sting of his palm against her cheek, startling her, bringing sudden tears. She placed a hand over the heated flesh. Never had he struck her!

"My child," he said, his tone no longer placating. "I am your father. And while you may not like my decisions, you are still my daughter and you must live by them. It is by my good graces that you will marry Jacob at all. Yes, he is a close relative, but you are the youngest of my children. It is not fitting that you marry before the oldest."

He shifted from foot to foot and glanced once more at the tent door, a look of sudden discomfort crossing his face. "And though it pains me to hurt you, Rachel, the truth is, sometimes in life things don't go our way." He raked a hand over his beard and scratched at the stubble. "Tonight we will celebrate, and Jacob will drink too much wine, and I will lead Leah to the huppa beneath the wedding veils. You will stay in your room. Tariq will guard you, lest you think to somehow thwart my plans."

He reached a hand to touch her flaming cheek. She flinched, but he grasped her shoulder and held her firm. "I would not mar this beauty, my daughter, but I will not hesitate to have you bound and silenced if you do not promise me this moment that you will accept my decision. Do you agree to keep silent?"

Tears blinded her from clear vision, but she nodded, know-ing in that moment that her father had the power to do as he wished. She had always known it at some level, but never in such a personal way. What joy could he possibly get in destroying the most important day of her life?

"Let Leah wed Jacob after me. Just please don't take this day from us." Jacob would be crushed when he discovered the ruse.

"Jacob would never accept her willingly. No. This is the only way."

Bitterness rose within her at the flippant way he said the words, as if he had calculated every possibility and chosen the only one that Jacob could not fight. "Jacob is getting a bargain then—two brides for the price of one," she said. Though Jacob's seven years had already produced double what need be paid for a wife. And she would be saddled with Leah for the rest of her life.

"Jacob will work for Leah as he did for you." Her father's self-assurance rocked her.

"What are you saying?" He had succumbed to delusion if he thought Jacob would stay here a moment longer than he had to. She wouldn't let him! If they could not escape Leah, then at least let them escape this man who would ruin their life's hap-piness in one selfish act.

"If you were worth seven years, Leah is worth as much. It is only fair."

It took every bit of her strength not to strike him. But her stinging cheek and his grip on her arm stayed her hand. *You don't know the meaning of fair.* But she could not say the words. She knew her father, knew what he was like. He just wanted Jacob's free labor for as long as he could get it. They would never prosper if every bit of Jacob's wages went to pay for her sister!

Truth dawned with the thought. "You are doing this to keep Jacob from returning to Canaan."

Laban released his grip and shrugged. "It is part of the bar-gain. I cannot simply give your sister to him for nothing. She is already risking life with a man who will not love her. I cannot make her feel as though she is worth nothing."

He sounded so magnanimous. But she knew the real reason. "You could have just asked him to stay." But Leah was part of this mess. It was Leah's desires he was caving in to. Farah must have been behind it too.

"The hour is late, and I would have your word, my daughter. Can I trust your silence, or will you force me to take it from you?" He tipped her chin to look into her eyes. She could not lie to him.

"You have my word." But as he walked her back to the house, taking the long way to avoid any servants who might see her weeping, her mind whirled with some way to warn Jacob. If she could get word to Bilhah or her mother, *someone*, perhaps things could still go in her favor.

6

Jacob's pulse quickened as he stood in the center of his tent and allowed Laban's servant Raheem to dress him. Rachel's scent still lingered in the air, and he knew by one quick glance into her side of the tent that she had been there. He fidgeted with the sash until Raheem took it from him and knotted the belt at his waist. Rachel would undo the knot and he would remove her veils. Soon. They would at last be one.

The thought made his blood pump like fire through his veins. He had waited so long. Oh, how he loved her! And yet seven years seemed like nothing to him now. She was his life! And he would shower her with every gift he could find for the sheer joy of spending each day with her. And one day soon, perhaps once the little ones came, he would return to his father and show him with pride the woman who had captured his heart.

He followed Raheem through the tent's opening and looked out across the field where Laban's house glowed like the noonday sun. Lanterns coated in pitch sat low to the ground, illuminating the huppa at the edge of the family courtyard. Music of flutes and lyres and the occasional beat of the wedding drum floated on the evening air. Laughter from the wedding guests rose with the songs praising the bride's purity. *Rachel*.

He followed the scents and sounds, his eyes searching, until at last he narrowed the search and found his bride. She was sitting on a raised dais, completely covered in veils so thick he could see nothing. Even her hands rested beneath the folds, hands he had come to love, not only for the foods they prepared or the tunics they mended, but for the long fingers and hennaed nails. His Rachel's love of beauty made her paint the nails and the skin of her feet in patterns of leaves and flowers and the smallest lambs. How he longed to touch the hennaed patterns along her ankle and . . . He shook his head. He would not think of it now. Not until . . .

He drew a breath as they approached the courtyard's edge and a trumpet signaled his arrival. Laban's plump form burst from among a crowd of guests, his flushed face like a man who had already partaken of too much wine.

"Jacob, my son. You are here at last! Come. Come." He wrapped a beefy arm around Jacob's taller frame, stretching to encase him in a warm embrace. "Come and eat and drink." He led Jacob to a table spread with foods both salty and sweet, delicacies that he would enjoy more after he had been with Rachel. But he could not voice the request. Patience. Restraint. Had he not waited seven years?

"Come, Zilpah, bring a flask and fill the bridegroom's cup." Laban's voice boomed the short distance to where the servant stood, and at his command she hurried closer and thrust a silver goblet into Jacob's waiting hands. "Drink, my son." Laban lifted a cup of his own and drank, then motioned Jacob away from the bride's dais to join his sons and the men of the city, who had come for a feast with more food than Laban had spared at sheep shearing time.

Jacob glanced over his shoulder at his waiting bride, then reluctantly followed, a dumb sheep to the slaughter, allowing Laban to dictate his every movement, drinking the sweetest of wines as had ever touched his lips until he was not sure he could hold another drop. The bright lights and scents of male bodies mingled with

the scents of rich meats and spiced breads. But in all of the feasting and laughter, the throb of the wedding drum lingered, and
one glance toward the bride's dais told him Rachel still waited.

I am coming, beloved. Soon.

Another cup of the sweet wine. He tilted it too far, spilling
a drop onto the smooth courtyard stones. Ribald comments
followed, until at last Laban stood.

"Your bride awaits you, my son. Wait here while I escort her
to the huppa."

Jacob's pulse had grown sluggish with more wine than he
was used to, and he swayed as he stood. Two of Laban's sons,
Melcher and Darab, appeared at his sides, steadying him, while
Laban trotted off to the dais and took his daughter's hand. *Soon.
I'm coming, Rachel.*

He watched as Rachel and her father disappeared into the
bridal tent to await him.

Rachel paced her small bedchamber until her legs grew limp.
She stopped at the door. Tried the leather handle. Still barred
from the outside. Her voice was hoarse from weeping, and her
screams had been drowned out by the music and laughter going
on outside in the courtyard. The music and laughter of *her* wedding feast! Yet it was Leah who sat beneath the veils awaiting
their hour. The thought brought the tears again. And then, for
the briefest moment, the wedding drums stopped.

She screamed loud and long. But the drum started up again
as the door burst open. Her brother Tariq crossed the threshold
in two strides, grabbed her arm, and slapped her cheek. Hard.

"You promised your silence. Let there be no more from you."
He pulled a linen cloth from his belt and stuffed it into her
mouth, then wrenched both arms behind her.

She squealed and tried to spit out the cloth, but it was wedged
just right, and he would not release her arms to free it.

"Not this time, you spoiled child." He pushed her onto the bed and quickly bound her wrists behind her. She fought and kicked at him until he yanked her around and shoved her against the pillows. "I will bind your feet if you don't stop this now!"

His tone and the look of anger in his eyes made her still.

"That's better." He got up and closed the door, his eyes never leaving hers, then returned and sat beside her on the bed. "Why do you make this so hard for yourself?" Tariq's tone had gentled, and she looked away from the pity in his eyes. "In a week, Father will give you to Jacob and all will be well. Why put up such a fuss for a few extra days?" He brushed a strand of hair from her eyes, then leaned back, looking at her. "I will take out the cloth if you promise not to yell again. Do you promise?"

She nodded. His expression held wariness. "I do not know why I should believe you." But he reached for the cloth and gently tugged it free. "Do not make me replace it."

She shook her head, her eyes filling again. Tears fell freely down her cheeks. She had no way to wipe them with her hands bound. Tariq used the cloth and touched it to her face. "There is no sense in crying over it, Rachel. What is done is done. You cannot change it, so accept it and live with it. There is nothing else to do if you wish to live in peace."

She studied him, this half brother who had been born before Jacob's mother even wed his father, a brother old enough to have fathered her himself. "Of course you would take Leah's side. Why should you favor a half sister over your own flesh and blood?"

Tariq rubbed a hand over his face, his beard seasoned with the years. "I would protect both of my sisters, even from themselves," he said after a lengthy pause. "Jacob can protect you both."

"Jacob doesn't want her!" The words were broken, a quiet sob, nearly silenced by the drum whose beat now told her that Jacob would have entered the tent to unveil his bride. "What will you do if he realizes before morning that my sister is in my place?"

Tariq tilted his head as if by doing so he could hear the friendly banter and merriment from the wedding feast. But they were too far from the courtyard to hear more than the music and distant laughter. That she was held prisoner, missing it all . . .

"Once he disrobes her, he cannot refuse her." Tariq's quiet words made her pause. She had not thought of that. To be alone with a woman in that way . . . it would truly be too late.

"You planned this well." Her words were as weighted as her heart.

"I did not plan this at all." Tariq looked at her. "I would have given Jacob what he wanted." No mention of her wishes. "He will be angry come morning."

"Or sooner."

Tariq shook his head. "Father made sure he had enough to drink." He stood, undid her bonds. "Get some sleep. Let Leah have this one night where she can feel the love you alone will know from this time forward."

He walked from the room and closed the door, leaving Rachel to ponder his words behind him.

Leah's heart pounded, skipping beats ahead of the wedding drum. Her father's reassuring words as he whispered to her once they were at the door of the huppa did not help. Her only thought was what Jacob would do when he discovered their ruse. Would he strike her? Would he put her out? Fear snaked through her, and she could not stop the shaking despite the warmth of the heavy veils and the heat coming from the lamps outside.

She stood inside the tent now, her filtered gaze making out a few shapes, yet not enough to move comfortably without tripping over her own feet. They had kept the lamps low outside, with none to guide within, lest Jacob see her clearly. How glad she was now that she and Rachel were similar in height and shape. And she had determined as she sat beneath the veils that when Jacob looked into her eyes, she would hold his gaze, unflinching. If she looked away, as she did so often without thinking, he would know. And she could not let him.

Resolve quickened her pulse as the drum picked up its cadence. In the distance, she had heard Rachel's cries, though her words were indistinct. Guilt filled her at what they were doing to her, to Jacob. Especially to Jacob. For though Leah could happily put Rachel aside and leave her in their father's home while she traveled with Jacob alone to Canaan, she would not be able to live with herself knowing how much Jacob would suffer.

Laughter grew closer, and she heard the sound of her father's voice. "Treat my daughter well, my son." A friendly slap on the back, perhaps.

"You have nothing to fear, my lord." Jacob's voice, strong, though slightly slurred.

Leah's pulse jumped as the voices ceased and the tent flap opened and fell back in place, closing them in darkness. She could feel his presence, though his form lay in shadows. He moved closer, his breath hot against her cheek.

"Rachel." He said the name like a caress. Leah cringed inwardly, her resolve weakening. His touch on her shoulder sent little waves of joy through her. Never had he touched her in any way, and now his hands probed her veils, seeking their release. "We are alone at last, beloved."

She nodded, not daring to speak. He would recognize her voice. Surely he would! Her mind whirled with what to do, all her mother had reminded her to do. *Whisper.* Of course. He would not be able to tell her voice if she kept it low, husky.

"Jacob," she said, so softly she thought at first he did not hear. But his fingers worked more quickly, pulling and tugging the fine linen from her face until at last he freed it.

She held her breath, waiting for him to continue. Did he recognize her already?

But his hands cupped her cheeks, and his head bent, his eyes closed. He kissed her eyes, her nose, until his lips rested on hers. Soft, tentative, but when she responded, the kiss deepened, taking her breath with it. He pulled back at last and looked into her eyes. She held his gaze, unflinching, praying the dim light would conceal the pale color, praying the kohl that she had used to match the look of Rachel's eyes would disguise her just enough.

A smile lifted the corner of his lips, and his gaze moved from her face to the rest of her veil-draped form. Slowly, carefully, he removed her robe. Then as if in a dance, keeping pace with the music outside, she placed her hands on the sash at his waist and undid the knot. His robe slipped to the tent floor where hers now lay in a heap. When at last the unveiling was complete, Jacob led her to the mat, whispering sweet words to her. Words she knew belonged to Rachel. Words she didn't deserve.

Yet words she clung to, pretending that for this one night, they were meant for her alone.

7

Jacob awoke the next morning, his head throbbing. Where was he? For a moment the thoughts would not clear, but then slowly, enticingly, the memories returned. *Rachel*. He let his mind travel over each moment of the night before, relishing the tender feel of her touch. How sweet the love they'd shared! And all the more so for having waited so long. He'd been almost surprised to find her so willing, so passionate. He smiled, though the action made his head hurt worse. Laban had filled him too full of wine! But the wine had not stopped him from enjoying each moment with his beloved.

He glanced at the woman still curled on her side, asleep. Love filled him. He rested his head on the soft pillow and closed his eyes. How different life would be now that they were together. Ima would be proud of his choice.

Thoughts of his mother made him yearn for home. Surely the danger of Esau's anger had passed. He would speak to Laban as soon as their wedding week ended and make plans to travel to Canaan within the year.

Rachel shifted toward him, drawing his thoughts back to this amazing bride. Dappled sunlight filtered through the tent's side as dawn broke free of night's hold. He turned, facing her. Stroked fingers through her undone hair, hair that spilled over her bare skin and the thin sheet that covered her. A shiver passed through her at his touch, and he smiled, watching as she slowly awoke and grew aware of her surroundings.

"Good morning, my love," he said, the words a caress against her ear.

She stiffened ever so slightly, then seemed to relax into his embrace. "Good morning, my lord."

No longer the whispers of the night, her words sounded strange to his ear. Perhaps the food and drink of night had somehow altered her voice. He sighed. Perhaps his own headache was to blame.

But as he lay with his arm draped over her, enjoying the feel of her by his side, a new thought shoved its way forward like a warrior with sword drawn. Memories of his own voice speaking deceitful words in his father's ear, words his father trusted despite his doubts. If only his father had listened closely and trusted his senses, he would not have been deceived.

The guilt cut through him as though it were yesterday, and with it an unnamed fear. Slowly, as one still awakening from sleep, he rose on one elbow and faced her. Hair the color of Rachel's, yet with ruddy streaks of the same red that covered Esau's frame from head to foot, spilled over creamy tan shoulders. His heart stopped.

He drew a ragged breath, his fingers moving of their own accord to brush the hair from her eyes. She lifted their closed lids. Met his gaze with eyes too pale, unable to hold his without skipping to some point behind him.

Leah!

"What are you doing here?" The words choked him, and he backed away from her, sure she had singed him. His limbs felt like fire as he pushed to his feet. "Why are you in my bed?" Trembling seized him as flashes of the intimacies they'd shared mingled with the flashes of memories of his father's shocked face, his brother's fury.

He did not wait for her to reply. He grabbed his robe from the floor, thrust his arms through the sleeves, and tied the belt in a careless knot, then stormed from the tent. Laban met him on the path to the house, where the servants hurried about cleaning the remnants of last night's merrymaking. Wedding guests had left long ago but would return to celebrate every night for a week. For a wedding that was false!

"What is this you have done to me? I served you for Rachel, didn't I?" Jacob's voice rose with each word. "Why have you deceived me?" The urge to strike Laban rose so swiftly Jacob nearly gave in to it. But his own accusing fingers pointed back at him, quashing only some of his rage. He faced Laban, hands fisted at his sides. "Tell me!"

Laban took a step back as if he did not trust Jacob's response, but before the man could speak, a figure emerged from the house draped in the same soft robe and tunic she'd worn the first day she met him in the fields with the sheep.

Rachel. Ah, Rachel! A deep groan fought its way through him, begging release. She stood there, her dark eyes filled with such pain he felt the dagger plunging to his marrow. They had both been tricked, kept from each other. For what?

Anger surged again, and he faced her father. "Why have you done this?"

Her father's dark eyes held his. Why had he never noticed before how calculating their gleam? "It is not our custom here to give the younger daughter in marriage before the older one."

"I was not told of such a custom. If this were true, why not marry the other off years ago?" He could not bear to say her name. "You had seven years!"

Laban's head bobbed as it always did when he intended to be amiable. "Finish this daughter's bridal week," he said, grasping one of Jacob's shoulders. "Then we will give you the younger one also, in return for another seven years of work."

Jacob stared at the man, dumbstruck. Another seven years?

His mother and father might not live long enough to meet Rachel if he stayed. But as he met Laban's gaze, he knew he would not be released of his debt so easily. Laban would keep him here by whatever deception.

He glanced in Rachel's direction. How lost and small she seemed. He would work a lifetime for her alone. And if that meant seven more years, he would do it. Not for Leah. For Rachel.

"She will be mine at week's end. I will not wait." Jacob would battle the man to the grave if he must.

Laban patted his shoulder, then stepped back, giving a curt nod. "After this daughter's week ends, the younger will be yours as well."

"Rachel will be mine." He grasped Laban's arm, his grip firm.

Laban glanced from Jacob's hand to meet his gaze once more. "Rachel will be yours," he said at last, shaking free of Jacob's hold.

Jacob stood a moment more, some of his fury subsiding as he watched Laban walk to Rachel's side and guide her back into the house. His pulse slowly returned to a normal rhythm. He would dress and go to the fields until the week ended, but Laban would surely hunt him down and force him into the huppa. For despite his need to flee, he could not. A bride awaited him, and he was duty bound to stay with her.

Whether he wanted to or not.

Leah crouched in a corner on the raised mat, the place where she had given herself to Jacob with all of her being. How different a morning could be! How different her life would be from this moment forward. No longer the pretense of allowing him to think she was Rachel. He knew. And in the knowing, he hated her.

She pulled the sheet to her chin, shivering beneath the soft folds, the chill not coming from the cool dawn as much as it was from the look in Jacob's eyes when he had realized her true identity. She closed her eyes, hearing again the angry words Jacob had flung at her father. Words she and her father both deserved. But there was no undoing it. For a moment she had held her breath, fearing Jacob would insist on putting her aside, demanding Rachel this very night.

When he had agreed to finish her wedding week, she could not stop the tears. The act, the willingness to cover her shame, filled her with gratitude. How she loved him! Could he feel even a small measure of affection for her?

She waited, her breath coming slowly, listening for his footfalls. He would return to the tent. Surely he would.

Silence greeted her. She sat still, telling herself to rise, to dress, but sudden fear of him paralyzed her. She curled tighter, huddled, suddenly wishing with a vehemence that surprised her that she had not been party to this deceit. She had hurt him. Stolen from him the love he had longed for.

The small victory she had felt over her sister now tasted like dung on her tongue.

Jacob stood at the huppa's door, emotion warring within him. To enter meant he accepted Laban's bargain to keep Leah. There had been no mention of putting her aside, and the thought had not occurred to him until this moment. He could turn back. March into the house and wait for the guests to arrive that very night, then declare Laban's deceit to all. Laban would lose his good name in the town, and his sons would pay the price. And if the men wanted proof, Jacob need only walk into the tent and bring his *bride* to stand before them. The family would suffer humiliation and most likely financial loss.

But Jacob could also lose Rachel in the process.

Doubt troubled him. He had paid for Rachel in good faith.

If he took her now, leaving Leah behind, he would be forced to flee. For exposing Laban would surely bring his wrath down on Jacob once the men of the town returned home. And then where could he go? What if his father would not receive him?

He was tired of running.

And if getting rid of Leah meant losing Rachel, it would exact too high a price.

He paused a moment more, still flirting with indecision. He wanted Rachel. Only Rachel. And he knew from watching Laban and the bickering and conniving that ensued between his two wives that he did not want to marry two sisters! But he could not deny that he had known her most thoroughly last evening. And to divorce her now would be her ruin.

He shook his head, feeling the throb of the morning's headache increase with the strain of choice. He glanced back toward the house. Saw two of Laban's sons standing in the courtyard, watching him. Undoubtedly sent by Laban, who did not trust him.

He held their gaze for a heady moment. It was in his power to hurt them, to hurt them all as he had been harmed. But guilt of his past sins proved too weighty a reminder. Leah was no worse than he, probably prompted by her father as he had been by his mother. The thought added to his loathing, both of her and of himself. For with Rachel, he could forget himself.

Leah would be a constant reminder.

❄✦❄

Leah glanced up at the light coming through the tent flap and, at the sight of Jacob standing there, released a breath that had become lodged within her. His look held censure and pain, and she longed to go to him. But still she waited. Would he send her away? Had he come only to tell her to collect her things, that the marriage was over?

He stood looking down at her for the space of too many

heartbeats. And she could not look away from the strength of his gaze.

"What will you do?" she said at last, unable to endure the brittle silence.

"Not what I want." He moved away from her to the small sitting area where they were expected to take their meals, to spend time together, to talk, to get to know one another. Then when evening came, he would emerge from the tent and take his place with the guests, while she waited, secluded, for him to return to her and fulfill his commitment. Which meant she hadn't much time to make him care for her, for him to get to know her for herself.

She moved from the mat and retrieved her bridal tunic, a garment she had poured much love into in secret, away from Rachel's prying eyes. But he would not care for the little details she had added, the intricate patterns she had woven along the edges of the sleeves . . . Her thoughts stopped short, and she wondered how she could think such things at a time like this.

He slumped to the pillows, rich cushions she had also woven with her mother's help. For Rachel, she reminded herself. Guilt washed over her, and she staggered. Hunger gnawed at her as she glanced at the table laden with fresh fruits and cheeses, put there by her maid Zilpah, who would have sneaked into the tent early this morn to leave the offering while they slept. But she could not eat.

She stepped closer to him. Small, tentative steps, then she sank to her knees at his side. She lifted her hands, a supplicating gesture. "I am sorry, Jacob." The look he gave her did nothing to ease the tension in her heart. "I was wrong. I see that now. It's just . . ." She looked away, tears filling her throat. She swallowed. Her tears would not sway him. She had seen Rachel use them to get her way and had determined she would not do the same.

She swiped them from her cheeks and looked at him again, forcing her gaze to remain fixed on his. "I wanted to marry you. I have loved you since the day you walked through my father's courtyard, and though you did not notice me, could not see past Rachel to see that I loved you—" She stopped at his upraised hand.

"Enough. Please." He shook his head, and a muscle moved along his jaw, his mouth a grim line. He closed his eyes. "We will speak no more of this." He looked at her, his smile almost conciliatory. "What is done is done. You are my wife. I did not choose you, but I will not send you away."

She released a long, slow breath. "Thank you, my lord." Relief rushed through her at his silent nod. He accepted her. Love for him filled her. Someday he would love her in return. Surely he would.

She rose slowly and moved to the table, choosing a plump, ripe date. She moved closer to him and lifted the date toward him in her palm. It was bold of her to offer it thus, but her confidence was growing in his presence. She was his and he hers, and this was their time.

He looked from her hand to her face. To eat together meant full acceptance. Bread and salt between them. And if he would but taste the date and offer her the second half, it would carry a richer promise. Would he accept her offering?

He touched calloused fingers to her palm. The exchange sent swift feelings of longing through her. She searched his face, praying he could read the love in her gaze. He lifted the date, his gaze holding hers.

He bit one end of the date and pulled the pit from its center. Looked at it for several heartbeats, until at last he held the date to her lips, the sweet flesh of the fruit a soft caress. She allowed him to place the date on her tongue, smiling at him.

His smile in return did not meet his eyes, and the fire of longing she had witnessed the night before was missing entirely now. But at least he had maintained the tradition, had shared the sweet date of promise.

She moved to the table again, this time piling fresh fruits and cheeses onto a small platter, which she placed before him. In time she would make him love her. In time he would come to her with passion once again. For her.

For now, his acceptance was enough.

8

Rachel sat on the same dais Leah had occupied a week earlier, palms sweating and heart beating fast. Laughter and music flowed in and around her, cocooned as she was in the tent of her maiden-hood. Jacob's voice rose above the fray now and then, quieting her with his distant strength. He would come for her soon.

The thought filled her with anticipation, longing. And yet . . . would he compare her to Leah now? Would she be found wanting in some way she couldn't understand or define?

They were supposed to have come to the tent untouched by another. And she knew he had waited long, saving himself for her alone. But that purity had been stolen from them. And the awful truth of it was they would never get it back.

The thought had stirred her blood to such anger the past week that she could not speak. She would surely lash out somehow, and yet the one she had wanted most to hurt had been secluded in the huppa for those seven days with Jacob. But no more. Leah was nowhere to be seen at this feast. Rachel's mother had insisted she stay away, and Rachel breathed with relief in knowing her sister could not ruin this night. Not again.

She glanced toward the men's table, watching through the thin slit she had fashioned in her veil. The maids moved like unseen ghosts among them, refilling silver goblets and replacing empty platters, the scents of the food mingling with the rich spikenard of the groom. This time when he approached the dais, he would know he was not being duped yet again.

"Is there anything I can get for you, mistress?" Bilhah appeared at her side holding a cup of spiced wine. But Rachel had eaten what little she could before the veils were placed over her head.

"I'm not hungry now. Thank you." Bilhah nodded and moved past her to the table and deposited the cup in her father's outstretched hand.

Boasts and praises were offered to Jacob, to her, until at last the drum picked up a different rhythm. The mood of the crowd shifted, and men shouted, "To the huppa!" Ribald comments and laughter followed, heating Rachel's blood.

She smoothed her hands along her gilded tunic, her heartbeat more erratic now, and tried desperately to remember the advice her mother had given at the last, advice meant to woo Jacob and keep him at her side, as her mother had done with Laban, besting Leah's mother. It was a game between the two women, and she had always despised their actions.

A swift sense of despair accompanied the thought. She didn't want a life like her mother's! But the thoughts faded as she watched Jacob move from the group of men to walk slowly in her direction. Her father jumped up from his seat as if he just now realized it was time and trundled down the short path, catching up with Jacob until they both stood in front of her.

"I must see her to the tent." Her father puffed, the short walk winding him.

Jacob did not even look in her father's direction, his gaze taking her in, the dark brows lifting as his eyes met hers. Surprise and a delighted smile curved the corners of his mouth, and she knew her break with tradition, allowing him to see her eyes, was a wise choice.

"Come, come, now. Mustn't keep the guests waiting." Her

father's jovial words barely caught her notice, but she dutifully stood and took the arm he offered her, allowing him to lead her to the huppa where she should have been taken the week before.

Her father lifted the flap and led her into the semidarkened room but backed quickly away as Jacob was already standing in the door waiting. When at last the flap closed them in, Jacob stepped closer but did not touch her, his smile slowly growing wider, his look caressing her.

"It is really you," he said, relief in his tone, in his smile.

"It is really me." She waited, anxious, longing.

He stepped closer still, the gap between them filled. His fingers worked the clasps of her veil, catching on the fine threads. "I'm sorry."

"You won't hurt the veil, my lord."

He bent closer and gently undid the clasp this time, freeing her of the veil that enclosed her. He lifted it from her head and tossed it aside. Turning, he sifted both hands through her unbound hair and pulled her to him, his mouth seeking hers. His kisses, no longer the gentle pecks they had stolen in rare private moments during their betrothal, quickly deepened, possessing her until her knees nearly gave way beneath her.

When at last he pulled back, he wasted no time in removing her robe. She lifted trembling fingers to his sash, unable to undo the knot. He placed both hands over hers, silently helping her. Had he done the same for Leah?

The thought of her sister made her breath hitch. She did not want to think about her here! The intrusion brought a rush of anger to the surface and with it the sting of sudden tears.

He seemed not to notice, and she blinked them away. She would not spoil their time together with complaints or let him see her worries.

"You're trembling," he said as he led her to the raised bed spread with fine linen sheets waiting for them.

"Am I?" But a shiver passed through her in defiance of her question, betraying her.

He traced a line along her shoulder, then tucked a long strand of hair behind her ear. "Do not be afraid, Rachel. I have longed for, prayed for this moment from the first sight I had of you. My little shepherdess." He smiled into her eyes even as his fingers moved over her back, pulling her against him.

"I'm not afraid." She leaned forward to kiss him. She would prove herself a worthy lover. Better than Leah. The thought bolstered her courage, and she pushed thoughts of Leah from her mind as she gave in to Jacob's sweet caresses. She was finally his. And he was hers.

At dawn the next morning, Rachel awoke first, her mind slowly clearing. She looked over at Jacob's dear form and smiled. He loved her! And she was at last his wife for as long as life lasted. She leaned closer, brushed a strand of hair from where it had fallen across his forehead. He stirred, blinked, then looked at her. At his quick sigh, she smiled.

"Rachel." His voice was music to her ears.

"Jacob." She leaned close, kissing his nose.

His arms came around her. "I love you, you know."

"I know." She laughed as his beard tickled her neck.

"I am sorry things turned out as they did."

"With Leah, you mean?"

He nodded, pulling back to look at her. "Things won't change between us. I will love you as I have always loved you. Don't ever doubt that."

She nodded, brushing her long fingers through his hair. "I wish . . ." She looked away. "I wanted you to myself." She kissed him softly, lingering.

He wound his fingers through her hair, breathing softly of

her scent. "And you shall have me to yourself. Things will be as we always planned."

"You would set Leah aside?" For the faintest moment, she almost hoped.

Jacob stroked her face, his calloused fingers gentle against her cheek. "I will do what I must by her." He looked beyond her, and she knew the thought pained him. "I cannot ignore her entirely."

"You can when she carries a child." She coaxed him to look at her. "Then you will have no need to be with her. While I, on the other hand, can have you to myself even when my belly swells with life." She kissed him softly again, pleased at the stirring of longing in his eyes. "Me, you will not get rid of so easily, my husband."

He laughed, wrapping both arms around her. "What a little temptress you are!" He buried his face into her hair, tickling her ear.

She laughed with him, warmed by the joy in his voice. "And don't you forget it!" She pulled him closer, then laughed again at the sound of his stomach growling. She gently pushed away from him and reached for his hand. "You are hungry, dear husband. Come, let us eat the food my maid brought for us." She tugged his arm, coaxing him to rise.

He grabbed his robe and donned it, then lifted hers from the floor and held it just out of reach. "I might enjoy watching you eat without this." She caught the wicked gleam in his eyes and tried to grasp the robe, but he toyed with her, holding it above his head.

She laughed, playing his little game until he snatched her in a warm embrace and slowly lowered his arm. "Hold out your arms." She did as he asked, and he fitted the sleeves over each one, then tied the belt at her waist. "I still say we would have had more fun the other way."

She slipped both arms around his waist and held him tightly. "I love you, Jacob ben Isaac."

He bent to kiss her again, and she reveled in it, wishing with all of her heart that this moment could last forever. His stomach rumbled again, an intruder to their love. But when he lifted his lips from hers, she led him to the table spread with a feast of fruits and nuts and cheeses and fresh goat's milk. As she fed him dates, he fed her apricots, love's finest fruit. And she knew she had captured his heart and would keep it, despite her sister.

At week's end Jacob led Rachel from the huppa and stopped at Laban's house to collect Leah and his wives' two maids, then led them to the field beyond, where his tent stood waiting for them. The tent, he now realized, was sorely lacking in size for so many women. One glance at Rachel's face when Leah emerged carrying a bundle of clothing and linens made him pause. He must set them to sewing goat's hair and expanding the tent without delay. They would kill each other under the same small partition he had meant for Rachel alone.

The excited chatter behind him turned swiftly to bickering, until at last Jacob stopped and called Rachel forward. He took her hand and placed it in the crook of his arm, setting out again a short distance ahead of the others.

"Can you at least try to get along with her, beloved?" His words came out sharper than he intended, and he drew in a slow breath, trying again. "That is, I had hoped this day would be one of delight for us. Can we make the best of a difficult situation?" He gave her a sideways look, watching her expression.

She looked ahead, avoiding his gaze, a soft pout on her full lips, her look contemplative. At last she faced him and smiled. "I will try, my lord. But I have seen the room you had set aside for me. It is not nearly large enough for four women."

He nodded. Ran a hand through his hair. "I have thought of little else since we awoke this morning. I will clip the goats this very day and insist your father sell me the hair for more tents. It is the least he can do." Though Laban might find it amusing to see him living in a household of women with no peace. One never knew how the man would act or what he was thinking.

They crested the low hill and found Jacob's tent standing as it had been, waiting for them, beckoning them home. He lifted the flap and ushered the women into his receiving area, past the partition to the opening in the wall that led to the second chamber. Leah entered after Rachel and stood just inside the opening as though trying to rearrange things in her mind.

"If we move your mat to that wall, there will be room for mine here." She pointed to the opposite wall. "Our maids can sleep between us." It left little room for movement, but he felt a measure of relief that they could work something out.

"We will trip over each other in the night, and where will we store the looms and other articles once we retrieve them from our father's house?" Rachel crossed her arms, her mouth a grim line.

"We can make it work if we try." Leah's tone held a hint of condescension, reminding him too much of Esau.

"We can try all we like, but it is still too crowded." Rachel's petulant response made him turn from the women and walk out of the tent. He understood. She deserved better, but it would help if she made more of an effort.

He grabbed his staff from just inside the tent and headed for the sheep pens. Let them deal with the situation and argue without him. For his part, he would confront Laban with the problem this very night and borrow some of the tents they used in the fields with the sheep. He would not be forced to live with a houseful of bickering women! Laban had thrust this upon him. It was up to Laban to make it right.

❊❊❊

Rachel stood at the door of her own tent a month later, shading her eyes against the glare of the setting sun. Bilhah stirred the stew over the open fire on the hearth just outside the tent's door, while Leah's maid Zilpah lifted the fresh bread from the clay oven. Leah had gone to visit her mother that afternoon, and Rachel had hoped her sister would remain, giving her one meal with Jacob alone. But one glance at the door to Leah's tent told her that she would not be so fortunate. Leah stood in the door but a moment, then crossed in front of Jacob's tent that separated them and joined her.

"Are you planning to keep him to yourself again tonight?" Her tone accused, and when Rachel met her gaze, the pale eyes flashed.

"He will eat with us, and you can speak with him if you must." She turned away, looking to the hills for some sign of Jacob.

"As it has been since the day we wed. Surely you can spare him one night in a month." The comment came out more pleading than angry, giving Rachel a twinge of guilt. Jacob had stayed away from Leah even when Rachel's time had come upon her because Rachel had requested it. He hadn't thought it fair but had listened to her argument. Hadn't Leah deceived them both? Didn't she deserve to pay for ruining their plans, their life's happiness?

She whirled, facing Leah. "You are fortunate Jacob allows you to stay with us at all. You don't belong here."

"He is my husband as much as yours." Leah held Rachel's gaze but a moment, then glanced in the direction of the path Jacob would take. "And in case you have forgotten, I am the first wife here."

"You are a usurper. You have no rights unless I allow them." She turned then, shaking, and quickly walked away up the hill. Leah would surely complain to Jacob now and lay Rachel's words before him. She must explain herself before Leah had the chance. She could not allow him to show favor to her sister.

As she crested the rise that overlooked the sheep pens, she saw him counting the sheep as they passed under his rod into the fold. She smoothed both hands on her skirts, her heart suddenly skipping a beat, uncertain. Jacob would not wish to be greeted with complaints. She must find a way to word her request without seeming to cause strife between them.

He looked up at her approach, a smile reaching his tired eyes.

"You are home," she said, looping an arm through his and reaching one hand to pet one of the lambs.

"And glad to be here." He pulled her close and kissed her cheek. "I had to rescue two lambs from a pit. One broke a leg in the fall." He pointed to a lamb with a bandaged leg resting quietly in a secluded corner of the pen.

"Were they being chased?" Sheep would naturally flee a predator.

"They were chasing each other and paid no attention to my call. The pit came upon them unaware, and before I could reach the first, the other had gone in after it."

"The one beneath, did it survive?"

He nodded, rubbing a hand over the back of his neck. "Just barely. If I had not seen it happen and had to find them later, the younger one underneath would have suffered more than a broken leg. Of course, they fought to get out, and it took all of my strength to lift them to safety."

"You must be exhausted." She stroked a tendril of hair from his eyes. "Come and eat and rest yourself. The food is waiting."

He smiled down at her and cupped her cheek. "I am hungry for more than food." His lips brushed hers, the touch so gentle it sent shivers of delight up her spine.

She wrapped both arms about his neck. "Then you must take your rest in my tent and let me feed you sweet dates and apricots after the meal."

He laughed. "My little shepherdess." He glanced once more at the sheep, and she could tell he was silently finishing the count.

"Your brother Bahaar is supposed to stand guard here tonight." He looked toward her father's house and then turned to scan the surrounding fields. "You have not seen him?"

She shook her head. "He is always a late one. He will come, though."

He hesitated. Normally he did not leave the sheep alone with none to guard. "Perhaps I will wait for him." The fold had no door but the shepherd, though he had blocked the way with stones set as pillars in an emergency.

"I will bring food to you here and we will wait together."

He looked at her, relief and gratitude twin expressions in his dark eyes. "Thank you."

She reached on tiptoe and kissed his cheek. "If my brother does not come, I will get a blanket and we will spend the night together here under the stars."

A smile lit his face, and she turned, hurrying back down the hill. He had made no mention of Leah, nor would he miss her. They would have their night together without her sister after all.

Leah stirred the stew and worried her lower lip, trying to decide whether or not to pull the pot from the fire. Rachel had gone over the rise to find Jacob and had been gone longer than she expected. Surely they were at the sheep pens and would soon return together to join the rest of them for the evening meal, as they often did. But when Rachel appeared running down the hill without him, then gathered up food and drink and walked again toward the sheep pens without a word to her, Leah's spirits sank. Rachel would keep Jacob to herself no matter what lengths she must go to, and there was little Leah could do to change the situation.

"You must eat something, mistress." Her maid Zilpah held out a platter with warm flatbread to dip into the stew. "If he returns, you don't want him to find you pining for him. Eat, busy yourself. When he sees all of the good you do for him, he will soften his heart toward you." She offered Leah a reassuring smile, but Leah found it impossible to return it.

"He will not return. Did you not see the blanket draped over Rachel's arm?"

"Perhaps she wanted to soften the ground where they would eat." Zilpah shrugged her round shoulders and lifted her pointed chin, her gaze looking beyond Leah to her father's house. "Would you like me to fetch your mother, mistress? Or get you something else?"

Leah looked from the low hill where the sheep pens stood, where Jacob and Rachel would likely spend the night together under the stars, to her father's house, where she could find comfort. But she had already spent the afternoon listening to the advice of her mother, who told her to be more forceful in handling Rachel, to speak to Jacob about her rights as his first wife. Rights Rachel insisted belonged to her and Leah had no strength to deny. One look at Jacob each day told her that her mother was wrong. The guilt of what she had done to Jacob and to Rachel grew with each passing day, and she was crushed by the realization that if Jacob did not come to her again, she would never bear a child and would die a barren widow in her husband's house because he did not love her and, in fact, wanted nothing to do with her.

"No, Zilpah, thank you." She stood, letting the wooden stirring stick rest against the clay pot. "I'll be in my tent." She was not hungry, and it would do little good now to wait for Jacob to come striding over the rise with Rachel on his arm. If he did not spend the night with her in the field, he would spend the night with her in her tent, and Leah could not bear to think of what they might do there. If she had the strength, and if she thought it would not simply delight Rachel further, she would pick up her tent and move it far from Jacob's and Rachel's.

But she could not quite bring herself to deny the kick over

her heart at the thought of losing him. And as she lifted the flap and slipped into the darkened interior of her tent, she heard again her mother's words of that afternoon.

If you want him to notice you, you will have to speak to him. Remind him of his duty to you as your husband. If you do not, I will have your father remind him for you.

The words were no idle threat, and her mother would make good on them soon if Leah failed to act. But she quailed at every thought of getting past Rachel's anger to Jacob. Jacob defended Rachel at every turn.

Then you must speak to him alone. But the only way to do so was to go out to the fields and find him while he was out with the sheep. And if she did so, she would have to be discreet, lest Rachel guess her motive. If she would have honesty with her husband, she would have to once again circumvent her sister.

Jacob kissed Rachel goodbye the next morning, picked up the lamb with the broken leg and draped it over his shoulder, then called the rest of the flock to follow him to greener pastures beyond Laban's fields. How he loved that woman! She had a way of making him feel more than just good. He felt alive when he was with her. The stars seemed closer, the food tastier, the wine more satisfying. Life with Rachel was nearly perfect, if not for the shadow of Leah's tent that rose with the sun across his path each morn.

Guilt nudged him at the thought of his other wife, then was swiftly replaced by anger and a profound sense of loss. If he had not allowed Laban to fill him with so much wine that night, if he had looked more closely into her eyes before taking her to his bed, perhaps he could have exposed Laban's deceit and prevented the strife he lived with now.

He shifted the weight of the lamb on his shoulders and used the staff to keep his balance, his thoughts making him feel old and used. He could not change what was past. And he could not rid himself of Leah, despite Rachel's attempts to keep them apart. He could not deny the woman forever. But Rachel would not make it easy for him.

He turned, taking a wider path through a dry wadi, then led the sheep to one of the low-rising valleys where the grasses still stood tall against the late summer breeze. Soon the winter rains would feed the wadis and give drink to the fields. But for now he moved farther and farther from home in search of untouched land.

He settled beneath a spreading oak tree and laid the crippled ewe beside him, feeding her from his own hand while the rest of the flock grazed nearby. The sun rose quickly as the hours passed, and he pulled the turban down to shade his eyes from its glare, glancing over the field to make sure none of the lambs had foolishly wandered off. He started at the sight of a woman coming toward him.

Rachel had made no mention of joining him today, but who else . . . ? He squinted as she drew closer, his heart sinking in recognition. Leah.

He stood at her approach, not wanting to face her, knowing he must.

"What are you doing here, Leah?" He studied her, reading determination and a hint of fear in her gaze. He gentled his tone. "Has something happened that you seek me?" He had just left Rachel a few hours ago. Had some harm come to her? Alarm filled him, but one glance at Leah calmed him. She would surely be agitated if she were forced to relay bad news.

"I must speak with you, my lord." She held his gaze but a moment, then seemed to find fascination with her feet. "That is, I need to speak with you alone. Without Rachel."

"It would seem you have managed to do that now." He bristled at his own impatience and winced at the hurt he glimpsed as she glanced up at him again, her expression apologetic.

"I know we did not start out well . . ." She looked beyond him again. "That is, I know you would not have married me at all if not for our deception." She drew in a long, slow breath, as if the words would come only one sentence at a time.

"What do you want from me, Leah?" He sensed her reasons without need of words, but she was here now. And he needed her to finish and be done with it.

"I want you to sleep with me." She met his gaze, unflinching. "I will never bear you sons if you never share my bed." Her cheeks flushed as she spoke, and he knew each word had cost her.

This time it was he who looked away. He'd known this was coming, but he hadn't expected it today. Here. Now. And yet here she stood, her manner brooking no argument. And from her look, he knew he owed her what she asked. She had every right to seek her father and confess Jacob's treatment of her. And if they involved Laban, there would be no end of trouble!

He glanced beyond her as if the thought of Laban might bring him forth at that moment, relieved when only the sheep stretched over the pasture before him. "I will come to you tonight," he said at last.

She nodded, and a shy smile tipped the corners of her mouth. "Thank you, my lord." She stood a moment more until the air grew uncomfortable.

"Is there anything else you needed?" He suddenly wanted her to leave, to give him time alone to think, to clear the air of her troubling presence.

She shook her head. "Only that it takes time for a woman to conceive. So perhaps you can come more than once in a month's time." Her pale eyes held such wistfulness, and the thought that she loved him pierced his already guilty conscience.

He nodded once. "I understand."

She smiled fully this time and turned to go. "I will prepare your favorite pastries tonight." She lifted her robe and picked her way over the rocky terrain without another word or back-ward glance.

Jacob watched her go, astounded by her boldness. Astounded and chagrined. Perhaps the woman was not so weak as she ap-peared. And in truth, he owed her the chance to bear sons. She was his wife, after all.

But as the day drifted on and the shadows lengthened, he could think of only one thing. How to explain to Rachel that he was spending the night with Leah.

❧ 10 ❧

"You can't go to her." Rachel stared at Jacob, her words choked, and she fought the urge to weep or cajole him into changing his mind. "I had hoped . . . that is . . ." She turned, unable to face him, the heat of shame creeping up her neck.

She felt his presence behind her, his gentle touch on her shoulders. He slowly coaxed her to face him. "What had you hoped, beloved? That we could pretend our life was as we had planned it? We cannot go back to those days. Our life includes your sister now, and we have to make the best of it."

Her lower lip quivered, and she blinked against the tears stinging her eyes.

He lifted her chin until she met his gaze. "What had you hoped, Rachel?"

"It doesn't matter now."

"It matters to you. If there is something I can give you, you know that I would." She searched his tortured gaze, realizing in that moment how much it pained him to leave her. "Please don't make this harder than it is."

"I wanted to be the first to conceive." The words were a whisper, an embarrassment. She couldn't blame him for not trying, as she had had his time exclusively since her wedding week, forcing Leah into a secondary role of more maid than wife. The power over her husband's affections, over her sister, had soothed the hurt of betrayal but a little. If she could bear Jacob a son first, then she could allow Leah the consolation of Jacob's time now and then.

"There is no reason to believe you still won't." He leaned close to her ear, his breath tickling, his kiss a gentle promise. "I will give her tonight, but tomorrow will be yours. She said herself that it can take a woman time to conceive."

"She told you that?" She could not imagine Leah having such an open conversation with him.

"She wants to bear a child, beloved, as every woman longs for."

"She can bear all she wants, just not first." She knew the words were harsh, but she could not hide the jealousy that rose like a living thing within her, sometimes so strong that it threatened to choke all kindness from her.

"Who knows but perhaps you are not already carrying the seed of promise within you?"

She blushed at his frank words and the way his eyes roamed over her, assessing, loving her with a look. Her time was still a week away, so perhaps . . . it could be true.

"You will give her only tonight?"

He tucked a tendril of hair behind her ear. "I cannot avoid her forever, Rachel. I will give her tonight, and perhaps others now and then. But tomorrow will be yours." He kissed her then, a kiss that did not linger, then cupped her cheek in a parting gesture.

She gripped his hand and squeezed. "I will be waiting," she said, forcing more cheer into her voice than she felt, watching him slip from her tent into the night.

When he was gone, she sank onto her mat and gave in to the bitter tears. She could not bear to share him. Could not bear to think her sister might conceive ahead of her. And in the turmoil, she could not decide which was worse, competing with her sister for her husband or competing to be the first to bear Jacob a son.

❈❈❈

Leah stood at the door of her tent the following morning, accepting Jacob's parting kiss on the cheek, then watched him stop at Rachel's tent and give her a lingering kiss full of promise. The familiar jealousy felt like a kick to her middle. She shouldn't compare. It did no good and only caused her further pain. He loved Rachel. He only tolerated her. Perhaps worse.

Emotion made her chest tight, but she drew in a breath to steady herself. He had come to her last night, and though their time was nothing compared to the first night when he thought she was Rachel, still he was kind to her. But she could not make him love her. He was too kind to say so, but she knew he resented her.

The thought threatened to make her spirits sink even lower, and she would not allow herself to ruin the memories of her time with him. Perhaps even now a child grew within her. She placed a hand over her middle and glanced heavenward. *Please grant me this mercy. You see how it is with me. Please give me a son to take my husband's place.*

It was a selfish prayer, she knew. And the chances of her conceiving after one night when she had not done so during her entire wedding week seemed unlikely. Then again, perhaps the Almighty would consider her plight and have mercy.

Three months passed, and Jacob found himself choosing to spend more nights with the sheep in the fields, avoiding his tents. How had his life become so complicated? A man could only give so much, and sometimes all he wanted to do was lay his head on a rock and stare up at the stars. To dream of the ziggurat and the angels of God gliding from earth to heaven, to know that surely God had a purpose for all of his struggles.

He should take joy in knowing Leah carried his child now. But the thought, which would normally have pleased him, lost all joy every time he stepped into Rachel's presence. He sighed.

Dragged a hand along the back of his neck as he looked over the field, mentally counting the sheep.

The afternoon sun blazed overhead, and it was time to call the sheep to take them to water. He lifted a flute he had fashioned to his lips and played a familiar tune, then called for the sheep to follow. As he walked he continued to play, then stopped short when he caught the sound of another flute matching his tune with accompanying harmony. He turned, searching the hills for the flutist. Surely a bird would not sound so similar or carry such a well-matched tone.

At last he spied someone walking toward him. He stood still, watching, his heartbeat quickening as the woman grew closer. She drew the flute from her mouth and tucked it into the pouch at her side, smiling up at him.

"I hope I am not intruding." Rachel's dark eyes were large, her lips parted, inviting.

"No." He looked at her, uncertain. He had spent the past several nights in the fields, moving farther in search of green pastures. "But it is not safe for you to have come here alone."

She shrugged. "I know where I am going." And he had to admit, she knew well the land surrounding her father's home.

"That does not mean someone might not come upon you unaware." Fear for her safety suddenly hit him full force. "You should not come alone."

"I know how to use a sling, Jacob." She touched the pouch at her side that held the stones she could grab in an instant, the sling hooked to its strings. "I've got pretty good aim too." She smiled at him again, her eyes alluring. "What I can't understand is why my husband prefers the company of the sheep"—she glanced purposely around her—"to me."

She stepped closer until he could feel her breath on his beard.

He held her upturned gaze and lowered his head, his lips grazing hers. "Perhaps because it is quieter here." He leaned away from her, gauging her reaction.

She lowered her eyes, her look apologetic. "I am sorry to have caused you such strife, my husband." She rested a hand along the collar of his robe. "My sister's pregnancy came as a shock, since you spend so little time with her." She glanced beyond him.

He touched her cheek, and she met his gaze. "Your child, whenever he is born, will be firstborn of my heart. Even if Leah should give me ten sons, yours will be first. The blessing will be his."

The promise came from a place deep within him, and he knew he meant it with every word. Rachel was his heart. Her children would be his heirs. And while he would not neglect Leah's children, he would not make his parents' mistake of confusing the issue of which son would rule after him. One wife and her firstborn son would have preeminence.

"Will you come home tonight?" She looked so small and fragile now, and he suddenly wished he had not stayed away.

He nodded. "Do you want to come with me to the well? We could make music as we walk, though your flute sounds better than mine."

She laughed. "I've practiced more." She pulled the flute from her pouch again and lifted it to her lips, played a merry tune, and then strode on ahead of him toward the well where he had first laid eyes on her.

He followed like one of the dumb sheep, struck by her beauty, her talent, and the way she could make him promise her the world. Would to God that she had been the first one to conceive. Would to God that He would look down on her even now and fill her empty arms.

Part

2

When the LORD saw that Leah was not loved, he enabled her to conceive, but Rachel remained childless.

Genesis 29:31

When Rachel saw that she was not bearing Jacob any children, she became jealous of her sister. So she said to Jacob, "Give me children, or I'll die!"

Genesis 30:1

11

The pains came upon Leah before dawn six months later. Winter rains had long since passed, and the promise of spring was in the song of the mourning doves and the whisper of gentle breezes in the gaily flowered fields. At first the constricting muscles across her belly had seemed insignificant, but as the day progressed, she sent Zilpah to summon her mother. Farah swept into Leah's tent and looked around as though trying to decide how best to proceed.

"How far apart are they?" She waved away a cup of water offered by Zilpah, her gaze on Leah.

"The rests between them are short. Sometimes barely a few breaths." Leah panted, pacing back and forth in her small sitting room.

"Do you still have your waters?" Her mother walked to her bedchamber and peered inside.

"Yes." Leah stopped, sudden fear gripping her. "Is that normal?"

Her mother nodded. "Yes, of course it's normal. But if the pains are coming so quickly, the waters will break soon. Then you will need the birthing stool. Where is it?"

Leah pointed to the half-circular wooden stool resting against the partition between the two rooms. Farah retrieved it and set it in the bedchamber, then fluffed the pillows on Leah's bed. "Did you lay a clean sheet down?"

"Zilpah did . . . earlier." Her breaths came in short puffs, and she placed both hands on her middle, cradling the child. "Come, sweet baby. Make your way into the world."

"Why is your sister not here?" Her mother glanced around again at the sparse room and frowned.

"I did not invite her. She would not have come." The thought accompanied another wave of contracting pain, as though the agony of her relationship with Rachel over Jacob could be drawn into her body and brought forth with the child.

"How long will the two of you fight over the man?" Her mother's tone carried disbelief and exasperation. She turned to Zilpah. "Go and fetch Suri. Tell her Leah is near to giving birth."

Leah stopped again and faced her mother. "I do not want Rachel's mother here either." She bit back the sting of tears, hating the emotion. "Why can't you deliver me?"

"Suri is a better midwife." Farah shrugged. "She attended your brother's wives and did a better job than I could do. Her hands are smaller but sturdy, and if the baby should need to be turned, you will be glad of it." She glanced beyond Leah to the tent door. "It does no good to be at odds with your sister or her mother, Leah. Women must come together and aid each other. Jealousy will destroy you both."

Leah started pacing again, wincing with another breath-stopping pain.

"Breathe, daughter. Short breaths if you must. But it is worse to hold it in."

"I still do not want Rachel to attend me. She has stolen my husband. She cannot have my son or place him on her knees. The babe is mine. No one else's." Though she hoped Jacob would claim the child, if it was a son, as his firstborn and heir. The words, the worries left her shaken, and she did not resist when her mother took her arm and led her to her bedchamber.

"Sit down and let me see how far along you have come."

Leah obeyed as hurried footsteps and the sound of voices filled her sitting room, Suri among them. She gripped her mother's arm and pulled her closer. "Promise me you will not allow Rachel to attend me."

"Leah, I don't see why you continue to hold such feelings inside of you. You are the first wife. You will bear the first son. Rachel would not think to try to claim him from you." Her mother carefully pried Leah's fingers from her arm, then patted her shoulder. "You are overwrought, my daughter. I warned you when you married Jacob how hard this would be, yet you agreed. But forget all of that now. You are about to become a mother." She lifted Leah's tunic and examined her progress.

"Promise me, Ima. Please. She has already taken my husband." Another pain accompanied the whispered words, swift and harsh like her life.

Her mother rearranged Leah's skirts as Suri and Zilpah burst into the room.

"Promise, Ima?" she begged through clenched teeth.

"Very well. I promise."

"Promise what?" Suri asked as she squatted at Leah's side. She placed a hand on Leah's middle, gently massaging.

"It does not concern you." Farah took her place at Leah's back and rubbed her shoulders.

Leah caught Suri's curious look but then closed her eyes as another contraction overtook her, thankful that she would not be expected to answer.

Rachel worked the spindle and distaff in the door of her tent, trying to blot out the sounds of Leah's moaning, then of the baby's first cries. Jacob should be here, pacing by the fire, but he had not come home from the fields the night before, and Rachel had chosen not to send someone to find him.

She closed her eyes, fighting the familiar guilt that heated her skin like unwanted wool. Why did she feel such a need to keep Leah in her place, to remind her of her past sins? Jacob did not love Leah, and Rachel did nothing to help change those feelings. And now God had given Leah a child. How could He, after what she'd done to them?

The spindle and distaff grew heavy in her hands, like the bitterness that felt like a weight in her heart. She pressed a hand to her middle to quell the uneasiness, the fear. Nearly a year had passed since her wedding night, and Jacob had been more than attentive to her. Leah rarely spent a night alone with him, yet it was Leah who was blessed and Rachel who suffered from what could only be a barren womb.

Was she barren? Tears stung her eyes. What other explanation could there be?

Why? Oh, Adonai, why have You blessed her and not me?

Did Jacob's God even hear her? Did the same God Jacob had met at Bethel in his dream of the angels hear prayer? Perhaps the God of Jacob did not hear the longings of a woman's heart.

Or perhaps He did.

God had surely heard Leah's prayers. The babe's lusty cries a few moments before were proof enough of that. Then why not hers?

She stood at the sound of voices and looked toward Leah's tent to see her mother emerge, looking haggard and relieved. She met her halfway, in front of Jacob's tent.

"How is she?" It was the polite thing to ask.

"Leah is resting. She gave birth quickly once I arrived. Quicker than most." Her mother walked to the fire pit and lifted a handful of ashes to scrub the blood from her hands.

Rachel turned and hurried to her tent to retrieve the jar of water she had drawn at the well that morning and poured it over her mother's hands.

"A boy," her mother said. "Perfect and strong."

"How nice." Though Rachel did not find the news the least

bit satisfying. "What will she name him?" She spoke, though the words did not seem like her own.

Her mother straightened, her dark eyes so similar to Rachel's, though her once beautiful black hair was now streaked with thick strands of silver. She touched Rachel's shoulder. "She named him Reuben."

Rachel winced at the name. "'He has seen my misery.'" So God really had blessed Leah instead of her.

"When she named him, Leah also said, 'Surely my husband will love me now.'"

Would he? Rachel looked away from her mother's searching gaze. To name him thus would be a constant reminder to Jacob of how Leah felt. He could not call his son's name without realizing that the son's mother was miserable, that she wanted his love. Would he give it now, leaving Rachel with nothing? Jacob's love was all she had.

"Jacob will be pleased," she said, wishing the words weren't true.

"Will he?" Her mother glanced in the direction Jacob would take when he returned.

"Of course. What man isn't pleased to see his son safely born?" She said the words to placate, fighting the rebellion, the hurt stirring in her heart.

"Has anyone told him that Leah's time was so close?"

Rachel shook her head. "I do not know. Leah might have sent a servant. It was not my place to tell." Nor did she want to. "Leah did not want me at the birth. She can tell Jacob when he returns."

Suri stood as if in indecision, her beautiful face lined with concern. "How many days has he been in the fields?"

"Three."

"How long does he stay away?"

"Sometimes a day. Sometimes a week. It depends."

"On?"

"On how much fighting and strife there is between us all."
To admit such a thing made her guilt loom larger. She sounded
petty and childish.

"Oh, dear child." Suri placed an arm around Rachel's shoulders and walked her toward her tent. "Do you still harbor so
much anger against your sister after all this time?"

Rachel's throat grew thick with unshed emotion. She nodded,
unable to meet her mother's concerned gaze. "She conceived a
month after her wedding week with him, Ima. Yet I remain a
wilting flower in his house! How can God bless her after what
she did? Jacob was never meant to be husband to her. He worked
seven years for me!" Her voice rose in pitch, and she stopped,
hating the whiny quality it took on when she was upset. She
cleared her throat and tried again. "He doesn't love her, Ima. It
is I who should have borne his first son. Not Leah. Never Leah!"

Suri led Rachel into the tent and stood in the sitting room,
facing her. Her hand was gentle and warm against Rachel's
cheek. "Dear, dear child. We cannot control the gods or determine their will for us. Perhaps it is your bitterness that keeps you
from bearing. Anger has closed many a womb, and you wouldn't
be the first barren wife to share her husband with another."

"I don't want to be barren!" She felt her defenses crumbling
under her mother's touch.

"And there is no saying you will stay that way. But until Jacob's
God or your father's gods see fit to bless you, try to get along
with your family. Let your husband care for your sister, at least
a little." She stroked her cheek. "Try to imagine what it would
be like if you were in Leah's place."

Rachel closed her eyes, the words wounding her. For a moment she imagined how it would feel if Jacob left her for Leah,
spent every night in Leah's arms away from her. The thought
was unbearable.

And yet it was Leah who held a babe against her breast. Leah
who would hand Reuben to Jacob to bless on his knees, whose

very name would cause Jacob to see her differently, to perhaps want to ease her misery, to love her as she wished.

"I try, Ima," she said at last. "It is easier to be angry and to keep my distance."

For though she knew her mother's words were wise, she could not give in to what it would mean to implement them. She could not allow Jacob more time with Leah or Leah's son. She needed him to give her a son of her own. She needed him for herself.

Jacob walked with hurried steps, thrilled with the news from the servant boy that he had a son safely born. Why hadn't he been told sooner? But what could he have done if he had? Comfort Rachel? She would be attending the birth, and he would be left pacing before the tent, listening to cries that would pain him to hear.

The thought made him pause and nearly stumble over one of the larger rocks along the path. No, it was better that he had remained in the fields, where he was blissfully ignorant of the goings-on in his household. The bickering between the sisters had grown worse as Leah's time had grown near. And somehow Rachel seemed to blame him that she had not been first to beget. Did she think him in the place of God to grant a child?

He rubbed the back of his neck, trying to ease the frustration from his mind, and lifted his gaze to the sun-drenched blue skies. *Why did You put me in this situation? I wanted only Rachel.*

But God had given him Leah as well, if, in fact, God involved Himself in such situations. He couldn't exactly blame God for Laban's deception any more than he could blame Him for his own. Was this strife payment for his sins? He should have offered a sacrifice . . . something! But he could not change things now.

He approached the sheep pens where Rachel's brother met him.

"It's about time you got here." Bahaar embraced him. "You

have a fine son. Hurry! Go and meet him." He nodded in the direction of Jacob's tents. "Your son awaits your blessing."

"You have already seen him?" Somehow Jacob thought Rachel's brother would be among the last to glimpse his nephew.

He shook his head. "Not yet. But Ima tells me he is strong and healthy." He shooed Jacob away with one hand. "Everyone has gathered and is waiting for you. Go!" He laughed as Jacob turned and moved toward his tents.

As he crested the rise, he saw that most of Laban's family filled the area in front of the tents, near the central pit where a fire blazed. Voices floated to him, and he paused a moment, taking it all in and searching for Rachel. Where was she? Surely she would not hide in her tent during the blessing of his son.

He slowly moved closer, his heart aching and joyous, an all-too-familiar mingling of opposite emotions.

"There he is at last!" Leah's mother, Farah, emerged from the crowd and hurried toward him. "We have been waiting," she said when she drew closer. "Leah is anxious to see you, for you to see your son."

Jacob nodded, meeting the woman's triumphant gaze, and he knew in that look that she was glad it was her daughter who had given Jacob an heir, the first sign of his strength, and not Rachel.

"Come." She placed a hand on his arm. "Bless your son."

He followed like an obedient ewe, accepting the well wishes of Laban and his sons, then followed Farah to Leah's tent. Still no sign of Rachel.

"You cannot touch her or you will be unclean," Farah was saying. "But you can speak to her and hold the babe."

"Am I not supposed to bless the babe outside, in the presence of witnesses?"

Farah stopped at the threshold. "You can do that after you see Leah."

He glanced around, still searching. He looked back at Farah. "Is Rachel in the tent?"

Farah could not hold his gaze but looked over his shoulder into the distance. "I assume she is in her own tent. I have not seen her."

Jacob touched Farah's arm. "Why did she not help her sister with the birthing?"

Farah looked at him then, and he caught the slightest flicker of indecision pass over her expression. A deep sigh escaped. "I would tell you that Rachel had no desire to be here. But the full truth is that Leah did not want her company. So they have not spoken, and Rachel is not here." She crossed both arms over her chest, and the crowd stilled as though listening to their every word. "You must do something to make them get along, Jacob."

Her comment raised his ire. "Me do something? I cannot control their jealousy. And I will remind you that we would not be in this situation if things had been done as I requested."

Farah shook her head. "No, but we cannot undo the past. And Leah has given you a son where Rachel has not. So come, see your wife and son."

Jacob stood still, warring with indecision. At last he turned and found a seat near the fire. He did not care what Laban said or did to him. He would see Leah in his own time. "Bring my son to me," he said at last.

Farah looked from Jacob to Laban, then moved closer to her husband. "This is not right, my lord."

Laban puffed on his pipe and looked from her to Jacob, then back again. "The man can do as he wishes with his wife," he said. "Bring him the boy, and let me see my grandson."

Farah's expression darkened, but she did not protest. She turned and went into Leah's tent, then returned with a swaddled bundle. She approached Jacob and held the sleeping boy out to him. "His name is Reuben."

He has seen my misery. Jacob took the boy and looked into his face, his heart pricked with sudden guilt. Whether he visited

Leah or not, she had sent him a clear message. She was miserable, and her son would be a constant reminder as to why.

"She said," Farah continued, "'surely my husband will love me now.'" She spoke loud enough for the entire company to hear.

Jacob's face grew hot. He could not conjure love from nothing. Love was a feeling, a passion, a deep caring, bringing with it purpose and a desire to protect from all harm. Love drew him to Rachel to spend time with her, to grant her every desire. When it came to Leah, he had no love left to give. Rachel used it up, pulled it from him, and wrapped herself in it, creating a tight bond between them. How could he even think to share such a thing with her sister as well?

The thought was ludicrous!

He glanced at Leah's mother, then down at the baby, his son, who had now opened his dark liquid eyes and seemed to look into Jacob's soul. Whether he loved the mother or not, this was still his son. The thought warmed him in a way he had never felt before. He stroked the boy's face with one finger and smiled.

"May you be blessed of Adonai, my son Reuben." He faced the crowd and lifted the boy for all to see, then pulled him close to his heart. "My son!"

"May he be blessed of Adonai!" Laban said, and his sons and the women of the household said the same.

The noise startled the boy. His lips puckered, and a moment later he let out a lusty cry. Men and women laughed at the joyous sound, and Farah held out her arms to take him. "I will return him to his mother," she said, tight-lipped.

"Tell Leah I said 'thank you.'" He would visit her later, after he found Rachel. Somehow he must find a way to ease her wounded heart, and somehow, God help him, he must bring some kind of peace to his household.

12

Rachel slipped away from the commotion, waiting until Jacob was distracted with Leah's mother, then worked her way up the hill to the sheep pens, following the tree line behind the tents. She could not bear to watch Jacob blessing Leah's son, nor stand by and watch as he entered Leah's tent, probably to give her a fond look and thank her for giving him such a sturdy firstborn. If Leah did not want her company, she shouldn't have Jacob's either!

She hugged her arms about her, shivering with anger—and fear. Her mother's admonition to make peace with Leah probably held wisdom. Jacob would surely think so. The thought stung. Would Jacob choose her sister now over her because Leah was fertile and Rachel was not?

She trudged higher, her steps weighted with worry. When she reached the pens, she found her brother Bahaar pouring oil over the head of one of the sheep.

"How do the animals fare?" She stepped into the pen and rubbed the head of one of the lambs. The flock had once been hers, before Jacob came and took over their care and she was forced to take on other chores. Perhaps she could talk Jacob into giving some of them into her care again, to get her away from her sister and the babe.

"The flock flourishes under Jacob's care," Bahaar said, glancing up from his work and assessing her. "Why aren't you with Leah?"

"Why should I be? She didn't want me." The reminder added to the hurt, the sense of betrayal she felt that God had blessed Leah and not her.

Bahaar sat back on his haunches and regarded her. "She didn't want you or you didn't want to be there?"

"Both." She moved a piece of dirt with the toe of her sandal. "She doesn't deserve to be a mother ahead of me." She challenged him with a look. Her brother was many years older than she, the second born of her mother and father, and the brother who had played with her as a child. Of her three brothers, Bahaar loved her best. She could tell him almost anything and he would not chide her unduly for it.

"Apparently Adonai did not see it that way." Bahaar stood and stretched the kink in his back. He stepped closer, looking down at her with affection.

She swallowed past the sudden thickness in her throat. "Why?" she asked once the threat of emotion passed. "Why should she have a child when she should not even have a husband? Not my husband!" The bitterness had grown in strength this day, and she wearied of its weight.

Bahaar laid a gentle hand on her shoulder. "I do not know. I am not God to answer such questions." He stroked her cheek, lifting her chin with his fingers. "Stop fighting the inevitable, Rachel. You will drive Jacob away from you and straight into Leah's arms."

"What?" She stepped back, stricken. "Never!" She crossed her arms in a self-protective gesture, wishing she could shut the world out and keep only Jacob in. "He loves me." The words came out a whisper, and suddenly she was not so certain. Even now he could be telling Leah how much he loved her. She had given him a son, after all.

"I'm not saying that will happen." Bahaar shrugged, his dark eyes doubtful. "I do know that a man does not want strife in his house. He will go to the ends of the earth to avoid it. Have you not noticed how many times Jacob does not return the sheep to the pens at night? Would he have done so in the early days of your marriage?"

"He did. Sometimes." Didn't he? "Sometimes he has no choice. You know yourself that it can take days to find green pastures."

"Yes, but Jacob has stayed away even during the early rains, when the grasses are green, probably taking shelter in a cave. Is that what you want him to do?"

She shook her head and worried her lower lip.

His gaze softened and he opened his arms, coaxing her forward. She fell into his embrace, warmed by his strength, his kindness. "Don't give him a reason to seek Leah's tent, dear one. Let him find your tent warm, inviting, and free of critical comments of Leah. Otherwise he will soon grow weary of you."

"I don't complain."

He held her at arm's length and gave her a knowing look.

"Very often . . ." She turned at the sound of crunching stones. "Jacob."

"Go to him," Bahaar whispered in her ear. "Remember what I told you."

She nodded and straightened her robe as she hurried to meet him coming up the path. "Why are you here?" She flew into his arms, and he lifted her, twirling her about. She laughed. "I am glad you are here," she said when he set her down. "But why aren't you with Leah?"

"I had to find you," he said simply. "When I heard that you were not with her and did not see you, I feared—"

"It is all right." She smiled up at him and kissed him. "I am sorry for the turmoil I have caused." Though she still could not quite forgive Leah for what she had done. "I do not wish to ruin the day your first son is born."

"You have not ruined it."

"Have you seen him?" She searched his gaze, seeking answers to her unasked questions. Did he visit Leah? Did he love her son?

"Yes. I held him and blessed him." His look grew wistful. "Leah's name for him was not comforting."

"No. She is looking for ways to express her misery."

"Seems like a child's name should not do the expressing. She could just tell me." He led her away from the pens to a copse of trees shadowing them.

"She is afraid her complaints will push you further away. I fear the same things."

He looked at her, his hand gentle against her cheek. "You have nothing to fear, beloved."

"I fear I have sent you away already. You do not come home as often as you used to." She looped her hands around his waist and held him close. "I miss you when you are gone."

"And I you. You know sometimes it takes me far to find good pastures." He looked away, and she knew he had only told her half of the truth.

"I know. But not always. Sometimes you want to avoid us."

His cheeks flushed, his look embarrassed. "I cannot bear the constant bickering," he said. He looked beyond her toward the tents where the family no longer celebrated, but where Zilpah and Bilhah and a few other women still worked to prepare the evening meal. They should go to Leah. Rachel should somehow manage to offer a hand of peace.

"I will do my best to change that," she said at last. "Have you been to visit Leah?"

"No." He looked suddenly uncomfortable.

"What if I went with you?" She would face her sister better with Jacob at her side.

"Will you not feed her misery if you do?" He raised a brow, his look doubtful.

"Perhaps. But will she not be miserable regardless? She has a son to love now. If we go to see her together, I will offer peace. There is no sense fighting over children. She has her son. You have done what you must for her." If Jacob stayed away from Leah, Reuben would be the only son she bore, giving Rachel time to conceive and pray God would lift her barrenness.

"I cannot avoid her forever." She knew he meant more than his words conveyed.

"You can for a time." She *must* conceive before Leah could bear another. "But come. Let us go to her now and then rest and eat. Then we can have our own celebration." She smiled coyly at him, and he laughed. Intertwining their fingers, he led them slowly down the hill.

Leah's heart stirred to the feel of the babe pressed close, seeking nourishment, the pull of his tiny mouth tugging her breast. Such perfect eyes and thick dark hair for one so small! And his nose still showed little dots of creamy whiteness over his light brown skin, left over from the womb. She touched a finger to the softness and laughed at the way he scrunched his face at her touch, his little mouth moving faster as though he could not eat quickly enough to get his fill.

She studied him, this gift of Adonai, and was moved by a new sensation, one she had never felt to such depth in all of her life. Joy. Unhindered, unequaled joy. How blessed she was! Adonai had heard her silent longings, had seen her misery. The thought awed and humbled her. Surely Jacob would love her now that she had given him such a son.

The low sounds of her mother and her maid talking in the other room drifted to her, and she briefly closed her eyes, the exhaustion of the day mingling with her joy. She looked down on him once more and stroked his soft dark hair. He was beautiful like Jacob.

The thought threatened to dampen her spirits, reminding her of the pain his distance evoked. She should have known he would not come to her even now. But she had hoped. Oh, how she had hoped! Did he hate her so much that he could not even visit her on the day of her son's birth? She had done what Rachel could not, what every man wanted, and yet as the sun had fully set, he still had not come.

She shifted, pulled the sleeping babe from her breast, and placed him over her shoulder, wetting his blanket with her tears. "It's okay, little one," she whispered, her voice wobbly. "You have your mother's love, and that is enough."

A stirring outside drew her attention, and other voices soon joined that of her mother in the sitting room. Jacob? Surely not. But she would know his voice anywhere, not only by the distinct way he said certain words but by the way her traitorous heart stirred to hear him.

She quickly covered herself and smoothed the bedcovers, tucking the babe in the crook of her arm, her heart beating fast. She feared her anxiety would wake the boy. The curtains separating the two rooms parted, and Jacob stood in the doorway, his frame blocking the light from the other room. A woman stood behind him, but it was too dim to see who she was.

"My lord," Leah said, for her mind would not work to think of another thing to say.

"Leah." He cleared his throat, and she sensed he was not at ease. "How are you feeling?"

He was asking about her welfare? Hope pricked her heart. "I am well. Thank you. Have you seen your son?" But of course he had. It was she he had not been to visit.

And yet here he stood.

"Yes. I blessed him this afternoon." He looked at her briefly, then set his gaze on Reuben. "He is a fine boy. You have done well."

The compliment brought tears to her eyes. "Thank you, my lord." She had not expected it from him.

He stepped farther into the room, allowing the light to spill from the sitting room, revealing the person who had been standing behind him. Rachel.

"Why is she here?" She should have known her mother would allow this, that Jacob would go against her wishes and bring his favorite wife! "I don't want her here!"

Jacob stood still, his look uncertain, his shoulders suddenly sagging. Rachel stepped closer to Leah's side. "Please, Leah. I have come in peace. I only want to congratulate you and to see my nephew." She knelt at Leah's side and touched her arm. "There should not be such strife between us. Jacob needs us to get along with each other."

Leah looked into Rachel's large dark eyes, searching. Was this a ruse just to appease her? "Do you mean it?"

"Of course I do."

"Then you will share our husband with me and not keep him all to yourself?" It was a bold question, but Leah knew if she did not ask now, then when? She was vulnerable, but in her weakness she might hold more sway to get what she had wanted for so long.

Rachel nodded. "We can share him, of course." She glanced back at Jacob, but Leah could not see the look that passed between them. Rachel turned to her again. "May I hold him?"

Leah tightened her grip on Reuben. She did not want to offer Rachel the privilege. But she nodded just the same. "In exchange for a night with Jacob." She looked from Jacob to Rachel, feeling like she had just made Jacob a pawn in some kind of female game.

Rachel's face flushed at Leah's bargain, and for a moment Leah wondered if she had risked too much. Why should Rachel care enough to offer Jacob to Leah in exchange for holding a baby for a few moments? But if she meant what she said about sharing him, then she should easily agree. It was little to ask, considering how few nights Leah spent in Jacob's arms.

"When your time for purification has passed and the boy is circumcised, he can come to you, yes." She glanced at Jacob, looking for his approval, but all she got in response was a man who seemed like he wanted to flee the room. Did he feel they were using him for their own gain?

"I'm sorry, my lord. I only wish to secure time with you. I hope you will forgive our bargaining." Leah looked steadily at Jacob, but he would not meet her gaze.

"Just do what you must." But she could tell he was not pleased with her request.

Still, if she were to have more children, she would need more time with him. If she had to beg, bargain, or steal his time to get it, she would.

"Agreed," she said, handing Reuben into Rachel's arms.

Rachel looked at her for a brief moment, then gazed into the baby's open eyes. A smile lit Rachel's face, and Jacob stepped forward and placed an arm on her shoulder, both gazing down at Leah's son. A pang, sharp and fierce, pierced her at the scene they made. A family. As a family should be.

But they weren't as other families, and the child was hers. Rachel could not claim him. Leah was a rightful wife to Jacob. She was Reuben's mother. Anxiety filled her for one swift moment until Rachel held out her arms, handing the baby back to Leah.

"He's beautiful, Leah. Thank you." Tears glistened in Rachel's eyes, and Leah's anxiety shifted quickly to guilt. Had she misjudged her sister? Was she wrong to have kept her away from the birthing? Here she was offering peace, and Leah was holding a grudge.

"Thank you," she murmured, taking the boy and settling him on her shoulder, then patting his back. She looked from her sister to her husband and forced a smile. "Thank you for coming." Exhaustion filled her, and as she watched them leave, a deep emptiness accompanied the need for sleep. They couldn't stay because she was unclean. But she saw the way Jacob placed a protective hand at the small of Rachel's back. Saw the look of affection that had passed between them as Rachel held the babe. And she knew that despite the fact that she was the one who had blessed Jacob with a son, Rachel would spend the night in his arms.

Jacob guided Rachel out of Leah's tent, walked past his own, and stopped at the threshold to hers. She held her head high, her back stiff, unwilling to allow Leah's mother or any servant who might be watching to see her turmoil. But she could not stop the disquiet in her middle or cease the shaking.

At the door to her tent, she turned to look at him. "Will you come in? I have some spiced wine I've been saving."

Jacob nodded once, took the torch from its stand, and lit the lamp they would carry inside. Rachel lifted the flap of the tent and allowed him to enter, then let the flap close behind them, encasing them in shadowed light. She took the lamp from him and set it on a stand she had secured to her tent post, then retrieved the flask of wine and two clay cups from a basket on the floor. Why was she so nervous? She felt like a new bride awaiting the wedding tent, and yet she had been wed to Jacob for nearly a year.

"Come. Sit with me, Rachel. Leave the wine." She turned, seeing Jacob had found one of her cushions and stretched his legs in front of him.

She did as she was told, setting the wine and empty cups aside. His arms came around her, and he pulled her head to rest on his shoulder. She shivered even in his arms, and he kissed the top of her head. "You're trembling." He rubbed her arms with his strong hands.

"I'm cold." Though that wasn't the whole truth. She was anxious and angry, and sudden tears filled her eyes. "I'm sorry."

"There, there," he soothed. "There is nothing to be sorry about. You were kind to Leah, you held the babe, and now we are together." He nibbled her ear. "A man might love his son, but he still wants his wife to pamper him." He turned her chin upward and kissed her nose. "You spoil me, beloved. I'm not sure I'm ready to share you, even with a child."

She smiled at the boyish look he gave her, the one she had loved since the early days of their courting when they would steal kisses in the olive grove. "You are only saying that to appease me. You know you want sons. Every man does. As every woman wants to bear them."

"Yes, but what most men won't tell you is that they feel slightly jealous of the love a woman gives her child. It's hard to share, even for a grown man." He traced a finger along the side of her face. "You know I would give anything for that child to be yours."

His suddenly serious tone made her look away. She would not cry. She would not complain. Bahaar had warned her, and she must keep her frustrations tucked inside her, lest they ruin the only thing she had left. Jacob's exclusive love. And yet already she had to share him with his son.

"I know." She closed her eyes against the threat of tears. She was a pitiful wretch!

"It's all right to cry, Rachel. Today you have good reason." His understanding warmed her, though she sensed the truth in what he did not fully say. Tears for no good reason—those he could not abide. Her brothers, her father—all men were the same. They understood grief. But not a woman's varying emotions.

She swallowed, determined to be strong for him despite his permission to give in to her feelings. How she longed to weep against his chest and feel his arms comforting her. Instead, she leaned close and kissed him. "I do not want to cry today, Jacob. I have you with me. It is a day to rejoice in that." Never mind that she had just bargained him to her sister for a chance to hold the babe, an action that reminded her too swiftly how much she ached for one of her own.

He smiled, his arms coming around her in a possessive, gentle hold. "Never fear over my love for you, Rachel," he said against her ear. "No woman on earth will ever take your place."

He kissed her until her shaking ceased.

13

Jacob dug the end of his staff into the dry earth and stopped at the edge of a low cliff to gaze at the valley below. Wind whipped the sides of the turban against his face, and he brushed the fabric away from his eyes. The valley held sparse patches of green against the reddish clay and sands. In another month the rains would wash the dry lands and the fields would sprout with life. But for today he would need to make his way down the ridge, guiding the sheep to one of the oases below. Which meant several nights away from home again.

The thought troubled him, but he told himself for the hundredth time that it could not be helped. He had even considered bringing Rachel with him, but Leah's time was too near, and Rachel had insisted on being there to help her sister, though he wondered at the wisdom of it.

He turned at the sound of bleating and called the sheep to follow, taking a quick count to be sure one hadn't wandered off. He understood the need to be near for birthing. He had attended many a birthing for his lambs. And it pleased him to know that Leah had softened some since Reuben's birth. This second pregnancy had made her more generous to Rachel, wanting to include her. In this he counted himself blessed.

But he still sensed the tension between them when they thought he would not hear or was not near enough to notice.

Did Rachel really think him so blind to her actions, her moods? How could she not understand that he loved her? Sometimes the strength of his love consumed him. He was driven by its force, controlled by its need. He wanted her. Only her. And sometimes in secret he thanked God for her barrenness.

She would kill him if she knew.

He rubbed a hand along the back of his neck and sighed, glancing behind him again at the flock as they neared a narrow path through the rock. His senses heightened to every sound, every bird call and whisper, every footfall. He scanned the area, one hand on his sling, taking careful steps over the rocky terrain. When at last he stepped through the pass onto the wider, drier soil, he moved aside, waiting, watching, and counting as each lamb made it through after him. At last satisfied that they were safe, he continued on toward the palm trees and grasses in the distance.

Rachel, his little lamb, could not possibly know how she made him feel inside. And he had so few words with which to tell her. No woman—not the women of his father's camp or the maids of the Canaanites from which Esau had found his wives—had come close to Rachel's appeal. And he feared losing her.

Women died in childbirth, as ewes did. Laban's own concubine had died that way, he'd been told, leaving a squalling newborn son. Laban had found Rachel's mother soon after, but neither Farah nor Suri had brought such a smile to Laban's lips as his oft-recounted memories of Refiqa.

He couldn't bear to lose Rachel in that way.

As the months passed and Rachel wept when her womanly time came upon her, Jacob knew nothing but relief. Let Leah bear his children. Leah was strong and sturdy and gave birth without much trouble, if the gossip was true. And should he lose her, her loss would grieve him as the mother of his children, but he would not miss her as he would Rachel. Rachel was his very life.

He glanced heavenward, wondering if the thought was

somehow blasphemous. *Forgive me.* But the truth was he nearly worshiped her, would do anything to please her, and desperately wanted to keep her near . . . and safe. He knew his thoughts were selfish, his longings born of something akin to greed. He had waited so long for her. Was it too much to hope that he could keep her for a time? They had been married only two years. His mother had waited twenty to have him and his brother. There was plenty of time.

He could not bring himself to pray otherwise. If he asked it of Adonai, He might grant the request and take Rachel in the process. A child of her womb was not worth the loss of her life.

And though he knew without doubt his fears were unfounded, he worried just the same.

Rachel stood in the corner of Leah's bedchamber, watching as Leah sat upon the birthing stool, surrounded by maids and mothers. Suri squatted low, waiting to catch the child, while Farah rubbed her daughter's shoulders and Zilpah allowed Leah to grip her arm until Leah's knuckles whitened and Zilpah winced at the pain she was inflicting. Leah's labor had been shorter than the last time, though Rachel had only known that by the strength of the sun at her labor's beginning and end, not by any personal experience of being there.

Perhaps she should have stayed away this time as well. Though there was something forceful and intriguing about birth that every woman longed to be part of, Rachel doubted her own good sense. Jacob had been right to question her motives. What good did it do to be here if it only instilled in her the reminder of her own failures?

Leah's grueling shout startled her, and a moment later the babe's hearty cry drowned out all other sounds. Suri quickly wrapped the boy in a clean linen cloth and took him aside to a table where a bowl of water, another of salt, and a stack of fresh linens waited. Leah groaned again, and while the others attended her, Rachel moved to Suri's side.

"Let me," she said, holding her hands toward her mother.

At her mother's dubious expression and glance back at Leah, Rachel knew the request might not be well received. She touched her mother's shoulder. "Please. Leah can do the same for me someday."

Suri nodded, handing the child to Rachel. "He's slippery, so hold him over the table while I wash his limbs."

Rachel did as she was told and took the child carefully while her mother dipped a cloth in the water that Bilhah had kept warming on the coals and gently but quickly rubbed the blood and fluids from his body. Heat from several lamps flickered nearby, causing sweat to form above Rachel's lip, but she dared not try to wipe it away.

"We must act quickly," her mother was saying, "lest he get chilled." Within moments she finished, then took a handful of fine salt mixed with olive oil and rubbed it over his soft skin. "Now place him on the cloth." Rachel did so. "Turn him slightly and bind these bands around his arms and legs."

Rachel took the linen strip and tucked it under the baby's upper arm, wrapping it tightly, though not too tight, down his arm to his fingers. Her mother looked on as she wrapped the other arm and finally the legs.

"Good. Now we tuck the blanket around him." She stepped closer, edging Rachel aside to show her, though Rachel had wrapped Reuben and the babies of her brothers more times than she could count.

"I know how, Ima." Just because she had no child of her own did not mean she was incompetent!

"Yes, well, it's just that with a newborn we must hurry. The longer his wet skin is exposed to the air, the more chance he could take a chill." Her mother looked at her, then handed the wrapped baby into Rachel's arms. "You did fine, dear one."

Rachel looked down at the baby, avoiding her mother's gaze, not caring that she had snapped at her. How beautiful the child was! He had Jacob's nose and chin, and Jacob's eyes, though glazed and new, looked back at her. Her heart twisted at the sight. Leah had borne another perfect son.

She looked at her sister, hovered over by the other women as they cleaned her and dressed her in fresh clothing. *Why do You withhold such blessing from me?* The bitter cry had flown from her heart straight to the heavens too many times since the day Leah had announced a second pregnancy. And still God was silent.

"Where is my son?" Leah's cracked voice broke into her thoughts. She looked to see that Leah now sat up in bed. "Bring him to me." The words were a command, not a request.

Irritated, Rachel bit back an angry retort and walked slowly toward her. She placed the baby in Leah's outstretched arms without a word, instantly aware of the emptiness of her own. She stepped back, smoothing her features.

"What will you name him?" Farah moved to take the place where Rachel had stood and peered down for a glimpse of her grandson. The older woman's movements were not as quick as they once were, and Rachel wondered if Farah was ailing or simply aging. But she did not ask.

"Because Yahweh heard that I am not loved," Leah said, her gaze fixed solely on her son, "He gave me this one too." Her cheeks flushed as she spoke, matching the heat in Rachel's middle. Jacob would hear of this. Every woman standing witness would tell him, whether Rachel spoke a word or not. "Therefore, his name is Simeon." *One who hears.*

How dare Leah flaunt her children, tossing their names like barbs against her!

"Surely my husband will love me now." Leah's words jolted her, and Rachel met her sister's defiant, challenging gaze.

"A child is no way to earn his love," Rachel snapped, her anger rising higher like a bright flame within her.

"What better way do you suggest? Since you do your best to keep him from me."

Rachel turned at the touch of her mother's hand on her arm, and another angry retort stopped on her tongue. She gave Leah an indulgent smile, however false. "I am sure Jacob will be pleased with your son." The words wounded her already bleeding heart.

She turned away, suddenly unable to take the stifling heated room, and pushed through the small crowd of women to the tent door, dragging in air once she stepped into the afternoon light. The sun had dipped to the point where Jacob would soon return, except she knew he would not be home this night. He would spend the night with the sheep in the fields, in a cave or out under the stars.

She could not bear to be without him now. Helping Leah with the birth had been a huge mistake. She could not abide her sister's taunts or the underlying longing in her pale eyes. A longing Rachel could ease with a few well-placed words to Jacob. But a longing she did not wish to grant as long as it was within her power to deny it. She could not, would not . . . not as long as Adonai remained silent.

If Rachel could not have her heart's desire, Leah would not have hers either.

❊❂❊

The sun dipped precariously close to the earth's edge as darkness spread its garment over the last vestiges of daylight. Rachel tucked the headscarf securely over her face and double-checked to be sure she had her pouch of stones, her sling, and her staff, along with food and a skin of water for the journey. Jacob would surely reprimand her for attempting to find him in the dark, but Rachel had been in the fields with the sheep on many a night. She was not afraid of the dark.

She was afraid of being alone. Especially now.

A runner could be sent to announce Simeon's birth, but Jacob would not hurry back. He had known Leah's time was near, and still he did not send the sheep off with one of her brothers. She understood his desire to get away. But he could not possibly have known how much Rachel would need him. Hadn't she assured him she would be fine? She had chosen to go to the birthing tent, had chosen to hold the child. And had suffered her sister's bitter tongue for it.

She slipped from her tent, looking this way and that, then ducked behind it and made her way along the tree line, over the ridge, taking the path Jacob normally took on his way to the fields. A torch would be helpful, and she had thought to bring one more than once but discarded the idea. She would let the moon guide her, lest she become a target for bandits.

The thought made her shiver, but she stiffened her resolve. Jacob would forgive her, even welcome her, once she safely arrived. He had told her he planned to head south and west, and she knew there were only two oases in that direction where he could be. She crouched low and hurried onward, glancing back now and then to be sure she had not been followed. When at last the moon replaced the sun at its position high in the sky, she had gotten far enough away to stop worrying.

Night sounds of crickets and the soft whoosh of bats' wings above her head caught her ears. She tilted her head, listening for any predatory animals—the cry of a wolf or the low growl of a lion. She touched the pouch, felt for a stone, and fitted it in her sling just in case. She had practiced long hours in the dark on nights when sleep would not come, and the fire alone did not keep such animals away from her flock. She knew how to defend herself and them. But she breathed a sigh of relief just the same when she at last came to one of the oases and spotted a flock of sheep sleeping near a fire.

She crept close, staying to the shadows, searching the area. If she came upon a different shepherd, she did not wish to make herself known. Though she knew many of the shepherds in the area, she did not trust them all, especially at nightfall. Men would do as men did, whether they feared consequences from her husband or not. She couldn't take that risk.

A single man rested before the fire, its light flickering over his robe and now and then revealing a portion of his face. She would recognize the robe and turban anywhere, but when she at last glimpsed his face, she moved closer.

He whirled about, hand on his sling. "Who goes there?"

"It's me. Don't fear." She spoke loud enough so that he could hear her voice, yet softly enough so as not to startle the sheep. She hurried forward into the light.

"Rachel?" His voice held surprise, but his brows drew together and she glimpsed fear in his eyes. "Did you come here alone? At night?" He looked beyond her as if searching for a guard or some man to have joined her.

"I came alone." She placed a hand on his chest. "Please, Jacob. Do not be angry with me. I know these hills, and I took great care getting here." She lifted her sling, revealing the stone in its folds. "See? I was ready to defend myself in an instant."

He looked at her askance. "You should not have taken such a risk." He frowned down at her, but she lifted both arms and placed them about his neck, leaned on tiptoe, and kissed him.

"I had to come. I needed you so badly, Jacob." She glanced beyond him but a moment, then met his gaze full on. "You were right. I should not have helped Leah with the birth. I cannot bear the way she flaunts her children at me." She lowered her arms and turned slightly away from him. "Nor could I bear to hold her son without thinking of what a failure I have been to you." Her shoulders sagged as defeat settled over her. She had carried the burden all afternoon, and now at last she could be free of it.

"You are not a failure." He stepped closer and placed a hand on her shoulder. "You could never be so in my eyes, beloved."

He turned her to face him and cupped his hands around her face. "What did she say to you?"

Emotion swelled with the memory, and she would not meet his gaze. "She accused me of the same old things, of keeping you from her, and said that with another son surely you would love her *now*. As if producing a child was worthy of something far more than I have given you." Tears came then, and he pulled her close. "Please tell me you will not give her what she asks. Please do not let her come between us. She has already stolen too much!"

"There, there. It's all right, Rachel. You know that I love you. I could not bear to lose you! And I will never love Leah as I do you." He kissed the top of her head and rubbed circles along her back. "Never doubt that."

"I don't." She wrapped her arms around him and held him close, relieved at the feel of his strong arms encasing her. Fire crackled and night breezes fanned the air around them. "I know you love me." She pulled back and looked into his earnest gaze. "It is just that she makes me so angry. She gives her children names that feel like arrows shot at me, and she says things to purposely make you feel guilty for neglecting her and me for asking you to."

His look turned thoughtful as he stroked her cheek. "What did she name this one?"

"Simeon." The word sounded bitter on her tongue.

"One who hears."

"Yes. She said God had heard that she was not loved, so He gave her this one too. Then she blamed me for keeping you from her. How can she say that when it was she who snuck her way into your bed on my wedding day? She is not loved for a reason!" Her voice rose in pitch as she spoke, until she realized she could wake the sheep and dropped to a whisper. He looked almost startled by her outburst, and she knew she should have held her tongue. She backed away from him and hugged her arms to herself to still her trembling. "Forgive me. I am tired and overwrought."

"Come here, Rachel." His quiet voice held no reprimand, though she surely deserved it.

She turned and went to him again. He took her hand and pulled her down to lay beside him in front of the fire. His arm came around her, and she nestled her head into the crook of it, gazing up at the stars.

"Can you count them?" he asked, one hand pointing heavenward.

"I couldn't begin to try," she whispered against his chest.

"On a night like this, I am reminded of the Elohim of Abraham and the Elohim of my father, Isaac. Yahweh promised my grandfather that his offspring would be like the stars of the skies—more than he could count." His grip tightened slightly on her arm. "That means there must be children, beloved. And God has seen fit to give me sons through Leah."

He stopped as she stiffened and pulled slightly away.

"Let me finish," he said, gently tugging her closer again. She relaxed against him. "I know you desperately want a child." He paused as though he had to carefully choose each word. "But at least I still have you. There is a risk in childbirth, and if something happened to Leah, I could bear it." He rose on one elbow to look into her face. "But not you, beloved. I cannot lose you."

She searched the depths of his dark eyes, their gaze so earnest and his words so impassioned they hurt. She touched his bearded cheek. "But a woman is worthless without a child. You yourself would despise me someday if I go through life at your side childless."

He shook his head. "That is not true. My mother was barren twenty years, my grandmother more than that, and God eventually gave them children. I cannot believe He would deny you." He kissed her forehead. "But even if He did, I would love you." He kissed her lips, his touch feather light. "Do you believe me?"

She nodded. "I know you love me, Jacob." He had never given her any doubt, so why did she fear? "I just wish . . ."

"We cannot change what is past and done, beloved. We can only move on from here and live the life God has given us." He rolled onto his back again and pulled her against him. "But please, it is late and I am tired. Let us speak of this another day."

She did not want to put aside her feelings so easily, but she could hardly ask him to give up sleep when dawn would come too soon. She had already asked more than she should in keeping him from her sister.

"When will you return to bless your son?" Despite everything, he should acknowledge the child.

"Tomorrow." His words were soft, and a few moments later his breathing changed and she knew he had fallen asleep. She curled closer against him, staring up at the stars, attempting in vain to count them.

❋ 14 ❋

The babe's strident cries woke Jacob from a much-needed rest.
He stirred among the cushions of his sitting room and rubbed the
back of his neck. The cries did not lessen, though he glimpsed
Leah pacing from her door into her own tent and back again,
trying to soothe the boy. The action did little, and his cries
were soon joined by that of his older brother. Was there never
a moment's peace?

He rolled over and tossed a pillow over his head, trying to
blot out the sound, but the cries pierced like arrows through
the cushions. He should have stayed in the fields with the sheep.
Ought not a man be allowed one day to rest from his labors?
He worked long hours on Laban's behest, and his flocks were
the strongest and most well mated of all Laban owned. But
he had just come from a difficult birthing of twin lambs. He
needed some respite!

The cries grew louder until other voices joined in, apparently
trying to calm both of the children, to no avail. Was something
wrong with them? Sudden fear mingled with his anger. He rose
and donned his robe, then walked with purposeful strides to
Leah's door.

"Is there not something to be done to quiet them?" His boom-
ing voice seemed to startle Reuben, whose cries immediately

ceased, and the boy ran quickly to Leah, who sat on a cushion trying to get Simeon to eat, tears streaming down her cheeks. Jacob's conscience pricked him, and the fear returned at the sight of her tears. "What's wrong with him?" He gentled his tone and stepped into the tent.

"I do not know." Her words wobbled on the threat of more tears. "I have tried to feed him, but he will not take it. I have walked with him until my legs won't hold me." She pulled Simeon close and hid her face in his blanket.

The sight of her filled him with guilt. Except to bless Simeon on his knees, he had rarely visited her tent even to spend time with the children, in deference to Rachel's wishes. He could not blame Rachel for wanting to keep him away from Leah for fear his love might be divided, but it was not fair to ignore the children because he did not love the mother. Why did women have to make life so complicated? If a man could have sons apart from them, he might just have wished for such a thing! But he knew in a heartbeat that he could not live a moment without Rachel. She was his life.

Still, the children were flesh of his flesh, and though they were babes in arms, they had not known enough of his touch. The image of his father's favoritism to Esau surfaced, and he winced, seeing his own actions in his father's.

"Perhaps I can help," he said, before counting the cost to Rachel that might stop him. He moved closer. "May I?" He held out his arms to take Simeon from her.

She glanced at him. The babe still whimpered, and he feared his movement would cause the screams to come again, but even before he could take the boy, Simeon's lips puckered and his cries ripped the air between them. Jacob stumbled backward and nearly left Leah and her maid to handle the children without him. Women were better with babes than men were. Give him a son when he was old enough to follow him into the fields. What did he know of infants in arms?

But at the look of relief in Leah's eyes, he took the babe from her anyway.

"Hold him close and walk with him. Pat his back too. It might help." She sat up, casting a wary eye on him. "If he senses your discomfort, he will cry harder." She released a long-held sigh. "Thank you, my lord. I fear there was too much garlic or too many onions in the stew last night. He has not been himself since I ate of it."

Jacob heard her words through the haze of distraction, his focus shifting to Simeon squirming in his arms, his son's cries louder than a cat's piercing scream. He walked with Simeon out of the tent and took the boy toward the sheep pens. Either his cries would scare the sheep or the sheep would calm him. *Please, Adonai, calm him.* Did God care about such a prayer? What father ever prayed thus for his son? Surely a loving one would, wouldn't he?

But Jacob's conscience taunted him with that thought yet again. He looked down at Simeon, so perfect, so angry for one so small, and knew he did not love the child as he ought.

"There, there. You are a strong one, aren't you? You will make a fine shepherd one day." He patted the child's back awkwardly at first, but as they continued to walk up the hill, he grew more comfortable with the task. The babe's cries stopped suddenly as he turned his head. At four months, he was no longer the wobbly infant he was at birth, and Jacob laughed as the boy's nose crinkled, seeming to pick up the scent of the sheep.

"A shepherd gets used to such smells, Simeon." He shifted the boy as they neared the pens and turned him to see. When they neared one of the gentler lambs, Jacob lowered the boy to the ewe's back and held him there.

Simeon dug both hands into the sheep's wool and squealed, his cry no longer angry but filled with delight that made Jacob smile. "So this is what you wanted? To be a shepherd already, my son?" He marveled at the word on his tongue. Until now, he had rarely thought of Leah's children as his sons, but of course they were.

When at last the babe tired and finally slept against Jacob's shoulder, he walked back toward the tents. As he passed Rachel's, he saw her standing in the doorway, arms crossed, her eyes red-rimmed and her smile uncertain. He knew by her look that her time had come on her again. The thought depressed him. For though he had hoped to spare her the threat of childbirth, he realized those concerns were unfounded, and he was wishing away a blessing for her that she wanted more than his love. If only he could give her what she asked!

He passed her, knowing he could not visit her tent this night, and carried the sleeping baby to Leah. Zilpah met him at the door.

"She is sleeping," she whispered, opening her arms for the child. "I will place him beside her."

Jacob studied the girl for a brief moment, reluctant to release the boy. "Let me," he said, surprising himself. He could not rush back to Rachel in her state, so there was no hurry.

He walked past Zilpah and crossed into the sleeping chamber where he spotted Reuben on a mat near his mother, napping, and Leah resting peacefully on her own. He knelt at her side and carefully placed Simeon beside her, tucking a blanket around him lest he roll away from her.

She stirred and opened her eyes. "Jacob. You have come." She blinked and brushed away long strands of silky hair, similar to Rachel's yet woven with those strands of red like Esau's, not quite as dark and lustrous as Rachel's.

He placed a finger to his lips. "Go back to sleep. Rest while the children do."

She shook herself, glanced at Simeon, and sat up. "Must you leave? There is plenty of room." She motioned to the other side of her mat, offering him to stay with her. She looked at the sleeping children. "Zilpah could take them to her side of the tent." She smoothed her tunic, unable to dispel the wrinkles. "We haven't talked in so long." Her earnest gaze held his, and he could not pull away. He so rarely gave in to her requests.

He glanced at the children. "Do not disturb them." It had been too hard to get Simeon calmed to wake him now.

She looked so disappointed that he quickly offered a hand to pull her up. "It is quieter in my tent." He smiled at the delight in her eyes as she hurried to don her robe and draped a scarf over her head. He led the way as the afternoon sun dipped toward evening shadows.

"Shall I bring food?" She stopped at her storage jars that held dates and nuts. There would be no cooking today on the seventh day, so they would eat the bread baked the night before along with fruits and nuts that needed no work to prepare.

"I have enough," he said, motioning her ahead of him. Her look held uncertainty, but at his nod she moved past him toward his tent. She glanced toward Rachel's, and he followed her gaze. Rachel stood in the door watching them.

He could not see Leah's expression from behind, but he could see Rachel's displeasure. He should go to her and explain himself. But he did not have the strength to handle her tears and still devote a listening ear to Leah. He nodded at Rachel as he lit the lamp, then entered his tent, closing the flap behind him.

Leah stood with her children near the central fire several paces from Rachel a few months later, waiting to bid Jacob farewell. She had wanted to share her news with him after the evening meal the night before, but Rachel had stolen him into her tent before the last dish was washed, leaving the nightly chores to her maid. Since the day Jacob had taken Simeon and calmed him and then surprisingly invited her to his tent, Leah had known. But she had waited, hoping for another moment alone with him.

Rachel had made certain that did not happen. Even during

the weeks of her uncleanness, she managed to keep Jacob from spending time with Leah. And then, of course, Leah needed to be sure. A woman could hardly know for certain the moment she conceived, but somehow Leah did. The quickening inside of her was a blessed force, a stirring that she could not describe with mere words.

Heat filled her cheeks at the thought as Jacob finally emerged from his tent ready to go. He saw Rachel first and wrapped both arms around her, his kiss lingering. Even from a distance, Leah could see the look of triumph in Rachel's shining eyes when he released her to turn to Leah. She stifled the urge to lift her chin and give her sister the condescending look she deserved. Not with Jacob so near. Guilt nudged her. Perhaps not at all.

She shook away the disturbing need as Reuben ran to greet him, and Jacob lifted the boy into his arms, rubbing his curly head. "Be good for your mother," he said, setting the boy beside her. Reuben stuck two fingers in his mouth and nodded, wide-eyed, saying nothing.

Jacob stepped in front of her and placed a hand on Simeon's head, smiling. He leaned close and kissed Leah's cheek. "Take care of yourself," he said. He turned, ready to walk away, but Leah touched his arm.

"May I speak with you just a moment, my lord?" He turned back, his expression a mixture of curiosity and annoyance. "I know you don't have long."

He faced her again. "What is it?" He glanced at the sky, and she sensed his impatience.

"I could walk with you to the pens, to speed things along," she offered, though she knew it was a right Rachel always claimed.

"Just tell me now." His knuckles whitened on the staff, but he gave her his full attention.

She lowered her gaze, suddenly shy to tell him yet knowing now she must, and quickly. She looked up, glanced beyond him to Rachel, who tapped her foot, her perfect brows knit in the tiniest of scowls. Let her be angry! Leah no longer cared what she thought.

"I wanted you to know," she said, looking directly into his dark eyes, "that I am with child." She spoke the words softly, reverently, her gaze full of love for him. "I hope it is another son for you, Jacob."

He looked at her, his expression moving from surprise to concern to pleasure. She knew in a moment that the concern was not for her welfare but for Rachel's reaction. The thought stung, but when he smiled at her a moment later, she felt only relief.

He touched her arm. "Thank you for telling me, Leah." He leaned forward away from Simeon, whom Leah still held in one arm and kissed her cheek again. "Take care of yourself."

He turned then and walked quickly toward Rachel, who followed him to the sheep pens. Leah stood watching them go, knowing he would tell her. Good. It would save her the trouble of her sister's pouting response. And perhaps, pray God, keep Leah herself from gloating, from purposely wounding her sister more. Why did she have the constant desire to do so? Shouldn't they have come to some acceptance of one another by now? But Leah could not stop the jealousy or the guilt she felt toward her sister. Jealousy that Rachel was first wife despite the marriage order and their age difference, for Jacob had made her so and listened to everything Rachel said, giving in to her every whim. Guilt in knowing she would not have Jacob at all except for the hand of deceit that had led her here.

A lump formed in her throat as she saw the way Jacob laughed at something Rachel said, and the smile that he sent her way held such love it made Leah's heart hurt. Despite their beginnings, was it too much to ask that he love her, or at the very least that he become attached to her because of the children? And now she would be giving him three.

She felt Reuben tug on her robe, still watching Rachel cling to Jacob's arm and chat on about some trivial thing. Perhaps she would go with him to the fields today and Leah could be free of her sulking. For despite the smile Jacob had cast Leah's way, she could not hide the disappointment she felt that he had not been more pleased with her news. Instead she had garnered only a peck on the cheek and the same words he always used: "Take care of yourself."

If only he would take care of her as he did Rachel.

If only her heart did not constantly wish it so.

❈

Jacob's arm tightened, and Rachel could feel the muscle flex beneath her grip as they crested the rise and descended out of sight of the camp to the dip in the land where the sheep pens stood. She studied his profile, watching the way the morning sun angled against his cheek, and saw the changing expressions in his dark eyes.

"What did she say to you?" She forced the question through clenched teeth, knowing yet hating the answer that was sure to follow.

He glanced at her but said nothing, continuing on until they reached the pens. She released her grip, and he nodded to the servant boy who had been awaiting Jacob's arrival. The boy took off running, hurrying back to her father's house for the morning meal, his gait gangly and awkward in its youth. Jacob looked away from her toward the sheep.

"Is she with child? Is that what she told you?" She knew she should wait for him to reveal it to her, but she could not bear his silence. "Please, Jacob, do not keep this from me."

He looked at her then and nodded. "Yes." He glanced beyond her. "I'm sorry, beloved."

She watched him a moment, but he would not meet her gaze. "Does this please you?"

An impatient sigh escaped him. "But of course it does. What man doesn't want many sons?"

She turned then and hugged both arms to herself. The morning breeze lifted the scarf slightly away from her face, its gentle warmth mocking her in its kindness.

"Please don't do this." He touched her shoulder and turned her to face him. "Do you not think I wish it were you?" He dipped his head until his gaze met her lowered one. "I would give a year's wages to have the son be yours, Rachel. You know this." He traced a finger along her jaw. "Please do not take away my joy."

His joy? How could he think such a thing could bring joy? Tears born of anger she could not release sprang to her eyes. "I'm sorry. I cannot think that a son of my *sister* could bring you joy."

He tilted his head, looking heavenward, and rubbed the back of his neck. "Rachel, please." He closed his eyes as though trying to rein in his impatience, then met her gaze once more. "Try to see this from more than your perspective. Try to be happy for me too."

She blinked and wiped the tears away, willing the anger to abate, longing to give in to the rage and the hurt. To flail her arms and beat against his chest with her fists . . . But he would not understand. To react in such a way, despite her feelings, would only stir his wrath and perhaps drive him once more into Leah's arms. She could not risk such a thing.

She swallowed and took a deep breath, offering him a conciliatory smile. "I am pleased for you, Jacob. I . . ." She looked beyond him, unable to continue.

He stepped closer and pulled her against him. "I know." He kissed the top of her head and held her, but she would not allow herself to weep. The bleating of the sheep beside them reminded her that he would never get the sheep to the fields if he did not start soon.

"You must go if you are to find pasture before the sun reaches its glaring point." She stepped back from his embrace, and this time her smile was genuine. "You will have our neighbors stealing the best spots if I keep you here much longer."

He released a long-held breath and gave her a relieved smile. "Come with me." He grasped her hand, intertwining their fingers for a brief moment. "It will do you good to be away from Leah for the day."

Emotion swelled again at his thoughtfulness. She did not appreciate this man the way she should. Hadn't he worked for her seven years, patiently waiting? And now he was working seven more for Leah, all the while waiting for Rachel to give him a son, never angry with her or disappointed that she had failed again and again. How was it that she could not see his love? Had jealousy over her sister blinded her so greatly?

"I would love to come with you," she said, squeezing his hand. "Thank you."

He smiled then and released her, turning to lead the sheep out of the pen to the path that led to distant fields and the well where they had met so many years ago. She waited until the last lamb trotted through the gate, then followed him.

✼ 15 ✼

Rachel hurried along the path to her father's house, heedless of Leah's calls to her from her tent, anxious to get away. She would die if she had to spend one more day with her sister, working at her side while the woman's belly swelled and she cast that constant look of pity in Rachel's direction. She had become the brunt of Leah's scorn since the day Leah told Jacob the news of this third child. The thought of Leah being so blessed tormented Rachel's every waking moment, and she could not bear another day. She must do something . . . Surely there must be something she could do.

Her heart pounded as she neared her father's courtyard, her feet scuffing the loose stones and then stopping abruptly when a stone caught between her foot and leather sandal. She lifted her foot and flipped the offending piece to the path, then rushed past the servants in the courtyard to search out her mother. She found her with Farah in the weaving room.

"Rachel! What is wrong?" Her mother set the shuttle aside and rose, hurrying to Rachel's side.

"Has something happened to Leah?" Farah's question caught Rachel up short, feeding the anger and hurt growing within her.

"Your daughter is fine." She managed the words through clenched teeth. "Though you might tell her to keep her pity to herself. She may carry Jacob's child, but it will be the last she carries if she keeps flaunting herself at me." She faced her mother then, turning purposefully away from Farah. "Can we take a walk?" She lowered her voice, though Farah could still hear. She did not need Farah telling Leah all that was in her heart.

"Of course, my child." Suri took Rachel's elbow, tossing an apologetic look Farah's way, then led her from the room.

"You didn't need to act so congenial to her," Rachel hissed.

"Yes, I did." Her mother's look held censure.

"She should make her daughter curb her tongue!"

"No mother has ever been able to do such a thing." Concern crossed her mother's face as she guided Rachel through the halls to the outer courtyard and beyond, the opposite direction of Jacob's tents. "What is this about, Rachel?"

Tears threatened and she looked away. Her mother's arms came around her shoulders, then turned her into a full embrace. "Oh, my child. Jealousy is such a terrible taskmaster." She patted Rachel's back. "Tell me what happened."

"I can't bear it anymore, Ima. She sits there at the grinding wheel, stretching her belly until it sticks straight out in front of her, patting it incessantly, and glancing my way with that pitiful look she has, but I just know she is laughing inside. She mocks me, Ima. As if it is my fault that I am barren." The word *barren* on her tongue tasted sour, and she felt suddenly sick. She placed a hand to her mouth and pulled away. She waited, drawing in slow breaths, until at last the queasy feeling passed.

Her mother's touch on her shoulder made her turn. "Come. Walk with me." Suri pointed to the tree line some distance away, and Rachel obediently followed. "First off, dear child, you must understand that when a woman carries a child and sits long hours at the grinding stone, her back grows stiff. The bigger her belly swells, the harder it is for her arms to reach the handle to turn the stone. So she stretches. So what? You arch your back when you stretch and your belly sticks out. It is natural. You will have the same trouble someday." She rubbed her work-worn hands over Rachel's younger ones.

"But she flaunts herself at me."

"And you know this because she looks at you with pity? How do you know it is pity? Perhaps it is gas and she is grimacing. You do not know what is in a person's heart." Her mother's tone held too much accusation, her excuses for Leah unconscionable.

"You mock me as well. I thought you would understand." Rachel was used to her mother's straightforwardness, but she did not expect it today. Did not appreciate it today.

"I do not mock you, my child. But you have been married nearly three years and still you are fighting with your sister. You must stop this foolishness. You will destroy Jacob's house if you don't." They were halfway to the tree line now, but Suri stopped and placed both hands on Rachel's shoulders. "You must stop thinking so much of yourself. Think of Jacob, of his children. Be a good aunt to them and Jacob will love you for it. And if that is too hard for you, find another way to accept your state."

"But what can I do?" She heard the petulance in her tone as she searched her mother's dark exotic eyes so like her own. "You shared my father, but at least you had sons of your own. Why does God keep them from me?"

Suri crossed her arms over her chest. "Who am I that I should know the mind of God? Perhaps He makes you wait to teach you to trust Him. Is that not what Jacob would tell you?"

She squirmed under her mother's scrutiny, not liking the direction of the conversation. Her mother had come to believe in the One God after listening to Jacob speak so often of Him. Laban did not care what his wives believed, as he embraced all gods, including the Creator. Leah had been the first to accept the singular teaching, and Rachel had soon followed. But she did not understand Him. And she did not like His ways, not if they meant she would bear no sons.

"Jacob would tell me he does not know why I must wait." She looked away. "What should I do, Ima?"

Her mother cupped her cheek and sighed. "Give Jacob your maid. Then whatever child is born to her can be born on your knees. The child will belong to you."

She startled at the words, searching her mother's face. "Why would I do such a thing? It is already impossible to share him!"

"Do you want a child or not?"

"Of course I do!"

"Well then, since you have had plenty of Jacob's time and your sister's fertility to prove the problem lies with you, there is only one way for you to have sons. Give the man your maid."

Rachel stepped back, stung.

"Or you could keep waiting."

No, she couldn't. Could she?

"But I can't . . ." She put a fist to her mouth and turned away, walking ahead of her mother to the trees. *Oh, God, why is this so hard?* Was she being too hard on Leah? At least Jacob was having the sons God promised him. Did it matter whether those sons came from her?

But she wanted children! She wanted to suckle a babe at her breast, to kiss a cheek so soft and pure, to gaze into eyes like Jacob's and know the babe was the product of their love. Surely she could wait for that. Hadn't Jacob's own mother waited twenty years? She would just find other ways to deal with Leah in the meantime.

She stood a moment, composing herself, then turned back and met her mother coming toward her. "I can't do it, Ima. Not yet."

Suri nodded, her look holding far more compassion than it had held when Rachel arrived in the weaving room. "Dear, dear child. How hard it is to love a man as you do. How hard to hold the strength of a love such as his."

The words brought tears again, but she merely nodded and brushed them away. If not for Jacob's love, she would be lost.

But if not for Jacob's love, she would not want so badly to please him. Love cost more than she had ever imagined.

❀✢❀

Jacob trudged the path home alone, the sheep left in the field with one of Leah's brothers, who had come to tell him of Levi's birth. Leah's third son. The thought pleased him more than it should, dampened as it was by the fact that the mother was not his beloved. But he lifted his gaze heavenward just the same and thanked God for the child. Perhaps Leah was getting her wish, as the boy's name meant "attached," and, in fact, Levi's birth did spark feelings of fondness in him toward the mother.

Rachel would not be pleased if she knew. But how could he deny the warmth he felt in the presence of the sons Leah had given him? What man didn't long to be a father? And already Leah had birthed three sons, more than his mother had given his father.

He quickened his step, anxious to see the newest child, his mind warring with how to respond to his wives when he arrived. He could not tell Leah she had pleased him. Somehow she would make Rachel feel worse if he did. No, the kind regard he found himself feeling for her would remain his own private affair. Rachel alone deserved his love and devotion.

He searched the blue skies at the cries of a hawk, and a steady breeze whipped the sides of his turban, lashing it in front of his face. His feet swirled bits of dust as he treaded the familiar path, and he wished just by this daily trek he could somehow stamp out the strife between the sisters. It should not matter that Rachel had no child to call her own. She had his love.

Why wasn't that enough for her?

He rubbed a hand over his jaw, feeling the grit of the wilderness still in his beard. He should take time to wash in the stream before returning home. He paused midstep. A turn in the path would lead him to the stream not far from Laban's property. The women could be there washing garments, but he could remain unseen if he picked a spot farther down the stream's path. Bushes grew in abundance along the banks, affording some privacy. And Rachel always appreciated the smell of him when he wasn't gritty with many days' sweat and dirt.

He smiled at the memory of her chiding him for coming to her tent with too much dust in his beard, insisting that he wash right away, then she changed her mind, took a cloth, and washed the dust away for him. Her kiss that followed had remained in his memory and often brought a smile to his lips.

Ah, Rachel! How beautiful and spontaneous she was! And if this would please her, he would stop and bathe. Then he would see to Leah and her son and try to keep his delight evident to Leah in some small way, yet hidden from Rachel in another.

Rachel knelt at the side of the stream, dipped her soiled cloths into the moving water, and let her tears flow with the stains she could not quite remove from her clothes or her heart. Beside her Bilhah scrubbed one of Jacob's tunics, a job Rachel usually reserved for herself, but with the passing months since Levi's birth she had allowed her maid more tasks related to her husband, all in an attempt to see if she could bear sharing him with yet another. She couldn't. How could she? And yet what choice did she have?

Laughter came to her from upstream where Leah and Zilpah washed their own stack of soiled linens and wools. The youngest, Levi, now four months old, lay on a blanket nearby where Leah could stop to feed him when he awoke, while the older two children played with a household servant some distance from the water's edge. Rachel's heart warmed to hear their childish squeals of delight, unable to deny that she had grown fond of Leah's sons. They were a distraction from the daily struggle with her sister. And yet they were also a reminder of all she did not have.

She glanced at Bilhah, trying to blot out the sounds of her sister and those with her. "I noticed a spot on the right sleeve of that one. He dripped some of the stew on it the other night. Take care not to rip it as you scrub." The tunic was one she had woven for him before their marriage, and though it was growing threadbare, she still favored it for the love that had gone into making it.

"I will be careful, mistress." She held up the sleeve. "See? It is already gone."

Rachel wrung one of her cloths and spread it on some tree branches to dry. "Good," she said, relieved. Perhaps she should make him another to replace it and not fuss so.

"Is anything wrong today, mistress?" Bilhah pulled the tunic from the water and twisted it from one end to the other. Water dripped beneath her sturdy young arms.

"Nothing unusual." She studied the girl, wondering what thoughts ran through her head. Bilhah had been little more than a child when she was given to Rachel at her marriage to Jacob, on the cusp of womanhood. Since then, she had grown into a woman. She was pretty in a plain sort of way, unremarkable yet loyal to Rachel in her struggle with her sister. She would understand if Rachel gave her to Jacob. Wouldn't she?

She had turned the thoughts over in her head for six months, since the day her mother had suggested it. Until now she had cast the thoughts out as quickly as they came, though in recent weeks they had lingered on the fringes of her mind, never quite leaving her alone. Had she waited long enough? What if Leah conceived again?

Her stomach hurt at the thought. She had begged Jacob to stay away from Leah, but some misplaced loyalty to Leah or something had made him ignore Rachel's plea. He had gone to her after her purification. And Rachel had waited, counting the days ever since.

She glanced Leah's way, not wanting her to see that she watched her. Leah bent over the blanket and lifted Levi high, tilting her head back to look up at him. His delighted giggle pierced Rachel's heart. She turned her attention to finish her task, then stood. She turned to walk along the banks to wait while the garments dried, moving the opposite direction from her sister.

But an hour later, as she gathered the clothes and folded them into her basket to carry home, she saw Leah walking toward her, Levi on her hip, Zilpah guiding the other children up the path ahead of them.

"I thought you should know," Leah said, her mouth tight. "Before I tell Jacob, that is."

Rachel looked into Leah's pale eyes, unable to miss the glint she saw there. "You are with child again, is that it?" She didn't need Leah to tell her. One night with Jacob seemed to produce endless children, while Rachel could spend every night in his arms with nothing to show for it.

Leah nodded, a slight smile replacing the grim line. "I do not tell you to upset you." Her voice gentled. "I wish it was you."

The words surprised her. "No you don't." She held Leah's gaze in challenge.

Leah glanced beyond Rachel, her normal lack of confidence showing clearly in her worried gaze. Rachel turned and started walking, not wanting to continue this conversation despite its surprising turn. But a moment later Leah shifted Levi and moved into step with Rachel along the path.

"All right. It is true that I am pleased to bear his children. But it is only because you have Jacob's heart. If I could trade places with you . . ." She glanced at her son. "I almost would."

Rachel huffed, unconvinced. "You and I both know it is not enough to have a man's love."

"I don't know that." Leah's voice was soft, wistful, and Rachel stopped, looked at her.

She studied her sister, wishing for the hundredth time that she could send her away and be done with the competition between them. "Well, you could have known it if you had married someone else."

Leah nodded too quickly. "I know that. If someone else would have had me, I would have. I know I am not lovely like you."

The admission pricked Rachel's conscience. "You shouldn't compare yourself to me. You are pretty, especially so when you are with child." Some foreign source within her urged kindness from her lips, though her heart felt little compassion to go with the words. "I am sure Jacob does not find you unattractive."

"Did he say so?" Her eager question and the look of such hope in her expression softened Rachel's own eagerness to wound where she had been wounded. She need not purposely hurt Leah. They were sisters, after all.

"Not in so many words." At Leah's dejected look, she amended, "But I can sense it. He does not say so to spare me, that is all." She looked away and started walking again.

They strode in silence for a time, Rachel's mind churning with Leah's latest news. Four children in four years! She closed her eyes, stricken, nearly stumbling with the heavy load of the basket on her hip, wishing yet again that it was a child she carried there. *How long, Adonai?*

As they neared the tents, she watched Leah walk ahead, taking Levi into her tent, no doubt to nurse him. Servants sat at the grindstone preparing the grain for the evening's baking, and a stew slowly cooked over the fire pit. Bilhah deposited the linens in Rachel's tent and hurried to help with the meal preparations, but Rachel stood looking on, feeling somehow detached from it all. Four children so quickly. And still she waited.

Well, she could wait no longer. She looked on her young maid once more, assured that the girl was no longer a girl. The outline of womanly curves showed along the profile of her garments. A shapely girl, well built to carry a son. A son that would belong to Rachel.

Jacob might not like her suggestion. But he must agree to it. She knew how to convince him. And she would use all of her womanly ways to do so. Though it would break her heart in the process.

❊ 16 ❊

The following week, Jacob dipped his bread into the bowl of red lentil stew he had made and handed it to Laban. Fire crackled in the pit nearby, casting shadows over the circle where Laban and his sons had joined him. The flocks rested in the pens a stone's throw beyond. Night had fallen quickly on the banks of the stream, and the air was festive with the coming sheep shearing. Morning would find them working hard, but tonight they ate and drank in camaraderie.

Laban took the bread Jacob offered and ate, the signal that his sons could partake as well. Jacob soon joined them, the mood high-spirited, abundant with food and laughter.

"Good stew, Jacob," Rachel's brother Bahaar said between mouthfuls. "With skills such as these, who needs women?"

Laughter followed the remark. "Bahaar only says this because his woman feeds his belly and nothing more," one of Rachel's half brothers said between mouthfuls of stew.

Tariq, Leah's oldest brother, tore a hunk of flatbread from the loaf Jacob handed to him. "Jacob has no lack where that is concerned." He glanced at Jacob, his meaning clear.

Jacob ignored the comment and scooped his own bread into the steaming pot.

"I hear Leah is expecting again," another brother said. "Rachel making your life miserable yet?"

"I hear Rachel is considering giving him her maid to wife." Laban took a swig from the flask of beer at his side and wiped his mouth with the back of his hand.

Jacob looked up, masking the surprise he felt and the sudden twist in his gut. "How would you know such a thing?" Rachel should be the one to tell him, not her father, if this was the truth. Was she considering this?

"Her mother told me." Laban belched and patted his ample middle. "Though Suri suggested it six months ago. I'm surprised Rachel hasn't told you by now."

"Perhaps Rachel did not wish to take Suri's suggestion." He had barely noticed Rachel's maid except when she placed food before him. Though now that he thought about it, Bilhah had placed food in front of him more often of late, and Rachel had encouraged her to sit with them at meals, if only for a few moments. Had she been preparing him for a change in their relationship?

No. Surely not.

"It's the only way Rachel can have children, Jacob," Tariq said, stating what was all too clear. Was his displeasure at the thought so obvious? "You know it is a woman's right if she is barren." He met Jacob's level gaze.

"You don't know that she is barren." Though what other explanation could there be? Leah was proof that the problem did not lie with him.

Tariq laughed and his brothers joined him, though Rachel's brothers were conspicuously quiet. "Unless you are not taking advantage of that time you spend with her . . ."

"So she is barren. It matters little to me. My mother waited twenty years. Rachel will not be barren forever." He clung to the thought, though even he wondered at its truth. With Leah bearing so easily, might Adonai be keeping Rachel from bearing to spare her, as Jacob had always secretly hoped? Perhaps Leah alone was to be mother to his sons.

"Not everyone is like your mother." Laban puffed on his pipe, his look thoughtful.

"Or my grandmother? Perhaps God has plans we do not know about." Sarah had given Abraham her maid and lived to regret her choice.

"So barren women run in your family, is that it?" Tariq scoffed. He took a long swig of his beer and capped the end.

"That remark does not deserve a response." Jacob felt his ire rising, not so much for the ribbing but for the fact that Rachel had become so desperate and kept it from him.

"Well, I say if she offers you her maid, listen to her," Laban said, smiling. "Give Rachel a child and the strife will lessen between her and her sister."

Jacob met his father-in-law's look without comment. To dredge up the cause of that strife would be to invite heated words. He stood instead. "I'm through with this conversation." He walked to the sheep pens where he would spend the night guarding the door, listening to their laughter behind him.

Rachel sat in her tent, the sides rolled up to let in the late summer breezes while she worked the spindle and distaff and watched the path Jacob would take to return from the sheep shearing with her father and brothers. She glanced at Bilhah working the millstone, grinding the barley for bread that evening. How often her gaze had turned to the girl of late. How often her mother's words moved through her thoughts like some incessant wind.

Give the man your maid. How easy it sounded! How hard it would be.

She had debated whether to tell Jacob, to ask his opinion, but the decision was hers to make. Of course, he would tell her to wait, to trust Adonai's timing. But he could not be sure God ever planned to give her a child. Somehow she must secure one herself.

He would tell her of his grandmother's regret in giving Hagar to Abraham, but at least it gave her a son to care for during the waiting for her own. Surely it could not have been so bad.

She closed her eyes, her hands moving in the familiar rhythm, and listened to the sounds of grinding, of bird calls, and at last of whistling. She opened her eyes and jumped up, dropping the spindle and distaff to the mat, and hurried through the tent. Jacob strolled toward her, a bundle of wool slung over his shoulder, a smile on his handsome face. She ran to him, foolish as it was.

"Jacob! How I've missed you!"

He caught her in a half embrace and kissed her. "And I you, beloved." He set the bundle on the ground and picked her up in a warm embrace.

She laughed as his beard tickled her cheek. "How did things go? I want to hear everything!"

He laughed with her, kissed her soundly, then set her down and took up his bundle again. "The shearing was a great success. Your father plans a feast when they return on the morrow."

"Why did they not come with you?" Her mother and the other women, including Leah, had been preparing all of the men's favorite dishes since sunup. Rachel had taken a turn, but when Leah had started telling her what to do and how to do it, she'd left. Let them prepare the food for the feast. She would wait for Jacob.

"Some of the sheep were harder to shear than others. They sent me on ahead to warn the women they would be late." He released the bundle at the door of her tent, then took her hand. "Come with me to tell them."

She squeezed his hand and followed, passing Bilhah still grinding on the way. Jacob glanced at her a moment. "Why is your maid grinding when the feast is to be with your father's house?"

Rachel looked at him, noting the raised brow. Since when had he noticed what her maid did? Had he been thinking about taking her, since Rachel couldn't give him children?

"She is grinding extra. Leah ran short." She tucked a strand of hair behind her ear. "Why do you look at her so?"

"Look at who?"

"Bilhah."

"Your maid?"

"Yes, of course my maid. Who else would you be looking at?" She glanced away, ashamed at her harsh tone.

"Why are you so upset?" He stopped halfway to her father's house to face her. "Is there something you need to tell me?" His gaze was open, tender, and she could not hold it.

"I'm sorry. It's just . . . Leah has been yelling at me all day, so I came here to get away." She looked up. "I'm just so glad you are home! Forget Bilhah." She would tell him later the plans of her heart. If she could go through with them.

He looked relieved, then took her hand again. "It's good to be home."

She smiled up at him. "Yes, it is."

❊❋❊

Dawn crept over the horizon, and Rachel could no longer lie at Jacob's side. She shifted, careful not to disturb him, and rose, snatched her robe from the floor, and headed to the tent's door. She would fetch her jug from her tent and get to the well before Leah or one of her maids could join her and start the fire for the flatbread. Sleep would not return again, and there was ample gray light to make the path discernible. But her stomach twisted every time her mind strayed to the truth that would not leave her. She was barren. And giving her maid to Jacob was her only solution to having children that would be hers, not her sister's.

She had lain awake most of the night despite Jacob's nearness, debating whether or not to broach the subject with him. Her decision was cinched when he inadvertently mentioned something Reuben had said that made him chuckle. Jacob simply must have children besides those of her sister's. She needed a child to make him proud and bring a smile to his eyes as Leah's children did. The thought had settled like a heavy stone in her middle.

She must tell him. Today. She could no longer put off what her heart told her she must do.

Jacob stirred and watched Rachel slip from the tent, his heart heavy. Though she had tried to remain still at his side in the night, he had awakened several times and known she wrestled with some disturbing thought. Had her father been right? Every indication, from her curt response at the mention of her maid the day before to her restless sleep, pointed to the truth. And it pained him to know how much she ached inside.

He rubbed a hand over his eyes, blinking in the soft predawn light, and gave in to a deep yawn, then pushed up from the mat and donned his clothes. He slipped from his tent to see Rachel emerge from her own, her water jug balanced on her head, her back straight but her gait slow, as if the jug were already weighted with water.

He followed at a distance, then caught up with her as she neared the path leading toward the well. "You're up earlier than usual," he said. Seeing her startle, he raised an arm to catch the jug, but she steadied it on her own, then looked at him.

"I couldn't sleep. There was no sense in trying any longer." Her tone was petulant, her fatigue evident.

"Can I carry it for you?" Though a man carrying a water jug was not a common sight, he would do anything to ease her suffering.

She glanced beyond him. "No. Thank you. I can handle it."

"I'm sure you can. I was only trying to help." He straightened the belt at his waist, though it was already secured with pouches and sling, as he searched for something to say to her.

She stopped midstep, surprising him. "If you would help me, give me children." Her plea came out choked, broken.

"Don't you think I have tried?" What more did she expect from him?

"Perhaps we are doing something wrong."

He couldn't imagine what. "We are doing all we can, beloved. What more do you want from me?" The words hung on a thread of desperation, and he knew she could sense his irritation. But he did not know what else to tell her. It wasn't his place to ask for her maid. And he didn't want to. He silently prayed she would not broach the subject. "We just need to be patient, Rachel. You will conceive in time."

"You do not know that!" She looked away. "I cannot bear to live like this, Jacob." She turned then and faced him head-on, her eyes taking on a fierce glint he had not seen in her before. He took an involuntary step backward. "Give me children or I'll die!"

The words hung between them, thick, impenetrable.

Jacob's breathing hitched and his anger spiked, warring with the irrational fear her words evoked. "Am I in the place of God, who has kept you from having children?" He couldn't lose her. Were children really that important to her?

She looked away, her face flushed. She lowered the jar to the ground between them and looked back toward the tents. In the distance, Rachel's maid already sat at the grindstone, the squeal and crunch of grain on stone sure to awaken the rest of the household. Rachel looked at her, myriad emotions moving over her expression, none of them pleased. He waited, watching her, hating the struggle, wishing he could take it from her.

At last he touched her arm. "Rachel, I . . ."

She shrugged him aside and crossed her arms, shielding herself from what she was about to do, from allowing him to comfort her. "There," she said, pointing to her maid, "is Bilhah, my maidservant." She swallowed hard and brushed a stray tear from her cheek, a tear he longed to wipe away. "Sleep with her so that she can bear children for me and that through her I too can build a family."

"Rachel."

"Please, Jacob. Just do as I ask." She snatched up her jug and returned it to her head, then offered him one more look. "Please. Her time has just recently passed. Go to her tonight." She strode away from him without a backward glance. He watched until she disappeared over the ridge, taking his heart with her.

Rachel reached the well thoroughly spent. What little energy she'd had upon rising that morning had disappeared the moment she offered her maid to Jacob. Now she was faced with the task of breaking the news to Bilhah. Or perhaps Jacob would do that himself.

No. It was her place to give the girl to her husband. In doing so, Bilhah would forfeit the status of maid to become Jacob's wife. A bonus for her. Rachel would have to find a new maidservant. The thought did not please her, not for lack of servants but for sharing Jacob's time yet again.

How weary her life had become! She lowered the jar to the well and wept as it fell slowly to the depths. She felt its weight as it filled and feared she would not have the strength to raise it again. The sky lit now with the pinks of dawn. Dew still tickled her feet where the grasses touched over the edge of her sandals.

She hefted the jar over the well's lip and sank onto the stone edge, looking toward the tents in the distance. She had no use for dew or sun today. She wanted only to curl onto her side and sleep, not caring if she woke again. *Jacob. Why has your God denied us this?*

She glanced heavenward, but the skies gave no answer. Of

course not. Adonai had chosen to bless her sister instead of her. Somehow she had been deemed unworthy. So now she must give another woman to her husband. Would she live with regret as Sarah once did?

She plopped the heavy jar onto her head and walked with weighted steps back to the camp. She met Bilhah just finishing the grinding and set the jar beside her in the hole meant to keep it from tipping.

"Come to my tent," she said, glancing briefly at her maid. She moved on ahead, her mind churning with how best to word her request. No. It would not be a request. Bilhah was a slave who was about to become a wife. There was no choice on her part.

"Did you need something, mistress?" Bilhah stepped into the dark interior. Rachel had yet to roll up the sides and did not bother to light a lamp. Darkness suited what she was about to say.

"Yes, come here and sit down."

Bilhah did as she was told, her expression quizzical. She folded her hands in her lap and waited while Rachel paced in front of her.

"There is no easy way to say this." She stopped abruptly. "I am giving you to Jacob to wife so that you can bear me a son. The child will be mine. I will name him and bear him on my knees so that I can have a family through you." She held Bilhah's startled gaze.

The girl quickly looked down at her hands sitting idle in her lap, now upturned in supplication. But she did not protest. She glanced up and gave a slight nod. "When?" There was nothing else to be said, as Bilhah could not refuse.

"Tonight." Rachel searched the girl's face. "You are clean?"

She nodded. "Yes, mistress."

"Good. Tonight then." While she still had courage to follow through with this. "I will take you to his tent, and you will become his wife." The thought twisted inside of her, but she did not show the girl her pain. "You may go now."

Bilhah stood, but she did not leave. Instead, surprisingly, she stepped closer and laid a hand on Rachel's arm. "I will pray that your God gives you a son either by me or by you or both."

By me. Rachel nodded. "Thank you."

Bilhah left the tent, and Rachel went into her chamber and wept.

❄ 17 ❄

Jacob stood too long at the sheep pens that night, counting the sheep twice, half wishing one was missing. He preferred the thought of going out after it to what awaited him in his tent. He shook his head, forcing back a deep sigh. He looked at the deepening dusk, rubbed the back of his neck. Surely God was punishing him for his many sins. Why else would He have denied him the one thing he wanted most in life? He had not worked for Leah, did not want Rachel's maid Bilhah. But the girl would be his whether he wanted her or not.

Most men would welcome the diversity of many women.

Jacob was not one of them.

He turned at the approach of a servant boy who would sleep with the flock this night. Memories of his own youth surfaced as he studied the boy's awkward gait, the carefree way his arms swung at his sides as he whistled, mimicking the mournful cry of a dove. How quickly the freedom of childhood passed. His son Reuben was not yet three years old and already weaned. Soon his sons would be grown like olive plants sprung up. Would Rachel still be barren then?

The thought turned his stomach as he nodded to the servant boy and moved slowly toward his tent. He approached the fire where Rachel and Bilhah waited for him. He sat, accepting the food Rachel placed before him, and ate in silence. Rachel refilled his cup several times, while Bilhah stood unmoving behind one of the smooth stone seats placed about the fire. When he finished, he stood. Rachel stepped forward with Bilhah beside her.

"You're really going to do this?" He looked at Rachel until her gaze at last met his.

"Yes." She took Bilhah's hand and placed it in Jacob's. "Here is your wife."

Bilhah's hand felt cold in his. He glanced at the girl, seeing fear in her eyes. His gaze did not linger as he sought Rachel's again. "You are my wife."

Tears brimmed in her eyes as she looked at him. "Yes, one of three."

He would argue she was the only wife of his heart, but it would do nothing to change the misery and pain mingling in her expression. He glanced down again at Bilhah's small hand in his and shook himself. Such a marriage required no formal feast. This was a slave wife, a concubine, and Rachel had sealed the bond with a word.

He glanced at Bilhah, wanting to send her to his tent to wait for him, but one more look at Rachel told him waiting would make it harder for her.

"Just go, Jacob." The words were a whisper, choked out through clenched teeth. "Do this for me."

He nodded, defeat settling over him. "For you," he said, knowing he could not deny her.

He gripped Bilhah's hand. "Come," he said, though he knew she would do so without a word from him. She had obeyed every command given her since she was a small child. Her need for daily bread had assured her quick obedience.

He led her into the tent, knowing he should speak to her, should help her to understand what he was about to do. But the words would not come past the pain in his heart.

✻✲✻

The next day Rachel met Bilhah already working the millstone, her expression unreadable. There would be no bridal week for her, and Rachel felt a stab of guilt and a certain sense of compassion that she was a wife now, yet so denied. She had thought to consult Jacob on the matter, to suggest he give Bilhah more than was required, but he had already left his tent and gone to the fields before she had arisen. Did he resent this new wife so much then?

She sat beside Bilhah and scooped up the pile of flour already ground, mixed oil from a flask she carried, and worked the dough with her hands. "Did Jacob say when he would return?" she asked after a lengthy silence.

Bilhah glanced up, her face flushed beyond the normal color brought on by hard work. "He did not speak much to me, mis—that is, he got up and left before dawn."

Birds chirped in the uncomfortable silence, mingling with the voices of Leah's children in the distance. Rachel studied her maid—no, no longer her maid—wishing she could read the girl's thoughts. But it would do no good to pry. Better to leave these things be.

"You will go to him again tonight," Rachel said, hating the necessity, wanting to pull Jacob into her arms instead and listen to all that was on his heart. But Bilhah would never conceive if she was not given the chance. Few were as fertile as Leah, and Rachel could not wait for Leah to give birth and conceive again before her maid bore a child. The thought stung. How used Jacob must feel! And yet did a man really care about such things?

"He would rather have you, mistress." Bilhah's comment, spoken so softly yet earnestly, brought Rachel's thoughts up sharp.

"Of course he would. But I cannot bear him children." And she was weary of this great struggle with her sister.

"Perhaps you may. In time."

Rachel looked toward Leah's tent as the commotion grew louder and the children's young voices clamored for Leah's attention. What would it be like to be surrounded by young ones and divide her time thus?

"I pray you are right, but for now we must do things another way." She searched the girl's plain features, saw a flicker of pain in her light brown eyes, but it was replaced quickly by acceptance.

"I will do as you ask, mistress." She tossed more wheat kernels onto the stone, grabbed the handle, and turned.

"Call me Rachel. You are no longer my maid in the same way." She slapped the dough onto a board and smoothed it with the palm of her hand.

"Yes, mistress."

Rachel sighed and shook her head. She would deal with such trivial matters another day.

Spring harvest saw abundant crops of wheat and barley, greater than her father had ever seen before, and the flocks birthed new young, all healthy and strong. Bilhah had conceived, lightening Rachel's mood. She fussed daily, weekly over her maid, praying, hoping that the birth would be as fruitful and healthy as the flocks in Jacob's care.

In the meantime, Leah's pains came upon her with her fourth child, but this birth was difficult, not at all as she had experienced the first three times. Rachel rubbed Leah's back as Suri tried to turn the child, and Farah draped cool cloths over Leah's sweating brow.

"Don't push yet, child. Breathe a little longer." Suri's soothing tone did little to ease Leah's suffering. "I see it is another son."

"There, see, Leah. Another son. All will be well as soon as you birth him." Fear snaked its way through Rachel, and she wondered if she would be able to endure such agony. "Breathe, dear sister." Despite their struggles, she could not imagine losing Leah. Not yet. Not with so many young sons to tend. Her envy did not extend to meanness. "You must try, Leah."

A guttural cry came from Leah's parched lips, and Rachel startled at the stark pain of it. She sounded more like a wounded animal than a woman.

"He is turned now. There. See!" Suri's triumphant voice broke through Rachel's fears. "Push now, Leah. With all of your strength."

Rachel helped Leah to sit up on the birthing stool and rubbed her shoulders as she bore down on the child. At last a lusty cry emerged from the boy, and Leah laughed and cried at his entrance into the world.

"A beautiful son!" Suri held up the baby, and Rachel's heart yearned at the sight of him. Of all of Leah's children, he looked the most like Jacob, despite the blood and fluids covering him. He had a head of dark hair just like his father and squirmed for attention.

Leah laughed and the others joined her. Rachel left her side to attend the babe, then brought him to Leah.

"A son," Leah said, her voice soft, exhausted, and yet reverent with awe. "This time I will praise the Lord." She closed her eyes and gave a contented sigh as the baby nursed.

"What name will you give this one?" Farah asked, stroking the child's soft head.

Leah opened her eyes and smiled. "Judah."

Praise. Rachel looked on at the pair they made, relieved that her sister had survived such a difficult birth. And strangely, despite the jealousy she could not quite release, she found gratitude in her own heart for this one. Judah. The name sounded like praise, the kind only Adonai deserved. And praise Him she did.

18

Leah sat in the shade of her tent nursing Judah, watching Zilpah play with Reuben and Simeon a short distance away. Levi napped just inside the tent, close enough that Leah could see him through the tent's open sides. She closed her eyes, grateful for the good health of the child in her arms. Birthing him had taken all of her strength, and she still had not regained it forty days later. The thought troubled her, but even more the fear that Jacob would have no more use for her if she could not bear him more children.

And yet why this great need to prove herself to him? Hadn't she already given him four fine sons? She looked down with affection on Judah's serene face and stroked the soft curls from his smooth brow. So contented. So guileless and free of the worries life would one day bring to him. What would this child face? *Please, Adonai, let this child be obedient to Your ways.*

She had not thought to pray such a thing with the first three sons and now realized she should entrust each of them to Yahweh's care. But her prayers, even her praise over Judah's birth, could not ease the desire for more children. For more of Jacob's attention.

Female voices came to her, and she glanced up, shading her eyes against the sun's angled glare to see who approached. But it was only Rachel and her maid returning from a visit to Laban's house. A visit Leah had no strength to make even yet.

"There you are," Rachel said as they drew near.

"Of course I'm here. Where else would I be?" She hadn't meant to snap but realized by Rachel's raised brows that she had spoken harsher than she intended. "Forgive me. I am weary today."

Rachel looked like she would offer a response but then seemed to think better of it. "Your mother sent these to you." She placed some of Leah's favorite pomegranates in a basket at Leah's side. "Do you want me to take one of the children for you?" She glanced at Judah, her look telling, the longing evident in her large dark eyes.

"I can manage." She tightened her grip on Judah ever so slightly. "Levi is napping, and Zilpah is with me."

Rachel shrugged as though it mattered little to her, though Leah knew the truth. Rachel glanced at her maid and lifted her chin. "Come, Bilhah. I want to cut these pomegranates and fix them the way Jacob likes them." She cast Leah a parting glance, then moved gracefully past Jacob's tent to her own.

Leah's stomach twisted, and she struggled against the inadequacy Rachel always managed to make her feel, the uselessness of her position in Jacob's household. It wasn't true. Jacob had even indicated stronger affection for her, especially since Judah's birth, of which he seemed doubly pleased over any of the other sons. But she felt it in Rachel's look just the same.

She watched Rachel's retreating back and Bilhah's slightly bulging middle evident now beneath her robe, the cause of Rachel's recent haughty spirit. She swallowed, surprised by the sudden anger and the unexpected sting of tears. She could not possibly be jealous. She had four healthy, beautiful sons! But as she examined her heart, she knew she could not deny it. She was jealous of Rachel's beauty and the coming child of Rachel's maid.

It was too soon for her to conceive again anyway, she told herself yet again. And in truth, she had no strength for the task. Her body needed time to recover, and soon she must tell Jacob that he could not come to her until she had healed, something that she expected would take much longer than she hoped.

Laughter coming from Rachel's tent set her teeth on edge. She glanced once more toward Rachel and Bilhah discussing some private sentiment they shared, keeping her out, as Rachel always did. And keeping Jacob to themselves far too often.

Anger fought its way to the surface of her heart, and she knew she could not quash the emotion. She glanced at Zilpah still sitting on the ground making pictures in the dirt with her sons. Two could play at Rachel's game. And she was already ahead with four sons to show her worth. If Rachel could give Bilhah to Jacob, she could give him Zilpah.

Then they would see just how haughty Rachel would remain.

Jacob lifted the cup of barley beer to his lips and sipped the lukewarm, frothy brew. The fire turned to glowing embers, clustered sparks like the stars above. Rachel had left his side some time ago not feeling well, and Bilhah slept in her own tent, more tired now that the babe had grown larger within her. The voices of Leah's children grew silent as Leah and Zilpah put them to bed. He should go to his own tent and rest, but he could not seem to gather the energy needed to rise. He took another drink instead and briefly closed his eyes.

Footsteps rustling the grasses outside the fire's circle drew his attention. He looked up to see Leah coming toward him. He stiffened, knowing by her look that she wanted something from him. He had little left to give, but he smiled at Leah's approach just the same, masking his impatience as he beckoned her to sit beside him.

"What do you need?" he asked, not wanting to belabor the

point. Were her cheeks paler than normal? It struck him that she had not seemed as well and strong as she normally did in quite some time. "Are you ill?" The thought troubled him.

She shook her head. "Not ill exactly." She glanced beyond him. "That is, Judah's birth was not easy on me, Jacob." She looked at him then, imploring, her pale eyes filled with a sense of sadness he had never seen in her before. "I am afraid I have still not recovered. To bear more children now would likely injure my health further."

He studied her, understanding dawning. She could not risk another pregnancy until she was strong again. Would she be strong again? Perhaps she would have no more sons than the four she now had.

"But you will recover?" Despite their beginning and the fact that he did not love her in the way he loved Rachel, he did hold some affection for her. He could not imagine his life now without her in it.

She nodded. "Surely in time. Yes." She twisted her hands in her lap. "Until then—"

"I understand," he said, wanting to spare her the embarrassment of stating it. He placed a hand on her knee, then reached for her hand and squeezed.

She looked up at him, tears skimming her lashes. Was she so fearful of losing her time with him? But one look into her eyes told him what he had spent countless hours trying to deny.

"I would like you to sleep with my maid Zilpah in my place, so that I may procure sons by her." She swallowed and made a valiant effort to keep the tears at bay. She had never cried in front of him, and he was moved to pity.

"You already have four sons, Leah. You need not bear me more." He meant the words to comfort her, but her startled look made him realize too late that she did not take the comfort he intended. "That does not mean you will live as a widow." He released her hand and placed an arm around her shoulders instead, pulling her head against his chest. "I will still care for you." He spoke softly against her ear, discomfited by her tears. "It's all right, Leah."

He hadn't meant to sound impatient and chided himself for not keeping his tone gentle. "That is, there is nothing to fear. You will be well and have more children in time." Though he knew his mother had never borne another after he and his brother were born. Perhaps that was all God had intended. How was a man to know such things?

"Will you take my maid then? Please?" She sniffed and dried her tears with her sleeve. She sat up to look at him. "It is my right, Jacob." He could not tell if the sudden glint in her eyes was her determination or the remnant of her tears.

"I do not see the need." But still, he felt pulled between the two sisters, until he wondered how long he could survive their jealousies and competition.

"If Rachel can give you her maid, then so can I. I want this, Jacob." She held his gaze, unrelenting, with a look that told him he would not win an argument with her.

He nodded, defeat settling over him, as though clouds had blotted out the stars, and yet they remained transfixed in the heavens, winking down on him. "When?" But he knew the answer.

"She can come to you this night. Or tomorrow." She touched his arm. "Please do not make me wait."

He stared at her. "Do you think me some kind of animal that you can call to come at your beckoning?" Both Leah and Rachel had treated him thus, and he had had enough. He stood abruptly, and she stood with him, alarm in her expression.

"No, of course not. Forgive me, my lord." She took a step back and hugged herself as though chilled. She truly did not look well, and he suddenly regretted his anger.

"I'm sorry, Leah." He pulled her close again and patted her back. "Send your maid to my tent. I will do as you ask." He was a victim of his love for Rachel and trapped by the yearnings of his beloved and her sister.

He released Leah and watched her walk back to her tent to call Zilpah to him. She would place Zilpah's hand in his, as Rachel had done with Bilhah, and they would be man and wife. He glanced at the heavens, the stars too numerous to count, and wondered just how many sons he must produce to no longer be able to count them.

※‡※

Rachel awoke with a start several months later to the sound of Bilhah's moans. She had insisted her former maid stay with her in her tent until the babe's birth and had worried and fretted over her like she would a small child. She hurried to the young woman's side and, at her anguished nod, woke a servant girl and sent her scurrying to her father's house to bring her mother.

"What can I get you? Some water? Does it help to walk?" Rachel's nerves tingled and her words rushed from her.

"I am fine." Bilhah drew in a long, slow breath just as Rachel's mother had taught her days earlier. She rubbed her lower back and paced the sitting area. "Some water, perhaps."

Rachel flew from the tent and retrieved some of the water from the jug still left from last night's visit to the well. They would need more, but she would send Zilpah or some other maid to get it. She caught herself at the thought of Leah's maid, no longer a maid but another of Jacob's wives and already carrying his child.

How could Jacob have done such a thing? He had told her that he could no more refuse Leah than he had her. It was a wife's right. But Leah had no reason!

She strained the water through a thin piece of linen to remove the gnats and set it where Bilhah could easily reach it, all the while her thoughts churning with the argument she and Jacob had shared the morning after he had taken Zilpah to his tent.

"How could you do this without even consulting me?" She had followed him to the sheep pens, keeping a short distance between them due to her uncleanness.

He had jerked to face her, his cheeks flushed, angry. "Since when do I need to consult you on every choice I make? I recall you made the same decision with your maid."

"Yes, but I had a reason. I did it to have a family through her. Leah already has four sons! She doesn't need more. She is only using you to stay ahead of me." Her voice had cracked on the words, and she sounded like a petulant child.

"Aren't you doing the very same thing?"

She could not hold the fierceness of his gaze, shamed even now by the accusation he had flung at her.

"No," she whispered as Bilhah's moans deepened, snagging her thoughts back to the birth about to take place. *I wouldn't do that to you. I had no choice, don't you see?*

The memory of her defense to him rang hollow in her ears now. He had looked at her long and hard, then shook his head and walked off, calling the sheep to him. He didn't see then, or now. And he had stayed in the fields for a week, letting the shame of her words continue to trouble her.

That he had at last returned held little comfort, for he had avoided her tent and everyone else's, retreating to her father's house after the meal or to his own tent alone. Would he come to hold Bilhah's child on his knees and claim it as his own? For her sake? Had his love grown cold?

Unshed emotion burned at the back of her throat, accompanying the guilt that condemned her one moment and justification that absolved her the next. She had done nothing any other woman wouldn't do. She was not wrong. Leah was the one adding to the conflict by giving Jacob a fourth wife. And a pregnant one now, though Rachel took some comfort in knowing that at least Leah was not carrying another.

The thoughts wearied her, and she pushed them away as her

mother and Farah arrived to attend Bilhah. The hours passed in agonizing slowness, but at last a son burst from Bilhah's womb. Rachel was the one, guided by Suri, to catch him, clean him up, and claim him as her own. She glanced at Bilhah, who looked on the boy with motherly affection and longing, and felt her heart twinge with the slightest hint of jealousy. The baby was not really hers, though by all legal rights he would be her adopted son. Still, she could not nurse him, and he would never bond to her as he would to the one who had borne him.

She glanced away from Bilhah's pleading expression, not wanting to give her the boy but knowing she must. She tucked the blanket closer around him and walked through the tent's door to the small crowd waiting near the fire pit. She searched for Jacob, relieved to see him sitting with her brother Bahaar.

She strode to him, lifting her chin. "You have another son, my lord," she said, holding the boy out to him.

Jacob met her gaze and smiled, though the smile seemed forced. She must speak to him. Apologize for her earlier outburst if she was ever to enjoy the presence of his company and the love they had once shared.

He took the child from her and rested him on his knees. "What will you name him?" He looked at the boy, touched a finger to his soft cheek.

"Dan," she said, grateful when he looked up once more and held her gaze. "God has vindicated me," she said softly. "He has heard my plea and given me a son."

He nodded. "A good name, beloved."

She released a long-held breath, relieved. "Thank you, my lord."

"Perhaps now you can find some peace?" His look held such hope and expectation that she longed to assure him all would be well. But the niggling fact still troubled her. Bilhah was Dan's true mother. How could she find peace apart from bearing a son of her own?

"I hope so, Jacob." If only Adonai would notice her too.

She took the babe from Jacob's arms and looked into the child's sweet face, knowing the peace Jacob hoped for would be a long time coming.

Jacob stood at the edge of a cliff, staff dug into the dirt, bracing himself against the wind. Dark clouds billowed overhead, the scent of coming rain in the swirling air. He glanced at the sky, its darkness matching his mood. The rare moment away from the sheep, away from the chaos of his household and the women fussing over another birth through Bilhah for Rachel's side, should bring some sort of relief. But relief would never come as long as Rachel remained dissatisfied.

He should never have listened to Leah and taken Zilpah to wife. For Zilpah had also borne him a son and then conceived again shortly after Bilhah. "What good fortune," Leah had said, as if the child's birth were part of a game of chance and she was fortunate enough to have won a round. And so Gad had joined Leah's family, making five for her, soon to be six, and two for Rachel.

He rubbed the back of his neck and sighed, glad for the feel of the wind's relentless strength pushing against him, flattening his robes to his body, whipping the edges of his turban about his face. Let it pummel him. The wind's beating was preferable to the cackling of the women in his tent, the fierce, endless restlessness of Rachel always vying for more sons. If she found another maid to give him, he would refuse. He was weary of her unhappiness and yet, in the same breath, felt his own unease, knowing he could never deny her. How he longed to give her what she asked!

How long, Adonai? Would God ever remember her and give Rachel a son? *Please. Let it be so.*

He had stopped worrying about losing her in childbirth.

None of the other women had been lost to him, and he realized that though such things sometimes happened, his worries were unfounded. Surely God would take care of her.

His prayers for her had come haltingly at first. But somewhere in the past year or so, they had become a daily necessity. As he watched the trees sway in the valley below him, felt the first fat drops of rain hit his cheek, he knew he would not stop seeking God's favor until He granted Rachel's deepest desire for a child. He could do no less than his father had done for his mother. If he did not do this, did not give her his heart in prayer and petition on her behalf, his love for her would be found wanting. He could not let that happen.

For though he would prefer to be rid of the need for such prayers, he would never be released from his intense love for Rachel. He was as bound to his prayers as he was to his love for her. And he would wrestle the wind to bring the answers forth if that was what it took to please his beloved.

✹ 19 ✹

Rachel held Bilhah's second son, Naphtali, against her shoulder and slowly paced inside her tent, relieved when his crying ceased and he at last slept peacefully. He was not as contented a child as Dan had been, and she wondered not for the first time if he was mocking the name she had given him—"my struggle." Her words to Jacob the night of his birth still rang in her ears. *I have had a great struggle with my sister, and I have won.* But had she?

She glanced at Bilhah, recalling the girl's violent efforts to bring him forth. For a time they had feared they would lose her, and Rachel knew she could not beg Jacob to sleep with the woman again anytime soon. Like Leah had after Judah's birth, Bilhah would need time to recover.

Rachel glanced at Naphtali's sweet face, thinking to lay him in the basket beside his mother, but she could not seem to release her hold on him. Already she loved this child as her own.

Almost as her own.

The thought brought the familiar restlessness to her heart, and she moved through the spacious tent to walk with the boy toward the pens where Jacob should soon be returning from the fields. She darted a quick look in the direction of Leah's tent and saw Zilpah, heavy with child, sitting with Leah in the shade of Leah's tent, both working the spindle and distaff while the children slept or played nearby. Reuben had gone with Jacob to the fields, already old enough to learn some of the easier tasks of shepherding.

If Zilpah bore a son, which Rachel fully expected, Leah's sons would number six while Rachel could name only two. She gently tightened her grip on Naphtali, forcing back the discontented thoughts. It did no good to feel such contention. The boy would surely feel her heart beating too fast beneath her tunic and wake up, crying again. Her struggle was not with the child, and she could not bear to upset him.

Mourning doves sang their sad dirge in the trees circling the edge of the tents, and the breeze softly rustled the hair she had let hang loose down her back. She approached the sheep pens, seeing Reuben running and jumping ahead of Jacob in the distance, the sheep following obediently behind them.

Her heart stirred at the sight of Jacob, so rugged and swarthy and strong. She caught the way his lips curved in that hint of a smile as he watched his oldest son, and she knew it pleased him to share his time with the boy. What man wouldn't want sons to follow in his steps?

She moved from the shadow of the trees and waited near the gate. His smile widened as he approached her, and his look made her heart melt. He patted Reuben on the head.

"Go on to your mother now, Reuben. Tell her all that we did today."

The boy glanced up at Jacob, his look full of pride and affection, then raced off toward his mother's tent, calling, "Ima!"

Jacob cupped his hands to his mouth. "Do not yell for her. She will think you are hurt."

The boy skidded to a stop, turned, and nodded. "Okay, Abba." He ran down the hill, his young voice again calling his mother's name, this time more distant.

Jacob chuckled. "He is anxious to tell her of his adventures."

Jacob met Rachel's gaze. She turned Naphtali so he could get a better glimpse. "And how is my youngest today?"

"He finally sleeps." She stepped closer and kissed Jacob's cheek. "I have missed you." He had spent little time with her of late, and she feared she was somehow the cause.

"I have missed you too." He touched her nose with his finger, then stroked the baby's head.

"Will you come to my tent tonight?" She needed him near, away from the others.

He glanced at her, raising a brow. "Of course. If that is what you want." His look told her she had only to ask.

"I'm sorry I've been so petulant since Leah gave you Zilpah." She wasn't really sorry, for she did not know how she could help such feelings, but perhaps saying so would ease her jealousy and make him believe her.

He took Naphtali from her and patted his back in a gentle rhythm. "It is not easy leaving your side to be with the others." His admission quieted her spirit. "You know how I feel about you."

She nodded, ashamed of her selfishness. "If only God would have seen fit to bless us together . . ." Her voice trailed off, the words too often said, nearly too painful to repeat.

He stopped, shifted the boy into one arm, and took her hand in his. "There is no need for more sons from the others, beloved. I would give you my time alone if you but ask."

She searched his handsome face, undone by his kindness. She did not deserve his patience. "Why do you put up with me? I act no better than a spoiled child sometimes."

He smiled. "Sometimes you do." He touched her cheek. "But most of the time you are simply a woman whose desire has been too long denied. Thwarted desire makes the heart sick, beloved. My mother felt the same."

"Your father prayed for her, though, and she had you."

"And I have prayed for you over and over again. Do you doubt it?" His look was so earnest, so open and sincere.

"I do not doubt you." A lump formed in her throat, and she swallowed unshed tears. "Why does Adonai not hear our prayers then? Should we offer a sacrifice? How can we make Him see and hear us?" The desperation she always felt crept into her voice, and she hated her inability to be happy and content with what she had.

"I do not know, beloved." He caught a stray tear from beneath her lashes. "We must wait and pray as my father Isaac did, and as my grandfather Abraham did as well. Do not fret over what we cannot control."

Heat filling her cheeks, Rachel swallowed hard and glanced away from him, wishing she were stronger, wiser. "Do you love them?" Her stomach twisted, and she suddenly wished to hold Naphtali, a shield between Jacob's words and her heart.

He shifted the child's weight again and lifted a strand of her hair with his calloused fingers. "I love only you, Rachel. You know this." A deep sigh escaped him, and his gaze shifted to the path in front of them and the tents beyond. She fell into step with him as he continued walking, fearing she had angered him by her repeated need for reassurance.

But as they neared Rachel's tent and he handed the boy back to her, he held her gaze, his own full of love for her. "Come to me tonight." He offered her a smile, then walked off to his own tent and shut himself in.

"How happy I am! The women will call me happy." The words burst from Leah's lips as she stepped out of her tent carrying the bundled son of Zilpah, whose travail had lasted throughout the night.

"Of course they will. And well you deserve it," her mother said, glancing Leah's way, her grandmotherly pride nearly as great for this child as it had been for Leah's own.

Leah lifted her chin, scanning the camp for Jacob. Surely

he had not yet left for the fields without checking on Zilpah's progress. But of course he could have. Rachel had managed to steal nearly all of his time since Naphtali's birth, an action that had not gone unnoticed.

She stifled the hurt that always accompanied that thought, squinting against the bright rays of dawn's early glow. There he was, sitting with Rachel beside the fire deep in conversation. She glanced at her mother, whose nod of approval gave her courage, and walked across the dew-drenched grasses to stop near Jacob's seat.

"You have another son, my lord." She waited, relieved when he met her gaze.

Jacob placed his clay plate on the ground, then shifted to face her, arms outstretched to accept the child. As she leaned down to place him in Jacob's sturdy hands, their fingers touched, and Leah's heart stirred with longing to feel his arms around her again. His smile, first at her, then at the babe, melted her heart.

"What will you name him?" Jacob touched the boy's soft cheek and the crop of straight dark hair.

"Asher," she said, crouching low to better see his face.

Jacob met her gaze. "You are happy then?" His earnest look searched hers. How she longed to tell him the truth. No. She would never be happy as long as Rachel kept him from her. She wanted her husband to be a husband to her again. But one glance at Rachel's tight smile stayed her words.

She nodded, unable to speak. She cleared her throat and tried again. "I am happy, Jacob. Happy in knowing you are pleased." She held his gaze, hoping he could read the truth in what she didn't say, wishing she could say it clearly.

But later, as she pondered Jacob's question, she could not deny the truth of her unhappiness. She needed Jacob's time and attention and, pray God, his affection. And she would find a way to have it. Soon. Whether Rachel liked it or not, Jacob could not be kept from her. She needed him. And she would see that he knew it.

⁑

Rachel spread the kneaded dough into a large, thin square, took the date filling from her mother and spooned the mixture over it, then sealed the edges and placed it above the hot embers. Heat from the ovens in her father's cooking rooms drew sweat along Rachel's brow, and she swiped at it with the back of her hand.

"I need some water. Do you want some?" Rachel handed the now empty bowl to her mother.

"You could bring me a cup."

Rachel left the room and moved to the outer courtyard where the breeze cooled her skin and water stood in large urns near the door. She took a cupful and drank, looking toward the path the men would take when they returned. Leah's son Reuben hurried toward her, clutching the wide green leaves of a plant, his gait swift and sure. He glanced at Rachel and moved to pass her, but Rachel stayed him with her hand.

"Are those mandrakes?" Rachel had seen the flowering green leaves when she walked the fields with the sheep but had forgotten their aphrodisiac uses.

Reuben pulled the plants close to his chest, his eyes wide. "They're for Ima."

"Of course they are. She is in the cooking room. Come. I will go with you." She quickly dipped another cupful of water for her mother, then followed Reuben inside.

"Ima, look what I found!" The women in the room stopped their work to look in Leah's direction. "Aunt Rachel says they're mandrakes."

Rachel glanced at Leah, who stooped to Reuben's eye level and took the precious fruit from his hands. "They are beautiful, my son." She touched his face, and his cheeks flushed pink despite his soft smile. "Where did you find them?"

He straightened, lifting his chin. "In the fields near the wheat where Abba is working. He said I could bring them to you."

Rachel's heart twisted, and she wondered what Jacob intended by saying such a thing. Did he know the fruit's value? They could be the answer to her barrenness! If she could eat them and feed some to Jacob . . . and if the tales were true . . .

She stepped closer to Leah. "Please give me some of your son's mandrakes." She would beg and plead if she must. Leah certainly didn't need them.

Leah stood up, her face flushed. Rachel felt the stares of everyone in the room and braced herself, feeling the anger in Leah's look.

"Wasn't it enough that you took away my husband? Will you take my son's mandrakes too?"

Warmth crept up Rachel's neck as she felt the censure of the women around her. She stiffened her back. She had done nothing wrong. "Very well," she said, pushing back a rush of guilt, "he can sleep with you tonight in return for your son's mandrakes." The mandrakes would keep another day for Rachel to use them herself.

Leah smiled, her look triumphant. She glanced at Reuben, placed several mandrakes in Rachel's hands, then turned to her son. "Lead me to the fields. I must speak to your father as soon as he is done working."

Reuben smiled, a toothy grin. "Sure, Ima. Come on."

Leah looked back at her mother, who shooed her off. "We can finish these. Go." Leah went without a backward glance while Rachel took the mandrakes to her tent.

20

Jacob gave a parting nod to Bahaar as the man took the path toward the threshing floor where he would spend the night threshing and guarding the wheat with Suri's other sons. Jacob's turn would come on the morrow, but for tonight he intended to enjoy Laban's feast and relax in his tent with Rachel at his side. He chuckled at the thought of her quick smile and how easily they had fallen into a comfortable family rhythm since he had finally learned to divide his time between his wives and children, saving the evenings when the stars hung low for Rachel alone.

His other wives seemed to accept the situation, he told himself, and Rachel seemed happier, which mattered most to him. He denied the little kick of guilt he felt when his gaze met Leah's. Of the three other women, Leah missed him most, but he could not bring himself to visit her tent when Rachel waited so eagerly. Even on the nights when he could not touch her, she listened to him speak of his homeland, his mother and father, Deborah and Selima and Eliezer's son Haviv, of Esau and his foolish wives and the competition that had always been between them. She was his friend, his confidante.

He quickened his pace over the rocky path, kicking up small stones with his sandals in his hurry to be with Rachel. She would serve him at the feast, of that he had little doubt, and tease him with those large, beguiling eyes of hers, eyes that had captured his attention even from a distance from the moment he first met her. He would taste the pastries she had promised to make for him and watch her while he drank with her father and brothers, knowing that there could be no distance between them as there once was. She belonged to him now. No more working those many years to finally have her to himself, though the truth was he still had two years left to work to complete his contract with Laban. But then he would be free to return to his homeland. Though he would have little to show for it aside from his wives and children. All the wealth he had now still belonged to Laban.

He glanced about, glad for the solitude and the fact that no one else was privy to his thoughts. The sun dipped at an angle that made him squint to see without shading his eyes. A hawk squawked and soared in the sky overhead, circling, at last diving to a field where some unfortunate prey would soon wish it had been more observant.

He pondered the irony of that thought, reminded of his own lack of observation. Had he been more aware of the schemes of men, his own included, he might be in a far different place today. Would he have stayed in his father's camp? Would he have found a different woman to share his life? But he couldn't imagine life without Rachel, no matter how difficult their circumstances.

The path took a turn as he neared the edge of the wheat fields, and he spotted a woman hurrying toward him, half walking, half running. Rachel? He shielded his eyes, his heart skipping a beat. Leah. She rarely came to him in the fields. What could she want? A moment of swift blinding fear for Rachel made his heart kick over again, but as he drew closer, he shoved the fear aside. "Is something wrong, Leah?"

She stopped, out of breath, placing a hand over her heart. "You must sleep with me," she said, her gaze bold. "I have hired you with my son's mandrakes."

He stared at her. "Perhaps you should explain yourself."

"My son found mandrakes in the field. He said he told you."

Jacob nodded, remembering. "They were growing wild in the field." He had wondered at the time how a five-year-old could recognize the leaves and fruit among the other plants of the field. "He asked if he could bring them to you." He rubbed a hand along his jaw. "I see he did."

"Yes, and Rachel bought them from me for the price of a night with you." She glanced beyond him, and her face flushed beneath her headscarf.

"Why would she do that?" He searched his mind for the uses of the fruit but could pull nothing from his memory.

"Mandrakes are said to remove barrenness."

He glanced away from her pointed look, suddenly uncomfortable. "If that is true, then it is Rachel I should be with tonight." He would like nothing better and wanted nothing more. But he knew that only God had the ability to give children.

"She offered you in exchange for them." She suddenly looked up, her boldness turning to a beseeching look. "Please do not deny me." She glanced away and clasped her hands in front of her, looking as if she wanted to say more but didn't.

A sigh escaped him, and one look at her told him she had noticed. But he could not help the weariness he felt at the struggles of his household. He looked at her hopeful face, the familiar guilt filling him. It was only one night. Surely he could put aside his own desires and give her that. He owed her more, just for the fact that she had given him so many sons.

He placed a hand at the small of her back and turned her toward home, falling into step beside her. "All right," he said, his pace slower than it had been when he thought Rachel was the one who would be awaiting him. "Let's go home."

❀✦❀

Rachel knelt in front of the tent and rocked the heavy goatskin back and forth, waiting for the milk to curdle. The skin was half as large as she was and suspended from wooden poles stuck in the ground, its feet and neck tied with palm fibers. She'd been at the task since Jacob left for the fields with the sheep just after dawn, grateful for work that could be done alone. She needed the distance from Leah and her children and the maids and their children. Always the children. And now Leah's belly swelled with yet another, a child conceived on the one night Rachel had bartered for the mandrakes, whose fruit had been worthless on her behalf.

She closed her eyes, her body rocking with the rhythm of the churning, silently keening for her own dead womb. Her chest ached with unshed tears. She was weary to death of weeping and weary of pretending all was well in Jacob's company. If she complained to him too often, he might grow tired of her and seek another, and she could not bear such a thing.

But how could God bless Leah again—and after only one night? It was completely unfair! What had she done to deserve this slight? Was this her reward for capturing Jacob's love? *Why, Adonai? Why do You not remember me too?*

A sob rose to choke her, and she blinked hard against the threat of more tears. The whole thing made no sense, and despite the many herbs and remedies she'd tried, the many prayers and even the sacrifices Jacob had offered—this goatskin a reminder of one of the more recent ones—still her womb remained closed.

The sound of the milk's sloshing changed, and she listened closely now for the sloshing to decrease and the feel of the skin to show the curds of milk within. A few moments later, she stopped the rocking and untied the neck. Hefting the heavy skin in both hands, she poured the creamy liquid into an urn, a treat she would save for Jacob, Bilhah's children, and, if there was enough, Jacob's other children as well. Everyone loved *qom*, the tasty water left from the cheese. Perhaps she would have a drink herself, if she could get past the queasy feeling and lack of appetite brought on by her grief.

When the last of the *qom* drained off, she carried the skin to the waiting clay pans spread out in front of her tent in the full heat of the sun and pressed the curds from the skin into the pans. Footsteps caused her to glance up, and she was briefly annoyed with the intrusion but grateful that it was Bilhah and not Leah.

"Can I help?" Bilhah shifted Naphtali to her other hip and placed a restraining hand on Dan, whose eager, curious fingers wanted to explore the white curds.

Rachel shook her head. "You have your hands full. I can manage." She smiled, though it was forced. She looked away, squeezed the rest of the curds into the last pan, and set the goatskin aside. A covered jar of salt sat nearby, and she took a handful and mixed it with a sprinkling of dill in one pan and parsley in the other. The third pan she left simply salted, the original *afiq*, which seemed more pleasing to the children.

When Bilhah did not move immediately away, she glanced up again. "Did you need something?"

Bilhah shook her head, but her look grew thoughtful. Naphtali squirmed in her arms, and Dan toddled off toward her tent. She gave Rachel a sheepish look. "I'm sorry. He won't sit still today, and Naphtali seems to think he must see everything Dan sees and go everywhere Dan goes."

Rachel rested a motherly gaze on Naphtali and smiled. "He has grown so quickly."

"Yes," Bilhah agreed. "And he is always hungry." She took a step back, and Rachel gave a slight nod, granting her leave. "I'm sorry about Leah," Bilhah said, pausing midstep, looking uncertain. "If I could bear more sons for you . . ." Her voice trailed off.

"No, no. Do not fret over this. It is too soon for you to bear another." Though in truth, Leah's first four children had been conceived and born only a year apart. Naphtali's birth had been too hard on Bilhah, and despite her longing for more, Rachel had no desire to use her maid in that way again. She brushed a strand of hair from her mouth and pressed the cheese with the palm of her hand into the pan. "There is nothing to be done about Leah." She looked at Bilhah, then returned to her task, pouring the last of the *qom* from the pressed curds into the urn.

Bilhah walked away, and Rachel blew out an unsteady breath. The only thing to be done about Leah was what she had already done for two years. And one night of weakness to seek answers for her own needs had brought about this child. She could not continue to deny her sister. If Leah would bear Jacob a child every time he came to her bed, then truly God must be in the giving. Perhaps she'd been wrong to deny her sister Jacob's company so long. The thought left her heart sore, vulnerable.

Would You ask me to give him up to her? He is the only thing I have left! Her prayer, wrought in anger and hurt through pain she could not escape, surged from a place deep within her, leaving her spent, weak. She pressed her palms to the last of the curds, her arms shaking with her weight. She could not give Jacob freedom to visit whichever wife he liked.

She needed him.

If she let him go so freely, Leah would surely win, and Rachel would be left with nothing.

Leah knelt beside her month-old son and tickled his belly, laughing at the coos and giggles she elicited from him. The sides of the tent were rolled up to let in the late afternoon breeze, bringing with it a welcome cool after the hot summer sun had made her eyes heavy with sleep. She had awakened with Issachar's soft whimpers to change him and delighted in the joy this new child had brought her.

"God has rewarded me for giving my maidservant to my husband," she'd told her mother and the women who had attended his birth. If not for Bilhah, Leah could be counted as single-handedly giving Jacob seven sons, building a tribe of princes for him. She bent to kiss the baby's belly and blew bubbles against his skin, laughing with him.

"How blessed we are, little one." She glanced up as she spoke, catching sight of Rachel hurrying past her tent with Bilhah, Naphtali in her arms. Had she heard? She had not spoken softly, and sound carried well with the tent sides open.

Guilt filled her as she picked Issachar up and nestled him against her shoulder. She leaned into the cushions, positioning him to nurse, her gaze shifting of its own accord to her sister. How hard it must be for her to watch every one of Jacob's wives giving birth and still, after six years, be denied.

The familiar bitterness she always felt when she tried to justify her blessings against Rachel's hold on Jacob's time and his heart soured her stomach. Even the tug of the babe against her breast did not fill her with the delight it normally did. She looked down at the boy, brushed the soft, straight dark hair from his forehead, and caught a glimpse of her own heart. She had not been kind in her thoughts to Rachel. She had endured and continued to promote the bitter struggle between them for love of Jacob.

But at what cost?

The ugliness of her heart made her squirm. Issachar seemed to notice and grew impatient with the flow of her milk. She tried to relax, but the burden of her heart would not ease.

Adonai, forgive me. Could You not look with favor on Rachel and give her a son?

The prayer surprised her, but even more the peace that followed the request. Had God heard? Should she speak to Jacob or to Rachel of her prayer? She pondered the request a moment, testing the peace, silently confessing the hurt and anger and betrayal she had fostered and felt all these years. Someone needed to bridge the gap between them, to make peace for Jacob's house. If she would not do so, Rachel never would.

The thought came with another wedge of guilt. It was unfair

to think such a thing. She could not know Rachel's motives or her heart. And Leah wielded the power of her many sons, who would care for her when she was old and Jacob rested with his fathers. Rachel had only the sons of her handmaid, who were not nearly as likely to care for Rachel as they would for their own mother. Surely it was time to hold forth an olive branch of peace to her only sister.

She drew in a breath, turning the idea over in her mind, feeling suddenly vulnerable and weak. Could she give up the right she should have to Jacob's time and attention? Could she go to her sister and pray for her, truly seeking her good?

She glanced at her son, at last contentedly nursing, then again spared a look toward Rachel's tent. God help her. She would do the right thing. For Jacob's sake.

And her sister's.

❊ 21 ❊

Jacob's knife slit the throat of a year-old male goat, prime among Laban's flock. The loss would come out of the pay counted toward the debt he owed the man, but it was a loss he must bear. If only God would hear and answer!

He searched his heart for words that could express his longing, Rachel's longing, but found none. The goat's body grew slick in his hands as blood spilled onto the stones of the altar he had painstakingly built. Fire burned in a torch held tight in the ground, waiting to consume the sacrifice. Laban appeased all gods on various occasions, but this was not a sacrifice he would think necessary. What did it matter if Rachel bore a son? Jacob already had nine sons, and Leah was carrying another, if her hints were true. And still Rachel waited.

How long, Adonai?

He had offered bulls and goats a few times in the recent past, but never with such a heavy burden upon his heart. Never with such a longing to see God answer his prayers. Could Adonai see the suffering of his beloved and feel the pain of his heart? Were his own sins the cause? To think so seemed far-fetched. God had blessed him with sons through three other women. To be denied a son with the woman he loved—would not the burden be hers alone to bear?

His great love for her told him otherwise. And as he cut up the goat and placed it on the altar, he felt the weight of his sins resting heavily on his shoulders. Surely he was sinful at birth! *One who grasps the heel*. A deceiver. Was he paying the price for such practices?

The rustling of grasses near the altar made him turn, his heart yearning at the sight of her, his beloved. How small she looked, head bent and draped in a white head covering. No jewels adorned her neck or ears, and her feet were bare. Her robe was simple, unassuming, and her hands were clasped in front of her. She stepped closer, and he longed to go to her, but she knelt in the grasses, head bent to the earth.

He stared, his heart constricting at her humility and the pain he had glimpsed in her large, luminous eyes. He reached for the torch, turned back to the altar, and lit the pieces of flesh until they caught fire. Smoke lapped the blood and animal flesh and rose to the heavens. Jacob set the torch back in its spot and came to kneel at Rachel's side.

Tears filled his throat, not from the smoke as much as from the sobs and soft prayers coming from his beloved's lips. He faced forward as well, palms splayed before him, his own prayers offered heavenward.

Forgive us, Adonai Elohim. Please, remember Your maidservant, my beloved, and grant her heart's desire. You have blessed me with many sons, but of this woman You have not given any. Look with favor on us, Your undeserving servants, and give us a son, as You did for my father and my grandfather before me. Remove the sting of her barrenness, I pray. He swallowed the unshed tears.

Please, hear my prayer.

He waited, searching his heart for any last words that he might utter to convince the Almighty to act on Rachel's behalf. As the last of the smoke died away and the sacrifice turned to ash on the scorched stones, Rachel rose slowly to her knees, and

Jacob took her in his arms. She rested her head on his chest, and he stroked her back, his silent tears falling softly now with her own, and he sensed that she still prayed, seeking God's face.

The sun dipped to blazing pinks and oranges by the time they stood apart. Jacob grabbed the torch and wrapped an arm around her shoulders, retrieved his own sandals from the edge of the clearing, and led her to the path home, feeling as he did the night he had met the Holy One at Bethel on the way to Laban's house. Truly God did not dwell only in Canaan's lands. His reach was long, and He could see them even here.

Surely He had heard their prayers.

Rachel awoke with a start, a queasy feeling in her middle. She rose quickly from her pallet and hurried to the clay pot, heaved over it, and lost the remnants of last evening's meal. She leaned back on shaking limbs and wiped her mouth with a linen cloth. Was she ill? She glanced at her sleeping mat, where Jacob had risen on one elbow, looking at her.

"Shall I send for your maid?" Concern etched his brow as he pushed to his feet and came to stand over her. "What can I do for you, beloved?" He placed both hands on her shoulders, and she leaned into his strength.

"I am all right now." She turned. "Help me up." He grasped her hand and tugged, holding her close.

"You are not ill?"

She shook her head. A sudden ravenous hunger came over her. "I am hungry enough to eat three loaves of bread and cheese and dates and—"

He placed a finger to her lips and laughed. "This is some strange illness you bear to be sick one moment and ravenous the next."

She gave him a sheepish look, then pushed from his embrace to change out of her night tunic and quickly dress. The scent of baking bread stayed her worry that she would have to wait until the flour was ground. She glanced up, catching his amused glance.

"What?"

"You are more beautiful than I ever thought possible."

She blushed at the compliment, her senses heightened with overwhelming love for him. Walking toward him, she offered him a bright smile. "And you, my love, are too kind." Her stomach growled loud enough for him to hear, and she placed a hand on her middle. "But you will have to excuse me. I must eat." She turned toward the tent opening, but he caught her hand.

She looked back at him, lifting a brow.

"How long has it been since your time?" He studied her, his gaze intense.

Heat rose again to her cheeks. She thought back, assessing, eyes growing wide with the knowledge he seemed to already possess. How could a man know such a thing? It was the woman's place to tell him.

She shook her head. "It isn't possible." Though on the second time through counting the days, she realized that well over a month had passed with no sign of her flow.

"Why not?" His smile warmed her from head to toe. He stepped forward and took both her hands in his. "Did we not pray? And have I not spent every night in your tent since that prayer?"

It was true. She felt suddenly weak with the realization. Another month would need to pass to confirm her suspicions, but her body already showed some of the signs—things Bilhah had told her to look for that she had also experienced. Leah had spared her the details, though her mother had given her some insight as well. She knew what to expect. And the gnawing hunger in her belly was only one of them.

"Oh, Jacob!" She was crying now, and his arms came around her in a gentle embrace. "I dare not believe it."

He patted her back, then rubbed circles along it. She glanced up, seeing the glint of tears in his eyes as well. He kissed her softly and looked lovingly down at her. "There is no reason to doubt, beloved. Adonai has heard, and He has answered."

Awe filled her at the thought, but in the next breath, she gripped his arms, fighting sudden fear. "We must not speak of it yet, Jacob," she said, her voice low. "Wait until I can confirm it with my mother, in another month or so. If we are wrong . . ."

"We are not wrong." His confidence boosted hers. "But we will wait, as you wish." He pulled her close again. "Adonai has heard, Rachel. You will bear me a son."

She sighed against him, her fears melting away with his words. Still, a sense of caution filled her. "I just want to be sure."

"Then it will be our secret." He released her then, and as her stomach growled again, he pointed toward the door. "Go!" He laughed. "Feed yourself . . . and the babe," he added softly.

She smiled, joy filling her, knowing in the deep places in her heart that it was true. She left the tent, listening to Jacob's joyful whistling behind her.

Months passed, and Rachel confirmed what Jacob had suspected. Joy became a constant spring within her every time she caught Jacob looking at her with awe, a secretive smile ghosting his lips. His attention to her heightened, and she basked in it. But at the same time, she found herself more aware of Leah and their maids. She had spoken privately to Jacob of her thoughts several nights before, and now as she sat with Leah spinning newly shorn wool into yarn, the words came back to her.

"I appreciate your nearness, Jacob." She'd grasped his hands and leaned forward, kissing him soundly. "But I don't want you to neglect the others on my account." The words had surprised them both, but she did not retract them. She had seen Leah's longing looks and felt a sense of gratitude that Adonai had been so gracious to her at last. She dare not risk His disfavor by her selfishness. No. Whether she liked it or not, God had given Jacob four wives. She could not keep him only to herself.

"I would have only you. You know that." He nuzzled her ear, and she sighed. He was not making this easy!

"I know," she said, wrapping both arms around his neck. Such love she felt for him! "But Leah carries your child as well, and it would do well for your household if you spent a night with her now and then. Your children need to know you care for their mothers." To say so reinforced her resolve.

"Your son shall be prince among his brothers," he said, and his look held more conviction than it had the last time he had suggested such a thing.

"Though he will be the last among them and the youngest?"

"He will be *your* first; therefore, he is my firstborn."

"Suppose it is a girl." Would God do such a thing after she had waited so long?

"It is a boy." His eyes blazed with fierce light, and she did not question him again.

Now as she sat with Leah, whose swollen belly indicated her time was near, she wondered how Leah's children would accept her son, especially if Jacob favored him above all of his brothers. They would hate him! As she sensed at times they hated her. She must not let such a thing come to pass. She must mend the rift with her sister as best she could.

Rachel paused in her spinning to place a hand on her middle. "His kick is strong." She smiled at Leah. "Your time draws near, my sister."

Leah wiped sweat from her brow and blew out a breath. "Actually, the pains are in my back this time. I fear the birth will be as difficult as it was with Judah." A wary look crossed her face, and the hint of fear filled her eyes. With Judah's birth, Leah had taken many months to heal, far longer than she normally did.

"I will pray that it goes well with you." Rachel's own fear

rose at the thought. Would her time be difficult? "I must admit, I envy how easily you have given birth in the past. I shouldn't worry . . ." Her voice trailed off, and she looked into the distance. Some women died in childbirth. Would God bring her this far to take her life? Would Jacob forfeit his love for her and be left with only her son? Or what if she carried the babe until the end and he died during the birth? She rubbed her middle, suddenly anxious to feel him move again.

"You must not fear," Leah said, bringing her thoughts up short. She met her sister's gaze. "Fear makes the pain worse. You must trust that Adonai will see you through it." She picked up her distaff and attached another bundle of wool to it. "He would not go so far as to answer your prayers only to take your life." Her gaze was fierce, protective even. "Or the babe's." She looked away as though suddenly embarrassed by her outburst. "I will pray for you as well."

"Thank you." Rachel found she meant every word. But a new thought struck her. "If something should happen to me . . ." She spoke haltingly, not wanting to speak but knowing she must.

"Nothing is going to happen to you. Don't say such a thing!"

Rachel held up a hand. "Please, I must."

Leah stared at her.

"I want you to raise him. If I should not make it." A sob rose up, but she forced it down. Nothing would happen. Adonai would protect her, as Jacob had said many times in the past few months. But just in case . . . "Promise me."

"You don't want Bilhah? She is your maid. I am your usurper, Rachel. You have hated me for years." Leah's look told her that the feeling had been mutual.

"You are my sister. I want you." Rachel's throat grew thick again, and she looked away. "Of course, I am hoping it is I who am allowed to raise the child." She laughed, the sound shaky to her ears.

Silence fell like a pall between them until Rachel picked up her distaff again, assuming the conversation was at an end. But many moments later, Leah cleared her throat, causing Rachel to look up again.

"I will do as you ask," Leah said, her voice tight. "And if God should see fit to leave you and take me, I would ask the same of you."

Leah's sons would not want her. But she did not voice the thought. The babe Leah carried and her youngest sons would not know the difference.

Rachel looked at her sister and nodded. "May Adonai give us strength to try Jacob's patience another day and through many children to come."

Leah laughed at the comment, and the air between them changed, sweeter than it had been in as long as Rachel could remember. She smiled at her sister, then lifted her gaze heavenward, praying her last words would be true.

Leah knelt at Rachel's side a few months later, working the pain from her back. "Breathe, sister. It does no good to hold on to it too long." How well she remembered Rachel doing the same for her a few months before.

Leah had not expected the pains to come on her so soon but was grateful the travail had not lasted as long as she had feared. A sixth son had been born nearly before her mother arrived, and she had held him close, proclaiming, "God has presented me with a precious gift. This time my husband will treat me with honor, because I have borne him six sons." Though with Rachel pregnant at the same time, Jacob's response to Leah held little difference until Rachel prompted him to stay near and hold the child. While Leah watched, Rachel had even taught him how to wrap the boy's bands as practice for her son when he was born, though Jacob had never tended even one of his children to that point. But he had complied with

Rachel's prompting, and Leah and Rachel had both laughed at his clumsiness.

And now Leah's son Zebulun lay sleeping in a basket in a corner of the tent, watched over by one of the young serving maids, while Rachel struggled in her own travail.

"I see his head," Rachel's mother said, her smile warm and more wrinkled than it had been when Leah had birthed her firstborn. Yet Suri remained a faithful midwife no matter which wife of Jacob bore down on the birthing stool. "A few more pushes, my daughter."

Rachel groaned and gave a loud cry as the babe finally slipped into Suri's waiting hands.

"A boy!" Suri's jubilant voice matched the boy's strident cries. Rachel laughed and wept as Leah helped settle her onto clean sheets plumped with cassia-scented cushions.

"I have a son." Her voice held such awe that even the twinge of jealousy Leah had felt at the moment of his birth vanished.

"Yes, sister. A fine boy." Leah stepped back as Suri handed the boy, now washed and swaddled, into Rachel's arms.

"I have a son?" The male voice was low, unmistakably Jacob's.

Leah stepped away from Rachel's side to allow Jacob a better view, unable to deny a soft nudge of jealousy.

Rachel looked up at Jacob's approach, her smile radiant. Jacob knelt at her side and touched his son's cheek and laughed at the way the boy stretched, tilting his head and emitting a contented sigh.

"What will you name him?" Jacob's gaze held such love for her sister it made Leah's heart twist with longing.

"Joseph." Rachel looked down at her son and touched the wisps of dark hair. "God has taken away my disgrace." She lifted her gaze to Jacob, her smile soft, her dark eyes not quite content. "May Adonai add to me another son."

Jacob twirled a strand of Rachel's hair between his fingers, and Leah felt like an intruder on something precious. She backed slowly away but did not miss the look that passed between them.

"May Adonai grant your wish, beloved. Let me bless him in the presence of the men waiting," he said when Rachel's fingers could not quite release him. Jacob took the child from her and shifted him with practiced ease onto his shoulder.

She let her arms fall to her sides. "Very well."

Jacob moved past Leah, carrying Joseph to the tent's opening. Leah followed to watch and listen. She was surprised to see that her father and many of her brothers and half brothers had gathered for the occasion that was not even the boy's circumcision. Jacob's older sons—Reuben, six, and Simeon, five—stood tall like little men when Jacob drew near.

"My son, Joseph," he said, holding the boy up for the men to see. "My firstborn . . . of Rachel." That he clarified his meaning made little difference. Leah knew with a certainty that Joseph was held before them as Jacob's firstborn rightful heir.

The emotion she had felt earlier in the tent swelled within her now, and she wanted desperately to go inside, to retrieve Zebulun from his slumber and hold him close, to gather her children around her and seclude herself away from them all. But Jacob's next words brought her thoughts to an abrupt halt.

"My father, send me on my way so I can go back to my own homeland. Give me my wives and children, for whom I have served you, and I will be on my way. You know how much work I've done for you." He pulled Joseph close against his shoulder and patted his back in gentle strokes. When had he become so good with small babes? But of course, Bilhah's sons would have received attention from him when they were in Rachel's care.

Her father stood and clapped a hand to Jacob's free shoulder. "If I have found favor in your eyes, please stay. I have learned by divination that Adonai has blessed me because of you."

Did her father actually think that Jacob would be swayed by such a claim? Leah stepped closer to the awning's edge to better glimpse her father's expression.

"Name your wages, and I will pay them." Laban's face was

open, earnest, and Leah searched his eyes for any hint of duplicity, unable from the distance between them to tell.

Joseph began to whimper in Jacob's arms, and he turned, glancing toward the tent. His gaze found Leah's, and she hurried forward to take the babe. "Thank you," he said.

She hurried to the shade of the awning, then stepped to the threshold and summoned Rachel's mother. "Take him to Rachel," she whispered. Suri's response was drowned out by Jacob's strong voice.

"You know how I have worked for you and how your livestock has fared under my care," he said.

Leah moved back to her place just below the awning, noting that Laban had stepped back a pace. The two men seemed to have squared off in challenge.

"The little you had before I came has increased greatly, and Adonai has blessed you wherever I have been. But now, when may I do something for my own household?"

It was a reasonable request. If they left now, they would have little more than the clothes on their backs. Still, Leah's heart hammered with the possibility, and she could not deny a rebellious longing to leave her father's household and set off to wherever Jacob led. But they could not leave so soon with Joseph a wee babe.

"What shall I give you?" Her father crossed his arms, and the glint in his eyes told her that he too had realized that Jacob could not immediately leave.

Jacob reached for his staff that leaned against a tent post and tapped it against the ground. "Don't give me anything," he said. "But if you will do this one thing for me, I will go on tending your flocks and watching over them." He had her father's full attention now and took a step back, his arm pointing toward the fields where the sheep still grazed. "Let me go through all your flocks today and remove from them every speckled or spotted sheep, every dark-colored lamb, and every spotted or speckled goat. They will be my wages. And my honesty will testify for me in the future, whenever you check on the wages you have paid me. Any goat in my possession that is not speckled or spotted, or any lamb that is not dark-colored, will be considered stolen."

"Agreed." Laban stepped closer and kissed each of Jacob's cheeks, Jacob doing the same in return. "Let it be as you have said."

Leah stood a moment longer and watched her father turn, motion to her brothers, and head back toward his house. She followed at a distance and saw the men circle back and head to the fields. Straight to the flocks. Before Jacob could claim his wages.

A sinking feeling settled in her middle. Her father did not intend good toward Jacob. He would rob her husband of his pay before he could act, while Jacob watched over his favorite wife and son.

She walked toward the tents, debating what to do. In the end, her love and loyalty to Jacob won out. She must warn him. Before it was too late.

Part

3

Jacob heard that Laban's sons were saying, "Jacob has taken everything our father owned and has gained all this wealth from what
belonged to our father." And Jacob noticed that Laban's attitude
toward him was not what it had been.

Then the LORD said to Jacob, "Go back to the land of your
fathers and to your relatives, and I will be with you."

Genesis 31:1–3

22

Jacob dug his staff into the ground and looked out over the flock the following morning, unable to shake the sense of complete betrayal and loss. Leah's warning rang loud in his ears. *My father plans ill against you, Jacob. I could see it in his eyes.* He should have listened to her. But he had been too taken with the joy of Joseph's birth to pay her heed or to care that her father and brothers had gone from his tents to the fields. Any number of reasons could have been the cause.

This he did not expect.

He faced the wind, glad for the force that drove against him, that battled the anger within. Better to face the unseen elements than to war against Laban's greed. Hadn't he battled the man for the privilege of wedding his daughters? And now it appeared they would pit their wits against each other yet again if Jacob was to earn even the wages that were due him.

Six years. He had agreed to six more years to work for Laban. He turned to gaze at the solid white flock. Not a streaked or spotted male goat, a speckled or spotted female goat or any with white on them, or a single dark-colored lamb remained of the sheep and goats Laban had left in his care. Laban had gone that very night of Joseph's birth and separated them all, given Jacob's wages into the care of his sons. Had even Rachel's brothers been party to this deceit? But of course they would have been. Bahaar, as friendly as he might be, was no match for his father. None went against Laban the patriarch.

He glanced heavenward. Deep, billowy clouds stood like strong towers overhead, briefly blocking the sun. What was he to do?

The thought sank like a heavy millstone to his middle. He walked slowly, lifted the staff with clenched fist, and tapped too hard on the earth, needing the action to keep him steady. If he did not fight against this, he would be as a drunken man, unable to stand upright.

He walked among the flock, noting those that were weak and those that were strong. A female lamb could breed every eight months, and if he were fortunate, they might carry two or even three young at each birth. If God was truly with him, there would be time in six years to produce at least a few spotted, striped, and speckled young. Was there a way to coax such a thing?

He pondered the thought as he led the sheep to the well and greeted his fellow shepherds, sons of Laban's neighbors, wondering what they were saying about him behind their hands, or at night when they gathered around the campfire and Jacob returned to his wives. Probably thought him the fool for engaging a man like Laban.

But Laban was not the only man who knew how to win at such games. Jacob's conscience pricked at the memories of his past and the prayers he had prayed to turn away from them.

"How am I supposed to find justice and gain my earnings otherwise?" He spoke to a male goat near him, which lifted its head as if to ask what it possibly could say to that. "What? Not even a sound from you?" The goat opened its mouth and bleated, then came and nuzzled Jacob's hand. "All right. I'm coming." He drew the stone from the well's mouth and filled the troughs, watching, thoughtful, as the animals came close and drank.

There had to be a reason some lambs were born white and

others were not. The normal thought would have been to mate black with white to produce speckled or striped. But his flock all looked the same, as white as the clouds above. He could ask a friendly neighbor to mate his black sheep with Jacob's, but he risked a dispute to ownership. No. If he would have his wages, he must find a way to coax the sheep to think spotted and speckled thoughts.

Did sheep think? He scratched the back of his neck, fully doubting he had any sense left in his own wayward thoughts.

He pondered and prayed for a coherent idea—or, at the very least, one that made sense to him—to do what would be impossible on its own.

And would not take far longer than six years.

Rachel draped a light shawl over six-week-old Joseph and walked with him to meet Jacob as he was returning to the sheep pens. The early evening breeze was gentle and warm, a respite from the earlier heat of the day. She had healed well since the birth and felt her spirit strengthened with each step toward the pens. It had been too long since Jacob had lain beside her at night, talking of his concerns for the future. Due to her uncleanness after the birth, he had stayed away from her tent except to stop in to glimpse Joseph before retiring to his own. She had been so exhausted and caught up with Joseph's care that she had barely noticed. But this morning she had realized how much she missed him.

She must remedy that now, must show him that she still cared to hear his concerns, the ones he didn't voice when they all joined under the shade of his tent for the evening meal, when the children were underfoot and the clamor kept them from discussing anything of importance.

Joseph stretched slightly in her arms beneath the soft fold of cloth covering him. She stopped, adjusting the scarf so he could see, then lifted him to her shoulder. What wonders did a babe notice in so small a body? Surely he was too young to understand anything beyond colors or light and dark. Then again, he did recognize her face, and he already knew his father's voice.

She kicked up dust as she followed the tree line to the pens just over the rise. Jacob's form came into view as she continued at a slow pace to the stone sheep enclosure.

"Rachel." Jacob called to her and hurried his step, his smile welcoming. "And who have you brought to see me?" His voice rose slightly in pitch, as it always did when he spoke to a lamb about to give birth or to his children when they were babes.

Rachel laughed and turned Joseph to face him. "Your son, of course." She could not help the pride that accompanied the words, and she smiled as Jacob bent to kiss first his son, then her.

"You have pleased me well." He cupped her shoulder and gave it a gentle squeeze. "Come, help me divide the sheep and goats."

She followed him to the gate where he inspected each lamb and each goat, then led them to separate partitioned areas for the night. "Is Bahaar coming to watch them?"

Jacob shook his head. "One of the hired servants will sleep at the gate."

This was not unusual, but never as good as when the flocks were watched by Jacob or one of her brothers. "What if there is trouble?"

"The boy will come to get me." He rubbed a hand over his jaw. "I could stay. But I need the respite of my own mat this night."

She looked at him more closely. "Have you not slept well?" She would not know, as he had spent his nights of late alone, choosing to be apart even from his other wives.

He patted the head of one lamb, sifting through the soft wool, then bent to remove several brambles from its head and body. "Where did you find yourself today, little one, that you are so covered in barbs?" He glanced up at her. "I have had little rest from the worry of how to provide for my family."

Her stomach did an uncomfortable flip at his words. She stepped closer, patting Joseph's back. "Is it so bad then? My father left you with nothing?"

Jacob continued to sift the lamb's wool for possible thorns and barbs, nodding as he worked. "He left me only the white ones."

Her breath caught. Shepherds knew that to produce white offspring, one only needed to mate male and female white sheep. The chance of them producing black or discolored young was rare. "It could take years to produce a flock to call your own." They needed the goats for milk for the children, and the sheep offered their wool to clothe their large household. But of course he knew this. She clamped her mouth against saying more.

"Longer than the six years I bargained for." Jacob tensed, a muscle twitching along his left brow. He looked at her. "I had a dream."

She tilted her head and gave him a curious look. "A dream?"

He finished with the lamb and stood, ran a hand over his beard. "I think God gave me a way to coax the sheep to bear spotted and speckled young." He looked at her, and she saw uncertainty in his eyes.

"Tell me your dream." She shifted Joseph, praying he would not fuss, and glanced at the last of the goats as they trotted into the pen to settle among the soft hay the servant had spread out that morning.

He patted the bottom of the last sheep as it passed his inspection, then moved to the gate and glanced toward the servants' tents, where their growing household of maidservants and menservants camped near their own. She followed his gaze. No sign of the servant boy yet.

He faced her then. "He will come."

"Yes. You are early." She smiled into his eyes. "Tell me your dream."

He met her gaze, then looked beyond her, weighing his thoughts. "You will think it foolish."

"Nothing you can say to me will make me feel that way." She shifted Joseph again. Jacob caught the movement and extended his hands. She placed Joseph in his strong arms.

"In my dream, I took poplar, almond, and plane trees and peeled white stripes on them and placed them in the water troughs during the mating season when the sheep and goats came to drink. The sheep mated before the rods and produced spotted, striped, and speckled young." He looked at her, searching her gaze as if looking for confirmation or skepticism.

She held his gaze, hoping he could see approval in her eyes. "I have never heard such a thing done before, but that doesn't mean it won't help." She touched his forearm and drew closer, smelling the soft baby scent of Joseph mingled with the more masculine scents of field and sheep and sweat from Jacob. "Surely if God gave you the dream, then He means for you to do what the dream suggests." She wondered at the doubt lingering in her own heart at the idea.

"Did God give me this dream?" His doubt mirrored hers. "Or am I just a desperate man in need of something who imagined the first ridiculous thing I could find?"

"Your thoughts are not ridiculous." She would not have him thinking this way. "You don't know whether this will work until you try it. Perhaps God is giving you a way to outwit my father." She glanced over her shoulder toward her father's house, then toward Jacob's tents. The servant boy came toward them at a slow jog.

Jacob handed Joseph back to her. "Perhaps you are right. It cannot hurt to try. And whittling rods will keep me from going mad trying to figure out something better." He laughed at that and she joined him. "Better to not worry over something I cannot control, in any case."

She settled Joseph on her shoulder again. The servant boy approached out of breath.

"I am sorry to be late, master." The boy was older than

Reuben by only a handful of years, but he had proven fairly responsible in the previous months.

"It is no matter. I am early." Jacob smiled at the boy, gave him a few instructions, and patted his shoulder, then placed a hand at the small of Rachel's back and walked her toward their tents.

"Surely God will watch over us, Jacob," Rachel said when they were out of the boy's hearing. "He gave us Joseph. Surely He can be trusted to give you flocks as well."

He nodded but said nothing for several moments. "We have no choice but to trust Him this time, beloved." He touched the top of Joseph's head. "We can no more create speckled sheep than you could conceive this child." He stopped, facing her. "But you did. God heard you and answered. So I will whittle the wood and see if the dream meant anything. If not, either way we will trust."

She nodded, wondering if indeed the whole idea was wise and of God or just the dreams of an overwrought husband with many mouths to feed and an entire household depending on him.

Lambing season came, and Jacob placed the rods of poplar, almond, and plane he had carved among the water troughs while the strongest of Laban's ewes were in heat. He had taken great care to choose two of the sturdiest rams to mate them, surprised and pleased to discover that every female that mated had conceived. He had fully expected to wait another cycle for some of those in heat to carry young, but Adonai, blessed be His name, had honored Jacob's silent pleas. Perhaps the dream had been a sign that He was indeed keeping His promises to bless Jacob and his household, as his father Isaac had once said.

Jacob leaned against his staff as he walked among the flock where they now grazed in the fields. Wistful longing filled him. He wanted to go home. To see his father and mother again, even Esau. Though the thought of his brother caused his stomach to tighten into a swift knot. Did his brother still hate him? If he returned, would he be in danger of his life?

He moved away from a patch of brambles and used the staff to guide a wayward young ewe back toward the flock, troubled by the memories he could never quite shake. He had done Esau wrong in stealing the birthright and blessing. But there was no undoing what was past. Still, he could not put Rachel and Joseph or his other wives and children in danger just because he wanted to see his mother and father again.

He glanced heavenward, squinting against the patches of sun streaming out from thick puffs of cloud cover, wishing his choices were easier.

Do You want me to return or to stay? The question borne of his heart yearned toward the Unknowable One, and he waited a moment, not surprised when there was no response.

He would wait to see if the lambs produced young that he could keep for himself and not the normal white lambs Laban would claim as his own. If God was merciful and truly blessing his efforts, the result would show him clearly.

In the meantime, he would send word to his father to see if it was safe to bring his family home.

23

Three-and-a-half-year-old Joseph took hold of Rachel's hand and skipped and kicked at stones along the path. Rachel laughed at his antics and finally released him to run on ahead once she spotted Jacob walking toward them looking dusty and hot, the sheep following behind him. They had reached more than the halfway point in Jacob's contract with Laban, and Jacob's wealth had increased faster than either of them could have imagined. The first season, the sheep had borne healthy, speckled young without a single miscarriage. Jacob's flock grew fifty-fold.

Her father had questioned each of her brothers and half brothers to be sure Jacob had not somehow snuck into the flocks by night and taken from what was his, but in the end he was forced to admit that the speckled lambs were Jacob's. The acceptance came with a price, however, as her father changed Jacob's wages to lambs with spots, not speckled or striped, making the likelihood of payment near impossible again.

But Rachel had laughed behind her veil at her father's flushed face when the lambs were born spotted and he had confronted Jacob that second time.

"What is this you have done to me? You have taken from my spotted lambs and switched them for the white ones." Laban's features were mottled in anger, and he stepped close to Jacob, staring him down. But Jacob stood his ground.

"I had no opportunity to do such a thing. Your sons keep your flocks several days' distance from mine. And my flocks are in the care of Reuben and Simeon, while I have kept yours apart. You accuse me falsely, my father." Jacob's tone had been conciliatory, and after a moment of silence, Laban finally looked away.

"I do not know if this is true. To test you, I have no choice but to change the terms of our agreement. This time only the striped shall be your wages. We will see if you speak truth. Even you cannot cause the animals a third time to produce as you wish." He crossed his arms, turned on his heel, and walked away without a backward glance.

Rachel sobered when she heard these new terms her father laid down, her fear rising. What if her father was right? The first time when the ewes produced all speckled lambs, Jacob's growing family had rejoiced. When Laban changed the wages to spotted, Jacob's wives had fretted over what they would do if the next lambing season fell in Laban's favor. Leah had tried to calm everyone and urged them to trust Adonai, but even Jacob worried, and at night when Rachel lay in his arms, she could feel his restlessness even in his sleep.

But a third switch? Could even Adonai perform such a feat? Spotted and speckled were more likely to produce white than striped lambs. Her laughter had turned to anger at her father.

Now Rachel drew closer and noted Jacob's knit brow even through his delight at seeing Joseph, and she knew the weight of her father's treachery weighed heavily on him. But she pushed the emotions and thoughts aside as she neared him, now holding a squirming Joseph.

"He wants to run. He is always busy, and I can barely keep up with him." She smiled and accepted Jacob's tired kiss on her cheek. "You look exhausted. Do you want me to take the sheep to the pens while you go bathe in the river? It would do you good."

Jacob took Joseph from Rachel's arms, tousled his thick dark hair, and laughed. "Is it my strength you wish to renew in the river or the smell of my sweat you wish to wash away?" He lowered Joseph to the ground, and each of them took one of the boy's hands as he skipped along between them.

"Both!" Rachel shared his laughter and listened as he told her about his day in the fields.

"I lost one of the ewes to a fox. I killed him with the sling, but not before he had torn the ewe apart."

Rachel shuddered. She had always hated the killing, but a shepherd had no choice when protecting her sheep. "How many losses does that make this year?" He kept track for his own sake but did not report the losses to her father. Why cause more dissension between them?

"In the past eight months, three have been captured by lions, two by foxes, and two by jackals."

"Up, Abba, up!" Joseph's childish voice drew their attention. Jacob glanced at her, and she smiled at the wink he gave her. "Up you say, my little man?"

"Up!" His insistence was more comical than defiant, and they both quickly obliged, lifting Joseph's arms together and letting him glide over the path. He squealed in delight.

They continued on, lifting and walking. "You will wear me out, my son," Jacob said as they neared the fork in the path that led to the river some distance away. He released Joseph's hand, but Rachel kept her hold. Jacob looked at her. "If you will take the sheep, I will go wash as you wish." His smile warmed her.

She wrinkled her nose, sending him a teasing look. "We will appreciate you not smelling quite like a goat, my lord."

He touched her head, his gesture affectionate. "I don't know why I bother, dear wife. I will just need another washing when the lambing takes place."

"Then you shall take another."

He laughed as they parted, and Rachel was glad for the

distraction of the sheep before returning to the tents to help finish the remains of the evening meal and nurse Joseph. She patted each pregnant lamb as it passed by her into the fold, praying the young would be striped this time, wondering if God even heard such selfish prayers.

For Jacob's sake, she added. If God intended to bless her husband, she would do well to remind Him that the prayers were meant for him.

❊✢❊

Leah sat in the shade of an oak tree, nursing her newest child. A girl, Dinah, now two years old, born two years after Joseph. She had hoped—oh, how she had hoped—that this seventh child would be a son, to give Jacob the tribal number of twelve. But perhaps Adonai intended to allow Rachel that privilege. Leah sighed and looked down on her daughter, so beautiful in one so young. She had her aunt's beauty, and Leah found the thought both pleasing and fretful. What fate awaited a comely child or a beautiful woman? Would she be barren as her aunt had been for so long?

But the thoughts were foolish to consider now with the babe not yet weaned. She stroked her daughter's dark hair, already to her shoulders, away from her cherub face. Dinah opened her eyes as though she knew Leah was watching and smiled, her gaze wide with childish secrets, then closed them again.

"I thought you would be in your tent." Leah startled at the sound of Rachel's voice.

"Sometimes the breeze is better in the tree's shade." She wiped sweat from her brow and positioned Dinah to the other side.

Rachel knelt near her and pulled a section of wool from a basket she carried and began to separate the strands. Joseph sank down beside her and found a stick to draw circles in the dirt. He glanced at Leah, pausing a moment. "Is she done yet?"

Leah smiled at her nephew. Though they were young, Joseph

and Dinah had taken to each other, with him entertaining her with stories as soon as he could string words together. Leah had marveled at his patience with his half sister, but since her own youngest sons, Issachar and Zebulun, had each other, she was grateful for her nephew's ability to distract Dinah.

"Almost." Leah patted Joseph's arm. "Go on with your pictures. What will you draw today?" The boy was a dreamer like his mother, either running and jumping, giving his mother's nerves a good shake, or sitting quietly as he was now and occupying himself.

"Oh, I dunno. Birds and trees and sheep." He lapsed into silence and set about to scribble in the dirt.

Rachel looked on him with pride, and Leah felt a little kick over her heart that Jacob took such delight in this son. But she allowed her own sense of pride when she watched Reuben, Simeon, Levi, and even seven-year-old Judah traipse after their father into the fields, already becoming fine shepherds themselves. Would Joseph grow up to tend sheep? She couldn't imagine him capable of killing a fox or lion or jackal when he grew flustered at the sight of one of his half brothers killing a scorpion. How could Jacob even consider this child as his heir? But one glance at her sister squelched her wayward, jealous thoughts.

"What is on your mind, sister? Or did you just long for my company?" Leah helped Dinah sit up and patted her back.

"I suppose I wanted your company." Rachel's smile made Leah silently repent of her jealousy of her sister's son. "And I needed someone to fret with about Jacob." She glanced beyond Leah a moment, then turned her attention to the wool in her hands.

"He does seem more tired and quiet than normal. Though you would know better than I how much he speaks."

Jacob lapsed more often into silence around the meals or conversed with his sons, teaching them things about shepherding, and rarely conversed with his wives, who stood nearby to serve. They often waited now to eat after Jacob and his sons were fed, and since Jacob spent his evenings in Rachel's tent, Leah was not often privy to his thoughts.

"He is terribly exhausted. Don't you see it upon his brow?" Rachel looked up, and Leah put Dinah on the grass near Joseph, then took some of the wool from Rachel to help her comb it.

"I see it some. I confess I am often distracted with the children." She would not admit that she had stopped looking to Jacob for companionship after Dinah's birth. She just didn't have it in her to keep hoping he would one day see her with greater favor.

Rachel sighed and tugged at a piece of tangled wool. "Well, he is working himself too hard trying to build the flock. He is training the boys, yes, but they are young. They cannot handle some of the greater tasks of trimming the sheep's hooves or lifting a lamb from a pit. They can barely handle the sling against those who come against the flock."

"Reuben and Simeon have learned quickly. Surely they are more help than you think. You weren't much older when Father sent you to the fields."

Rachel gave a conciliatory nod. "Yes, of course they are a wonderful help to him. But Father has made things so difficult. He has changed Jacob's wages six times in four years, and I have no doubt he will do it again in the two that Jacob has left to serve him. First it was speckled, then spotted, then striped. But no, that is not good enough to prove Adonai is blessing Jacob. Then it was speckled and spotted with only brown spots. Then it was striped but only black stripes. Father is impossible!"

Leah let the wool fall to her lap. "I did not realize."

"Jacob did not want to complain. But it is wearing on him. He hides his anger, but I know he is counting the days until we can leave this place." Rachel glanced at Joseph as though fearing the child would tell what he had heard. But he had wandered a short distance from them with Dinah, gesturing toward the treetops and talking, Dinah looking on with rapt attention.

"But what can we do?" Protectiveness toward Jacob and anger toward their father caused Leah's hands to clench into tight fists. She leaned forward. "I would love to see Father squirm as much as Jacob has done in the eighteen years he has been with us. I think Father delights in besting him."

Rachel nodded. "And Jacob is starting to sense a change in Father's attitude to him. Have you noticed? I think Bahaar still considers Jacob a friend, but he will not go against Father. What of your brothers? Do they resent our husband?"

Leah picked up the wool again and pondered the thought. Did they? She had paid little attention to them and rarely spoke at length with their wives. She was too busy with her own children to notice. "I do not know. Have you spoken to your mother? Perhaps she knows. I have had little time to speak to mine." She regretted the way that sounded the moment she said it. "That is, I haven't really been up to going to the house since Dinah's birth."

Her sister seemed not to notice the impression Leah gave that Rachel, who had only one child, would have more time to spend with her mother than Leah did with hers. Both mothers often saw the wives of their sons, who had rooms extended in their father's house, unlike Rachel and Leah, who lived in tents with Jacob on the farther reaches of Laban's property nearest the sheep pens.

"My mother has not been feeling well of late. When I am with her, we do not discuss anything that could upset her." Rachel ran the comb through another section of wool.

Leah looked at her, surprised at this news. "I had not heard this. How long has she been ill?" She saw the shadow pass in front of Rachel's luminous eyes.

"About a month. She has lost weight—she has no appetite. And she could not attend the last birthing of Tariq's daughter-in-law." She bit her lower lip and looked away. "I worry about her."

Leah leaned closer and touched Rachel's arm. "We must pray

Adonai's favor upon her." She couldn't imagine giving birth without Suri's help. She was the best midwife in all of Laban's household and had saved many a woman from undue pain and even death. "I must ask her to teach me her secrets," Leah said. "Perhaps I can help until she is well."

Rachel nodded and called Joseph to come. Leah glanced up to see the pair of children had wandered closer to the distant trees that led to the sheep pens. Joseph took Dinah's hand and quickly obeyed. Leah marveled at the child's lack of rebellion and couldn't help but feel the twinge of envy that Joseph had been given far more of Jacob's time than her sons ever had. Perhaps that was why his spirit was one that was quick to obey.

"I don't know what we can do to help Jacob," Rachel said once she was satisfied that Joseph was within a safe distance.

"We should do something to make Father think twice before changing his wages again. Something he would find painful." Leah lowered her voice, half amazed at her own rebellious thoughts. "That is, if there was such a thing."

"The only things he cares about are his pipe, his beer, and his gods."

"His gods most of all. He paid a hefty price for those images, and some are as old as Tariq. Ima said that Father bought them when Rebekah still lived here, long before Jacob or you and I were born." Leah tucked her combed wool into Rachel's basket, brushed the lint from her robes, and stood. "I can't see what we could possibly do to his gods that he wouldn't discover. Then our husband would have to pay for whatever damage we did, and it would take us even longer to leave this place." She called Dinah to her. "I must change her and start the grinding."

Rachel stood as well and took Joseph's hand as they headed back to their tents. "You are right, of course," she said in parting. "I just wanted you to know."

Leah's heart warmed as she held Rachel's concerned gaze. Perhaps they would be closer now. At the very least, she was glad she was the one Rachel had included. No one else loved Jacob like Leah did, and perhaps Rachel was finally coming to see that.

"Thank you for telling me."

Rachel nodded, then turned her attention to what Joseph was saying. Leah watched them but a moment, then hurried with Dinah to her tent, wondering what she could do to her father's gods to make him think twice about hurting Jacob.

24

Jacob sipped his barley beer, watching the crowds of men—workers and sons of Laban—enjoying the fruits of their labors after a successful sheep shearing. Laughter and the swell of voices drowned out the sounds of the fire crackling in the pits and in the tall sconces that cast long shadows on the walls.

Jacob moved along one of those walls of the courtyard now, catching patches of conversation as he headed to where Bahaar and Laban's other sons sat with full plates before the fire. He stopped at the sight of Rachel coming toward him from the cooking room with a large flask and held his cup out for her to refill it.

"Did you notice the difference in the sheep this year?" Jacob turned at the sound of Tariq's voice. "Jacob's sheep were heartier and stronger than our father's. Does anyone besides me see a problem with this?"

Jacob slid into the shadows and pulled Rachel with him, holding a finger to his lips. He cocked his head to better hear and glanced around, hoping he was not noticed.

"Jacob has taken everything our father owned and has gained all this wealth from what belonged to our father." The voice belonged to Rustam, son of Laban's concubine Refiqa. Murmurs of agreement followed the comment.

"He took only what our father agreed to pay him." Jacob recognized Bahaar's voice, his heart lifting to find one supporter among his brothers-in-law. "Though it is curious that he has done so well while our father's flocks have clearly weakened."

The skin prickled on Jacob's arms. Perhaps not so supportive. He glanced at Rachel, whose wide eyes told him she had heard and feared for him, for them. Surely Laban's sons would not harm him. But as the voices continued to argue and agree, Jacob forced himself to pull away. He drew Rachel into the house, into one of the inner rooms, and shut the door.

"I want you to take Joseph and go home," he whispered, afraid even the birds of night might hear his comment and repeat it to Laban or one of his sons.

"But I will be missed. There is still so much food to prepare and pass to the men—" She cut her words off at his touch on her shoulder.

"You heard your brothers, beloved. They suspect me of cheating them."

Rachel nodded and took his hand. "They will not harm us here, Jacob. We cannot just run away. My father will be slighted if you send all of us to our tents and leave his celebration." She released his hand and touched his forearm. "They have had too much to drink. By morning they will forget everything."

He didn't agree. She had not worked beside them shearing the sheep, had not seen the malevolent glances his way when they thought he would not see, when one of his sheep came before the shearers. But now was not the time or place to fully express his concerns, his fears.

"You are right, of course." He touched her cheek. "But as soon as you are finished, I want you to leave. I will send Leah shortly after you. The children are young and must be put to bed. No one will argue that."

Rachel looked at him a moment, considering his request. "I

had thought to check on my mother before we go. To see if she needs anything."

He gave a slight nod. How could he refuse her anything? Especially when Suri's health had continued to decline. "Go to her as soon as you can, then take Joseph and leave." He knew he was probably being overly protective of them, but he could not shake the feeling of unease in his gut. "You will go?"

She nodded, her dark eyes holding him captive, her smile erasing some of the fear troubling him. "I will go, Jacob. I think you worry too much." She stood on tiptoe and kissed his cheek. "But I will leave as soon as I'm able."

He drew in a breath, though the action did little to soothe him. She picked up the flask she'd set by the door, and he followed. He would go back to the fire and give them warning of his approach, lest Laban's sons suspect he had overheard them. Then he would see how they acted in his presence.

Rachel's heart beat too fast as she walked to the fire where her brothers and half brothers sat talking among themselves. She approached Tariq, making her presence known, and was satisfied when the conversation shifted to concerns over the wheat crop rather than further discussion of her husband. She moved from man to man, refilling their cups, resting a pointed look on Bahaar. He glanced beyond her, but she read the guilt in his eyes. He did not appreciate Jacob's success any more than the others, but at least he felt some type of remorse for his comments.

She looked up as Jacob approached the men, their smiles forced but half welcoming before she moved to stand in the shadows, listening. Her brothers made room for Jacob to join them, but the air was tenser now, and the jokes carried barbs that seemed especially sharp. Rachel stood near, her hands clenched tight about the flask, and for the briefest moment wished for the sling she used to carry when she shepherded the sheep in the fields. But she wouldn't really use such a thing against her own kin. Still, she couldn't help the protectiveness that rose within her for Jacob and for her son.

She hurried away, wondering where Joseph had wandered off to. Jacob's earlier distress suddenly filled her with worry. She must tell Leah and take the children back to the tents. Perhaps it was time for them to leave her father's household and travel to Canaan as Jacob had long hoped. Jacob's contract with her father would be completed at month's end, and her father had done nothing to make any of them want to stay even a week beyond. She stopped near the outer courtyard searching for her son, spotting Leah's older boys playing games with Bahaar's children. Would they truly go and leave this all behind?

Thoughts of her mother surfaced, bringing a sense of loss. Her stomach twisted in an uncomfortable knot. How could she leave her when she was so ill? And how could she live without her? Or bear another son without her aid? To leave her behind . . . But her mother could never come with her. Her father would hunt them down to bring her back.

She worried her lower lip, her anxious thoughts racing ahead of her feet as she hurried through the house searching for Joseph. There were too many rooms and too many children. She should have told him to stay close to her. But at six years old, he could hardly be expected to hang on to her robe and ignore time with his cousins.

She found Leah in one of the sleeping rooms holding Dinah, Issachar and Zebulun and Joseph already sleeping on cushions beside her. "There you are. I expected them to be playing with their cousins."

Leah glanced up. "They held races in the field behind the courtyard and nearly fell asleep eating their meal."

"Let me help you take the children home."

Leah shifted Dinah's sleeping form onto her shoulder. "We

should have taken them long ago," she said, exhaustion lining her face. "These feasts wear me out."

Rachel bent to coax the boys awake and took Joseph and Zebulun by the hand while Leah took hold of Issachar's. They moved quietly through the house, passing Farah in one of the halls.

"Have you seen your mother, Rachel? She's asking for you." Farah glanced at Rachel, then looked at her daughter. "Let me help you. Are you taking them home?"

Leah handed Dinah to her mother and took Zebulun's hand from Rachel's. "Shall I take Joseph for you?"

"No, he can come with me. We won't be long." She left them and took a side hall to her mother's room, where she found Suri lying on her mat. Rachel hurried to her side. "Are you in pain, Ima?"

Her mother's face looked pale and drawn, but she shook her head and offered Rachel a weak smile. "I am well, my daughter. Just tired. So very tired." She looked from Rachel to Joseph, and her smile widened. "Come to see me, dear child."

Joseph, still groggy from a full day of work and play, climbed beside his grandmother, his touch gentle as if he sensed her weakness. She pulled him near and stroked his soft dark hair. "Such a beautiful boy you are, Joseph. Yahweh has great things in store for you, my son." She kissed the top of his head, and Rachel's heart stirred with a mixture of joy and pain. Joy over her mother's blessing and pain over the fear that she would soon lose her.

"Can I get you anything, Ima?" Rachel wanted to linger but sensed that her mother needed rest. "Shall I call for your maid?"

Suri shook her head. "No, child. Seeing you was all I needed. I fear I wore myself out trying to help until Farah shooed me away." Her gaze traveled beyond Rachel, and Rachel turned to see if someone was there, but they were alone. "Go now, Rachel. Take Joseph home." She kissed Joseph's cheek then, and Joseph crept closer to Rachel. Rachel bent to kiss her mother's sallow cheek.

"I will come tomorrow, Ima." Surely a good night's sleep would make things right.

"Tomorrow," she said, her voice drifting off.

After a few moments, when she saw her mother's even breathing in the soft rise and fall of her chest, she took Joseph's hand and left the room. They made their way to the main sitting room of the house, then toward the outer courtyard, passing her father's shrine to his gods as they went. Rachel paused at Joseph's tug on her arm.

"Why does Sabba Laban keep images, Ima?" He no longer sounded sleepy, and a grave frown creased his young brow. "Abba says we are to worship only one God, Elohim."

She squatted beside him to better meet his gaze and kept her voice low. "Abba is right, my son. Sabba Laban should not keep these."

"Then why does he?"

"He thinks they bring him good fortune. And one day he will pass them to his heir, the son of his choosing, as his inheritance." Her father had long believed that the passing of his gods to his oldest son, or whichever son he deemed most worthy, would pass down the riches and blessings he had enjoyed in his life. Jacob had scoffed at the idea, and Rachel had agreed.

But as she led Joseph to their tent, a new thought crept into her mind. If her father thought all of his earthly blessings were wrapped up in those images, and if that blessing would pass to his heir, wouldn't it be the perfect deception to give them to Jacob? None of her brothers were as deserving. And if they continued to choose to believe such lies about the idols, why not let them lose the very thing they hoped to gain?

But as quickly as the thought to steal them came, she passed it off. She would have no opportunity to do so without being found out. And Jacob might not appreciate her duplicity or her attempt to put her father in his place.

❄❄❄

Morning dawned bright and clear, and Rachel roused before the children, before Leah, to draw water from the well. She loved the cool tingle of the dew on her feet and the peace that came with the earth's waking. Normally she would wait for Leah or Bilhah or even Zilpah to join her, but today she needed to think, to pray. It had been six years since she'd borne Jacob a child, and she could not shake the longing for another. If Adonai were gracious, she could perhaps bear another son before Jacob deemed it time to pack up and leave. For though the idea of leaving had pleased her in the night during the heat of anger toward her brothers, morning had brought the contentment of the familiar. She could not go. Not yet.

Still, as she lowered the jar to the well's depths and then turned toward home, her emotions again grew conflicted. Why did life have to be so difficult? So many struggles she had endured against Leah. So many struggles Jacob had endured against her father. And already she saw the signs of struggle in Jacob's children. Few of his older sons looked on Joseph with favor. They resented his place in Jacob's heart as his firstborn, and the looks they gave him when they thought Rachel did not see were less than kind, their words often harsh toward him.

If anything happened to Jacob, how would she protect her son from Jacob's oldest, sometimes mean-spirited sons? She had seen the way Reuben eyed her son, and Simeon and Levi were not quiet in their teasing of him, until she quickly intervened. Judah was the only one of Jacob's four oldest who seemed to hold a hint of kindness in him, but he was too young and often swayed by his brothers. Rachel did not exactly fear them—they were children, after all—but sometimes, when the night sounds lingered outside the tent and sleep would not come, she crept close to Joseph's mat and slept at his feet to protect him.

She steadied the heavy jug on her shoulder with one hand and took the path toward Jacob's tents, but as she neared the camp, expecting most to still be abed, commotion made her heart grow still. She moved closer, her recent thoughts giving rise to fear.

Had something happened to her son? Surely not. But her heart beat faster just the same. She hurried and set the jug in its ground hole and peered inside the tent, heart pounding now, relieved to see Joseph still sleeping. She breathed a sigh, then turned to scan the camp.

"Rachel!" Jacob's sharp voice from the direction of her father's house gave her a start, and she whirled about and hurried toward him.

"What is it?" One look into his dark eyes made her stomach tighten with a sick feeling of dread. "Tell me."

He touched her hand and pulled her along with him. "Your mother." He swallowed, the effort strained. "Come."

Rachel ran at his side as he led them to her father's house, suddenly aware of her father's servant running ahead of them. Distant keening filled her ears as they neared, and the sick feeling grew. Her knees suddenly felt weak. She forced herself to keep going, her breath coming hard, until at last they stopped outside her mother's room. Farah greeted them.

"I'm so sorry, Rachel." Moisture skimmed Farah's lashes, and Rachel wondered if her tears were real.

"Let me see her." Rachel pushed past her brothers' wives into the small room her father had portioned for her mother and for her when she was a young girl. Dawn's bright colors filtered through the small window, casting streams of light on the woven rug beside her mother's bed, where her body lay still, devoid of even the thin color it had held the night before.

Rachel stared, disbelieving. Her mother had still breathed just last evening. This could not be!

The sound of the keening women coming from the direction of the courtyard drew closer. How had the professional mourners already heard when she had just been told? She felt a sense of invasion and wished she could shut the door to weep for her mother in peace.

She knelt at her mother's side and slowly, carefully touched her cheek. The lack of warmth took her aback, and she leaned away, stuffing a fist to her mouth, tears filling her throat. She covered her face with both hands and moaned. Jacob's touch did not stay the tears when he knelt beside her. He pulled her into his arms and held her, letting her weep.

"How can I live without her?" she said, her voice hoarse against his robe.

"Hush, now. Everyone goes to the grave sometime, beloved. This was just your mother's time." His soft words did not soothe, but she nodded in feigned acceptance.

"I was not ready."

"Death never asks permission, beloved."

She had nothing to say to that, but his gentle touch on her back slowly calmed her. He was right, of course. Death came as the end of all life, and no one knew when it would snatch one from another. Hadn't she known it was coming? Hadn't she sensed it in her mother's look the night before? In her mother's parting words to Joseph?

"She knew." She lifted her head and wiped the tears from her face, meeting Jacob's gaze. "Last night she asked for me. I took Joseph to see her and she blessed him. She knew she would never see him again."

His eyes misted at her words, and her heart beat with love for him. "She loved you." He kissed the top of her head. "As do I."

She looked from his dear face to her mother's colorless one and sighed. "At least we still have each other." She turned to him and took his offered hand, letting him help her to her feet.

He leaned close to her ear. "Yes, and that is all that matters."

❧ 25 ❧

Jacob lay awake long into the night, going over the scenes from Suri's burial and the mourning feast that followed. At first he thought Laban's exclusion of him in carrying the bier and his subsequent scowls and distant looks were simply the result of grief, nothing more.

But as he sat with his brothers-in-law and Laban around the table that night, he could not help but notice the exclusion from conversations. Where Laban would normally have sought his advice on a particular problem with the sheep, he had turned to Tariq and Rustam and his other sons, not once even glancing Jacob's way. The slight could not have been more obvious.

He shifted on his mat, unable to get comfortable, wishing now he had asked Rachel to share his bed. But she had nearly fallen asleep during the meal, as Joseph had done, and when he carried the boy back to his bed, she had curled up beside him, asleep within moments. If only he had been so fortunate.

He rolled onto his back, staring at the tent poles above him, suddenly restless and moody and unable to stay abed. He rose, donned his robe and sandals, and left the tent. Stars greeted him as he glanced at the night sky, their bright lights nearer tonight than he'd seen in months. A soft breeze lifted strands of his damp hair, cooling the sweat his restlessness had produced. He moved past his tent and stopped but a moment at Rachel's. All was quiet in the camp, the fire banked while they slept.

Jacob walked slowly on toward the fields, past the sheep pens where the servant boy lay sleeping at the gate, protecting the sheep against the night's predators. Beyond the boy, the moon illuminated the white patches on the speckled and spotted sheep and goats, a portion of his hearty flock. God had blessed him in the six years he had worked for his wages, until his flocks outnumbered Laban's both in size and in strength. Only Adonai could have granted such success with the whittled tree branches to produce so many speckled young. And he had no doubt his success was the reason Laban's attitude toward him had changed.

He rubbed the back of his neck to forestall a headache he'd been fighting half the day. How could he stay where he was no longer appreciated or wanted? And yet how could he leave? His service to Laban had ended, but what if Laban tried to stop him? Laban's nine sons and many adult grandsons along with his servants far outnumbered Jacob and his servants. Jacob's sons were still children. No match for their wily grandfather and uncles.

He came to the rise of a hill and stood in a swath of moonlight, gazing up at the stars. *Oh, Adonai, what should I do?* He had not prayed so earnestly nor felt so compelled to do so since he had begged God to give Rachel a son. Not that he had forgotten his God, only that the urgency of his prayers had changed with the need.

Never had he felt so in need of guidance as now. He waited, listening, and sank down on the grass, aware of the night sounds, his ears attuned to the song of crickets and the whoosh of distant wings far above. Darkness shrouded him, and he sensed a thickening of the air as though a distinct presence rested above him. His breath grew labored, and he tried to open his eyes, but they would not lift.

"Go back to the land of your fathers and to your relatives, and I will be with you."

The voice was a whisper, softly spoken to his heart, yet the source was unmistakable, the same voice he had heard the night he fled from his brother.

Is it safe from Esau now?

The question went unanswered, but the presence seemed to hover. Perhaps God would speak again if he asked a different question. But no other question filled his mind like the sudden realization that he would be leaving the hostility of Laban to return to the hostility of Esau. And yet God had said, "Go."

He had no choice but to obey.

Jacob rose before dawn the next morning, splashed tepid water over his face, and walked to Leah's tent. He lifted the flap, surprising the servant girl who was just lifting the water jug in her arms, and moved toward the area where Leah's oldest boys still slept.

"Jacob?" Leah rose from a corner of the dark sitting room.

"I did not mean to disturb you. I came for Judah." He had given the task ahead much thought, and after weighing the attitudes of his oldest sons, he had considered nine-year-old Judah to be the one most able to do as he was told without running off distracted.

"Let me get him for you." She rose, but he stopped her with an upraised hand.

"Don't trouble yourself. I can get him." He had rarely entered the sleeping area of his children, and it was early enough that dawn's pink light had barely grown visible, but he was accustomed to the darkness now.

She nodded. "If you're sure." For a moment it occurred to him that she wanted to help him, but he would need her help in other matters soon enough.

"I'm sure." He moved to the sleeping quarters and found Judah, arm flung over his head, blissfully sleeping. He questioned the wisdom of entrusting a nine-year-old with the task. But he shook the disquiet aside and touched Judah's arm.

He lifted his head, his light brown hair falling over one eye as he quickly sat up and shook himself. "Abba?" He blinked and rubbed his eyes. "Is it morning?"

"Yes, my son. It is early, but it is morning. I want you to come with me to the fields today. I have an important job for you, but you must come with me now." He straightened and waited as the boy seemed to consider what he'd said.

At last he nodded and rose, quickly dressed in the semidarkness, and pulled his sandals over dusty feet, hurriedly tying the knots. "I'm ready." His eager voice gave Jacob pause. How rarely he had singled the boy out to spend time with him. He must remedy that in the future.

Judah hurried to the jar that held a mixture of dried dates, figs, and almonds and filled a small pouch, as Jacob had done in his tent the night before. Leah stood at the tent's door, and Jacob nodded to her as he passed through. Judah stopped to kiss his mother's cheek, causing Jacob a moment of guilt that he had not done the same. He stepped aside and waited for Judah to give his mother a parting hug, then walked with his son to the sheep pens.

Silence hung between them, and Jacob decided the boy was still too sleepy to speak. For his part, he tried and discarded a number of comments, finally deciding on none. At last they came to the sheep pens, and Judah entered, went to his favorite lamb, and dug his small fingers into its wool. Jacob smiled at the look of delight on the boy's face, and when Judah met Jacob's gaze, the boy's joy warmed his heart.

"I'll call them and you follow behind," Jacob said as he set out for the fields, his staff easing his step as they climbed a low hill, then descended into a lush valley below. He would miss the fertility he found in these lands where the river ran nearby and the rains came in predictable intervals. Canaan was more prone to drought, and the terrain in parts was more patchy and weak. But Canaan was home, and his heart stirred at the thought of returning.

"Shall I build a fire for you, Abba?" Judah's young voice brought his thoughts up short. They had come to a place where the sheep could spread out to graze, and Judah stood beside him near a terebinth tree, chewing a date. He spit the pit away from them and gave Jacob a toothy grin.

Jacob smiled and rumpled the boy's head. "Fires are kept at night, and only when the wind is calm." He pointed to the leaves above him. "See how they sway? The breeze is too strong to keep a fire safe."

Judah nodded, his small brows furrowed. "What did you need me to do?"

That the boy wanted to please him made Jacob wonder why it had taken him until now to get to know this child. But images of Joseph surfaced, and he knew why Judah and his brothers had gained less of his attention.

"The task is for later, when the sun is halfway to the midpoint. For now, you can walk with me among the flock and keep watch for foxes or lions." He touched Judah's shoulder and guided him to circle the pasture where the animals grazed, giving instructions on how to care for lambs when they were first born, and explaining why only one ram was needed for breeding many female lambs and how the rams would fight if they were together.

"Like Simeon and Levi fight over girls," Judah said, making a face. "Girls are boring." He glanced up at his father, and Jacob smiled.

"Girls won't be so boring when you are older." He chuckled as Judah stuck out his tongue.

"Not to me! Girls cheat at games and they don't like frogs."

Jacob laughed. "No, I imagine they don't. Especially when you put them in their bed." He gave Judah a knowing look.

The boy shrugged. "Wouldn't catch me crying over a frog in my bed."

The comment brought back memories of the antics he and Esau had played on some of the servant girls in the camp during the few years they had enjoyed each other's company. How quickly things had gone awry as their interests changed and they became the separate favorites of their parents.

A check in his spirit gave him pause. Did he not favor Joseph as his mother had favored him, as his father had favored Esau? What kind of future awaited his sons with sharing his time? He glanced at Judah, silently vowing to show the boy more attention.

Jacob kept a close eye on the path of the sun as he sat, watching Judah whittling a branch as he had taught him to do months ago.

"Judah."

"Yes, Abba, I'm here."

"I want you to run home now and bring your ima and aunt Rachel out to see me. They will need you to show them where I am. Can you remember the path we took?" It wasn't so far that he could have easily forgotten, but Jacob made him repeat the directions just the same.

"I won't forget, Abba." Delight shone in Judah's eyes, and he ran off to do Jacob's bidding.

The sun had risen halfway between its starting point and the middle of the sky by the time Judah returned with Rachel and Leah. Jacob greeted the boy, thanking him, and sent him to watch the sheep, far from where Jacob's words would be heard.

"What's wrong, Jacob?" Rachel asked, coming closer. Leah held back a pace, but her face held equal concern.

Jacob leaned on the staff in his hand and looked to Leah, then let his gaze linger on Rachel. He drew in a breath, then spoke the words he had rehearsed in his mind, praying the women would not find fault with them. If they would not cooperate with him, parting from Laban would be that much harder.

"I see that your father's attitude toward me is not what it was before," he said, gauging their reaction, "but the God of my father has been with me." At their mutual nods, he released a breath and continued. "You know that I've worked for your father with all my strength, yet your father has cheated me by changing my wages ten times."

"He is despicable," Rachel said, her beautiful mouth forming a scowl. "He wanted you to fail."

Jacob nodded. "Perhaps that is true. However, God has not allowed him to harm me. If he said, 'The speckled ones will be your wages,' then all the flocks gave birth to speckled young, and if he said, 'The streaked ones will be your wages,' then all the flocks bore streaked young. So God has taken away your father's livestock and has given them to me."

"God has been very gracious to you," Leah said, her look thoughtful. In that moment, he thought her almost beautiful.

"He has." He glanced at Rachel again, relieved to see the eager light in her eyes. "In breeding season," he said, glancing to where Judah petted one of the smaller ewes, still thankfully out of earshot, "I once had a dream in which I looked up and saw that the male goats mating with the flock were streaked, speckled, or spotted. The angel of God said to me in the dream, 'Jacob.' I answered, 'Here I am.' And He said, 'Look up and see that all the male goats mating with the flock are streaked, speckled, or spotted, for I have seen all that Laban has been doing to you.'" Jacob paused but a moment. "Then He said, 'I am the God of Bethel, where you anointed a pillar and where you made a vow to Me. Now leave this land at once and go back to your native land.'"

Jacob searched each face before him. "Will you come?" When they both spoke at once, he felt a heavy weight lift from his chest.

"Do we still have any share in the inheritance of our father's estate?" Rachel asked, taking one of his hands.

"Does he not regard us as foreigners?" Leah stepped forward and took the other. "Not only has he sold us, but he has used up our bride-price for his own gain, payment that belonged to us and to our children." Bitterness tinged her voice, surprising him. He expected her loyalty to reside with Laban.

"Surely all the wealth that God took away from our father belongs to us and our children," Rachel added. Her own tone matched Leah's, and he wondered how often the sisters had discussed the situation outside of his presence.

"So do whatever God has told you," they said in unison.

Jacob pulled them close, holding both of them to him as he had never done before. "Thank you," he whispered, kissing Rachel's forehead, then Leah's. "Begin packing things for the journey, but do not alert anyone in Laban's household, not even your mother." He looked at Leah. "Laban cannot know we are leaving." He released his hold, and they stood before him again.

"When will we leave?" Rachel tucked a strand of loose hair beneath her headscarf.

"Your father departs at the end of the week for the far pastures to shear his sheep. We will go while he is away."

"So, a week?" Leah fidgeted with the sash at her waist, clearly anxious to be off and starting already.

"A week," Jacob said. "I will speak to my steward to ready the camel's packs and gather food for the journey. We will store it far from the house and the camp. When the day comes, we will load the camels and come for you."

"We will be ready," Rachel said, stepping forward to kiss Jacob's cheek. "You are doing the right thing," she whispered in his ear.

She hurried away then, and Leah looked at him for an awkward moment as if trying to decide if she should offer him a kiss as well. In the end, she turned and hurried after her sister.

❧ 26 ❧

Rachel folded the half-woven tunic she was making for Jacob and tucked it into one of the camel's saddlebags along with her wool, spindle, and distaff, the last items to add to packs she had been filling for days. Joseph's small robes and tunics were already tucked in with her clothing and everything they could spare, all packed neatly in camel cushions and saddlebags and hidden in the dark corners of the tent, lest someone from her father's household come to call and notice something amiss.

She glanced up at the sound of voices outside her tent, quickly set the bag aside, and peered into the darkness, relieved when she recognized her sister and Zilpah. Dawn was still many hours off, the perfect time to slip away unnoticed, before the women of her father's household awoke to travel to the well and begin preparations for the morning meal.

"Are you ready?" Leah's soft whisper held anxiety, urgency.

Rachel nodded. "I put the last items in the bag just now." She looked toward the sheep pens where the earth rumbled beneath camels' hooves and the soft murmurs of men's voices drew near. Bilhah emerged from her tent, and the men came forward to load the camels.

Jacob stopped before them and looked from one woman to the next. "Are you ready to go?"

"We have only to wake the children," Rachel said, glancing at Leah. They would eat a meal of unleavened bread and dried fruit as they traveled, stopping only when necessity forced a rest.

"Good. Come. I will show each of you to your camels and those of your children. You can bring your packs and set them nearby. The men will fasten them securely." Jacob took Rachel's hand and led her to the first camel, motioning for Leah and his two concubines to follow. "You and Joseph can ride together. If it becomes too difficult, I will take him from you for a time." He released her hand, and she was glad of the clear night and the moon's glow, which allowed them to see.

"I will go get my things." She turned to leave, but he caught her arm. She looked at him, curious.

"We must keep the children as quiet as possible. Don't wake them until all is packed." She saw the worry in his eyes, reminded of several conversations they had had that week.

"Do not worry, my lord. My father is three days' journey away, as are my brothers. We will be far from here before anyone can tell them we are gone." She had reassured him of the same thing twice before, but her words could not shake the fear from his gaze. She touched his arm. "It will be all right."

He nodded and bent to kiss her cheek. "Your father has the power to do us great harm. He could take you back by force."

"He wouldn't do that."

"Wouldn't he?" Jacob's doubt fueled an anxious one of her own. Her father's hostility and bitterness had grown more verbal of late. Ever since her mother's death, her father had found one reason after another to blame Jacob for his losses—his loss of a healthy flock, which wasn't true, or of income, which had no lack—and now he carried his ill feelings on the loss of his wife.

"My father imagines things that aren't real. He thinks too much of himself. And he doesn't have Adonai's blessing."

Jacob touched her hand. "Be quick about your work." He turned then to show Leah and the maids to their camels while

Rachel hurried to her tent, hoisted several saddlebags in her arms, and deposited them near her waiting beast.

She finished all but waking Joseph and packing her tent, her thoughts whirling with Jacob's doubts and fears. Her father would return to find them gone and would take off after them. Of this she had no doubt. His best trackers would have no trouble following their trail, and at their reduced pace with the herds and flocks and children, he would catch them. When he did, what then?

She twisted the sash at her waist, about to go into her tent to wake Joseph, when another thought made her pause. First her father would consult his gods. Hadn't he done so when he saw his riches increase under Jacob's watchful care? She remembered the way he had wheedled Jacob into staying six more years for wages that should have already been his, had her father not stolen the bride-price of his daughters. Her father had confessed to using divination to discover the source of his wealth.

Had his gods truly spoken to him? She glanced heavenward at the blinking sea of stars that would light their way until dawn. Had Adonai spoken to her father through his gods? Jacob had always insisted there was only one Creator. Surely Adonai would not reveal their plans to Laban now.

No. The God she had come to know, the God who had given her Joseph, favored her husband, not her father.

Still . . . her father's gods must have some mystical power, because her father knew things about God's blessing that he shouldn't have known, couldn't have known otherwise.

A camel snorted, shaking her thoughts, and she stood before her tent, sudden indecision filling her. Perhaps it was she who was deluding herself now. How could images of stone and gold speak?

But her father believed they did. And everyone knew that the gods of her people were sought after for everything from prosperity to healing. Hadn't she sought them herself in years past?

Her father would return after the sheep shearing, or sooner if someone sent him word, and immediately consult his gods for guidance, to determine the direction Jacob had gone and the best way to defeat him. Why should he have such an advantage?

The thought spurred her to action, and she turned and ran from her tent to her father's house. The moon cast eerie shadows over the white bricks of the house, and Rachel slowed her pace, tiptoeing through the courtyard, careful not to allow her sandals to slap against the stones. She opened the door, grateful to find it unlocked, and eased her way to the familiar hall where her father kept his shrine, darting quick glances about the darkened interior and taking shallow breaths so as not to awaken a servant.

A small clay lamp still burned near the images as though her father feared the gods might be afraid of the dark. She nearly laughed at the thought that images of stone had feelings or fears. She looked down at the small golden objects and wondered how her father could imagine a piece of wood and precious metal had any power at all.

Memories of Joseph's furrowed brow and worried words from the night her mother died rose in her thoughts.

"Why does Sabba Laban keep images, Ima? Abba says we are to worship only one God, Elohim."

"Abba is right, my son. Sabba Laban should not keep these."

"Then why does he?"

"He thinks they bring him good fortune."

Not this time. She snatched the images from their perches and tucked them beneath her robe. Glancing quickly about to be sure she wasn't seen, she retraced her steps to the door, barely daring to breathe, hurried out through the courtyard, and ran all the way back to Jacob's camp.

By the time dawn broke night's hold and brightened the sky, first in soft gray light and then in a burst of brilliant pink hues, Rachel had settled into the camel's rhythm and stopped glancing behind her to see if they had been followed. Her heart had slowed to its normal pace as well once she had tucked her father's idols into her camel's cushions, where they hung now from the animal's sides, softened by some combed wool and hidden from obvious view.

Guilt had followed her rash act, chasing her as she quietly woke Joseph and settled him in front of her on the camel's back. She had shoved the feeling aside more than once as Joseph leaned into her, soon falling asleep with the swaying movement of the animal. Her own ability to sleep had not come. How certain could they be that a servant had not heard them and watched them leave in haste in the dark of night? Even now, one of the younger boys could be headed toward her father's camp with the news of their departure.

She chafed at the desire to urge the camel into a faster trot, knowing the flocks Jacob was driving up ahead could not be rushed. Nor could the children handle a faster pace. But her heart skipped a beat with every thought of her father, and even her prayers seemed hindered by her guilt. Had she done the wrong thing?

But it was too late to return the images now.

The sun rose higher even as the thoughts plagued her. Sweat trickled down her back, and she was grateful for the headscarf that kept the bugs and wind from lashing her face. She should bury the images in the ground at the first stop they came to. But the thought was foolish, and she knew it. She had little respect for her father, but to bury his gods would be the ultimate show of contempt, and despite everything she could not quite bring herself to do so. If he caught up to them, which he surely would, she would return them to him and confront him, telling him how he did not deserve to keep anything of value because he had cared so little for his own daughters, selling them like chattel.

She formed the words of the imagined conversation in her

mind, where she saw herself casting the idols at her father's feet, telling him that he owed them what they were worth and much more. If only she had such courage.

Her stomach rumbled as the sound of the gurgling water of the Euphrates filled her ears. The flocks and herds and camels up ahead came to a stop, and she looked up to see Jacob's camel lumbering toward her.

"This is the narrowest place to cross over," he said as he turned his mount to walk beside hers. "We will eat here and stretch our legs while the men drive the flocks and herds across. Once you are rested, I will guide you and the others over as well. I will rest easier once we have crossed the river."

She glanced at his turbaned brow, seeing the worry lines creasing it, knowing how much this escape was costing him. The thought made her own guilt pale in comparison. But she also knew in that moment that she could not share what she had done with him. It would add to the weight of his worry, and she would spare him whatever she could.

He led them closer to the river before commanding his camel to kneel, hopping down, and guiding the women and his older sons to do the same. Then he showed each one how to lead the camels to the river's bank to drink.

Rachel wrapped her hand over Joseph's on the camel's lead, half stumbling in an effort to gain her bearings on firm ground again. The children laughed and ran in and around the camels' legs until Jacob scolded them and sharply warned them against provoking the animals and receiving a swift kick. Protectiveness made her tighten her hold on the reins and put herself between Joseph and the camel's knobby legs.

Watering the flocks and camels and herds took until the sun had passed the midway point, the children had been fed, and they at last had made it across the river, where Jacob commanded they continue on until nightfall.

By the time they settled at the foothills of the hill country,

Rachel's anxiety had lessened, her exhaustion palpable. Joseph lay sleeping on a mat near the fire in the open, since they had all decided to leave the tents packed, as Rachel had done many a night in her youth while watching the sheep, but tonight she could barely keep her eyes open as she lay beside her son.

She felt Jacob's arm come around her, grateful for his presence, grateful he had chosen her above the others. She leaned into him while keeping her arm around Joseph, a threesome against the night.

"Tomorrow will be tougher going once we enter the foothills of Gilead," he whispered in her ear. "Are you up for the climb?"

She yawned, then breathed in his familiar scent. "Wherever you go, we will go, Jacob. All the way to Canaan." She sighed as his arm tightened around her.

"My mother and father will love you," he said softly. "May God take us there swiftly."

"Yes," she said, her mind fighting to stay focused on his words. "Swiftly."

Weeks passed as they traveled south and west until at last they set up camp in the hill country of Gilead. One morning, as the dawn dispelled the dew, Rachel set aside the millstone and then rose, her anxious heart keeping time with the drum of camels' hooves coming toward them.

Jacob emerged from his tent, barking orders to the children to gather near their mothers and wait in their tents. Rachel grabbed Joseph's hand, quick to obey, but stood watching at the tent's door. Jacob's steward, Omid, and other male servants gathered near and spread out along the perimeter of the camp, a small army against an invader.

But as the camels came into view and her father and brothers approached, Rachel's heart slowed with an unhappy mixture of anticipation and dread. Did she have the courage, as she had imagined so often in her mind in past weeks, to toss her father's gods at his feet and make him aware of his guilt? Would he listen? Her heart thumped faster and her palms moistened at the scenario she envisioned, but she could not make her feet move from their place to retrieve the images or to disobey Jacob's order to stay in her tent.

What would her father do to Jacob if he knew? Surely he would find some way to lay blame at her husband's feet, and Jacob had suffered enough from her father.

The thought assuaged her guilt for a moment, caught up as she was in the brooding scowl on her father's face as he dismounted his camel and stormed to Jacob's side.

"What have you done? You've deceived me, and you've carried off my daughters like captives in war," he said, his voice rising with every word. "Why did you run off secretly and deceive me? Why didn't you tell me, so I could send you away with joy and singing to the music of tambourines and harps? You didn't even let me kiss my grandchildren and my daughters goodbye. You have done a foolish thing." He crossed his arms in that telltale way he had and looked down his nose at Jacob, an action that he often used to intimidate those beneath him.

Rachel's heart hardened at the sight, heat creeping up the back of her neck. She fisted her hands, longing to rush outside her tent and pummel her father with her fists. How dare he!

"I have the power to harm you"—her father's words cut into her thoughts—"but last night the God of your father said to me, 'Be careful not to say anything to Jacob, either good or bad.' Now you have gone off because you longed to return to your father's house. But why did you steal my gods?"

Rachel's heart skipped first one beat, then another. She blinked, fighting the urge to sway. Suddenly her rash act seemed foolish indeed, especially as she saw Jacob's face darken and his brows furrow in a deep scowl. He shifted from foot to foot, but his gaze held her father's, unyielding.

"I was afraid," he said, his voice holding little trace of the fear he admitted, "because I thought you would take your daughters away from me by force." His voice held an edge. "But if you find anyone who has your gods, he shall not live. In the presence of our relatives, see for yourself whether there is anything of yours here with me, and if so, take it."

Rachel's knees weakened, nearly collapsing beneath her, and she watched in a daze as her father quickly did as Jacob had offered. He marched to Jacob's tent while her brothers stood with Jacob outside, waiting. Sounds of items being moved and shoved aside filled the quiet camp as the implications of Jacob's words fully penetrated. Would Jacob truly order her death?

She swallowed hard, her mind whirling. She could not possibly confront her father now. Jacob had given his word, and even if he would change his mind and have mercy, her father and brothers might not. Dare she risk her life for a pair of useless images?

A shiver worked through her, and she forced herself to act as her father emerged from Jacob's tent and moved to Leah's. He would be at her door in a moment. She glanced at Joseph, who sat with his arms tucked around his knees on his mat, eyes wide, and put a finger to her lips for him to remain silent. She walked to her sleeping quarters outside of Joseph's line of sight, took the camel cushion with the images, and laid a blanket over them.

Her father would surely discover her ruse, but what else could she do? She settled herself on top of the cushion and waited. Normally she would rise and kiss his cheek in greeting, but if she stood, the camel cushion would be searched. There was nothing to do but make an excuse for not showing him hospitality. One more deceit added to her guilt.

She waited, heart thudding with slow, anxious strokes, her mind struggling to keep pace with the activity around her. Leah's voice could be heard telling their father to take care with her goods, and Rachel wondered if he had left things intact or was just making a mess of Leah's careful organization.

At last the tent door darkened with the shape of her father, and she heard him rummaging in the sitting room where Joseph sat.

"Greetings, Sabba Laban," Joseph said, his voice cheery despite the worry she had seen in his face.

Her father grunted a response, making Rachel's anger rise a notch. The man had no manners. All he cared about were his foolish gods! She would throw them in his face if the situation weren't so dire. Why had Jacob made such a rash comment? Were such images worthy of death? But of course to steal them was a punishable offense, though death seemed a harsh sentence.

The thought of losing her life for her own rash act fueled her anger, her fear. She looked up as her father at last entered her sleeping chamber and offered him an apologetic smile. "Please don't be angry, my lord, that I cannot stand up in your presence. The way of women is upon me."

He looked at her, his gaze assessing. She held his gaze, unflinching, for the space of several heartbeats and forced herself to relax. At last he nodded and continued his search, revealing nothing. When he left her tent, Rachel's limbs turned to liquid, and she sagged against the cushions, releasing a deep sigh. She was safe. At least for now.

But she would not rest until her father left for good and she could rid herself of the accursed images.

※ 27 ※

Jacob stared at his father-in-law, his nemesis, barely holding his anger in check. He took two steps forward, aware of Tariq and his brothers' subtle movement closer to their father. He didn't care. Let them try to come after him! Laban's search of his goods was humiliating and uncalled-for! He pointed a finger straight at Laban.

"What is my crime? What sin have I committed that you hunt me down?" He stepped closer until his breath nearly touched Laban's cheeks. "Now that you have searched through all of my goods, what have you found that belongs to your household? Put it here in front of your relatives and mine, and let them judge between the two of us."

Laban lifted his hands to ward off a blow and took a step backward, saying nothing. His silence raised Jacob's ire, his heart beating fast, his mind whirling with pent-up words. "I have been with you for twenty years now," he said, his voice rising in pitch. "Your sheep and goats have not miscarried, nor have I eaten rams from your flocks. I did not bring you animals torn by wild beasts; I bore the loss myself. And you demanded payment from me for whatever was stolen by day or night. This was my situation: The heat consumed me in the daytime and the cold at night, and sleep fled from my eyes." How well he remembered! "It was like this for the twenty years I was in your household. I worked for you fourteen years for your two daughters and six years for your flocks, and you changed my wages ten times." The injustice, the sheer audacity of the man looking back at him now with such an impassive look, heated his blood. He clenched his hands, his nails digging into his palms.

Jacob drew a breath, willing his anger to still. It would do no good to strike the man, despite the urgent, pleading need to do so. Tariq and his brothers would retaliate, and the end would only bring harm to his family.

"If the God of my father," he said, dragging his emotions under control, "Elohim of Abraham and the Fear of Isaac, had not been with me, you would surely have sent me away empty-handed. But Elohim has seen my hardship and the toil of my hands, and last night He rebuked you." Jacob took a step back, further distancing himself from Laban, and crossed his arms, a barrier between them. He glanced from Laban to his sons and back again.

Laban's look held unease, but a moment later he straightened, lifted his chin. "The women are my daughters, the children are my children, and the flocks are my flocks. All you see is mine." He spread his hands wide.

Jacob's grip tightened on his arms to force a calm he did not feel. He stared, incredulous. The man would claim all Jacob had worked for? He blinked, slowly looking from Laban to his sons, for the first time sensing a hint of unease from his brothers-in-law. Perhaps even they could see the falsehood in their father's words. Perhaps they were not quite so unaware of just how deceived Laban really was.

Laban laughed, a rueful sound, as though he could somehow lighten the mood. He pointed in the direction of Rachel's and Leah's tents. "Yet what can I do today about these daughters of mine or about the children they have borne?" He met Jacob's gaze again, extending a hand. "Come now, let's make a covenant, you and I, and let it serve as a witness between us."

Jacob studied Laban's dark eyes, noticed the streaks of white lining his beard, saw the slight lift of his mouth in the familiar way he smirked when he was at his most congenial, when he was trying to coax a man to see things his way. He still thought himself in control of the situation, and yet God had protected Jacob even through Laban's accusations.

Jacob stood straighter, breathing a silent prayer of gratitude. He nodded, then walked without a word to the edge of the camp where an outcropping of rocks protected them from the elements. He lifted a large stone, carried it to the place Laban stood, and set it up as a pillar.

"Gather some stones," he said to his oldest sons as well as to his brothers-in-law. They moved quickly to do his bidding, brought the stones to the spot Jacob had picked, and piled them in a heap.

"The place shall be called *Jegar Sahadutha*," Laban said.

"And we shall call it *Galeed*." Both meant "witness heap," but even in this, Jacob broke from Laban's hold. He would keep to the language of his fathers, not his uncle. His fathers' heritage, not Laban's.

"This heap is a witness between you and me today." Laban raised his hands as if in benediction and blessing. "May Adonai keep watch between you and me when we are away from each other. If you mistreat my daughters or if you take any wives besides my daughters, even though no one is with us, remember that God is a witness between you and me."

Laban turned briefly to face his sons, then looked back at Jacob, acknowledging Jacob's sons with a nod. "Here is this heap, and here is this pillar I have set up between you and me. This heap is a witness, and this pillar is a witness, that I will not go past this heap to your side to harm you and that you will not go past this heap and pillar to my side to harm me. May the God of Abraham and the God of Nahor, the God of their father, judge between us."

"May Elohim of Abraham and the Fear of Isaac judge between us," Jacob said, again reminding his sons and wives who were listening that they had broken loyalty to Laban and his gods to be wholly devoted to the God of his fathers. "Let us offer a sacrifice to complete the agreement."

Rachel spent the night confined to her tent, feigning illness during the feasting, still afraid to leave her father's gods even to share in the evening meal. The weight they had brought to her heart since she had lifted them from their stand in her father's house had become like a millstone tied to her neck. How she longed to be rid of them! And she would be, the first chance she got to bury them away from her tent.

The jangle of camels' bells woke her before dawn, and she was half surprised to find her father and brothers already preparing to leave. She cast about for a place to hide the camel cushion, quickly placing it behind another pair of sacks that still held clothes and some of the weaving equipment she had yet to remove. Satisfied that things did not look out of place, she donned her robe and clutched it tight about her to still the sudden trembling. Perhaps she truly was ill.

She moved to the other side of the partition to wake Joseph, helped him dress, and then met the other women and children in the center of the camp, where Jacob was already speaking to her father and brothers. She shivered, glad for the morning chill that might make the others think her cold rather than reveal the nervousness that now gripped her middle. Joseph sidled closer to her, still groggy, and she pulled him in front of her, her shield, and she his protector.

Her father's laughter jarred the birds' happy morning calls, as if even the land where they were standing would be glad to be rid of him. She braced herself as he stepped toward her.

"Ah, my daughter. Feeling better at last, I hope?"

She nodded, swallowed hard. "A little."

He leaned close and kissed each of her cheeks, then bent before Joseph and did the same. Joseph clung to his grandfather in return and kissed his peppered beard. "I will miss you, Sabba Laban." Tears clung to her father's lashes when Joseph released him, and Rachel felt the sudden loss of him as well.

She longed to fall into his embrace and hold him close, to feel his protective arms around her. But he had long ago given up that privilege when he treated her future with such contempt. She reminded herself of the things he had done, even the pilfering of their goods, searching for what she would not give him. Still, despite everything, he was her father and she loved him.

"I will miss you too, Father," she said, pulling Joseph against her again. "May God go before you and watch between us."

"While we are absent from one another," her father finished the benediction. "Bear many more sons, my daughter." He looked for a moment like he would say more, and she wished belatedly that she could have offered him some comfort. But he had ruined the bond they had shared in her childhood by his own choices. It took all of her strength to remember that fact.

"Farewell, Father." She gave him a soft smile and an affirming nod before he turned to Leah and his other grandsons. When at last the goodbyes were said, Laban mounted his camel, and her brothers did the same.

She watched them go with an aching heart until the last camel disappeared into the distance. Joseph ran off to find his half brothers, and sometime later when all were fed and the men were busy with daily tasks, Rachel took the camel bag with her father's images, walked a safe distance to a tree in the woods, and buried the gods deep in the earth.

Part

Jacob also went on his way, and the angels of God met him. When Jacob saw them, he said, "This is the camp of God!" So he named that place Mahanaim.

Jacob sent messengers ahead of him to his brother Esau in the land of Seir, the country of Edom.

Genesis 32:1–3

So Jacob was left alone, and a man wrestled with him till daybreak . . .

The man asked him, "What is your name?"

"Jacob," he answered.

Then the man said, "Your name will no longer be Jacob, but Israel, because you have struggled with God and with humans and have overcome."

Genesis 32:24, 27–28

❋ 28 ❋

Jacob stood on an outcropping of rocks, staff in hand, looking to the west where the hills of Gilead dipped to lush valleys and the Jabbok River rushed to the Jordan on its way to the Dead Sea, in the area where his uncle Lot once lived. Oak and pear and pine flocked the hillsides, while a sea of pink oleander covered the slopes all the way to the fertile plains. They'd traveled for days since leaving the camp at Mizpah after Laban's departure, the covenant and the pillars they had set up reminders of the goodwill that now rested between them.

Yet Jacob's heart beat heavy with the memories and dread of the future. Would he find acceptance in the house of his father? Did Esau still hold hatred against him? The fears were never far from his thoughts.

Up ahead, almost too far for his eye to clearly see, his servants drove his flocks—first goats, then ewes, then rams, followed by herds of camels, cows, bulls, and donkeys. The God of his fathers had surely blessed him, as He had promised when he first left his father's house with only the staff he carried now.

The sound of children's voices drifted to him on the rise, and he looked down to where his wives and sons and daughter passed before him toward the place where they would make camp. Satisfied that all was well, he walked to his waiting camel and mounted, tucking the staff into a sling at its side. The camel took the downward slope at a careful pace, then snorted its pleasure when they touched even ground and ran at Jacob's beckoning toward the women and children. He paused as his beast aligned with Rachel's.

"All is well, my lord?" The smile in her eyes was all he could see beneath the veil that blocked the sun and wind from her beautiful face.

He smiled and nodded. "All is well. We will make camp soon. I am going up ahead to secure the location."

She acquiesced with a silent tilt of her head while Joseph waved and bounced, obviously eager to get down. Jacob laughed, the lighthearted feeling boosting his spirits.

He coaxed the camel forward, passing the herds as he went. As he neared the goats, he noticed the shadows had lengthened and the servants kept the animals in their respective groups apart from each other. Jacob glanced at his chief shepherd and waved, calling out orders to stop for the night. As he took the camel's reins to return to the women, he spotted men walking toward him, their bearing tall and distinguished, their clothes bright as noonday.

He halted and commanded the camel to kneel, then took his staff and slowly walked toward them. To wait for his steward or a few of his servants would have been wise, but the men approaching seemed familiar in a way that made the hairs on his skin tingle. He had met them before. And they were not as normal men.

Memories of Bethel the night he'd fled his brother surfaced. He had encountered God on that trip, in the dream of the zig-gurat and the angels of God walking up and down the stairs.

His knees weakened beneath him, and he leaned more heavily on the staff as he approached. "This is the camp of God," he said, though none could hear.

He planted his staff in the dirt and waited. Angels as numer-ous as they had been the night of his dream approached and circled him, moving forward and back, floating just above the surface of the earth. A sense of assurance and peace filled him. God was in this place. He gazed on the messengers who surrounded him but did not speak. And yet his heart heard the music of their silence and recalled Elohim's words all those years ago.

I am Yahweh, the Elohim of your father Abraham and the Elohim of Isaac. I will give you and your descendants the land on which you are lying. Your descendants will be like the dust of the earth, and you will spread out to the west and to the east, to the north and to the south. All peoples on earth will be blessed through you and your offspring. I am with you and will watch over you wherever you go, and I will bring you back to this land. I will not leave you until I have done what I have promised you.

Until. Elohim would not leave him until He had fulfilled His promise. Jacob was standing on the cusp of that promise, his family behind him, the land before him. God had not forgotten him.

"This place shall be Mahanaim, Elohim's camp and my camp, for Elohim has met me here," he said, his voice sure despite the tremor that passed through him.

The angels left him then, disappearing from his sight. The sun had not moved from its place in the sky despite the time it had seemed to take for the angels to approach and move around him. He turned, shaken, the sense of awe he had known at Bethel as tangible as the beat of his heart. He closed his eyes, trying to get his bearings, and looked up at the sound of camels approaching. He would make camp in this place and stay for a time, then cross the Jabbok and head to the Jordan before making the long trek south to his father at Hebron.

Rachel settled Joseph in her tent for the night, then wrapped a cloak about her and stepped into the moonlight, searching the campground for some sign of Jacob. He had spoken little during the evening meal, and she sensed something had happened on their way to the camp. But her attempt to get him to speak in the company of the others had failed, and now her sense of exhaustion nearly outweighed her need to know what troubled him. She looked with longing at the mat beside Joseph and almost gave in and curled up beside him. She could question Jacob another time. If he didn't want to tell her, then she should sleep while she could.

But a deeper need to see him, to comfort him, pulled her from her tent. She found him near the fire, speaking with his steward. She slowly strode closer and stood where he could catch her eye without being interrupted. He smiled her way and bid his steward good night, then walked toward her.

He took her hand and squeezed. "Walk with me."

She intertwined her fingers with his and smiled when he looked down at her. "What happened to you today?" They moved from the circle of tents to the edge of the forest, where the night breezes rustled the oak leaves above them.

His grip tightened, and he led her farther to a place near the edge of the camp where they could sit on some upturned rocks. "God met me in this place," he said, settling beside her. He tilted his head, and she followed his gaze heavenward, longing to see what it was that put the edge of awe in his voice. "Before you arrived, his angels came from that spot." He pointed to a place in the field just beyond them. "It was almost like the time I met Him at Bethel, on my journey to your father's house. Now we have come full circle back to the land He has promised to me and my descendants, and He met me again."

She searched his face, drawn by the light in his dark eyes. "What did He say to you?"

Jacob stroked his beard with his free hand. "He did not speak this time." He glanced beyond her in the direction the angels had come as though hoping to see them again, then looked back at her. "But I sensed His words from the time before. And I sensed His pleasure in me." His crooked smile reminded her of Joseph, and she knew how much such pleasure meant to him. Despite the blessing Jacob had won, his own father had favored his brother.

"I am happy for you, Jacob." She leaned close and kissed his cheek, touching the other cheek with her palm, stroking his beard. "You are the favored of Adonai. You will surely be blessed from this day forward." A feeling of pride filled her that she could share in such blessing, that her son would one day rule at his father's right hand. "Will we go directly to see your father and mother in Hebron then?" He had talked so often of the anticipated reunion that she fully expected him to take over for his father as soon as they could return.

He nodded. "This is my hope. We will stay here for a week to give the animals time to feed and the children a chance to rest. But then we will continue south to my father." He stood, pulling her to him, and lifted her in his arms, twirling her in a joyous dance. "We shall be home at last, beloved. Ima and my father will love you." He kissed her then, a slow, gentle kiss that made her knees weak.

"Perhaps we should continue this in your tent." She whispered the words against his ear, and he laughed, filling her with joy she had not known since Joseph's birth.

"Perhaps we should." He slipped his arm around her waist and guided her back the way they had come, continuing the kiss as the tent flap closed them in.

Jacob lay awake long after Rachel returned to her tent to stay with Joseph lest he awaken and fear her absence. His body ached with weariness, and yet anticipation of the future kept his mind churning with possibilities. What would his father say to him? Was his mother well? Was Deborah still living? He had had little word of them during his stay with Laban, the last message coming over a year before. Surely he would see them again soon.

But as the night sounds settled into the quiet that preceded the dawn, Jacob dreamed of Esau, not his father. All the anger and grappling they had done as children, all the ways Jacob had deceived his brother came to him in memories he had long tried to suppress. The rift between himself and Esau could cause serious problems for him as he entered his father's camp.

Did Esau still reside with their parents? Had he taken over his father's affairs in Jacob's absence? What would cause him to give up the right to control them now, if he had? Esau had two wives and several sons when Jacob left him, and he had added at least one more wife after Jacob fled, if the gossip was true. No doubt the man had probably fathered more sons during the ensuing years. But was he well? Did he have livestock and servants as Jacob had?

The vision of the angels that had met him hours before filled the place where the memories of Esau lingered. And with the vision came the sense of his own unworthiness and the weight of the guilt he had carried for years.

He awoke with a start, sweat beading his skin. God had not spoken in words when He'd sent the angels to Mahanaim, but His guidance could not be more clear.

Jacob must reconcile with Esau. Before he returned to his father.

The thought made his insides quiver. Sleep would not return this night.

"But why, Jacob? Wouldn't it be better to avoid trouble than to search for it head-on?" Rachel's words raised his own doubts the following day when he spoke to his wives after the morning meal.

"I would love to avoid facing my brother, particularly when

he left me with the threat to end my life, but it seems this is the path God has led me to." He rubbed the back of his neck and sighed, wishing he could have avoided this conversation. But his wives must be told what lay ahead. He just didn't expect Rachel's gaze to hold such fear. Perhaps he had spoken too warily of Esau in the past.

"I think if God is leading you to meet your brother, then you must do as He says."

He turned at Leah's voice and assessed her. Were her thoughts truly her own, or was she making the suggestion to increase her sister's fear? But no. Leah feared Adonai. She would have spoken from her heart for Him, not in meanness to her sister. Surely such jealousies were long past.

Rachel touched his arm, drawing his attention back to her, and he wondered by the scowl lines along her brow whether that last thought was true. "But think of the children, Jacob. Wouldn't you be putting them—putting all of us—in danger if Esau were invited to our camp? If he comes alone, then he will fear for his own life. But if he comes with his sons as my father just did, they could be armed as my father's sons surely were, and attack while we are sleeping."

Her fears were not unfounded, but if he listened, if he allowed her fears to become his, he would shrink back from what he knew he must do. Hadn't the angels of God just met him? Surely Adonai would be with him. He must trust that He would protect him, if this indeed was His plan.

But was this His plan? The doubts floated near him like pestering insects as he listened to the arguments back and forth between Rachel and Leah.

"I understand your fears, and I will do all in my power to keep you safe," he said, no longer able to bear their bickering. "But I believe this is the right thing to do, and I must do it." His tone was sharper than he intended, but the words had their desired effect.

Rachel gave a slight nod. "As you say, my lord." Her tone held constraint, and he regretted that he could not be more reassuring.

"Adonai will be with us," Leah said, placing a comforting hand on his arm. He met her gaze and for the first time felt gratitude for her faith, for her purpose in his life.

He smiled his response and thanked them both. As they went back to their daily tasks, he walked toward the herds to speak to his chief steward. He would find out where Esau now resided and send messengers to greet him, seeking audience.

Then he would see what God would do.

29

"We found Esau living in the land of Seir as you had discovered, my lord," one of Jacob's young male servants said a few weeks later. "And we repeated the words you told us to say—how you have been staying with Laban until now and have cattle and donkeys, sheep and goats, menservants and maidservants. We told him that you were sending the message to find favor in his eyes, just like you said."

Rachel looked from the messenger to Jacob, saw his stiff shoulders, his tense jaw. Her own heart beat to an anxious rhythm, and her breath was unsteady in her chest.

"What answer did he give you?" Jacob's brows drew down, the worry lines clearly evident beneath his striped turban. His knuckles whitened on the top of his staff.

"He said he is coming to meet you, and four hundred men are with him." This from the same messenger, but the other men with him nodded in agreement.

"Four hundred?" Jacob's voice was low, barely a whisper. His hand trembled in its grip, and it took all in Rachel's power not to rush to him, to hold him up. But her own knees wobbled, and a sudden pall fell over the group.

"So many." Jacob looked about for a place to sit, and his men took his arms, guiding him to the stones set about the campfire. One of the men offered him a drink from their skin of water, and he took it, though some of the water sloshed from his shaking. What could they do? What could they possibly do against four hundred men?

"It's the size of a raiding party," Omid said, sitting across from him. "We have enough men to stand against him, my lord. They are not trained in battle, but we have surely faced many a predator against the flocks and herds. We could go on ahead and meet him before he ever gets to the women and children."

Rachel forced strength into her limbs, taking comfort in the steward's words. She moved closer, seeking a way to join Jacob, to be a silent comfort at his side. She stood in his line of vision, but his gaze seemed to stretch beyond her as though he was seeing into another time or place.

The steward cleared his throat and sought to regain Jacob's attention. "My lord?"

Jacob shook his head as if to clear it and looked at the man, not acknowledging Rachel.

"Shall I gather the servants and prepare to battle him?"

Jacob stroked his beard. When had the streaks of silver cropped in among the hairs? He had always seemed so full of vigor, nearly invincible to her. But right now he looked like the years had suddenly aged him, and the fear, her fear, had overtaken him.

Regret filled her, and she moved closer, slipping into the seat at his side. He finally sensed her presence and looked at her with an expression she could not read. He took her hand, and his was cold to her touch. He did not speak for a lengthy moment. At last he faced his steward.

"We will divide the camp into two groups. The men who can handle a sling or a sword shall be in the first group, with some also in the second to protect the women and children. If Esau attacks one group, the group that is left may escape." He drew in a ragged breath, then lowered his head into his hands.

"It will be as you say, my lord," the steward said. "Do not worry. We will move quickly. The groups will be separated by nightfall."

Jacob looked up and nodded, the lines of distress and fear evident in his face. The men left to do his bidding, leaving Rachel beside him. They sat in silence as the women and children slowly gathered around him, aware of the silence, of Jacob's fear.

He stood at last, leaning heavily on his staff to address them. "Gather everything and pack the camels. We will move across the river by nightfall." His gaze took in the group, sorrow gracing his words, his gaze. He turned and walked abruptly to his tent, leaving them behind him.

The wind picked up, whipping Jacob's cloak against his body as he walked toward his tent like a drunken man. He lifted the flap, letting his eyes adjust to the dark interior, glad that he had failed to lift the sides at dawn lest his wives and sons see his misery. Lest they taste his fear.

He stumbled to the cushions and the colorful woven mats that covered the floor, gifts from each of his wives to brighten this receiving room. They had outdone themselves trying to create the finest work for him, and he had gladly praised the work of their hands. Would they live to do so again? To create, to build, to share in his days?

Oh, God! He couldn't bear to lose Rachel! And if he thought on it a moment, Leah either. They had become his life, his heart. Even his slave girls Bilhah and Zilpah were his, had borne him children. Would Esau come and destroy all he had been given, all he had built?

The fear moved through him, a living thing, a snake slithering through the dry places in his soul. *Your brother Esau is consoling himself with the thought of killing you.* His mother's words, long thought a distant memory, sounded in his ear like she stood with him in the room. *When your brother is no longer angry with you and forgets what you did to him, I'll send word for you to come back from there.* But word had never come.

Esau is coming to meet you, and four hundred men are with him.

Four hundred men. The standard size of a band of outlaws or a raiding party. A formidable host.

He sank to his knees on the mats, suddenly aware of too many aches in his bones. He stretched out his arms before him, his face to the ground. Words formed in his heart, the silent prayers of a desperate man. But he would not keep them silent. He lifted his voice, choking on emotion as he spoke.

"O Elohim of my father Abraham, Elohim of my father Isaac, O Yahweh, who said to me, 'Go back to your country and your relatives, and I will make you prosper.'" He paused, seeing in his mind's eye the angels, hearing again the Voice who had promised. "I am unworthy of all the kindness and faithfulness you have shown your servant. I had only my staff when I crossed this Jordan, but now I have become two groups." The reality of the blessing sank deep within him, carrying with it seeds of comfort. He rose to a sitting position, hands raised to the tent's ceiling.

"Save me, I pray, from the hand of my brother Esau, for I am afraid . . ." He paused again, emotion making the words thick in his throat. "I am afraid he will come and attack me, and also the mothers with their children." As the words left his lips, the memory of the promise filled him, renewing him. He stood slowly, beseeching yet consumed with a strange sense of boldness.

"But You have said, 'I will surely make you prosper and will make your descendants like the sand of the sea, which cannot be counted.'" Surely God would remember. Surely He could be trusted to keep His promise.

Jacob wiped the tears that had slid into his beard and swallowed hard, his mind working with what to do next. An idea surfaced, filling him with hope. He grabbed his staff, straightened his cloak, and hurried to find his steward.

❊❊❊

Rachel spotted Jacob the moment he stepped foot outside his tent. She set down the water jug she carried and hurried to his side, grateful that Joseph was occupied with his half sister Dinah, helping Leah pack. Though her fear made her want to keep Joseph with her, there was no use worrying a six-year-old.

"Jacob," she called to him, grateful that he slowed and waited for her to catch up. "Where are you going? Can I come with you?" She would not say it to him, but she needed to be with him, to see his face, in case . . . No. She could not lose him.

He looked at her a moment, his expression thoughtful. "I am only going to see my steward. Then I will visit the overseers of each of the flocks and herds. There is nothing for you to do."

She tucked a strand of hair beneath her headscarf and gave him a pleading look. "I would be with you. That is enough."

"Have you packed already?" His comment held little conviction, and she knew he would appease her.

"There is little to pack. We have not been here long enough to take everything out of the baskets. Leah and the others had more to do than I did." She did not suggest that she could be helping them. Not when she knew he needed her, whether he admitted such a thing or not.

His half smile and the way he took her hand, looping it over his arm, answered her question. "We must hurry."

Her grip tightened as he crooked his arm, pulling her along, his staff digging into the earth to aid their going. "What need have you of your steward? I thought you had already sent him to divide the camp into groups."

"I am sending Esau a gift," he said, his breath coming quickly as the ground sloped upward before them. "If he will accept it, I will appease him, and he will spare my life."

He stopped at the top of the rise and lifted a hand to shade his eyes against the afternoon's glare. The hot winds of summer were still months away, but the breeze had a warmer than normal edge to it. She traced the hairs on his arm with her fingers, causing him to look at her.

"You fear him greatly."

He nodded, but the earlier distress did not fill his gaze. "I fear him. And yet I know God has promised me things that cannot be fulfilled if I die, if you all were taken from me." He swallowed and briefly closed his eyes. "I am finding it hard to trust."

She nodded, leaning close to his side. "As am I."

He took her hand and continued walking. "From the best of the flocks I am going to give him two hundred female goats, twenty male goats, two hundred ewes, and twenty rams. You can help inspect them."

So many. "I would be happy to help. I have not forgotten how to choose the choicest lambs." She smiled up at him. "You have taught me much."

He smiled into her eyes. "Everything I did was for you, beloved."

The warmth in his gaze melted some of her fear, and on any other day she would have teased him and coaxed him to chase her among the grasses. But the seriousness of his brother's visit, a visit she should have welcomed if his family had not been so at odds these many years, kept her from considering such foolishness.

"I would tell you that I also plan to give him cattle, camels, and donkeys from the herds. Each will be sent in its own drove, with distance between them. Perhaps as my brother comes upon each one, he will be more impressed as he goes. He never could turn down a good meal, even if it still walked on all fours."

She laughed. "Your brother sounds like a man of many appetites. Let us hope he does not plan to eat the camels and donkeys."

Jacob stopped again, scanning the horizon, at last spotting his steward talking to one of the overseers near the flock of goats. "You are right, my love. My brother was always a man of passion, of heated emotions and rash thinking. He came to quick conclusions and could not sit still. It is funny. My father loved him best, yet it is I who am most like my father."

She turned her head to better see him against the sun's setting as he waved the two men closer. "Your father was a quiet, introspective man as you are?" She had seen his ability to laugh and joke with her father and brothers but had also been privy to his silent moods. And she had seen him pray, had seen his tears, as the sheen of the sun's orange glow now showed them dried upon his cheeks.

"My father was much quieter than I." He looked at her, touched a hand to her cheek. "Come, now. Let us prepare the gift for my brother. Then I will take you back to camp to finish packing. I want you all across the river by nightfall."

"Will we cross in the dark then?" Already the heat of the day had passed, and she would be missed preparing the food they would eat in haste.

He glanced at the sky. "Or we will wait until morning." He seemed suddenly unsure. "I do not know."

"Waiting one night shouldn't hurt."

He gave a slight nod as the men approached, then turned to lay out his planned gift before them. Rachel moved to where the goats grazed and began searching for the ones she thought might please the brother she had never thought she would meet. And wished now they never would.

30

Jacob finished the last bite of flatbread and wiped the crumbs from his mouth with the back of his hand. He stared into the fire, mesmerized by the sparks licking the air as though ever grasping what was just out of reach—much as he had done most of his life. "Heel grabber" was what the adults in his life had called him, and he had been struggling to overcome the name and its implications ever since.

The gifts for Esau had been quickly selected and were on their way south toward the mountains of Seir, where Esau now lived, to intercept him as he made his way north to Mahanaim. Rachel had convinced Jacob to wait until morning to cross the river, but as he stared into the flames, he could not shake the sudden restlessness, the need to have things settled now. And as he looked up at the sound of his sons bickering and his wives rushing to get the little ones to bed, he realized he could not wait—whether they liked it or not.

He glanced at the slice of moon overhead, joined now as it was by stars too numerous to count, reminding him again of the promise. God would take care of him. Surely He would. Jacob chided himself over the doubt that lingered as he gripped his staff and pushed to his feet, no longer as weary as he had been when he had first heard the news of Esau's coming. He stepped from the shadows of the fire and walked toward the women's tents. Leah emerged, carrying a basket in her hands.

"Are you ready to cross the river?" he asked.

"I thought we were waiting until morning." At the sight of Leah's tired expression, Jacob hesitated.

"I would rather we do so tonight." He questioned the wisdom of his urgency for a moment, but her smile put him at ease.

"We are ready to move at your word, my lord. Let me call the children to help finish loading the camels." She waited for his approving nod, then hurried to do as she'd said.

"We are going tonight?" Rachel's voice made him turn, and he braced himself for her opposition. But she too seemed accepting. "I will get Joseph then." Her smile did not reach her eyes, but in the dim night's shadows, he could not tell her thoughts. She hurried from him as well, and he went to find his steward.

With the help of his men, the women and children would be across the narrowest part of the river within a few hours. Then he would face the struggle he sensed within. One he would gladly have avoided if not for the weight upon his heart and the knowledge that he could not face his brother until he faced himself.

"Aren't you coming with us?" Rachel's dark eyes searched his face, her fingers clasped in his.

He shook his head, lifted her hands to his lips, and kissed her fingertips. The last of his possessions had crossed over on the final camel's back, and in the clearing beyond the river's edge, the men and women were quickly setting up a makeshift camp for the night. A fire already glowed in a circle of stones, and torches illuminated the perimeter where the women and children would sleep.

"You will be safe here," he said, his gaze shifting from the camp to her. "I will join you on the morrow."

"You have nothing to sleep on, no cushion for your head."

Her lip curled in a slight pout, which quickly faded at the look he gave her.

"I slept with a stone for my pillow at Bethel, beloved." He glanced toward the river a short distance from them and released her hand. "It is not sleep that I need this night."

She gave him a quizzical look, but he ignored it, anxious to get back across the river, to be alone, to pray. He lifted his staff and felt her eyes upon him as he moved to the water's edge, girded his robe above his knees, and steadied the staff in the water to help him as he stepped across the large rocks his older sons had taken with such easy strides on their way across.

Exhaustion nearly overtook him as he climbed the bank and stumbled to the clearing where his tents had been. The embers of the fire had been put out, the black ash visible only in the moon's distant glow. He sank to the earth near the dead fire, his hands on his knees, emotions rising and falling within him.

He couldn't do this. How could he face Esau after so much time and in such a way? If God had wanted to bless him, why did He make it so hard? Why not allow him to be firstborn? His father would have never questioned his right to rule, would have blessed him without deception, and he would never have had to flee his homeland to fight for his very existence, for his wives, his children, his possessions, these twenty years!

Grief and anger rushed him like a charging bull, crushing him. He lifted his arms to ward off the imagined blow and was startled to touch the skin of a man. Exhaustion fled as he sensed a presence over him, a man who suddenly grabbed hold of his arms and twisted his body, flattening him to the ground.

A loud grunt escaped him as the air whooshed out of him. His opponent held him fast, pressing his face against the dirt. Jacob struggled to breathe but quickly regained his strength and shoved up from the ground. Twisting, he grabbed the man's leg and waist, bringing him down—and this time Jacob got the better of him.

But the man was no weakling and soon twisted Jacob around again, gaining the upper hand. The wrestling continued, taxing every muscle, every fiber of Jacob's being, and with the grappling, though no words were said throughout the night, Jacob's heart beat with questions. Every doubt and fear, every injustice, every deceit, every hint of anger that had crossed his mind poured like sweat from his limbs, and he knew he did not wrestle with a normal man. Neither of them would have had the strength to survive such a night if not for a strength beyond Jacob's own.

No. But like the angels he had met twice before, this man was real, yet though he pushed and shoved and turned Jacob this way and that, he also imbued his power into Jacob, giving his weakness a vigor he did not possess. And somehow in the struggle Jacob knew his silent thoughts were being heard.

Night breezes turned cool in the midst of their fight, and the stars faded, chased away by the coming hint of dawn. And still they fought, one trying to free himself of the other's grip, neither prevailing. At last, as the gray predawn light gave way to its pink overtones, the man touched Jacob's hip socket, wrenching it out of place.

Weakness overcame him, and Jacob's legs shook, begging rest, barely holding him upright. Tears came unbidden, and with them the awful realization of just how wretched he was, how deceitful, how fallen.

"Let me go, for it is daybreak," the man said, his grip loosening on Jacob.

But Jacob, despite his urgent need for release, for an end to his struggle, couldn't bear to let the man go. The sense of loss over such a thing was sobering, acute, and with the overwhelming longing, he wept.

"I will not let you go unless you bless me," Jacob said, his breath heaving with the effort to speak. *Please, Adonai, don't let me walk away without some reward for my struggle.*

"What is your name?"

Their striving had ceased, though Jacob still gripped the man's arm. "Jacob," he said, though he sensed the man already knew.

"Your name will no longer be Jacob, but Israel, because you have struggled with God and with men and have overcome."

Israel. Jacob tested the name in his thoughts, pleased. *Thank you*. The man nodded, and his smile sent sweet warmth through Jacob, bathing him in acceptance.

"Please tell me your name." Suddenly Jacob longed to know, needed to know who this was whose bright gaze could have won their battle without a fight, if the darkness had not kept his face from Jacob's view. His grip slackened slightly, and he was overwhelmed by a look that seemed to hold the purest of love.

But with the love came the slightest shake of the man's head. "Why do you ask my name?"

And Jacob knew he would not reveal it. But the man's next words of blessing flowed through Jacob like a tender healing balm, replacing his fear, his doubts, his questions, with peace.

Jacob released his hold as dawn fully rose and blinked as the man vanished from his sight. He looked at the ground where they had wrestled, the evidence of flattened earth and the two sets of footprints the only sign that Jacob had indeed not been alone. Awe and unworthiness swept over him, and he realized with stark truth that his wrestling had been with Elohim Himself.

His breath floated in front of him in the chill of early morn, and he tried to stand but fell back from the pain in his hip. That he lived at all with only a displaced hip after such an encounter shook him to his very core.

"This place shall be called Peniel, because I saw Elohim face-to-face, and yet my life was spared."

He searched near him for his staff and crawled over to it, then using it to aid him, he stood and slowly limped away.

❋❋❋

Rachel rose before dawn, grabbed her water jug, and headed to the river, anxious for some sign of Jacob. She had spent a restless night half praying, half worrying that something awful had happened to him. Why did he want to spend the night alone where wild animals could find him? He had no protection except his staff and the sling he carried at his side.

Her heart beat faster as her feet neared the bank of the Jabbok, the dew of early morn clinging to her sandals, tickling her feet. She felt the brush of the grasses reach her calves and steadied herself where the land dipped to the water's edge. Squatting beside the pebbles and rocks, she lowered her jar to the rushing stream below.

Movement across the river brought her gaze up to search for the cause. She hefted the heavy jar in her arms, set it upright beside her, and stood. Rustling sounds and the thump of uneven footsteps caught her attention, furrowed her brow, but when she saw Jacob emerge from the trees lining the shore, she released the breath she had not quite given vent to through the long night. He was safe! She smiled as he lifted his gaze and found hers, and hurried closer to where he was slowly attempting to cross the river.

"What happened to you?" She could not mistake the pronounced limp or the heavy leaning on his staff. She touched his arm and helped him climb the bank before retrieving her water jug and falling into step beside him.

"I was injured." His look held a peace she had not seen earlier. "I spent the night wrestling with a man . . . no, not a man." He looked at her, the light in his eyes radiant, as if he had gazed at the sun and the brightness had lingered. "I have striven with God and lived, beloved." He placed a hand on his hip and swallowed. "He touched me. It was the lightest of touches, despite our grappling throughout the night. But it was enough."

Rachel leaned closer to see that his leg beneath his robe was indeed bent slightly and he could not stand fully upright. "Why would He hurt you?" She was finding this God of her husband's more confusing as the years passed. "If He promised you blessing, why wound you? Is that not more like a curse than a blessing?"

Jacob stopped his walking and put both hands over the head of his staff to hold his balance, looking at her, his gaze kind, tender. "Perhaps we would not recognize the blessings we have if not for the pain we face along the way." He glanced beyond her, and she could hear the sounds of the camp awakening, the millstone grinding, the children's young voices rising. "Besides," he said, drawing his gaze back to hers, "I met Elohim face-to-face and lived to tell of it. To come away with only a limp from such an encounter is a small price to pay."

She studied him, saw the awe in his dark eyes and a new sense of humility. "I imagine you are right," she said at last, though not at all sure she agreed. "Though I do not like the suffering, the waiting for Him to act, the fear of what He will do to us or let us face. I do not see how striving with God will help you face your brother." She hated to dash the joy in his expression, but she could not stop the fear from filling her own. "The messenger last night said Esau is getting closer. He could come even today, and what will we do?" She lifted the jar, and he moved slowly with her toward the camp.

"I will climb the rise to see if he is near," he said, though his pace did not hurry, perhaps could not hurry due to his limp. "Then I will decide what we will do." His look held reassurance, and she drew in a breath, trying to keep calm. But she knew her own struggles were every bit as difficult as Jacob's had been the night before.

She had not seen Elohim face-to-face, and she was not hindered by God's wound, but neither did she have His peace. She was not sure which one she wanted more.

✳✳✳

The wind carried the scent of oak and pine as Jacob stood with his steward on the rise of a hill above the camp. He lifted a hand to shade his eyes, the other arm dependent on the staff to hold him. The staff, his only article left from the days in his parents' household, had become an extension of himself in recent years. Now even more so.

A distant stirring of dust along the road drew closer, the camels' hooves moving to the pace of a master in a hurry, as he would expect of a raiding party, not a traveling caravan.

"Esau approaches," he said to the steward. He glanced at Omid, who had come to him from Harran after his children were born, not part of Laban's household, a man who had proved trustworthy during the years he had built his flocks and herds.

"What would you have us do?" Omid said.

Jacob stared at the approaching host, surprised at the peace that still cloaked him. Or perhaps the fear had turned him numb to what might happen. He had so little control.

"Divide the women and children into groups. Put the maid-servants and their children first, Leah and her children next, and Rachel and Joseph in the rear. I will go ahead of them to meet my brother."

The steward nodded and moved ahead of Jacob to do his bidding while Jacob made his way slowly down the path. When he was satisfied that the women and children were spread out with plenty of space between them and the approaching Esau, he limped toward the trotting camels and bowed low once, twice. He rose with effort and moved ahead several paces, then bowed again. By the seventh bow, the allotted amount he would have given any reigning monarch, Esau had drawn near enough to hear his familiar voice.

The camels came to an abrupt halt as Jacob rose slowly, warily. *Please, Adonai, if ever You have heard my plea, save me now.*

He glanced heavenward, then at Esau, and was startled to see his camel kneeling and his brother jumping to the ground, then running toward him. Jacob braced himself for the blow that would surely come, but Esau threw his arms around Jacob's neck and kissed each cheek. Emotion rose swift and harsh, the past rushing in on him. He looked into Esau's familiar face, saw the tears running freely down his cheeks, and could not hold his own tears in check. Moments passed in silence, each one clinging to the other, weeping.

At last Esau stepped back and glanced beyond Jacob. "Who are these with you?" he asked.

"They are the children God has graciously given your servant." Jacob turned and motioned for Bilhah and Zilpah to step closer. Their children beside them, they came forward and bowed at Esau's feet. Leah and her children followed, until at last Rachel and Joseph did the same.

"I could almost be jealous of you, brother. I myself have five fine sons and eleven grandsons. I see you are a long way from grandsons." He laughed lightly and cupped Jacob's shoulder. "But you have a fine family."

"Thank you, my lord." They exchanged a smile. How well Jacob recalled the Canaanite women Esau had married, the women his parents had found sorely taxing. Would his parents think more highly of Rachel and Leah?

Esau rubbed a hand over the soft curls of his red beard, his lips curved in a slight frown. "What do you mean by all these droves I met?"

Jacob lowered his gaze and kept his tone subservient, as he would to a king. "To find favor in your eyes, my lord."

"I already have plenty, my brother. Keep what you have."

Jacob lifted his eyes at Esau's use of the familial term, reminded yet again of the struggles they had shared, the blessing he had stolen from his brother. He must make some restitution for the injury he had caused Esau.

"No, please!" he said, his tone pleading. "If I have found favor in your eyes, accept this gift from me. For to see your face is like seeing the face of God, now that you have received me favorably. Please take my blessing that was brought to you, for God has been gracious to me and I have all I need."

"But it is not needed. Despite our father's choice," Esau said, the slightest shadow crossing his features before it disappeared in a wide smile, "I have become prince of a large company. I have no need of your gifts, my brother." His look seemed guileless, but a check in Jacob's spirit would not let it go.

"I would be pleased and honored if you would accept this tribute, my lord." Jacob dipped his head in a gesture of subjection, then met his brother's gaze once more. "Please."

Esau seemed to hesitate a moment but at last shrugged his shoulders and then lifted his arms wide. "What can I say to this? Yes, I will accept your gift." He motioned to his men, who turned to retrieve the herds and flocks from Jacob's servants.

Jacob breathed a soft sigh, still wary yet relieved.

"So then, let us be on our way," Esau said, turning his attention back to Jacob. "I'll accompany you."

Jacob's heartbeat quickened, but he masked the alarm filling him. "My lord knows that the children are tender and that I must care for the ewes and cows that are nursing their young. If they are driven hard just one day, all the animals will die. So let my lord go on ahead of his servant while I move along slowly at the pace of the droves before me and that of the children, until I come to my lord in Seir."

"Then let me leave some of my men with you." Esau's gaze skimmed his frame, and Jacob knew he had to have noticed the way he leaned too heavily on his staff.

"But why do that?" Jacob straightened, ignoring the pain. "Just let me find favor in the eyes of my lord."

"You have acquired a limp," he said, searching Jacob's face.

"Yes." Jacob lowered his gaze once more as a servant to his

master, silently pleading for this reunion to end. For though he was grateful to find acceptance in Esau's eyes, he did not fully trust him. The sooner he could get Rachel and Joseph and the others safely away, the better.

"All the more reason you could use my men to guide you safely through the mountains." Esau said the words, but they lacked conviction. "But I suppose you have a point. My men would chafe at having to slow their pace to keep up with yours." He touched Jacob's shoulder.

Jacob looked up. "Thank you, my lord."

Esau embraced him once more, kissing each cheek. Jacob, not wanting to slip from the role of servant, did not return the gesture but bowed instead and kissed Esau's feet. He did not invite Esau to linger, to share a meal, or to spend the night around the campfire.

"Until we meet again, brother," Esau said, helping Jacob to stand.

"Until then." Jacob watched Esau turn, mount his camel, and lead his men back toward Seir.

Jacob found his steward and directed his servants to pack their belongings and head north and west toward Succoth. The exact opposite of his brother.

❊ 31 ❊

TEN YEARS LATER

Leah stood near the edge of Jacob's camp and wiped sweat from her brow. The gates of the city of Shechem were less than half a day's walk from the camp, too close for Leah's comfort. She had grown used to Succoth, where Jacob had chosen to stay for a time after hearing of his mother's death. Somehow hurrying to see his father had lost its earnestness as he grieved the woman who bore him. He had even gone so far as to build a home like Leah and Rachel had known in Harran, a house of stones with shelters for the flocks and herds. Things had been pleasant there, and Leah missed the protection of the stout walls and the clay oven he had built for them to bake their bread.

If only they could have stayed . . .

But when a caravan had come bringing Deborah, Rebekah's old nurse, with news of Isaac's desire to see him, Jacob's guilt at having neglected the man had grown into restlessness to continue to travel southward to see his father before it was too late. Deborah had stayed on with them then, though even she had seemed anxious to immediately return to Isaac. If not for the flocks' mating season, they would be traveling even now, rather than settling again near a city she feared.

She shook her head to dispel the disturbing thoughts. She

had no real reason to fear the inhabitants of Shechem. Jacob had found them most agreeable when he had asked to purchase land near the city. And the women had been kind to her when she shopped in the marketplace.

But their idols and the temple worship had reminded her too much of Harran and the gods her father and relatives had worshiped, not at all like the One Creator God Jacob adored. Not like Adonai, the Lord who had given her six sons.

She twisted the wet rag she had brought, letting the dirty water drip to the side of the path, then rubbed the back of her neck and turned at the sound of her daughter's voice. "Ima, can I go to the city to the shops? Adi will come with me. We won't be gone long. I promise." Her daughter, Dinah, gave her a pleading look, her beautiful dark hair escaping the pale blue scarf she wore that denoted her a virgin daughter of her father. The girl was too much like Rachel and too unaware of her appeal to men.

"It is not safe for women to go alone to town. Not without your father or brothers." And Adi, a servant's daughter, was younger than Dinah—no protection at all!

"Then let Joseph take me." Dinah and Joseph had remained close despite the distance between Joseph and Leah's sons. Distance brought by Jacob's constant favoritism toward Rachel's only child. Leah felt the muscles clench in her jaw. She forced herself to take a long, slow breath.

"There is no need to go to town. When your father plans a trip or if one of your brothers has need to go there, then we will consider going along." She looked at Dinah, ignoring the girl's curled lip and the tiny scowl lines between her eyes.

"You never let me do anything exciting. Why must my brothers always go with me? I'm old enough to watch out for myself. And I can run faster than Joseph or Issachar, and they can almost catch a fox." Dinah crossed her thin arms over a well-developed body and met Leah's stern gaze.

"*Almost* does not count. Even foxes get caught in traps. You do not know what traps await you in a foreign city with foreign gods." Leah touched Dinah's cheek, but the girl flinched and turned away. At fourteen years she should be betrothed to a worthy man, a man who could put that restless spirit to good use raising his children. Maybe then she would realize the anxiety she brought to Leah with her bent toward adventure and even a hint of rebelliousness. If only her father would listen and find a suitable husband for the girl.

"I don't care about the foreign gods, Ima. I want to shop in the marketplace, meet the women, maybe talk to girls my own age." She glanced at her servant Adi, a girl three years younger.

Leah studied Dinah's dark, brooding eyes. "If you have questions of womanly things, you can talk to me or to your aunt Rachel."

"I don't have questions. I just want to explore, to meet girls my own age." Dinah glanced toward the city gates seen easily in the distance, her look full of longing. Leah inwardly cringed at the desire in her eyes, wanting to pull her back, rein her in as she would one of the young donkeys, praying her daughter would not be as stubborn as such an animal.

"Will you take me to their festival?" Dinah's question held a hint of accusation, her small mouth pursed, so much like Rachel's. Half of the young men in the camp had turned their heads at the sight of her. How much worse would it be in a town full of uncircumcised heathens?

"You should want no part of such a festival, my daughter."

Her sons had brought rumors on their return from occasional visits to the city about the heathen practices that went on during those festivals—the way the virgin girls danced and how the men of the city would capture the virgin of their choice, whisk her away to their place, and take her as their bride. She had nearly cuffed Simeon's ears when he had laughed at the rites and suggested he wouldn't mind participating. The last thing she needed was for him to bring home a captive Shechemite bride, some unsuspecting young maiden who would not want to leave her homeland, who would expect to be captured by a man from her own city. She shook her head, wondering not for the first time where that boy's thinking came from. Levi was no better. Sometimes all six of them made her want to shake them, but in the next breath she could hold them close and lavish her love on them. They might not have Jacob's favor, but they would surely have hers!

"I don't see what's so wrong about it. The girls dance in colorful costumes until their lover comes and steals them away to his house to be his bride." Dinah pressed her hands to her heart, her head tilted to the side, eyes closed, as if the idea were some pleasing, happy tale. "For some of the poorer girls, it is a way to be wed without a dowry."

"Who told you such things?" Why on earth had Jacob settled them so close to the town? "The men who take their bride in such a way may keep her as a slave or a concubine, not a wife." Her voice rose as she fought to talk some sense into the girl. "You are the daughter of a prince, Dinah. You do not want this, and you should not think it a good thing."

"Bilhah and Zilpah are slaves, and Abba cares for them quite well." Her comment stopped Leah's breath.

"So you would rather be a slave?"

Dinah rolled her eyes. "Of course not. But I don't see why I couldn't go to watch. You could come with me, Ima." Her pout turned to a pleading look that Leah often had trouble resisting. The girl could coax the wool from a sheep without shearing it.

"We will speak no more of this, Dinah," Leah said, forcing sternness into her tone. "You will not go to the city without your father or a brother, preferably two. I will not risk it." She placed a hand on Dinah's shoulder and beckoned Adi to follow, leading them back toward camp, her heart picking up its pace as her irritation shifted to the all too familiar fear.

"You worry too much, Ima," Dinah said in quiet challenge.

Leah closed her eyes and drew in a slow breath. She would keep her temper in check, though the girl seemed to know exactly how to exasperate her.

"Oh, and Abba has called everyone to a sacrifice. He built an altar and said to come find you."

Leah tsked. "Why didn't you say so at once? All this foolish talk of festivals." If Jacob had sent for her, she must hurry. She lifted her skirts and motioned each girl to hurry along.

"And Aunt Rachel is sick again. She was asking for you."

So much to happen in the few minutes she had slipped away from the camp? They had barely finished the morning meal. Why couldn't Jacob and Rachel have said something to her there? But she squelched the thoughts. Rachel had complained of illness often of late. Could it be? Was she again finally with child?

Leah's own womb had closed several years ago, and Joseph was already sixteen years of age. Could Adonai have blessed Rachel with another after all this time?

Leah's steps slowed the slightest bit as the thought hit her. She was not sure she was ready to hear whatever Rachel had to tell her. Her sons already competed with Joseph for their place in Jacob's life. Another son of Rachel's would put them even further from Jacob's heart.

Her pulse fluttered, and her stomach twisted uncomfortably. She glanced at Dinah skipping ahead of her now, unaware of the power of her beauty. How long could Leah protect her?

Somehow she must. She would speak to Jacob this night. She would make him see that Dinah must marry, as her mother had made her father see that she too must marry when he agreed to give her to Jacob in Rachel's place.

※✣※

Rachel forced herself up from bending over the clay pot, the contents of the morning meal now filling it. She shuddered, wiped her mouth with a linen towel, and crawled to her mat, a hand pressed to her middle as she lay back. The queasy feeling passed several moments later. She closed her eyes for a brief moment, pondering the changes her body had undergone in the past few months. Jacob, though he had guessed the truth with Joseph before she had, did not suspect. And this time, after so many years of waiting, she feared being wrong. What if her symptoms were simply the result of an overwrought mind?

She rose from her mat, half longing for the raised cushioned bed she had used in Succoth, quickly fixed her disheveled scarf, and walked slowly from her tent. Jacob's household, his servants and wives and children, moved past her toward the clearing at the rise of a nearby hill where Jacob had called them, to an altar he had set up. She wrapped her robe more tightly around her and fell into step with Leah, trailing behind her daughter.

"Dinah said you wanted to see me." Leah glanced at her, sizing her up as though she already knew. "You are sick?"

"I think it is more than that." Rachel kept her voice low, her gait slowing. "I haven't told Jacob yet."

Leah nodded, and the two walked in silence until they neared the rise of the hill, the altar clearly visible from where they stood, the rest of the household gathered around the perimeter.

"Is there a reason you are waiting?" Leah met Rachel's gaze, her pale eyes holding a hint of compassion.

"I wanted to be sure. After all this time . . ." She looked away, ashamed of the tears rising up the back of her throat. She swallowed. "I'm afraid," she whispered. "It's been so long."

Leah touched her shoulder. "I am sure you have nothing to fear. But of course every birth brings uncertainties. It is natural for a woman to feel as you do." Her tone was gentle, reassuring, putting Rachel's mind at ease.

"You think so?"

Leah embraced her, a spontaneous action so unexpected they both laughed as they pulled away. "You must tell Jacob soon, of course." Leah smiled, and Rachel saw no guile or even a hint of jealousy in her gaze.

"Thank you." She brushed a stray tear from her cheek and turned to the sound of Jacob's voice giving thanks to Adonai as he spilled the blood of the sacrifice and lit the fire on the altar.

Smoke rose to the heavens, and Jacob's voice rang out over the assembled camp. "This altar shall be called El Elohe Israel, God, the God of Israel."

Rachel listened as he extolled Adonai's praises, recounting the things He had done for them since the day Jacob met Him at Bethel over thirty years before. When he finished, he prayed for forgiveness, for mercy on them all.

Rachel placed a hand on her middle over the place where a new life formed. *Oh, Adonai, have mercy also on this child that I carry. Let him be healthy and let him live to please his father.*

When the gathering dismissed, she returned to the camp. Tonight, when Jacob came to her, she would tell him.

❋

Leah waited for Jacob to finish speaking to his steward, telling Rachel she would join her for the weaving after she had spoken to him of her concerns for Dinah. Rachel had nodded her understanding. Through the years, when Leah had fretted over Dinah's restless ways, Rachel had assured her the girl was just spirited and longed for adventure. Much like Rachel had been in her youth. Rachel had put her mind at ease on more than one occasion.

But this was not a time for commiserating over a young girl's desires. Dinah needed a husband, and only her father could make that happen. Surely Jacob would see this. He was not as blind as her father had been or so greedy that he would make them wait. Surely.

She smoothed her hands over her robe, suddenly nervous to approach him. But at last his steward departed, leaving Jacob alone. Leah climbed the hill to meet him, knowing it would take him time even with the aid of his staff to come down the hill to her level.

"Leah." He smiled at her, his look welcoming. "What can I do for you?" He lifted the staff and motioned for her to walk with him, taking the path with the lower incline.

"I must speak with you about Dinah." She studied the path before her, glancing his direction once as she spoke. "It is time we found a husband for her."

He paused in the path, leaning heavily on his staff. "She is only fourteen." He rubbed a hand over his jaw.

"Fourteen is old enough to bear children, my lord. She has been nubile for over a year."

He seemed startled by this revelation and looked beyond her as if seeing a different time and place. "You were much past her age when we wed, Leah. She has plenty of years to mature." He touched her shoulder, and she looked into his dark eyes, searching.

"I do not think it wise for us to wait, Jacob." She twisted the belt at her waist and sighed. "She needs a home and children to settle her."

He looked at her for several moments, saying nothing. At last he nodded. "I will consider it." He touched her elbow, continuing their walk down the hill.

It was all she could do.

Sunset fell like autumn leaves over the camp as Rachel set the last dish to dry on the woven mat inside her tent. She straightened, pressing a hand to the small of her back, longing desperately for sleep. But Jacob waited for her inside his tent, and tonight she would tell him her news. She had thought to tell him the week before, but he had been too distracted with the business of the flocks and herds and the men from the city coming to invite him to the Festival of Virgins. Jacob had graciously declined, though some of his sons had argued with him afterward about going. He had sent them to the fields with the sheep to keep them from following the pagan pleasures.

Rachel did not know who was more relieved, herself or Leah, that Jacob had made such a swift decision. With Leah's sons either already men or on the cusp of manhood, it was no wonder some were anxious to marry. But not that way. Not with pagan women.

She shook the thoughts aside, grateful that Joseph had not been among those asking for such a thing. God had given her a good son, a son who followed in the footsteps of his father, a son who carried his father's favor. The thought pleased her. Though sometimes worry slipped in when she compared Jacob's treatment of Joseph to that of Leah's sons. Would Joseph one day suffer for such favor the way Jacob had done, when she was no longer there to protect him?

She shivered, dispelling the very idea, and moved from her tent to walk the short distance to where Jacob waited. Stars began their evening dance, taking turns brightening the sky. She glanced up. *So shall your offspring be*, God had promised Jacob.

He smiled at her approach and took her hand, drawing her into his tent. "Your hands are cold," he said, wrapping his fingers more fully around hers.

"Are they?" She stepped closer and kissed his cheek. "I had not noticed."

His gaze swept over her, and he touched her nose with a soft kiss. "I've missed you. I am sorry to have stayed away so long."

"I've missed you too." She slipped her arms around his waist and rested her head on his chest, listening to the steady beat of his heart. "But I am here now."

They stood in silence for several moments until at last he pulled her into the sitting area and settled her among the cushions she had made. He drew a flask of wine from a basket, poured two silver cups, and handed her one. She sipped, then ran her finger over the rim and looked at him, a smile touching her lips.

"What is it?" He had always been so observant of her moods. "Something has pleased you, beloved. Tell me." He swirled the liquid in his cup, watching her.

"I have something to tell you." She glanced away, suddenly shy. It had been so long since the last time. What if something happened to the babe? Though none of her sister wives had ever miscarried, there was always the chance.

He set their cups down and moved closer, encasing her hands in his own. "It is good news?" His boyish smile made her laugh.

"Yes, of course it's good news!" She traced the line of his beard along his jaw. "The best of news, Jacob." Her words were soft, a caress.

His hand moved to her waist and rested there. Her stomach fluttered at his touch, and the look of love in his gaze dispelled all her misgivings. The babe would be fine. She had nothing to fear.

"How long have you known?" he asked, his smile wide, crinkling the corners of his eyes. "And when will he come?"

"What makes you so sure it will be a boy?"

He pulled her close and kissed her softly, tenderly, possessively. "Because it will be," he said against her ear. "But if it is not, then she will grow up to be a princess of greatest beauty like her mother."

His kisses trailed along her jaw until he found her lips once more. His breath was warm, minty, and when he gazed into her eyes, her breath hitched. His dark eyes searched hers, reading into her thoughts, reminding her in a moment all that they had shared. He had loved her with a passion she had never quite grasped, and in the way he looked at her now, she knew that love had never abated. The strength of it weakened her even as his kiss silenced every fear.

God would give him twelve sons, saving the last to come through her. She was indeed blessed.

❊ 32 ❊

The camp was unusually quiet several days later during the height of the Festival of Virgins in neighboring Shechem. Rachel and Leah sat companionably in the weaving tent while Bilhah and Zilpah stacked the flax to dry in the sun.

"I thought Dinah would join us today." Rachel tucked a purple weft thread through the striped red, blue, green, and yellow warp threads of the loom. Joseph would look wonderful in the coat when it was completed, but she let Leah think she was making it for Jacob. There was no sense causing upset when it would be up to Jacob to approve whether Joseph could wear it so soon. Such a coat would set him apart as firstborn and heir, and the thought brought to Rachel's heart both pride and a hint of fear of the repercussions.

"She should be here." Leah snapped a thread with her teeth, then yanked it tight into a knot. "She asked to go pick some of the wild grapes. She took her maid with her." She glanced at Rachel. "I have been uneasy since she left."

"I am sure she will be fine. She did not go far?"

"To the field south of the camp." Leah pulled a new thread from the bag and tied it to the loom. "She needs to wed."

Rachel studied her sister, surprised at the urgency of her tone. "Surely there is still time." She had been more than twice Dinah's age when she married Jacob. "Have you a man in mind?"

Leah's head lifted. "Jacob's steward has a son who seems to look at Dinah as she passes."

"Most of the young men glance her way when she passes." Rachel chuckled. "I doubt Jacob wants his daughter wed to a servant."

"Then who? There are no relatives to choose from. He won't send to Esau for a cousin or to our father for one of our nephews."

Rachel paused in her weaving. "Do you want me to speak to him?" She rarely offered to speak on behalf of her sister or the servant wives because it only caused friction, reminding them all that she had Jacob's ear. If he would not listen to them, she could often get him to see things their way.

Leah worried her lip, seeming to ponder the thought. She opened her mouth to speak when a commotion from outside the tents drew their attention. Rachel glanced through the open sides of the tents to see Dinah's servant Adi running toward them, weeping.

Leah jumped up, letting the shuttle fall to the floor, and rushed from the tent. "What is it? Tell me quickly!"

The child's hair was disheveled, her clothes dirty, as though she had fallen in the dirt or been involved in a great scuffle. Rachel rose to join them, fear mounting at the look of terror in the child's eyes.

"Dinah . . . She told me—" The girl choked on a sob, and Rachel could tell by the look on Leah's face that she wanted to shake the child. Rachel went to the cistern and returned with a cup of water. The child took it and gulped it down.

"Now, tell me, Adi, where is my daughter?" Leah's calm voice belied the lines of worry and strain along her brow.

"She went to Shechem by herself. She said she wanted to see the women of the land, but I know she wanted to attend the festival. She has talked of nothing else for weeks." Adi shrank back from Leah.

Rachel stepped closer and put an arm around the girl. "How

long ago did she leave?" She looked at Leah. "We can send someone after her."

Adi shook her head. "It's too late. He already took her and . . ." She buried her face in her hands. "I followed her." She peered through the gap in her fingers. "I know I shouldn't have, but . . . I didn't know he would hurt her. I waited outside the city gate for her to return. I hid in some bushes and watched, listening to the songs. At last Dinah came out, only I almost didn't recognize her because she had on a new colored veil and was swaying and dancing and singing as she walked home. I followed her and was just about to run to catch her and call her name when a man came toward the city all dressed in fine clothes. He saw Dinah, and before I could call her name, he approached her, grabbed her about the waist, and carried her into the trees."

Rachel gasped, and Leah grew so pale Rachel feared she would faint. She took her sister's arm, supporting her.

"Dinah screamed and screamed, and I was so scared!" The girl's words were drenched in broken sobs. "I didn't know what to do. If I ran home, it would be too late. But then her scream-ing stopped and she started to cry. I crept closer and saw them. He was stroking her hair and speaking to her like he cared that he'd hurt her."

Leah swayed in Rachel's arms, and Rachel led her quickly to a bench to sit. "Dinah," Leah moaned, the word barely audible.

Rachel turned to Adi. "Where is Dinah now?"

The girl stuck a fist to her mouth. "He took her. She was cry-ing so hard, and then he pulled her to her feet and lifted her in his arms, like Master Jacob does a hurt lamb. He spoke to her, but I couldn't hear. And he carried her to the city."

Leah stared blankly, barely moving. Rachel touched her shoul-der. She must tell Jacob. They must get Dinah back. "The man probably thought she was one of the virgins from the festival and claimed her," she said in Leah's ear. "If that is the case, he took her to his home to be his wife."

Leah jerked as though struck and met Rachel's gaze. "He defiled her!" The words hung in the air like poisoned smoke.

"I will go and get Jacob." She gently squeezed Leah's shoulder.

"She should have wed." Leah stared, unseeing.

"Let me get Jacob," Rachel said again, feeling the weight of the news with such force she nearly stumbled as she hurried from Leah's side. She glanced back at her sister sitting so stoically, her head bent in sorrow Rachel could barely fathom.

Dinah, Dinah, why did you run off unescorted? Such a foolish, rash choice.

Jacob looked up from the lamb he was tending, his ear catching a frantic, high-pitched sound. Was someone calling him? He reached for his staff and pushed to his feet, cupping a hand to shade his eyes. There in the distance, a woman—was that Rachel? His heart thumped hard at the sight of her rushing toward him, her robes billowing behind her, her arm waving to catch his attention. Had she lost the babe? He shook his head at the thought. She would be lying on her mat if she had. It would be Leah or one of the other women running to him now. He limped toward her, hurrying his gait, frustrated at his inability to close the distance faster.

"Jacob!" Rachel stopped and leaned forward, hands on her knees, her breath coming in spurts. "You must come at once."

He touched her shoulder, alarm rushing through him. "Calm down, beloved. Tell me what happened." He reached for the flask of water at his waist and offered her a drink.

She took it and drank greedily. "Dinah," she said, still gulping air. "Dinah has run off to Shechem to the festival and was captured by a man." She looked at him, her expression anguished. "He defiled her, Jacob. One of the servant girls told Leah and me the story. She followed and saw . . ." She glanced beyond him. "She saw too much."

Jacob stared at her, his body rocked with her words. How

could this be? Dinah was but a girl, barely old enough for a man to notice. He closed his eyes with the weight of his own denial. That was not true. Leah had told him, had warned him that she was ready to wed. But he had not listened. Not so he actually believed her.

"You must do something, Jacob. You must go to Shechem to retrieve her . . . something!"

He clung to the staff for balance as his mind reeled with her urgings. "Do we know who took her?"

Rachel shook her head. "The servant girl said that Dinah went off to Shechem alone. She followed but waited outside the town for Dinah to return. When she did, she was wearing one of their scarves, probably like the virgins wear in the festival." She clutched his arm. "Oh, Jacob! The man met her on the path home and dragged her into the trees!"

His pulse slowed as though his blood forgot the path through his veins. He swayed, his hand cramped around the staff. "You have no idea who this man was?"

Rachel's large eyes filled with tears as she shook her head.

He forced stiff limbs to move and pulled her close. "Come. I will send for my sons. In the meantime, take me to Leah."

She slipped an arm around his waist and walked with him in silence back to camp.

"This is an outrage!" Jacob's son Simeon paced the path in front of Jacob's tent, his brothers nodding their heads, spouting blistering curses on every man in Shechem.

"Such a thing should not be done in Israel." Judah, the least boisterous of Jacob's sons, stood, fists clenched, locking gazes with Jacob. "Something must be done."

"What do you suggest?" Jacob met Judah's gaze but did not hold it, looking instead to Reuben, his firstborn. "We don't know who took her."

"We will go to the town and knock down every door." Simeon stopped before Jacob, his face flushed, hand on the hilt of his sword.

"And kill every man in it until we find her." Levi's comment brought Jacob up short.

"An extreme measure, my son," Jacob said. The look in Levi's eyes troubled him. "Would you punish an entire town for the acts of one man?"

"It was their festival that started all of this!" Levi's voice rose above the din of his brothers' mumbled conversations going on around him.

"And Dinah was the one who chose to attend it." Joseph's words brought a hush that lasted but a moment.

"Would you not defend our sister?" Simeon demanded.

The shift in anger toward Rachel's son made Jacob wince. This was not good.

"Of course I would defend her. I only wish she had waited for one of us to take her there."

Silence followed the remark.

"Your brother is right," Jacob said, trying to defuse the heated air between them. "Your sister made a foolish choice. But that does not change the fact that a man took advantage of her."

"We will sneak over the wall and search the town this very night," Simeon said, pacing again.

One of the servants approached as Jacob's sons continued to argue and spoke to Jacob. "My lord, horses are coming down the path, carrying the king and his son."

His words carried to the group, bringing a halt to the conversation.

"Perhaps he knows who did this and is coming to make atonement." Jacob looked to his sons, his expression stern. "We will be civil to him, to see what he wants."

"If he has our sister, he will be fortunate to leave us with his life." Levi's quiet, weighted comment made Jacob's blood run cold. When had his sons become so bitter, so violent? Yet he could say nothing better. And he took solace in knowing his sons would act on Dinah's behalf, even if he found it difficult to do so.

Leah stood in the shadows, her robe tucked tightly around her, unable to stop shivering despite the heat from the nearby fire. Rachel's arm slipped through hers, and the two waited mutely as two men dressed in resplendent robes rode to the edge of the tents and dismounted.

"I can't stand this." Leah clenched her jaw, the cold coming from deep within her causing her teeth to chatter against her will. "I'm so cold."

"Let me get you a blanket." Rachel slipped into her tent and quickly returned, wrapping a soft woolen blanket around Leah's shoulders.

Leah glanced at her sister, then toward the men Jacob and his sons now approached. "What do you think they want?"

"Perhaps they came about Dinah." Rachel escorted her closer to the fire and coaxed her to sit.

Leah shook her head. "The men will want to sit here."

"They will not mind if you stay."

Leah sat, her gaze fixed on the men, while Rachel stood behind her, kneading her shoulders. The gesture would have warmed her in another lifetime, but she could not seem to manage a single emotion other than fear.

The men moved toward them, and she tried to push up from the stone seat, but Rachel's gentle resistance stopped her.

Leah barely acknowledged her, her limbs too weighted to rise, though she wanted to. Jacob glanced at her as the men drew near the fire and offered their guests seats opposite her. Jacob took the seat at her side and reached for her, his warm hand folding over hers.

"I am Hamor the Hivite, and this is my son Shechem, prince

of the land. We have come to speak to you of your daughter, Dinah." Hamor spread his hands toward Jacob, palms open in supplication. He was a handsome man by some standards, though clean-shaven and square-jawed, with eyes too calculating, too sure of himself. Like her father. The young man beside him looked younger than Joseph, barely old enough to wear the princely robes or carry the burdens of a man. Surely not old enough to wed!

"I am aware that my daughter is captive in your town," Jacob said, his voice even, though Leah could hear the edge of anger and feel the tenseness of his hand around hers. "Whatever you have to tell me had better include her return safely to my tents."

Hamor sat back, his expression confused. "But . . . your daughter attended our festival. She wore the veil of the virgin maidens. My son . . . that is, we thought she was aware of the purpose." He rubbed a hand over his jaw but quickly recovered his composure. "Forgive any misunderstanding, my friend. We come in peace to tell you that my son Shechem has his heart set on your daughter. Please give her to him as his wife. Intermarry with us—give us your daughters and take our daughters for yourselves. You can settle among us; the land is open to you. Live in it, trade in it, and acquire property in it." Hamor's words rang in the silence.

Leah's heart thumped hard, awakening the dead feelings within.

The young man, Shechem, stepped forward and fell to one knee before Jacob, his gaze taking in her sons as well. "Let me find favor in your eyes, and I will give you whatever you ask. Make the price for the bride and the gift I am to bring as great as you like, and I'll pay whatever you ask me. Only give me the girl as my wife."

The request swirled in Leah's head like a vivid nightmare. No man would want Dinah after what Shechem had done to her, but to do as they asked, to intermarry with uncircumcised heathens . . . She could not finish the horrible thought. Agony filled her, and she nearly gave in to the desire to sway and moan Dinah's name aloud. To weep over the death of her daughter's purity, her future—for unless they gave her to this man, her womb would most surely be dead, her life ruined beyond hope.

Leah glanced at Jacob, who had stiffened beside her, then in turn looked to each of her oldest sons. Simeon caught her gaze, his mouth a thin line. He turned to Hamor. "We can't do such a thing. We can't give our sister to a man who is not circumcised. That would be a disgrace to us."

Levi stood, hands clenched tight at his sides, and Leah feared he would pull his sword that very moment and put an end to both men's lives. Instead, he took a step nearer, his gaze conciliatory. Yet she knew that look. "We will give our consent to you on one condition only: that you become like us by circumcising all your males. Then we will give you our daughters and take your daughters for ourselves. We'll settle among you and become one people with you. But if you will not agree to be circumcised, we'll take our sister and go."

Leah shivered again, the cold becoming a living thing within her. She barely felt Jacob's hand tighten around hers. She knew her sons, knew the violence hidden in their hearts, and feared to think what plans they possessed.

But Hamor and Shechem did not detect her sons' deceit. They both stood, smiling and bowing toward Jacob. "It shall be as you have said." They made swift goodbyes and took off on their horses back to their city.

It was only after they had left and Rachel had helped her to her tent that Leah realized they had not offered hospitality to the men, did not break bread or offer drink to them. But the men should not have expected such a thing after what they had done.

Yet in the quiet of night, Leah knew that neither man realized just how deplorable Shechem's act had been to Jacob and her sons. Nor did they suspect the harm her sons surely plotted against them.

33

Rachel woke with a start three days later, her heart beating too fast. She rose and searched the mat beside her, aware of Jacob's absence. Voices drifted to her—loud wailing—and the lowing of sheep and goats drew nearer. She quickly donned her robe and ran her fingers through her rumpled hair, hurrying from the tent. Torches lit the compound, and a large company of women and children stood huddled, crying, near the edge of the tent rows, while all six of Leah's sons, Dinah in their midst, stood before Jacob.

She moved closer, saw Leah emerge from her tent and rush into Dinah's arms, both weeping. Fear moved through her as she took in the company of women and children. What was this? Joseph appeared at her side and took her arm. She looked into his concerned eyes, so like his father's, and drew strength from his hold.

"What is the meaning of this?" Jacob's voice boomed in the darkness, silencing the noise except for the occasional fearful weeping of some of the children.

Simeon and Levi stepped from the gathering of Leah's sons and faced him, chins raised, defiance in their dark eyes. "These are the captives of Shechem. While the men were recovering . . ." A smirk crossed Simeon's face. "We killed them."

"They deserved to die for what they did to Dinah." Levi's hatred fell like a hot blanket over burning skin.

Rachel's legs lost their strength and her breathing grew jagged. Joseph's arm came around her, his muscles tense. She glanced at him, saw the fire in his eyes. He had not been party to this. She looked from Joseph to Jacob, who leaned heavily on his staff, and it seemed he aged in moments as she watched him. She sought a deep breath but felt it lodge in her throat.

Jacob coughed and ran a hand over his beard, his low voice like a wounded animal. "You have brought trouble on me by making me a stench to the Canaanites and Perizzites, the people living in this land." He looked slowly from one son to the next, seeking to drive home his point with sharp fury. "We are few in number, and if they join forces against me and attack me, I and my household will be destroyed."

Their silence lingered but a moment. "Should he have treated our sister like a prostitute?" Levi spat into the dirt at his feet, whirled about, and stormed off, Simeon following.

"Let me go to him, Ima," Joseph whispered in her ear. "He needs me now."

She nodded, hating to lose the strength of his support but knowing his father needed it more. She let him go and made her way to Leah's side, then escorted her sister and a still weeping Dinah into Leah's tent, wondering what on earth they were going to do with a city full of widows and their children.

Jacob walked the length of the camp, his heart as heavy as the stones he had chosen for the altar he had first built on coming here. Now those stones seemed to mock him, as though his guilt were no longer cleansed, his sacrifices a stench in God's face. Just as the acts of his sons were a stench in the nostrils of the men in the cities surrounding Shechem. That none had come to avenge the murders of Hamor, Shechem, and their clans brought little comfort. He was responsible, and yet he was powerless against the vigilant anger of his sons.

He dug his staff into the dirt to help him climb the low hill to the altar, his knees weakening as he approached the place where he had once felt God's favor. How was it possible such disaster had come upon him? God had saved him from Esau's hand, but He had done nothing to stop Dinah's shame or the acts of Simeon and Levi. And Reuben, Judah, Issachar, Zebulun, and Zilpah's two sons had joined in the greedy taking of booty. Even Bilhah's sons had taken captive brides from among the women of the town, leaving Jacob to deal with foreigners and their wayward gods.

He bowed low, kneeling in the dust at the foot of the altar, his heart yearning for the man who had wrestled with him that long-ago night. To feel His strength imbued into him again, to feel the blessing of God on his head would do much to ease the pain he felt now.

Oh, Adonai, what am I to do?

He waited in the silence, listening. A stiff breeze moved the branches of the nearby oaks, each limb dancing a different rhythm to an unfamiliar song. Birds twittered and chirped, and the voices of many children coming from the tents of the captives carried to him where he knelt. He closed his eyes, put his face to the earth.

Go up to Bethel and settle there, and build an altar there to God, who appeared to you when you were fleeing from your brother Esau.

The words joined the music of the birds and the dance of the trees, and he could not escape the thought that he should have gone to Bethel months ago. If he had not stopped here . . . But there was nothing to be done with what was past.

He pushed to his feet, a slow sense of rightness, of peace, settling in the place where the weight had been. They would purify themselves, rid themselves of the foreign idols the women had

brought with them from Shechem, and change their clothes—
symbols of the past, of all that could defile them. He would
bury the lot of it under the oak tree that stood on the path to
Shechem and lead his family in faith to Bethel.

Rachel placed a hand over her protruding belly and held
Jacob's hand as the two walked the fields near Bethel several
months later, the sheep grazing nearby. "Do you remember when
we first met?" she asked, smiling up at him. His beard was not
nearly as dark as it had been back then, and the lines along his
brow had deepened since Dinah's defilement and Deborah's
recent death. But when he looked at her, the light in his eyes
still held a love so great it took her breath. She blushed like a
young girl at his boyish smile.

"I will never forget that moment, beloved." He squeezed her
fingers, then brought them to his lips and kissed them. "You
captured my heart from the moment I set eyes on you, my sister, my bride." He stopped walking and bent to kiss her, a soft,
gentle reminder of how much they had shared.

She looked at him, her heart yearning with longing and love
so strong it almost caused a physical ache within her. How
long would she have him? How long would she live to show
him her love? The thought had troubled her too often of late,
especially since the loss of Deborah. Though she had not known
the woman long, her death haunted Rachel, and she couldn't
quite escape the reality of its finality.

He smiled down at her, then continued to lead them toward
the altar where he had first met Adonai on his way to Paddan-
Aram, when he escaped Esau's wrath all those years before. A
stone pillar still stood where he had placed it, and as they approached it now, he stopped several paces away, his gaze lifting
beyond to a man walking toward them.

She instinctively took a step behind Jacob, placed a protective hand where the babe lay. "Do you know him?" she whispered, suddenly aware of a stillness in the air around them.

"I have seen him before." Jacob bowed as the man approached, and Rachel knelt, unable to bend as far forward. She peeked at the man through hooded eyes as he stepped up to Jacob and placed a hand on his bowed head.

"Your name is Jacob," He said, His voice like music and rushing waters and joy all wrapped in one, "but you will no longer be called Jacob; your name will be Israel."

Her pulse jumped, her heart racing at the sound of His voice. A tremor rushed through her, and she could not meet His bright gaze.

"I am El Shaddai, the All-Sufficient One. Be fruitful and increase in number. A nation and a community of nations will come from you, and kings will come from your body."

She felt a stirring inside her at His words, and the babe moved as though he too yearned for the promise, a promise this child would bear a part in fulfilling. Tears sprang to her eyes, deep emotion warring with gratitude and unworthiness. She covered her face with both hands, shivering as the man continued to bless Jacob.

"The land I gave to Abraham and Isaac I also give to you," He said, "and I will give this land to your descendants after you." His words ended, and the air around them moved again, the birds singing louder, endowed with new life.

Jacob rose slowly to his feet and stared for the space of many heartbeats into the place where Elohim had stood. At last he turned and helped her up, his expression unreadable.

He took her hands in his, tears shining like pinpoints of light in his eyes. No words passed between them. Moments later, Jacob released her and limped to the side of the path unaided, picked up a heavy pillar as he had once moved the heavy stone from the well the day he had met her, and set the pillar upright where Elohim had stood over him and blessed him.

He took the flask of water from his belt, untied it, and poured it over the pillar, then took a smaller goatskin of oil and did the same.

"This is Beth-El," he said, "house of Elohim. For Elohim has met me here twice, and I am blessed."

She nodded, meeting his gaze, still too shaken for words, and let him lead her back toward the camp.

Leah glanced at Dinah's bent head as the girl turned the millstone in its rhythmic circle, grinding the grain as if they could store her cares within its crevices. Dinah's voice never rose in song since the trials at Shechem, and Leah found herself longing for the arguments and rebellion she had once faced rather than this detached, sad silence. But as before, she could not find the words to help her daughter, and every attempt failed in Dinah's continued brooding.

Leah released a sigh as she fell into step with Rachel on the way to the well. In the weeks since Jacob had decided to move away from Bethel to return to his father's house in Hebron, Rachel had grown large with child, and the weight of it seemed to draw her inward, as though she carried a secret along with the babe.

"Let me get the water this time," Leah said, aware of the way Rachel's shoulders sagged as she walked. Even the empty jug seemed too heavy for her.

Rachel glanced sideways at her and smiled, her expression as captivating as always, putting Leah at ease. "And have you think me weak?" She laughed, the sound musical.

"I think you are about to burst with that child, and I don't want you to have it halfway to the well." Leah's scolding brought more laughter from Rachel, and she waved Leah's concern away.

"I'm fine." But her secret smile made Leah wonder.

"Have the pains begun?" But no, she would not smile if they had.

Rachel placed a hand on her lower back. "Some slight aches in my back. Nothing more." She shifted the jug slightly on her head and continued walking. "I wonder what Father Isaac is like. Jacob speaks so highly of him. I look forward to placing our son on his knees." She glanced at Leah. "I am sorry you did not have the chance to give him a babe to hold. I wish we had made this trip long ago."

Leah's heart stirred with the genuine compassion in Rachel's gaze, and she saw no trace of the rivalry they had once shared. "You have changed," she said without thinking.

"Have I?" She smiled again, causing the slightest twinge of jealousy in Leah's heart. "I am sorry it has taken so long." She touched Leah's arm. "Please forgive me for the things I've said, the bitterness between us."

Leah shook her head, guilt touching her. "I am as much to blame. We have had a hard life sharing a man." She looked away, too aware of Rachel's sincerity. "At least you have always known he loves you."

Rachel lifted her hand from Leah's arm, and silence fell between them. At last she spoke. "He loves you too, Leah. Not in the same way. I don't think Jacob is capable of the same type of love for more than one person at a time." She paused in her walking and faced Leah. "Sometimes his love is so fierce, it staggers me," she confided. "It is as though he depends on me for his very breath." She looked away. "Sometimes I fear . . . I fear what will happen to him when I am gone, if he outlives me."

"Don't say such a thing. Jacob is far older than either of us. We will bury him long before he buries us." She said the words to make them true, suddenly realizing how much it would hurt to lose her sister. She could not bear the thought. Even if it meant she would have Jacob more exclusively.

They walked on, coming soon to the well, and drew the water they needed before turning back to camp. "What are you going to do with Dinah?" Rachel asked, apparently done with thoughts of death and love. "I feel so bad for her."

Leah's heart grew heavy again with the impossible situation. "What can I do? She barely speaks. She will never marry—what man would want her? And so she will never bear children. I wish . . ." She shook her head. She wished her sons had not been so rash. "There is no sense wishing for what cannot be undone."

"No. There isn't."

As they neared the camp and saw Dinah still bent over the stone, working her fingers raw, Rachel touched Leah's arm. "See if she can watch some of the children of Shechem. A babe in arms, even if it is not her own, can do much for a breaking heart."

Leah met Rachel's gaze, reading in her dark guileless eyes the memories of her own empty arms of years past. She spoke from experience.

"I will see what I can do," Leah said.

The pains in her back grew stronger as night waned, and Rachel could no longer keep silent. She sent a servant to fetch Leah, who quickly returned with the camp midwife, Bilhah, Zilpah, even Jacob.

"You should not be here, my lord," Rachel said as he squeezed her hand and bent to kiss her sweaty cheek.

"I know." He gazed at her, his smile gentle, the softest hint of concern lining his brow. "I love you, Rachel. I always have."

"I know." She drew in a sharp breath as another wave of pain washed over her. "You should go."

He nodded, at last releasing her hand. He left the tent, and the women crowded around her, all giving advice at once. The midwife examined her and proclaimed the birth a long way off, but the pains did not abate.

Hours passed, and Rachel moved from pacing the tent to collapsing on her mat, her strength slowly ebbing. She looked at Leah, caught the fear in her gaze, and her heart beat fast with dread. Why wouldn't the child come?

The midwife bade her to lie down again and checked her progress. Her breath no longer raced within her. She struggled to speak as Leah drew close and took her hand.

"If anything happens to me . . ." she said, her voice brittle as dried leaves.

"Nothing will happen." Leah squeezed her fingers, but Rachel could not respond. She closed her eyes, imagining the man who had spoken to Jacob and blessed him standing over her now. *I am El Shaddai, the All-Sufficient One. Be fruitful and increase in number. A nation and a community of nations will come from you, and kings will come from your body.* Kings would come from her! Would to God that it were true. And if not her, then surely Leah.

She opened her eyes and looked at her sister, suddenly wishing the years had been kinder to them, that they had settled their differences in their youth.

"Don't be afraid, for you have another son," the midwife said, her words distant.

Leah's face faded from her view.

"Ben-Oni," she said. Tears slipped down her cheeks, and her eyes slowly drifted closed.

Leah bent over Rachel, waiting, her breath catching on her tears. "Rachel?" The babe's lusty cry came in response, but Rachel did not move, her chest no longer rising and falling with labored breaths. Her skin had paled with the effort of the birth, her bright lips cracked, her cheeks streaked with tears.

Leah rested a hand on Rachel's chest, her own heaving with sobs. A flurry of activity broke around her as Bilhah cleaned and wrapped the babe and the others washed Rachel's limp body for burial.

Rachel! Leah wanted to scream her name, to shake some sense into her, to demand she return from that place of Sheol. She felt Bilhah's presence at her side, the squalling babe in her arms, tears falling freely onto his soft blanket. She offered Leah the child.

"Jacob must be told," Bilhah said.

Leah took the boy and nodded, moving silently through the tent into the courtyard where Jacob waited with Joseph. Her sons had dispersed to their tents, though some of them were still with the sheep in the fields. Simeon and Levi had kept their distance since Shechem, even since the sacrifice at Bethel and Jacob's command to purify the camp. Her thoughts drifted to them now, to their births, to the children God had blessed her with. And now Ben-Oni made twelve sons of Jacob.

But what kind of life would he have as the son of Rachel's sorrow? The thought pricked her heart, and she wished she had been the one to die in her sister's place. How would Jacob bear such loss?

She approached Jacob and Joseph, the babe held close to her heart. She met Jacob's gaze across the circle where the fire still burned low and the men sat in quiet conversation. He stood at her approach, and she could not stop the tears as she held the babe out to him.

"Ben-Oni," she said. "As she was dying, Rachel named him 'son of my sorrow.'"

Jacob sank back to the seat, the staff falling to the dirt beside him, hands resting on his knees as if trying to hold himself up.

Joseph's voice rose beside him in a deep, guttural moan. "No!" He rocked back and forth, seemingly unaware of Leah's presence, and Jacob buried his head in his hands, weeping.

Leah stood, uncertain what to do, longing to fall to her knees and weep at his side, but the babe's cries broke through their sobs, causing both men to quiet. Jacob looked up, saw her there, and seemed to realize why she waited. He lifted his arms, accepted the child, and rested him on his knees, tears still streaming into his beard.

"He shall not be Ben-Oni, but Benjamin, son of my right hand." His voice filled the courtyard, and Leah glanced beyond him, seeing that all the family and servants who were in the camp had gathered. She caught Judah's look as he stood near his tent, saw the hurt in his gaze. By Jacob's words, Rachel's son had been elevated to a place above her own sons, beside Joseph.

She should have known, had always known Rachel's children would rise above hers. She had come to terms with the idea long ago, but her sons did not share her sentiments. She must do what she could to keep peace among them. With Rachel gone, there was no one else who would look after Rachel's children to keep them safe.

Movement caught her eye, and she saw Dinah emerge from the shadows to sit at Joseph's side. She touched his arm, and the two held each other. Perhaps Dinah would find solace in Rachel's sons, in caring for Benjamin and consoling Joseph.

Leah moved closer to Jacob, aware of the babe's quiet cooing. He would need a wet nurse soon. But for now, she sat beside her husband and placed a hand on the babe's head. Jacob looked at her through his pain, and she determined she would do whatever it took to ease it. She was his first wife now in every sense.

"Do not worry, my lord," she said softly. "I will care for Rachel's Benjamin." Her brow furrowed. "That is, if you want me to."

He nodded his thanks, words seeming to fail him, and handed the babe back to her, then picked up his staff and rose, limped across to Rachel's tent, and let the flap close behind him.

❊ 34 ❊

Jacob touched Rachel's hand in the darkness of her tent, where a single torch cast shadows over the room that hours before had been full of life and hope. Stars blanketed the sky outside her tent, making it impossible to choose the place for her grave this night. He looked into her face, the skin ashen, drained of color, her beautiful smile hidden, yet her lips somehow faintly showing a hint of the smile he once knew. She had teased him with a similar look when she acted coy and wanted to get him to see things her way. She had always succeeded, partly because he loved giving in to her.

He studied her, wondering what she saw now on the other side in Sheol. His eyes closed, seeing again the ziggurat with the angels and the visitors at Mahanaim, and the man he had wrestled with across the Jabbok River. Rachel, of all others in his life, had witnessed his last encounter with God, had heard His blessing, had seen His look of love. She had spoken of it in awe several times since, and he could not help wondering if she was with Him now.

Would to God that he could join her!

He buried his face against her stiff side and wept, wishing dawn would never come. Let them find him dead at her side, two lovers joined forever in death as their love had joined them in life.

How could he bear to go on without her?

He raised his head, brushed a strand of her hair, no longer soft as it had been, and tucked it along her shoulder. He left his hand resting against her cheek, not caring that she could no longer feel. A sob rose within him, choking him.

Rachel! Rachel, come back to me.

He lifted his head, gazing heavenward, seeing only the wooden tent posts and cords, a shroud about him.

Why did You take her from me?

The questions swirled inside of him, complements of the same thoughts he had struggled with when he had wrestled with God, and he knew he could not utter them aloud. Could only keep them close to his heart. There was no reasoning with good and evil in this life. Memories of his father and Uncle Ishmael discussing God's goodness when he was but a lad surfaced. And with the memory he caught a glimpse of his father's sufferings on God's altar.

He drew in a breath, unsettled. He could not live without Rachel. And yet he had no choice but to do so. Joseph and Benjamin needed him. Leah needed him. That thought surprised him, but he could not explore it now.

He laid his head beside Rachel's, his tears wetting the floor at her side. Dawn would come, and he would bury his most beloved wife beside the road to Bethlehem at Ephrath.

And he would raise a pillar in her honor.

Leah stood surrounded by her sons, watching as the servants lowered Rachel's body to the earth beside the road and covered her with dirt. Jacob and Joseph kept their distance from the rest of Jacob's sons, the rift as wide as it had ever been. She had spoken to her sons as they walked along the way, begged them to be a comfort to their father and brother, but only Judah had given the slightest hint of agreement. She looked to him now, but he glanced away as though she asked too much of him.

Jacob moved to the side of the road where a pile of stones lined the path. Joseph hefted the largest in his arms, carried it to his mother's grave, and set it upright. Jacob looked up and addressed them.

"In memory of Rachel," he said, his voice hoarse from his night of weeping. He looked from one son to the next, his gaze resting on each of his wives and his daughter as well. "She loved you all." He swallowed, his Adam's apple moving in his throat. "May Adonai accept her."

Leah brushed a stray tear from her cheek, glancing once more at Judah. But it was Dinah who moved away from her brothers, first to Jacob to kiss his cheek, then to Joseph, who held her close. Judah's feet seemed loosed by her actions, and he came close to embrace his father and brother. Leah breathed a sigh. Perhaps one son would pave the way for goodwill between them all.

They stood for a time talking softly in small circles until at last Jacob left them to walk alone in the fields. Leah longed to follow. They were camped near the road due to Rachel's travail that had come upon her sooner than they had expected. They could not stay there for long, and soon Jacob would want to continue the journey to see his father in Hebron.

Rachel's eyes would never rest on Jacob's family. Only Leah would meet the famous patriarch. Sadness followed the thought. Isaac would have loved Rachel, as everyone did.

Leah moved to her tent, letting Jacob go off to grieve alone. There was time enough to sort through the problems Rachel's death left them. Time enough to comfort him as only she knew best.

The seven days of grieving passed, and Jacob continued the journey south toward Hebron. Dusk fell as he walked, his limp more pronounced than it had been in years, and he looked out over the land that stretched before him, land that he had known all of his life. How many lessons he had learned at the hands of his father and mother in this place with these people. How Rachel would have loved to have known them both!

Benjamin's cries drifted over the camp as he neared his tents. Leah had found a wet nurse among the Shechemite widows and had brought the woman as a servant into her tent to care for him. Jacob spotted Judah and Joseph in conversation near the fire, and his heart warmed to see their attempt at getting along. If only Rachel had lived to see it.

His steps slowed as he neared Leah's tent. Benjamin's cries abated, and Leah sat under the awning, spinning wool, as he had seen her do a thousand times in the years of their marriage. The sight was somehow comforting, beckoning him.

He turned aside and walked closer. "May I join you?"

She looked startled for a moment, then quickly stood, motioning for him to take her seat among the cushions. "I will get another," she said, hurrying inside for another large pillow. "Some wine, my lord?"

He nodded, waiting as she retrieved the flask and silver cups he had given her. He breathed deeply of the sweet aroma, then sipped long from his cup. Grief rose and fell as he sat beside her in companionable silence. He looked into her pale eyes, not remarkable like Rachel's but familiar.

She offered him a quiet nod, then picked up her spindle and worked the distaff, sitting beside him as the servants worked in the camp around them. Children's voices mingled with the evening song of birds in the trees above them.

He met Leah's gaze, wondering if they would grow old together.

The thought did not displease him.

Note from the Author

When I began researching Rachel's story, I had a good idea of what was coming. What I didn't realize was just how much Jacob (and Rachel by her connection to him) would struggle throughout their lives. Jacob's very name means "heel grabber," or "deceiver"—as if he was born with a bent toward seeking his own way, always grappling for what he desired.

When Jacob was old, and many years after he had laid both Rachel and Leah to rest, he was quoted as saying to Pharaoh, "My years have been few and difficult" (Gen. 47:9). I would say that is a bit of an understatement! Earlier in Genesis, God said to Jacob, "Your name will no longer be Jacob, but Israel, because you have struggled with God and with men and have overcome" (32:28). Jacob knew struggle even in the womb.

And Rachel knew struggle from the moment her wedding night was stolen from her and given to her sister. I cannot even begin to imagine the heartache that must have held for her. I do believe that Jacob and Rachel wanted and intended to marry only each other. Here was a man who wanted a monogamous marriage and ended up with forced polygamy. Sometimes life dishes out things we would not choose.

In this version of Rachel's story, I gave Rachel and Leah different mothers in order to set up the earlier conflict and to give Laban an even deeper reason for possibly wanting to deceive Jacob. Perhaps Laban was jealous of the love Jacob had for his daughter. Perhaps he was just consumed by his own greed. In any case, the Bible is silent on the mothers of Rachel and Leah; their creation is my own.

The struggles Rachel and Leah carried in sharing a husband, however, were theirs. The Bible gives us a good glimpse of just how personal things got in the names Leah chose for her sons and in Rachel's bitter cry that she would die if she could not bear children! I wonder if Jacob didn't feel rather like a pawn in some childbearing chess game.

My favorite part of this story, though, is not in the struggles of the women over their want of children or over Jacob's love, but of the struggle Jacob faced when he wrestled with God. Have you ever carried fear as long as he did? While he surely stuffed the fears and guilt aside to live his life, Jacob never quite forgot what he had done to his brother, and he did not know peace at a heart level until he settled the matter (and many more matters, I'm sure) with God alone.

And isn't that the way it is for each of us? Life is filled with struggles, some nearly impossible to bear. We grapple and fight and flee and live with guilt, and yet what our hearts are longing for is restoration and reconciliation. For Jacob, that meant facing his brother. For Rachel, it meant realizing that God was more important to her than raising children, and it meant coming to some sense of peace with her sister. I'd like to think Rachel and Leah were friends in the end.

That's not to say that all relationships can be restored. We can live at peace with men only as far as it concerns us. And Esau was not a man Jacob could trust. He was a man Jacob could forgive and seek forgiveness from. Still, in the end, they went their separate ways.

Someday, when Jesus (Yeshua) reigns on earth, all things will be fully restored. But until then, we, like Jacob and Rachel, will struggle. And sometimes we will wrestle with God's best for us.

Like Jacob, I hope we can come away from such encounters changed and yet blessed.

In His Grace,
Jill Eileen Smith

Acknowledgments

Authors work and research alone, but we also work in a community. Through the years of email support loops, I have met some wonderful friends. Together we encourage each other and pray for one another. To thank them as a whole seems like such a small gesture, but I would need to fill a book to mention all of those who have touched my life and blessed my career.

As for the writing of this book, my biggest thanks goes to my first reader and critique partner, Jill Stengl. Thank you, dear friend, for helping me through another story!

Other mega thanks go to my editor, Lonnie Hull DuPont, whom God first put in my life in 1991 as a sneak peek of the fact that He wanted us to work together. It took until 2007 for that to be realized in His perfect timing. Thank you, Lonnie! You're the best!

And to my line editor, Jessica English. I'm so glad we got to meet and have lunch in person this year! Your style of editing is so uplifting and encouraging! Thank you for making my work look good!

To all of the great people I get to work with at Revell—Twila, Michele, Claudia, Deonne, Robin, Janelle, Jennifer, Lindsay,

Cheryl, Donna, Mary—thank you for believing in me and for all you do to support this work. I love you guys!

To Wendy Lawton—I loved getting to know you better at the Books & Such retreat this year. You are a rare gem, and I'm so glad God made us a team.

To Randy, my heart's true love. I'm so glad I never had to share you like Rachel did her Jacob!

To my California guys, Jeff and Chris, who make me so proud to be your mom! (And jealous of your sunshine!)

To Ryan and Carissa, who will be married by the time this book sees print! I can't tell you how happy I am to get to love the two of you! I'm pretty happy about having a girl in the family too!

To my mom, whose love of reading got me started in the first place. I'm so glad we still have you here on earth to celebrate the joy of living!

And above all, to the Elohim of Abraham, the Elohim of Isaac, and the Elohim of Jacob—the God who is true and living through all of the struggles of all generations.

Selah.

Jill Eileen Smith is the author of the bestselling *Michal*, *Abigail*, and *Bathsheba*, all part of the Wives of King David series, and of *Sarai* and *Rebekah*, books 1 and 2 in the Wives of the Patriarchs series. Her writing has garnered acclaim in several contests. Her research into the lives of biblical women has taken her from the Bible to Israel, and she particularly enjoys learning how women lived in Old Testament times. Jill lives with her family in southeast Michigan.

Contact Jill through email (jill@jilleileensmith.com), her website (http://www.jilleileensmith.com), Facebook (https://www.facebook.com/jilleileensmith), or Twitter (https://twitter.com/JillEileenSmith). She loves to hear from her readers.

Meet
JILL EILEEN SMITH

at **www.JillEileenSmith.com** to learn
interesting facts and read her blog!

Connect with her on

 Jill Eileen Smith

JillEileenSmith

Can love heal
the rift between two souls?

"This incredible author's ability to re-create biblical settings and transform dialogue delivers a God-given message that is just as relevant today as it was thousands of years ago."

—*RT Book Reviews*, ★★★★

THE WIVES OF KING DAVID series
will transport you back in time

Bestselling author Jill Eileen Smith brings to life the Bible's most famous stories of passion, betrayal, and redemption.